'Funny and brutal, heartf... ... Kenny O'Neill, a ... ...ith real
a captivating anti-hero in ... ...
emotional depth. The plot ... ...es along, pausing only to rip at your heart
and knee you in the groin. Highly recommended.' CRAIG ROBERTSON

Also by Michael J Malone

BEYOND
the
RAGE

Michael J Malone

CONTRABAND

Contraband is an imprint of Saraband

Published by Saraband,
Suite 202, 98 Woodlands Road
Glasgow, G3 6HB
www.saraband.net

ISBN: 9781908643704
ebook: 9781908643711

Publication of this book has been supported by Creative Scotland.

ALBA | CHRUTHACHAIL

Printed in the EU on sustainably sourced paper.

2 4 6 8 10 9 7 5 3 1

Prologue

There was usually some sort of shouting match in his house after he went to bed. Sometimes it began immediately after he shut his bedroom door, sometimes it would happen just as he was falling asleep, but most often it had to wait until his father came home late.

On the occasions he went to bed while Dad was still 'out', his mum would be extra nice to him. She'd make sure he'd eaten some supper, she might even let him off brushing his teeth, and she'd always tuck him in. Which was embarrassing, he'd try to tell her. But she didn't care. It didn't matter if he was almost a 'big teenager'; he was always going to be her little boy.

He might even get to stay up late and watch some TV. He didn't much care what programme was on, so long as he could brag to his pals at school the next day that he'd been up past his normal bedtime. But as soon as his mum heard the tell-tale sound of his father's key being twisted in the lock, he was sent running to his bedroom, with a pat on the backside and a panicked 'Hurry, son. Bed.'

It wasn't that she was shy of fighting with her husband – he overheard her tell her mother on the phone one night – she just didn't want 'the wee fella' to watch.

He thought that was crazy: the notion that not being able to see their faces bright with yelling at each other made things any easier on him. He was quite able to fill in the pictures, thank you very much. In his mind's eye, his mum was always standing and his dad was on the sofa, with a cup of tea in his hand. His mum would be doing most of the talking and while she talked she would be pointing, her finger sharp as a knitting needle. Dad would pretend he wasn't bothered until eventually he would lose it. He would then stand up, towering over her and the shouting would begin in earnest.

Kenny could see him carefully putting his cup on the coffee table. In his imagination, his father always had just enough reserve to save the crockery before he went mental. There was never any physical violence. Dad was always telling him that men should never hit women and that any man who did was a 'real cunt'. But there was always plenty of shouting.

He could rarely work out what they were arguing about. The odd word would make it up through the ceiling/floor and the occasional phrase, but for the most part the words ran into a meaningless melee of sound; one a gruff bass and the other a shrill soprano.

One night he woke up to a real humdinger. The Partick Thistle FC clock on his bedside table was shining 01:15 into his bedroom in bright green and both his parents were screaming at each other. But this time they were in the bedroom next door. He heard one word that night. Gun.

Then it fell silent. A silence that was just such a contrast to the noise he had been listening to he wondered if he had temporarily lost his sense of hearing. Then his mum began crying and he could hear a low, soothing rumbling sound from his dad. Not long after that the bed began creaking.

That was almost the worst thing about the fights; the way they made up afterwards. Don't let the boy see us fighting, but when we start shagging just inches away through the wall to him, he'll have to put up with it. Grown-ups were crazy and their relationships were fucked up as far as he was concerned.

The noise-making at this stage was in the same proportions as the fighting. His mum made most of the noise, while his dad just gave a big groan at the end. Meanwhile, he was laying feet away, face brighter than the clock.

He discussed everything the next day with his pals at school. Davie Morgan got really excited at the mention of the gun, telling everyone that Kenny's dad must be a gangster. Ben Kelsey got most excited when he heard about his parents shagging. Kenny's mum had a cracking pair of tits, Ben said, and he was going to have to have a wank later on while thinking about them. Kenny had to be pulled off him by a passing teacher.

The teacher was a student called Bob – and a pretty cool guy – and in Bob's opinion Ben Kelsey probably wasn't at the stage where he could manage to beat one off. But that wasn't the point, Kenny argued after his face fell when he was given two hundred lines. He pretended later to his pals that his lines read, *I will not fight my pals in the school grounds when they say my mum has nice tits.*

Then there was the night just five days before his thirteenth birthday. Dad was out and Mum didn't let him stay up late, which he remembered thinking was odd. She sent him off to bed as soon as Big Ben began to chime at the start of the *Ten O'Clock News.* He protested, 'Aww, Mum.' She said, 'Aww Mum nothing, get your skinny wee arse off to bed.'

He didn't get tucked in that night and he must've fallen asleep quickly because he was really fuzzy-headed when it started. It was a low noise with the one note. Then it rose in pitch and volume and made his hairs stand on end. He tip-toed down the stairs and the sound got louder. The thing that freaked him out was that it sounded like it was his dad that was making it.

And there he was, on his knees in the kitchen leaning over his mum, who was slumped over the kitchen table. He remembered thinking later how weird it was that he was able to take in everything in the room with one glance. He noticed everything. The blonde of his mother's hair, the empty bottle of brandy in one of her hands, the small, white medicine packet in the middle of the table and his father's continuous howl of guilt and protest.

'Nooooooo.'

1

'So that concludes our business for the day then, Mr O'Neill,' the man across the table from him said as he spun the combination locks on his briefcase. 'A pleasure as always.' He stood up and stretched out a fat hand.

'It's Kenny. How many times do I have to tell you to call me Kenny?' he said as he leaned back in his chair, ignoring the hand before him and trying not to make a face of disgust at the amount of hair growing on the back of the other man's fingers.

'We may be involved in a business that is... less than legal, Mr O'Neill. But it is a business nonetheless and it behoves us to act in the manner of business people.'

'If that's the case, why are we meeting in a Little Chef on the A9 instead of the Hilton? And who the fuck says "behoves" nowadays?'

A tight smile formed on the man's face as he considered his response. He was aware of the rumours that surrounded Kenny. Who wasn't? But he would be keen to assert his own ego, while maintaining some sort of relationship. It would also be nice not to get his arse kicked.

'Mr O'Neill...'

'Kenny.'

'Mr O'Neill...'

'Kenny.'

'Kenny, your sense of humour is part of your legend, so I don't take offence.' A shrug. 'In my view a man should always look to better himself and that means a certain look...' – he paused to correct the position of his tie – '...deportment, vocabulary...'

'Yeah, yeah, yeah, Dimitri. In the real world... in the twenty-first century, like, businessmen don't wear ties. They call each other by their first names, they meet in offices and if anybody gets above themselves they slap them down...'

'There's no need to bring up the threat of violence, Kenny,' Dimitri said in a broad Glasgow accent that as far as Kenny was concerned just did not go with the name. Dimitri's voice wavered for a moment. He swallowed and then squared his shoulders as if he had just remembered how he needed to act the part. Kenny did have a reputation.

'...They slap them down by refusing to do business with them ever again,' Kenny pointedly finished what he was saying. He wanted to add 'you pompous twat' at the end of the sentence but restrained himself.

'Do I not give you good product, Kenny?' Dimitri held both hands out, palms up like an actor waiting to accept applause.

'And that, my friend' – Kenny stood up – 'is the only reason why I agreed to meet you.' He held a hand out, despite his better judgement and almost too eagerly Dimitri took it in his moist paw and shook it.

'Now, Dimitri,' said Kenny, wiping his hand on his trouser leg, 'take your briefcase, your tie and your deportment and get the fuck out of my face.'

Once the man had huffily walked out of the restaurant, Kenny pulled his phone from his pocket. Just as he was dialling a number, Dimitri walked back in.

'The toilet,' he mouthed as he walked past. 'Just needed the toilet.'

Kenny looked to the ceiling. Where did these people come from? You just can't get the right class of villain these days. His phone rang out. A voice answered.

'Kenny, m'man.'

'Well?'

'It's good. It's all good.'

'Excellent,' Kenny said. 'Usual terms?'

'Of course, Kenny. Of course.'

'Excellent.' Kenny was taking a step back from the coalface. He no longer wanted to be at the front of the deal, offering the goods to the buyer. That was the dangerous side. The role that meant greater personal risk with the small matter of police capture, trial and jail time. No, fuck that. He wanted to make the maximum amount of money, with the minimum amount of risk and that entailed setting himself up as a middle-man. That meant anonymity.

'Excellent,' he repeated. 'Call me by my name once again over the phone and I'll tear your fucking heart out.' He hung up before the other man could say anything. He'd had enough of idiots for one day.

Not that he was averse to getting his hands dirty. Cometh the hour, cometh the knuckle-duster. He was more than willing to hand out some lessons, and lessons learned the hard way tended to stick, in his view.

He caught the eye of the waitress as she was folding purple napkins around knives and forks for prospective diners. She carried on with a couple more before she huffed and walked over. She pulled a pad from a pocket in her apron, licked at her teeth and said, 'Help you?'

Kenny looked at her name badge. It read *Versace*, for chrissakes. He couldn't bring himself to say her name.

'I was going to ask for another coffee, but I can see you have more important things to do rather than serve the one customer you have in the room. So I'll just have the bill, please.' Now that she was closer to him, he considered that she was probably about fourteen and she'd be thinking that social niceties were reserved only for grandparents holding out a wad of notes and the cool kids in her class at the high school.

As if she had just remembered her training, Versace straightened her back and stretched her mouth into a smile.

'Was everything okay for you, sir?'

'I've tasted worse.'

She processed that with a raise of her eyebrows and a faraway look.

'I'll... I'll just get your...' She turned and walked away. As she walked, Kenny studied the swing of her backside. If you liked that kind of thing – pubescent – and he knew some men who did, she was not too bad. He, however, preferred them with a little more curve, a little more years and with a price tag. Then you knew exactly where you stood. Sex, as far as he was concerned, was all about a form of barter. He got some rest and relaxation, the girl got some cash. If you knew the cost up-front before the wood took then nobody got hurt. And by nobody – if he ever took the time to analyse it – he meant himself.

His phone rang. The ringtone was the theme music for *Looney Tunes* and was set for his cousin, Ian 'Mabawser' Ritchie.

'Ian, elucidate.' Kenny loved using big words with Ian. It really fucked with his mind.

'Eh?' was the response.

'Expound.'

'Dude, you talk some amount of shite.'

'And dude, you're from Milngavie, no Manhattan, so cut it with the Americanisms.'

'Anyway, cuz, I was won-der-ing...' He dragged the word out by way of a delay tactic. Like he knew what he wanted to say wasn't going to get a good reception but he knew he had to say it anyway. '...Seeing as it's your big Three-Oh today, if you wanted to come round my mum and dad's tonight?'

'Shit. I forgot about that.'

'You forgot your own birthday? It's your big Three-Oh.'

'Think about it, Ian. When did I ever celebrate...?'

'Oh, right,' Ian said. The penny clanked to the bottom of his sieve-like mind. 'It's just that Mum felt that it was time to... bygones and all that.'

'Fuck, Ian. Do I have to?' Kenny rubbed at his forehead. He could deal with all kinds of hard-cases – murderers, rapists, thieves – but his Aunt Vi knew how to tweak the old guilt reflex. He'd managed to avoid her... them, for two years now. Since that last time when he threatened Uncle Colin. The man was a twat and he'd always be a twat, no matter how nice his wife was. He'd gone to live with them when his mum died and his dad vanished and Uncle Colin never let a day pass without reminding him how lucky he was that they'd taken him in rather than letting him go to live in an orphanage.

'You know how much Mum cares about you, dude. You're her sister's son...'

'I know, I know, I know.' Kenny was leaning over the table, still rubbing at his forehead. Fuck. He didn't think he could bear to be in the same room as his Uncle Colin without wanting to wipe that sneer off his face with a cheese grater.

'She's got something for you.'

'I don't need any presents, Ian. I have enough stuff.'

'This isn't stuff, Kenny. It's a letter.'

'A letter?' Kenny sat up straight in his chair. Something twisted in his gut. He could sense this was important.

'She said to tell you only if you were moaning about coming over. A last resort, bribe kinda thing.'

'The letter, Ian?'

'It's from your dad,' Ian said and Kenny could picture his cousin's face scrunched up as he issued the words. Only he in the world knew how important his father's absence in his life had become. 'I swear to God, Kenny, this is the first I heard of it.'

'So it's not a new letter?' No one had heard a word about or from him in the last seventeen years... and five days. Or so he thought.

'Apparently it arrived when you were eighteen and Mum has been keeping it until you were old enough to–'

'Fuck,' said Kenny. His old man was still alive. Or at least he had been when he was eighteen. 'What does the letter say?' He swallowed. If he is alive, where the fuck has he been? Acid scored his stomach. He took a deep breath. Dropped his shoulders. Forced some calm. Seventeen years was a long time.

'Like she's going to let me read it. She's not even let Dad read it.'

'That would all but kill the old fucker. He'd be desperate–'

'He doesn't even know about it,' Ian continued and Kenny whistled. That was something. For her to keep something from her husband. When he found out, there would be hell to pay. He'd whine about it until he gave them both ulcers.

'Time?' asked Kenny.

'Oh, it's...' He heard a rustle and the next words that came from Ian sounded distant. Like he'd placed the phone away from the side of his face to look at the time. '...It's three thirty.'

'Naw, ya numpty,' said Kenny. 'What time tonight?'

'Six o'clock, ya numpty. When else?'

'Aye. Right enough.' It was a standing family joke that Uncle Colin had to eat at six o'clock sharp. It didn't matter what else was happening, where they were or who they were with, Uncle Colin had to be sat at a table with a fork and knife in each hand and a plate heaped with meat and two veg in front of him.

'Afore you go, Kenny... if you can see your way to having some stuff...'

'I don't do drugs, Ian. I've never dealt them and I nev͟ ͟ ͟'͟'͟'

'Not since that last time.'

That last time.

There were few career choices for a man like Ian. Too full of testosterone as a teenager, he'd messed up. The army offered a way out. A way to grow up. He revelled in the command system: having someone to tell him what to do and when. He'd gone all around the world and loved it. Then came Afghanistan. He'd returned a changed man. From nice, aggressive and simple, he became nice, addicted and simple. 'That last time' referred to two years ago. The doctors prescribed methadone. He ran out of the stuff and tried to go cold turkey. It nearly killed him and Aunt Vi had begged Kenny to get her boy a fix. He'd done what she asked, saved Ian's life and earned Uncle Colin's hate for the rest of his life.

'It's just a wee bit of weed, man. My usual guy has gone and got himself arrested...'

'That's cos it's fucking illegal. Not to mention fucking stupid.'

'Don't need the lecture, dude.'

'See you at six,' Kenny said and hung up.

'Mmm, gorgeous,' he said.

'Not a little bit too cheesy?' she asked.

'You can never have enough cheese,' he grinned.

She looked him up and down. 'Nice teeth, all your own hair, oh...' – she took in his flat belly – '...and no paunch. Who are you and what have you done with the nice Glaswegian who should be here?'

'You speak perfect, but slightly accented English. Your clothes have a European look to them. You seem to be actually interested in what some of these puffed-up peacocks have to say. Who are you and what have you done with the nice Glaswegian who should be here?'

She laughed, her head tilting back, her teeth flashing.

'At least one of us is from Glasgow,' she said.

Kenny shook his head. 'I'm from Ayrshire. What are you, French?'

'Swiss.'

'Is everything in your life ordered and precise?'

'I'm Swiss-Italian. Much more relaxed. What about you? Do you conform to the cliché of the west of Scotland male?' She placed the rim of her glass against her bottom lip.

'Let me see...' He looked to the ceiling as if searching for the right words. 'I hate rugby, love football. Hate beer, love wine. I exercise regularly–'

'I noticed.'

'Shh, don't interrupt when I'm impressing you.' They laughed together, his deep notes of amusement folded among her light song. 'I floss twice a day, don't talk about my feelings ever, but I cry like a girl when an athlete collects his gold medal at the Olympics. I hate deep-fried Mars bars and I love it when I have a beautiful woman's undivided attention.'

'And I love it when a non-conformist conforms.'

A man coughed at their side. He was in his mid- to late-fifties, sporting a gleaming set of teeth and wearing his large belly like it

15

was a badge of success.

Alexis offered him a smile and faced Kenny.

'Excuse me,' – she placed a hand on his forearm – 'I am other-wise engaged this evening. It has been a pleasure talking to you. I hope your work with the council goes well.' As she walked away the big belly guy took a grip of her arm and Kenny could hear him saying, 'What were you talking to that guy about?'

'He was just keeping me amused while you were talking busi-ness, Tommy.'

As Kenny watched them getting closer to the bar, he saw Tommy move his mouth to her ear. She shrank back as if he had issued some sort of threat. Or maybe that was what Kenny wanted to see, for in the next moment she was whispering something in his ear and they both laughed.

For the rest of the evening, Kenny kept an eye on them, trying to work out what their relationship was. That it might be, or could be, sexual in nature became apparent as the evening wore on. At least that was how Tommy clearly wanted it to be judging by the way his great paws couldn't stop touching her, but Alexis' behaviour never ratcheted up beyond mildly flirtatious.

Eventually, Kenny mentally slapped himself on the forehead as he realised the truth of the situation. How could he not? He waited until Tommy walked off, presumably to go to the toilet, before approaching Alexis again.

She was wearing an expression that was one part quizzical, one part wary and several parts amused.

'Do you have a card?' Kenny asked her.

'But of course,' she answered with a tilt of her head. She opened her purse and delicately picked one out and handed it to him.

He read the gold embossed lettering on white card. All it con-tained was her name and mobile telephone number.

'Very discreet.'

'Of course. I find that you Brits are a little less accepting than the Continentals in these matters, but even more... needy.'

'I think I must be more Continental when it comes to negotiable affections,' he replied before pressing his lips to the card and placing it in his breast pocket.

A smile from Alexis aimed over his shoulder alerted Kenny to the fact that Tommy had returned. He brushed past Kenny so hard that he had to put a hand on the bar to steady himself. The older man stood beside Alexis.

'I think we should be away now,' he said, completely ignoring Kenny.

People had lost a few teeth for less, but remembering where he was Kenny decided to let it pass. Now was not the time for violence. In a loud enough voice to carry along the bar, Kenny addressed the couple. 'Tommy, it's so nice to hear that you've recovered from the prostate surgery. Hope it hasn't affected you too much.' He shook the other man's hand with enough pressure to crack a knuckle. 'You treat this young lady well, okay?' He laughed with exaggerated heartiness. 'Cos if you don't, I'll hunt you down.' With a wink to Alexis, who was struggling to hide her mirth from Tommy, Kenny turned and walked away.

He was met at the door by Liam Devlin. The smaller man walked towards him with brisk steps. Ever the politician, airbrushed with the certainty of his position in the world; his suit and tie looked as fresh as they undoubtedly were first thing that morning. 'Do you know who that is?' he asked Kenny.

'No. Don't care.' Kenny grinned at his own petulance.

'Tommy Hunt is not a man to mess with. He knows people.'

'I'm happy for him. I know people too.'

'Dangerous people, Kenny.'

'Wooo.' Kenny laughed and made a face. He then sobered and looked Liam squarely in the eye. 'I am dangerous people.'

He called Alexis the very next day. They arranged a meeting that night and partied vigorously for two days. The sex was tender, it was hard. They fucked like animals, they giggled like teenagers, they lingered, connected at the groin for hours. It was fun, it was furious, it was expensive and it was worth every penny. And by the end of the two days Kenny was in a place he had promised himself he would never be.

He was in love.

• • •

She'd left him a text and a message. That wasn't like her. She normally left all the running to him, after all he was the one who was paying for it. The text was an address that he had never visited, but one that he vaguely recognised. For her to leave him a voicemail there must be something wrong. He thought about the other message that was waiting for him, the letter from his father. He desperately needed to know what was in that letter. His Aunt Vi had kept a hold of it all this time, so why now? He'd had many birthdays between eighteen and thirty, why was this one so important? What level of maturity had she imagined he'd reached that would allow him to process whatever the letter contained?

Curiosity won in the short term. He pressed dial on the phone. A voice told him he had one new message. Before he could decide whether or not to listen to it, the message came on line and Alexis' voice filled his ear.

'Kenny. Please call me. It's urgent. Please. You know I wouldn't...' There was a suppressed sob and then the call ended.

4

He typed the address from the text into his sat-nav and soon he was on his way down St Vincent Street and headed towards the Merchant City.

This is one of the oldest parts of the city. In medieval times it was dotted with orangeries, rose gardens and the odd merry monk. Now it's an area of bars, clubs, boutique hotels, concert halls and very expensive apartments.

One of which contained a weepy, but hopefully unhurt escort girl. By some minor miracle, Kenny managed to park his vehicle at the secure entrance to Alexis' flat. He locked the car, walked the half-dozen steps to the buzzer and pressed. As he waited for an answer, he looked around him. There was the odd couple strolling arm in arm. The occasional passing taxi and a plethora of parked cars. Nothing appeared to be out of the ordinary. He peered in to some of the cars nearest to him. Just in case. But no one seemed to be lurking in wait for an over-protective punter.

'Hello,' a tinny voice issued from the speaker at the side of the door.

'It's me,' he said. 'It's Kenny.'

The buzzer sounded and he pushed the door open. Kenny hated lifts, so he took the stairs. As he ran up, taking two at a time, he tried to imagine what state Alexis might be in; the reason for her upset and why he was the one she turned to.

Six floors later and he was breathing easily. Fit and strong is the new black, he thought as he knocked on her door. She opened it immediately, offering him a weak smile and enough time to see she was wearing no make-up, her hair was badly needing a wash and the heavy bruising down one side of her face.

She turned and walked down the passageway into her living room. Kenny was full of questions, but he knew Alexis well enough to know that she would come round to the answers in her own good time.

She folded herself into the corner of a giant brown, velvet-covered sofa and fixed her eyes on the fifty-inch plasma TV, where Billie Piper was doing her thing. Despite his need to know what the hell was happening, Kenny couldn't help but look around the room. Although he had been 'seeing' Alexis for over a year now, they only ever met in hotels. This was the first time he had actually been allowed in to her refuge.

It was classy. As he expected. Large colourful prints hung on the cream walls, the curtains were luxurious fabrics, and the furniture was sparse but clearly expensive.

'Whenever I need to laugh with irony I watch this crap,' Alexis said, nodding at the TV.

Billie Piper was whipping some guy on a bed. He was wearing nothing but ~~...~~ ...head, indicating he had no idea what they were watching.

'It's Belle Du Jour. She's a call girl and she makes it look like it's all glam and no pain. That your soul doesn't get sucked out of your body every time someone pays you to suck their cock. That the *Pretty Woman* myth is alive and well.' Alexis chewed the inside of her lip and crossed her arms; her right hand slowly began stroking her left shoulder. She looked down at her lap and then up at Kenny through her fringe.

'Sorry. You didn't need to hear that.'

'What the hell happened, Alexis?'

She bit her top lip and looked into the distance. Elements of her real character played across the stage of her eyes. Kenny read pride warring with consequence; uncertainty tinged with self-loathing.

He moved over to her and knelt by her feet. Saying nothing, he examined her bruised face. He touched it lightly. Nothing appeared to be broken.

'Do you have any numbness? Any tingling?'

Alexis chewed on the inside of her cheek and shook her head.

'Are you hurt anywhere else?' Kenny asked, dreading the answer. He realised his fists were clenched and that he needed to hurt somebody. Who could have done this? What sick fucker would hurt a beautiful woman, any woman like this?

Alexis looked into his eyes. 'Don't, Kenny. Don't.' She pressed herself further into the cushion of the sofa. 'Don't be so nice...' Her eyes filled with tears.

'Are you hurt anywhere else, Alexis? Should we call–'

'He got his guy to rape me, Kenny.' Her voice was just above a whisper. Her head fell forward and sobs wracked her body. Kenny sat on the sofa beside her and took her in his arms. She gave in to his need to console her and allowed the emotion to carry her. He said nothing, simply held her, stroking her head. Two sides of him struggled for attention; his worry for her well-being and his demand to kick some bastard until his head was mush.

After several minutes, she managed to rein herself in.

'I need a shower, or a bath. I need to clean myself.'

'Should you...? Don't you need to...?'

'Kenny, I'm a prostitute. The law doesn't want to concern itself with people like me. Besides, I've already had two baths. Any... DNA has been washed away.' She stood up and brushed past him. She took two steps, moved faster and began running down the hall. A door slammed. Kenny found himself standing at the door of the living room looking down the empty hallway and feeling completely useless.

He walked slowly down the hall, listening for any sounds. The second door down was closed. He tested the handle. It was locked.

Sounds of weeping came from the other side.

'Go away,' Alexis shouted. 'Leave me alone.'

Kenny considered doing just that. He looked towards the front door and back down the hall to the living room. She had called him. Part of her must want him to be here. She didn't invite just anyone to her living space. Besides, his muscles ached with the need for action. He had to do something. He had to find out who hurt her and pay them back, with interest.

He walked back down towards the sound of the TV and sat on the sofa. Leaning forward, elbows on his knees he considered what he should do. He spotted a door off to the side. Could that be...? Yes, it was the kitchen. He walked in, switched on a light and walked over to the kettle. He filled it with water and switched it on. When all else fails, resort to cliché. A nice cup of tea will surely help.

As he waited for the kettle to boil he looked around the kitchen. White doors, chrome appliances; everything spotless. Like it was a show home, or about to be sold. In fact everything about the entire flat had that same feel. Unlived in.

He made two cups of tea and left one steaming on the worktop. He walked back over to the sofa and sat down. Sipping his tea, he looked around himself. Yes, this place definitely had that same feeling; that the owner barely lived here. He considered what he really knew about Alexis. She was born in a small village on the Swiss border with Italy. That she was around the same age as him and that she gave a damn good blowjob. Pathetic. And this was a woman he supposedly had feelings for.

He stared across the room. And realised with a start what he was looking at. It was a phone seat. God, people still had them? It was some kind of dark wood with velour padding and on the shelf sat an actual honest-to-fuck phone. Not a mobile, hand-held computer, but a small simple piece of technology with a large round dial and a thing you hold against the side of your head to speak into.

Beside the phone sat a leather-bound book. Like a diary. Or, an appointment book. Kenny, you eejit. He walked over and picked

22

it up. Of course. It would let him know who Alexis had been with earlier on.

He opened it up. The pages crackled with a satisfying quality as he looked for that day's page. He looked down the entries. Three entries in blue ink on crisp vanilla paper. At ten, she had noted, *Doctor*. At twelve, *The Chip*. The entry for 4pm read simply, *DT*.

He closed the book and placed it back down on its space. The Chip? There was a popular eaterie over in the West End called The Ubiquitous Chip. Might she have been having lunch with someone there?

DT. Who could that be? Other than that the page was empty.

He looked back across the room at the sofa. Under where he had been sitting he could see a handbag. One of those capacious things that women loved and would spend their last penny on. In every man's experience such a bag was crucially important to a woman, held their entire lives and yet they could never find anything when they wanted it.

Back at the sofa, he picked it up. He only considered for a moment if what he was doing was in any way wrong. He always felt that looking in a woman's handbag was a big no-no, a violation even. But today was no time for social niceties. He had to find out what was going on.

Her mobile phone was tucked into a pocket. He pulled it out and read that only one bar was showing – it had a poor signal and it was about to run out of juice. There was one unread message. With barely a pause and only the tiniest feeling of guilt, he opened it. The message had two words.

Lesson learned?

Kenny checked the sender. TD. Well, that was a coincidence and who the hell was TD? Whoever he was, he was going to be very sorry he had messed with his girl.

His girl? Get a hold of yourself, O'Neill.

He looked down at the phone and scrolled through the contact list. He wondered if he knew any of the people here. There were a few first names of women and a list of initials. There he was. KO. When he and Alexis were together she never discussed any of her other punters. They had the occasional laugh at some of the weird, silly ones, but Alexis was a professional; no names were ever given. He scrolled down to TD.

Just then he heard a door open and the pad of feet as they moved in his direction. He dropped the phone in the bag and managed to kick it back under the sofa before Alexis appeared at the doorway.

She had brushed her hair out, put on some make-up and was wearing an ankle-length sheer gown that hid nothing of the shape underneath. Despite himself, he responded. Blood surged into his groin.

'You have money?' Her expression was all business. He nodded.

'You need to fuck me and you need to pay me,' she said as she walked towards him.

'Alexis, I...' He stood up, arms wide.

She reached him and opened her gown. His eyes slid from the swelling of her breasts down to the spare line of hair above the pout between her legs.

'This is not a good idea,' he heard himself say as she tugged at his belt.

'You need to take this big hard cock...' She stroked him through the material of his trousers.

'Alexis, I don't want to hurt...' He felt shame at his arousal heat his neck. He placed his hands on her shoulders, pushing her back a little.

'Kenny,' she said, her expression shifting. A hurt, little girl peered out from behind thick, mascara'd lashes. 'You need to do this for me.' The working girl was back. 'Leave your cash on the table there.' Her hand moved back to his groin and she gripped his shaft as he pulled his wallet from his back pocket and pulled out two hundred pounds.

'It's all I've got on me,' he said. 'I didn't expect...'

'Shh.' She placed a finger over his lips. 'For tonight, that will do.'

24

In the bedroom, her ankles locked behind his back as he moved in and out of her wetness. She raked his back and buttocks with her nails.

'Harder, Kenny. Fuck me harder,' she shouted into his ear and he lost his sense of guilt and gave in to the role she was demanding of him. He grunted and thrust, working up into a rhythm she was looking for. He surrendered to the sensations, to her urgency and came in a hot rush.

Panting, he rolled over on to his back. His usual post-orgasmic feeling shaded with distaste. No, disgust. He shouldn't have given in to her. He should have been more supportive. More of a friend.

Alexis jumped off the bed and put on a white towelling robe. She pulled her hair back from her face, her expression strained through with a number of unreadable emotions. 'Now you need to get the hell out of my apartment.'

'But Alexis...'

'Kenny, don't make me ask you again,' she said as she crossed her arms. 'Just go.'

5

He turned the radio on full blast as he drove home, as if to crowd out the confusion in his mind. It made sense to him that she'd want to force some sort of normality into her life. What was normal for her was a transaction. When it came to that form of negotiation she held the power. She decided what happened and when. She made the choice.

He got that. But how could she face another man after one had forced himself on her and hurt her? Surely she should never want to breathe the same air as another man again.

The bass-line of an old Luther Vandross track filled the car.

'...she's a super lady, uh huh...'

Ahh, the irony. He switched channels and found a station playing some hard rock. That was more in keeping with his mood.

The roads were quiet. Most people would surely be curled under a quilt, having given up on one day and sleeping on the expectation that the next might be an improvement.

Sleep. That would be nice. He suddenly realised how tired he was.

Shit. Fuckity fuck. He'd forgotten all about his Aunt Vi and the letter. He looked at the clock. 11:30. They'd all be in bed now and his name would be muddier than mud. He'd go first thing in the morning, with a bunch of flowers and a pair of earplugs to drown out the moans of his Uncle Colin. How that woman had stayed with him all these years, he'd never know.

He was on the Great Western Road driving out towards Kelvinside when the bright beam of car headlights filled his mirror. He looked up, trying to judge who it was. Police? He turned down the volume on his stereo. The car lights appeared closer and he could hear music coming from the other car. Not police then, just a joyrider.

He pressed his foot down on the accelerator. His car surged forward. It might only have been a Ford, but it was the top of the range and had plenty power to spare. The lights from the other car faded into the distance and then came back as the driver faced up to the challenge that Kenny now presented him with.

He heard a shout and looked in his mirror. There were two guys in the other car. He couldn't make out both of them, but he could see the driver was not happy. Good. Kenny had a surfeit of anger to deal out and if this guy wanted some, he was happy to oblige. For his own part he never could understand that urge to assert your position on the road, that rage that built up in some people. We all have somewhere to go and the roads are wide enough for us all. Why lose it just because someone gives us an imagined slight while we are behind the wheel of a car? A similar incident while out walking would barely merit a look, but a car engine purring in front of some people was enough for them to act as if you had just threatened to rape their kids.

Kenny jumped on the brake. A squeal of tyres sounded from the other car as the driver fought to avoid a collision. Then Kenny pushed down on the accelerator and surged away. Within seconds the other car was back on his tail and through the mirror Kenny could see that the driver's face was contorted with fury, as he screamed a challenge at him. The passenger on the other hand, was sitting with his arms crossed, looking decidedly uncomfortable. They were young, but not so young that he couldn't deal them a lesson. The driver: shaved head, square face; he would have guessed early twenties. Kenny shifted the mirror to get a quick look at his passenger. From what he could see, he had some height on the driver and a couple of years. He had blonde hair, cut army-short and was a finer featured version of the other. Brothers or perhaps cousins?

He turned left at the next junction. Pulled to a stop and stepped out of the car. He was more than happy to see how this was going to play out. Two of them, against one of him. Just the odds he needed.

Kenny could see now that the other car was a Golf. It screamed to a halt behind his car and the two guys stepped out. Straight away he could see that they were gym bunnies. Despite the fact it was a cold night in March they were both wearing T-shirts. Tight enough to show off the heft of their muscle. A muscle that was earned, no doubt, while posing in front of a full-length mirror for hours and hours. A muscle that would give them a false sense of security when they teamed up against a solitary man.

Oh well, thought Kenny, their funeral.

'You got a death wish, mate?' the driver asked as he stomped towards him. He was just under six feet, all shoulders, pecs and biceps. Working out to a pattern that would show best when he was wearing T-shirt and jeans. His thighs nowhere as developed as the top half of his body.

'C'mon, Mark,' the passenger said, 'we don't want any trouble.' He was looking over Kenny, appraising him. Smart, thought Kenny while he in turn checked him out. He would be more of a challenge than his buddy. Just over six feet, he was leaner and more in proportion and he walked with a grace that suggested a more rounded fitness regime. If Kenny didn't take him out first, this might get interesting. Perhaps too interesting. The tall one would have to go first.

'What the fuck you playin' at, mate?' The driver was working himself up to the necessary pitch before he waded in to mete out some punishment. 'We're going to fuck you up so bad, you'll be eating through a straw for months.'

'Mark,' the passenger said, 'enough. Let's go.'

'I'm going to have you, mate,' Mark said. 'And my brother here is going to wade in and kick your arse because that's what brothers do.' He turned to face his brother. 'They help each other. Now get some steel, bro, and help me waste this wanker.'

Kenny simply stood before them, arms loose by his side, feet shoulder-width apart, saying nothing. Giving them nothing back. The man who doubts is the man who loses, his old fight teacher once told him. Sow some doubt and the first battle is won.

'What, can you no fuckin' speak, ya poof?' Mark said.

'Aye, probably been up at some gay bar getting pumped in the toilet, ya fanny,' his brother joined in, half-heartedly. This guy clearly didn't want to be here, but judging by the way he was still moving nearer Kenny and by the way he was working his hands, he would do what was necessary to help his brother.

Fine by me, thought Kenny. Still saying nothing. He looked over their shoulders at the junction. As he expected, there were a couple of CCTV cameras trained down the main road. Whoever was operating them hadn't yet thought to check on this side of the junction. Good. No witnesses.

Kenny maintained his position, feeling his connection with the ground. His certainty. He thought of Alexis and the bruise on her face. He thought of her need to have paid sex with him. Man, that was fucked up. He imagined his anger as a white ball of anger, he allowed it to spread and fill his muscles. He revelled in the feeling of the violence that was to come. He waited till the men stepped a little closer and then attacked.

6

Kenny's motto was to get in quick, maximise the damage and then get back out again. The smaller brother – Mark – he pegged straight away as the big mouth, and the taller one as the real danger in the situation. Take him out and the other guy would be much more manageable.

He jumped inside the guy's range, just as he was about to launch a punch. It didn't come anywhere near connecting. Kenny brought up his right leg, and stamped down with his foot on the other man's knee. The joint moved in a direction knees were never intended to.

The man fell down with a scream. He wouldn't be getting back up again soon. Kenny turned to face his smaller brother, who was coming at him like a windmill. He was all about power and he expected that would always be enough for him to win any fight. He'd clearly never come up against anyone like Kenny.

He waited till the last moment, wheeled to the side. Mark lost his balance. He righted himself. Kenny kneed him in the gut. Breath exploded from the other man's lungs. Kenny wheeled again and brought an elbow crashing on to the side of his face.

Mark groaned. He stepped back. His expression was one of fear. He was breathing hard. He hadn't expected this and Kenny looked like he had barely expended any effort.

Kenny took another step closer. Mark looked round to see where his brother was. Kenny was between him, the cars and his brother.

He turned and ran.

'Aw, for fuck's sake,' Kenny exclaimed. 'Come back,' he shouted at Mark's rapidly retreating back. 'I was only getting warmed up.'

He turned to the brother who was struggling to stand up. Kenny looked from him to the other one, who was still running. His anger left him as if flushed out with the brief spell of action. He ground his teeth at his own reaction. Shit. They were barely out of their teens. He should know better.

'Maybe you shouldn't stand on that,' he said. 'Might do it irreparable harm.'

'I could still get you when I'm one-legged.' The young man hopped up and down and held his fists out.

Kenny laughed. 'What's your name?'

'Is that so you can tell all your bum-chums who kicked your arse?'

'You've got spirit, son,' Kenny said and lunged forward as if to attack. His opponent tried to hop backwards and fell. He groaned with the pain.

'See, if I wasn't in so much pain, I'd have you.'

'What's your name?' Kenny repeated. He looked down at him sprawled on the ground, cradling his knee and his mouth contorted with pain.

'Calum,' was the reply as he moved into a sitting position. 'And I could still kick your arse.'

'One-legged? That would be a feat.' Kenny laughed. 'Oh, get it?' He giggled, his laughter fed by the adrenalin that was still feeding his system. 'A feat? One-legged?' He laughed some more. Forced himself to calm down and joined Calum on the ground.

Calum flinched as if expecting another blow.

'Nah, you're awright, mate,' said Kenny. 'The moment has passed.' He looked down at Calum's leg.

'How's the knee?'

'Fucking agony. Don't know if I can stand on it.' He made a face as he tried to flex the whole limb. 'Aaaah,' he groaned. 'Can't move it.'

'Shit, man,' said Kenny. 'You're going to have to get that seen to, Calum. And soon. We're talking ligament damage.'

'You for real?' Calum squinted over at him.

'What do you mean?'

'You face up to a road-rage merchant. Near break my leg... and now you're offering sympathy?'

'About the leg thing – I'm really sorry,' said Kenny. And he was. He could see that there was more to this young man than abusing other road users. There was something about the way he held himself. The calmness before the fight and then the refusal to give in despite being quickly taken out of the action.

'Yeah, what was that move?' Calum asked. 'I've done some martial arts...'

'That was from the street, Calum. I could see in a blink that you were the dangerous one. I had to take you out quickly so I could concentrate on the lesser fighter,' Kenny said. 'Your brother's a pussy by the way.'

'Who you callin' a pussy?' The shout came from further down the street. Mark must have reconsidered his flight and returned to see if there was any fight left or if his brother was okay.

'You're a pussy, Mark,' Calum shouted. 'You fucking ran.'

'See how quick he took you out, brother. I wasn't going to wait for that.'

'So you fucking ran.'

Kenny stood up and looked down the street. Mark was hunched over behind some cars. Despite his obvious fear he was making his way back up towards his brother. Can't be all bad, thought Kenny.

He took a step towards Mark. Mark took a couple of steps back, stopped and then took a step forward.

'I'm not a pussy,' he repeated, looking about seventeen years old.

'What age are you?' Kenny asked.

'Twenty-two. How?' Mark scowled.

Kenny tutted. 'No, buddy, the question is, why?' It was one verbal tic that pissed Kenny off; too many people these days used

'How?' as their default question.

'Eh?'

'Brought up by Red Indians?'

'How?'

'Mark, shut the fuck up,' Calum joined in. 'You're comin' across as a total loser.'

'Aye, ya dobber,' shouted Mark. 'You're the wan wae the fucked-up knee.'

Kenny groaned. He was going to be here all night.

'Mark,' Kenny shouted. 'Get your arse up here.'

'No fuckin' way. You're going to do me like you did him.'

'As I said to Calum, the moment's passed. Now I just want to be pals.'

'I'm no that stupid, mate. Once you're in that car and offski, I'll come and get my brother.'

Kenny shook his head and took the few steps back to Calum, who was now sitting on the kerb. His face was shaded with pain, but he was resigned to the situation, waiting to see how it worked out.

'You going to be alright?' Kenny asked.

Calum raised his eyebrows.

'I know, I know, why should I care?'

Calum read something in Kenny's expression. 'Might not be able to work for a few weeks.'

'What do you do?'

'I'm a bouncer in the evenings. Work with a security firm covering a few nightclubs in town. I'm a student during the day.'

'The bouncing thing figures. You look like you could take care of yourself... and you won't get hit by that same move again,' Kenny smiled. 'What are you studying?'

Calum made a face. 'Philosophy.'

'You're kidding me, right?'

'"I have had women, I have fought with men; and I could never turn back any more than a record can spin in reverse. And all that was leading me where? To this very moment..."'

'Bet girls love those lines. Who said it?'

'Jean Paul Sartre.'

'What does it mean?'

'Fucked if I know.'

They both laughed.

'What's going on up there?' shouted Mark. 'You two fallin' in love, or somethin'?'

'Shut the fuck up, Mark,' Calum and Kenny both replied at the same time.

'I feel we should share a smoke,' said Kenny.

Calum grinned. His eyes moved down the road in the general direction of his brother. He shrugged.

'Sorry about the car chase thing and the road-rage crap.'

'You're better than that, Calum,' Kenny said. 'Why'd you do it?'

'Mark's always hyped. Always got to prove he's the big man. But it usually ends up with me stringing along and protecting him, or...' – he looked down at his leg – '...taking the beating.' He shrugged again. 'Blood's thicker than water, mate.'

'Aye,' Kenny stood up and wiped the dirt from the seat of his trousers. 'But when the person with the blood connection is thicker than shite, you have to let them go to it on their own.'

'You learned that lesson?'

Kenny said nothing. He pulled his wallet from his pocket and plucked out a business card.

'Once you've got your knee in a brace give me a call. I could use somebody like you. You can bring your pussy brother once he's grown up a wee bit.'

'Who are you callin' a pussy?' the shout came from down the street.

7

Next morning, Kenny was up at his customary time. He'd never needed an alarm clock. Regardless of how late he went to bed, he was always fully alert at 6:30am. He ground some coffee, filled the espresso pot and left it to work its magic while he had a shower.

He sent off a quick text to Alexis: *You okay?* He didn't expect an immediate reply, thinking she must still be sleeping, but every couple of minutes he looked at the screen just in case.

The gym was his next stop and some core work. Another shower and he was off to see the nearest thing he had to a family.

'Aww, they're lovely, son,' Aunt Vi said as he handed her a bunch of flowers. There was no sign of any disappointment she might have felt at his no-show the previous evening. Her features were arranged in their usual set-up meant to convey warmth and welcome. This was a look she'd worked hard at, as if trying to compensate for the bulldog features of her husband.

'Didn't think garages would have flowers at this time of the morning,' Uncle Colin said, looking like he'd just read Nostradamus and he'd taken it that the world ending prophecy was meant for him alone.

'Just as well I know a florist then, isn't it?' Kenny offered the older man a thousand-watt grin, knowing that a sign of that much pleasure would truly piss him off.

'Och, it's good to see you, son.' Vi placed a hand on his arm. They were not a demonstrative family and this was as close as she came to showing affection. Kenny smiled in answer, feeling some surprise at how pleased he was to see her.

Sitting on the cream, leather three-seater sofa, Kenny looked around the room. Apart from a TV of biblical proportions, it hadn't changed since he was last here. Still the lace coverings on every surface and a collection of porcelain dolls dotted here and there. He was desperate to ask about the letter, but he didn't want his Aunt Vi to feel that it was the only reason he was here.

'You'll have had your breakfast?' Uncle Colin said, lowering himself into his chair and reaching for the TV remote. Most people would turn the TV off, but as Kenny expected he changed channels and turned the volume up slightly. The TV flicked from news, to sport, back to news and then settled on a reality He's-the-Father-of-My-Baby-and-He's-Shagging-My-Mother show.

'Colin,' Vi said, 'don't be so rude. We have a guest.'

'Guest? Where? All I can see is that great lump of a boy who ate us out of house and home.' It was a familiar refrain and Kenny saw the mouth move but didn't allow the words to register.

'A wee cuppa, sweetheart, and then you can tell me everything you've been up to.' Vi leaned forward, hands clasped together as if she was talking to a five-year-old.

'That would be nice, thank you,' said Kenny. To run from the room as if his jacket was on fire would have been his preferred action, but he sat back into the cushion of the chair. If nothing else, Vi was owed the courtesy.

'You still ducking and diving?' asked Uncle Colin, eyes fixed on the screen. 'Made your first million yet?' The words were conversational, but the tone suggested a serious lack of interest in the answer. He was playing the role his wife was looking for from him. If it was left to him, Kenny would still be standing at the door.

'I'm keeping busy, Uncle Colin,' Kenny said, fighting with the volume of the TV, which suddenly rose in pitch when a member of the audience ran up on stage and started punching the man who was shagging the mother. The rest of the audience were cheering him on, their faces brazen with the need to see someone pay. Lynch-mob TV, thought Kenny. Don't you just love it?

Both men fell silent as the drama carried on. Guards rushed on to the stage and a man was huckled off it. Now the daughter was haranguing the mother and the presenter was standing between them, pretending to calm them down. His face had that smug I-Fucking-Love-My-Job look on it.

'Right, son. Here you go.' Vi walked in carrying a tray. 'Still like your tea, son?'

'You can't beat a nice cup of tea,' said Kenny, who'd barely drunk a sip of the stuff in the last two years.

'I've got some croissants there as well, son. Just you tuck in and Colin,' – her voice raised slightly and some steel came into its tone – 'if you're going to watch that crap, go and watch it somewhere else.'

'This is my house and I'll watch what I like, Violet.'

She just looked at him.

'Right. Fine.' He stood up. 'Banished to my own kitchen,' he moaned as he walked out of the room.

'He's a lovely man, really,' Vi said as she took his seat, pointed the remote at the TV and turned the sound down. 'Just hides it well.'

'I heard that.' A shout came from the kitchen.

Vi rolled her eyes and spoke in a conspiratorial whisper. 'He'll be standing at the kitchen doorway listening to everything we say. Nosey old so-and-so.' As she spoke her eyes were shaped with a mixture of long-suffering wife syndrome and not a little affection. An affection that always took Kenny by surprise. His uncle was a man who repelled that particular emotion in almost everyone else.

'He never had the charm of your dad, Kenny, but he's always been a good man to me. He's never let me down.' Vi settled into her chair and with a smile offered her usual defence of her husband's behaviour. There was a time when his Uncle Colin's words would have had Kenny running out the door and kicking it on the way past. But now he could make allowances.

'I'm sorry about last night, Aunt Vi,' said Kenny. 'A friend of mine was...'

'S'alright, son,' she replied. 'You're a busy man...'

'He's a crook, Violet. A bigger crook than his father ever was. I don't know why you let him in that door,' Colin shouted from the kitchen. Vi rolled her eyes.

'What about that nice boy you used to be friends with? The one who became a policeman?' This was the only way that Aunt Vi ever commented on his career choice. She'd bring up Ray McBain and hope the fact that he was a decent member of society might shock him into an act of conscience and make him turn his back on a life of crime.

'Yeah, Ray's fine. He's an Inspector now.'

'Yeah, the friend becomes a detective,' shouted Colin from the kitchen. 'Our two become a junky and a thief.'

'Excuse me, son,' said Vi and walked to the door. From there she looked down the hallway and addressed her husband. 'He is the child of my late sister and I love him like he's my own. I don't care if he's...' – she struggled for the worst possible crime – '...a paedophile, I'll still love him. I've not seen him for two years and it's all because of you and your petty mouth. So, if you want me to carry on cooking your food, laundering your clothes or any of the other hundred wee jobs I do for you, then you'll keep your mouth shut, Colin Hunter.'

She turned to face Kenny, bit her bottom lip and looked to the side as if waiting for a reply. The silence surprised them both. She raised her eyebrows and flushed; embarrassed at losing control. She returned to her seat.

'I meant that, son,' she said, her eyes moist. 'I've missed you... I understand why you don't want to be in the same room... but it would be nice to hear from you now and again.'

Kenny accepted this most gentle and most effective of rebukes. He looked over his aunt and felt guilt sour his mouth at his neglect of her. She hadn't changed much since he last saw her. Her hair was

38

still shaped in a blonde bob that came down to her shoulders. She still wore her favourite wool twin-set and long skirt over her thick-set body. She'd be around sixty now, thought Kenny as he read the lines on her forehead and the loosening of her skin along the jaw-line. Never one for much make-up, her face was bare apart from a warm peach colour on her lips.

Kenny felt a rush of affection for her. Must be getting old, he thought.

'Sorry, Aunt Vi. It was never deliberate and it was never you. I just...'

'I know, son. You don't owe me an explanation. I know you'll always be there if I need you.'

She smiled and, reaching forward, patted his knee. Her smile was laced through with empathy, apology and regret. Then she breathed, displaying some nerves for the first time.

She swallowed, took another deep breath.

'The letter.'

8

Now that the moment had come, Kenny was unsure that he wanted to know what the letter contained. He was a grown man. He had proved he could survive and flourish despite everything. What did it matter what it said?

But there were so many questions. What really happened that evening? He lost both parents at the same time. He remembered worrying that it was all his fault. He picked through every conversation he had with both his mum and dad in the weeks leading up to that night and found a hundred things he'd said that might have been the cause. His twelve-year-old mind sought importance in the banal and found it. He moaned so much about his bike, he had flunked school, and he had been 'lifted' by the police for throwing eggs at passing cars. All or any of this was to blame.

Then came the nights he would lie awake certain that suicide was catching, that he would find himself with a knife at his wrists ready to slash and nothing would stop the muscle from carrying out the action. He became obsessed with a nearby bridge; maybe he would find himself climbing over the wall, like waking up from a sleepwalk, and then jump into the dark, cold waters below.

'When your mum died,' – Aunt Vi cut through his thoughts – 'I was so angry. She was my sister. Why didn't she come to me and talk? Then there was the guilt. Why didn't I go to her and talk? It was so confusing.' She rubbed at her forehead, her eyes shaded with the hurt. She closed them and refocused. Showing that the pain had never gone away, it was there like an unwelcome relative. 'I can only imagine what you went through.'

'It was a formative experience,' Kenny said with a weak smile.

'And then some... I worried that I didn't offer you enough support and then when the letter arrived...' She shrugged and Kenny could read her trepidation.

'I was eighteen and a tearaway. If you'd given me the letter, who knows what I would have done?'

'God.' She held a hand over her heart. 'Every time a knock went at the door I was convinced it was the police to tell me you and Ian had been killed in a gang fight.'

'If it wasn't for Ian, I would have been,' Kenny said, remembering dozens of fights he had started. And the times Ian had backed him up. He was nothing but energy and anger. He yearned for the connection of fist on bone. The satisfaction of letting go consumed him. The only time he felt alive was when he was trading blows with another boy. 'I must have been a nightmare child.'

'Still. You were here. You were my sister's boy. I needed that connection, and it felt... that your acting out was my punishment for failing my sister.'

'Complications of the human mind.'

'Is that a book?'

'It should be,' he grinned.

'What do you remember of your father?'

'Some... bits and pieces...' He tailed off. In truth, he remembered much more of his father than his mother and it felt like some sort of weakness. Both parents earned his anger. Both abandoned him. The method was different, but the effect was the same. Whenever he tried to recall his mother's face he struggled, but his father's sprang into his mind as if he had just seen him an hour earlier. Did he think the suicide was more of a betrayal, was that it?

He knew from a young age that his father's primary source of income was illegal. This knowledge caused him shame at first, but then... His dad took risks, his dad was an important man, people were afraid of him. He earned respect the hard way. All of which was of course a bath-sized portion of bullshit, but to an impressionable child was electrifying.

He wanted nothing more than to grow up to be just like his dad.

Saturday afternoons were his favourite time. Dad would take him to Firhill to see his team, Partick Thistle. Dad thought it was too easy to support the big two – Celtic or Rangers – and thought it was a sign of a free-thinker to go for the less obvious. He remembered moving through the crowds, viewing a world of bobbing heads from his perch on his father's shoulders and how people used to gravitate around him. It seemed everyone knew Peter O'Neill and everyone wanted to speak to him. It made Kenny feel important that his father was such a man. Kenny could see that the backslaps, the handshakes, were hesitant; born of fear rather than respect.

It was intoxicating.

'Actually,' said Aunt Vi, 'it was more than one letter.'

'What?' Kenny sat straighter.

'He sent one on your birthday, each year from your eighteenth. They stopped when you were twenty-one.' Vi chewed on the inside of her cheek. 'I'm sorry, son. You weren't ready for... I'll go and get them for you.'

She was gone for a couple of minutes. Kenny could hear her footsteps up the stairs and across the ceiling. His Uncle Ian stuck his head in the door.

'Is she...?'

Kenny nodded.

His Uncle Colin looked at him, thought about speaking and then listened to his wife returning.

'S'pose given where you came from it couldn't be helped,' he said, shrugged and then returned to his spot in the kitchen. What was that, thought Kenny. Understanding? Was he being excused? Or written off? Like he could give a shit.

Aunt Vi handed him a green shoebox with the legend *Clarks* on the outside. Her expression was unreadable.

Kenny accepted the box from her and resisted the urge to open it straightaway. He needed to be alone.

Aunt Vi walked to the front door, knowing exactly what was in Kenny's thoughts. Gratefully, he followed. At the door she stretched up on tiptoes and grazed his cheek with a kiss.

'Whatever you're feeling is right, Kenny. Don't doubt yourself, just process it.'

'Christ on a bike,' sounded from down the hall. 'Somebody's been watching too much Oprah.'

• • •

Kenny placed the box on the passenger seat, turned the key in the ignition. Before he drove off he had a look at the screen on his phone to see if Alexis had left a message. Nothing.

There was a knock on the car window and his Aunt Vi's face loomed before him.

'Sorry, son,' she said when he rolled down the window. 'Can I ask you something?'

'Sure,' said Kenny, wondering if this was something about his cousin.

'Let's drive.' She opened the door, picked up the box and sat down. She offered him a smile in lieu of explanation. 'My nosey old man will be at the window. He thinks I just popped in next door.'

'Where do you want to go?'

'Wherever.'

Kenny put the car in gear and drove off. Minutes later a giant superstore hove into view and Vi gestured that they should go in there. Thinking that this was all a bit strange, Kenny did as she asked. He found a parking space close to the entrance and turned to her.

'Good,' she said, 'I need to get something for tonight's tea.'

'Eh?'

She laughed. 'Only joking, son.' She tapped his shoulder with her fist. 'You got to laugh, don't you?' She paused and looked out of the window. 'Or you'd never stop crying.'

Kenny said nothing. She'd get to the point in her own good time. He looked down at the box she was cradling on her lap. He really needed to see inside.

He felt her hand on the side of his face.

'You must laugh when you hear people say that childhood is the best years of our lives,' Vi said softly. Kenny turned to face her and saw that her eyes were shaped with regret, apology and any number of unnamed emotions. He felt his throat tighten in response.

'You have nothing to be sorry for, Aunt Vi.' He heard the emotion in his voice and coughed. 'You did your best.' Mentally he gave himself a shake. Normally he had all the emotions of a breezeblock. What was happening to him?

'You had so much anger in you, Kenny. I used to think that if I touched your skin I would get burned.'

Kenny smiled as memories of teenage tantrums filled his head. 'God, I was a little shit. Don't know how you put up with me. No wonder Uncle Colin was always threatening me with an orphanage.'

'Over my dead body, son. Nobody was putting my sister's child in a home,' Vi said and patted his hand.

They settled into silence for a few moments. Kenny looked out of the window at shoppers going in and out of the superstore and wondered what dramas were being played out in each of these people's lives.

'This note arrived addressed to me. It was on the floor of the hall the morning of your birthday.' She handed him a small piece of card. The front bore a painting of flowers in a vase. The colours were pastel, the arrangement generic. It was the kind of card old women would send each other, Kenny thought. He opened it up. Three words were typed in the middle.

Does he know?

Kenny read it. He held it up. 'What the hell is this all about?'

'I think it's from your dad.'

'Really?' Kenny sat and stared at the card. 'Know what?'

'That your dad is still alive, is my guess.'

'If he wants me to know that, why doesn't he pay me a visit?' Kenny was stung. 'Fuck.' He looked out of the window and everything he had been ignoring all these years crashed in on him like an articulated lorry.

Silence.

'Do you remember much about that night, son?' Vi asked eventually.

Kenny didn't need any clarification. He knew instantly what night she was talking about.

'I remember going to bed and then waking up when I heard my dad wailing. Then when I walked downstairs... there they were.'

'Exactly where were they?'

'I must've gone over this with you countless times over the years, Aunt Vi,' Kenny said.

'Bear with me, son.'

'Right. Well...' And Kenny explained how his father was on his knees at his mother's feet and how she was collapsed over the table.

'What were your impressions, Kenny? From an adult looking through the child's eyes.' She stared into his eyes, desperate to hear what he had to say.

'They haven't changed over the years, Aunt Vi. Mum was dead. The pills and the drink suggested how... and Dad sounded like he wanted to join her.'

'Was he saying anything? Did he speak?'

'It was mostly just an inarticulate noise. Or...' – he reconsidered – '...a long "no".'

'Anything else, son? Think.'

Kenny looked at her face and saw for the first time what his mother's suicide had done to her sister. All those years later and still she was haunted by it. Kenny was sure it would never leave her.

He cast his mind back. He was there in the room again. His heart was thundering against his ribs; his stomach twisting as realisation crept up on him. His twelve-year-old self was frightened more by the out-of-control grief from his father than the still shape of his mother. His father's torment was present, an energy that caused a vacuum of thought around him. The shape of his mother was distressing but one where the full implications had yet to strike home.

Again, he could see his dad. The moment when their eyes met. His father's expression formed an apology. It was like he was taking full responsibility. He mouthed a single word.

'Sorry.'

There was no volume in the memory and that was how it presented itself to Kenny now. His father's open mouth forming two syllables. The sound gone, sucked into the black hole of his grief.

'It was like Dad was apologising to me,' Kenny said, the sound of his voice sounding too gravelly in the confined space. 'Do you think' – Kenny turned to face Vi – 'that, knowing what kids were like, he was trying to tell me not to blame myself?'

'No,' said Vi. 'I think he was telling you he was blaming himself.'

'What?' Kenny looked at her. Where was she going with this?

'I've been worrying at this for the last seventeen years, Kenny. I knew your mother better than she knew herself and if she was the type to commit suicide then my name is Shirley Temple.'

Kenny looked at the steering wheel. Examined the dashboard. Looked out of the window. Then he turned to her and spotted the tear that was sliding down her cheek. 'Are you sure you're not just looking for something else, Vi? Nobody ever completely knows someone else. Your sister, my mother, died and yes it was a tragedy.' He gripped her knee. 'Suicide is such a betrayal. The grieving process is never quite over. I know that better than anyone. '

Vi shook her head. 'Your mother and I lived in each other's shadows. We were closer than peas in a pod. Our dad used to call us The Twins. Here's The Twins, he'd say, even though we were born three years apart. So don't tell me I didn't know my sister, Kenny. I knew her and what you've just told me has convinced me more than ever...' She pulled a paper hankie from her handbag and dabbed at her cheek.

'Your mother didn't commit suicide, Kenny. She was murdered.'

9

The water was dark and deep and frothing, rushing below and under him from his position on the bridge. He fancied the water was angry, surging towards the next obstacle content in the knowledge that nothing could withstand its power.

The riverbanks were a steep tangle of brambles, broom and nettles. Here and there it looked like the local youth had gone in for a spate of ornamental gardening and their ornament of choice was the ubiquitous supermarket shopping trolley.

He leaned forward, the wall of the bridge reaching his midriff and planted his elbows on it. He looked into the brown depths and at the memories trapped under its shifting surface.

The first letter was a disappointment. The writer was tentative, frightened even, subsumed by the need to make friends. The information was scant, the apology brief as if they were afraid to mention the reason for the writer's absence and that any mention of it would have the reader reaching for a match and an ashtray.

Kenny learned nothing about the writer of the letter and was so confused by its blandness he almost refused to believe that it was written by his father.

The next two letters, which would have arrived when he was nineteen and twenty, were equally as nondescript. If they had been food, they could have been compared to watered down consommé.

Kenny threw the letters back in the box after he had finished reading them. They offered him nothing. It was as if the writer was going through the motions. As if the act of writing the letters was some form of punishment. Like he was only writing them to please someone other than himself and the intended recipient.

He dropped his aunt back at her house. She was tripping over herself to apologise. He was tired, numb and counting the minutes before he could be on his own again. Emotions too many to number were crowding his mind, demanding attention and an emotional articulacy he didn't possess.

His answer was to drive to the spot where his he had spent many evenings as a teenager contemplating death and whether the cold would kill him before the water swamped his lungs.

The fourth letter was different, reflective and if you knew where to look, layered with meaning. It was also quite clear that when he wrote it his father was drunk.

The first three letters had been addressed to Kenny. This one was headed *Dear Kenneth*, as if now that he was twenty-one he had outgrown the boyish air evinced by the derivative, Kenny. As far as he was concerned it was patronising. A poorly penned attempt by a stranger to reconnect with his son.

He recognised his impatience and decided that as this was the last letter he should read it as if coming to the whole experience fresh. He exhaled sharply, sought his centre as he did when he was about to fight someone. A relaxed mind was a more receptive mind, he told himself.

He read.

> *Dear Kenneth,*
> *Happy Birthday, son. 21, eh? Time for you to get the keys of the house and all that.*

Then there were some lines that had been scored through so harshly it made them illegible.

...Sorry about that, this is only my ninth attempt at this letter and I'm running out of paper. And booze. And booze is needed for this, I'm thinking. You know, typical Scot. Emotion can only be examined in a state of inebriation and the problem is that once pissed you overdo it, don't you?

So, you're 21 and I haven't seen you for ages. It was just weeks – or was it days? – before your thirteenth. I always remember your mum kidding you that you were turning into a man. Just like your dad. Some dad I turned out to be. So that's the last time I saw you. Apart from that one time I stood by the school gates when you would have been in fourth year at the academy. You looked so well and strong and confident striding among a group of your mates that I didn't dare come over and speak to you.

Kenny broke off from reading at this point. His eyes were misting and he could no longer see the print. He coughed. Fuck, my dad was close enough to speak to me. Why didn't he? He would have given anything for that moment to be returned to him. What would he have said? He saw his father before him and his stomach shifted and surged.

...I just stood there like a big lump. Desperate to say hello. I even practised for the moment when we faced each other. 'Hi, Kenny. I'm your dad.' I said it over and over again. Like it was a prayer. But when I saw you it all vanished and I could no more walk or talk than I could fly. I got a wee bit emotional that day. So much so, some woman came over and asked if I was okay. She even handed me a hankie. I told her to piss off. That'll be the last time she speaks to a stranger, so I've done her a favour, eh? You looked like you had my height and your mother's good looks.

Does it hurt you to mention your mother? She was an amazing woman. Softened my rough edge and made me more of a man. Cliché but true, it was a privilege to be married to her and I've missed her every day since.

And you. I've missed you...

Oh fuck off, thought Kenny.

*...You probably don't want to hear it and who can blame you?
A boy needs his father and I abandoned you when you needed
me most. The change from boy to man is a difficult time and if
you were anything like me – a cocky, aggressive bastard – it can't
have been easy.*

*If you're as bright as I think you are, well, you are your moth-
er's son...*

Turn it down, Dad, for crying out loud.

*...you'll have noticed a change in this letter from the pre-
vious ones. Well, it's because I've been given another chance.
I met a lovely woman just after I sent your last letter. We've
had one baby, a girl, and there's another one on the way.
Having these other kids has me thinking about you more and
more. I'm older and wiser and full of what might have been.*

Kenny felt a hot spike of jealousy score his gut. He realised that
this was the wee boy of twelve who still lived at his core. The grown
man felt a vague sense of happiness. He had a sister and perhaps a
wee brother?

*...The thing is I have to stay away. Two reasons. One is my
new wife has no idea of my past and it needs to stay that way or
she's gone and I can't lose another family. The other is that your
life may depend on it.*

Oh, come on tae fuck, thought Kenny. Somebody's been watching too many TV soaps.

...That probably sounds a bit too dramatic, but it's true. It's

no secret that I was involved with some unsavoury types and one of them and me had a serious fight. Unfortunately, and I will take the guilt of this to my grave, people died. A mother and a son. It was a horrible accident but no one believed me. The family of the deceased told me that if I didn't vanish then you would too. The threat was unmistakeable. My choice was to stay and you'd be the one to suffer the consequences. Or run and you would live. This man was determined I would lose as much as he did.

I've said enough. My difficulty here was to explain without telling you too much. I don't want you to go looking for revenge. These are people that no one messes with. Let me repeat that – no one.

I hope you can find it in your heart to forgive me, or at the very least think that I'm not all bad.

Yeah, right, Kenny thought. He read over the last few paragraphs time and time again. He struggled to take the information in. His dad was responsible for people dying. He was a killer.

The letter was signed simply.

Dad.

10

The way he saw it, Kenny had two choices. When faced with news that involved a possible surfeit of emotion either he exercised until he dropped or he got pissed. He'd already had his daily dose of the first and he couldn't do the second on his own.

He picked up his phone and dialled one of his contacts. A deep voice answered in a familiar manner.

'What the fuck are you wanting?'

'Detective Inspector Ray McBain, you are cordially invited to an afternoon of debauchery.'

'If I knew what it was, I might be tempted.'

'Booze and lots of it.'

'I don't know, Kenny.' McBain's tone grew serious and Kenny could hear him walking. 'There's stuff going on here.'

'Delegate, m'man, and tell them you've an important suspect that needs to be waterboarded with whisky.'

'That serious?'

'Mmmm.'

'Okay, consider me a willing debauchee.'

'If that's not a word,' said Kenny, 'it should be.'

• • •

People who have a wont to launder their falsely earned money quickly realise that few methods are more effective than washing their money through businesses that deal mostly in cash. When people buy a round of drinks they rarely do so with a credit card or a cheque. In the drinking business, cash is the ermine-cloaked asset and therefore the bar becomes a handy place to integrate your pennies.

Kenny owned a number of pubs and cafés throughout the city and it was in one of these that he arranged to meet Ray McBain. He chose one that was in a quieter part of the city and one that was 'owned' by a faceless corporation. None of the employees knew he was the boss and he could visit without causing a stir.

It was called The Blue Owl and was originally offered to the Glasgow punters as a bar where jazz and blues musicians could jam and congregate. The 'owl' part was presumably to denote the late-night nature of the venture. Which was a bit of a misnomer because it failed to get a licence to sell alcohol beyond midnight. The business never quite got off the ground; the musicians decided they were too hip to be seen this far from the city centre and the owner was forced to sell. The building remained a bar, but despite the best efforts of an array of eager landlords it wobbled from one cash-flow crisis to another. Until Kenny and his 'company' took over.

Strangely, these new owners managed to make a success of the business without increasing the footfall.

• • •

Kenny was on his third Glenmorangie – ice and water – when McBain turned up. Reading what Kenny was nursing before him, he ordered the same. The barmaid took enough time from her dedicated reading of *Real Lives, Real Loves* magazine to pour him a measure.

While she was temporarily busy, Ray looked around himself. He took in the low ceilings, the soft lighting, the giant saxophone over the bar and the two other customers, who were tucked away in far corner. By the way they were sucking the face of each other he guessed they were in love.

'Right, buddy,' the barmaid said, sliding the glass towards him.

She was tall and stringy, with cropped packet-blonde hair and wearing a black blouse and skirt. Her expression was as devoid of personal expression as her clothing. Bored to distraction, she named the price.

'Charmed,' said Ray, holding his glass towards her and toasting her complete lack of it. She threw him a twisted smile and went back to her tale of the man with two heads who married the woman with three hands.

He placed his glass on the table, sat on the chair across from Kenny and exhaled long and deep. 'Sorry, mate,' Ray said. 'Crime never rests.'

'*Au contraire*, my friend, yes it does.' Kenny held his glass up, mimicking Ray's interaction with the barmaid. 'So,' – he assessed his friend – 'which part of the Luther Vandross weight yo-yo are you currently on?' He was of course referring to the now-deceased soul singer who was just as famous for his agonised deliberations about weight on the sofa with Oprah as he was for the numerous albums he produced.

'Rushing back up to being a fat bastard.' Ray lost and gained the same twenty pounds on a regular basis.

'You should get yourself to the gym, man.'

'What, and deprive the ladies of all this loving?' Ray grinned. 'It's not the size of the nail that counts, it's the fifteen stone knocking it in.'

'Right. Fifteen stone.' Kenny had the good manners not to snort. 'Talking about which, you getting any?' He delicately enquired about the state of his friend's love life.

'Yup,' said Ray. 'I had sex with an actual person the other night.'

'Was she blind or drunk?'

'Blind drunk,' Ray answered with a laugh. 'She expressed her gratitude by leaving her phone number on the bathroom mirror and a pair of panties in my fridge.' He took a sip.

'You'll have to have a shower and steam up the mirror before you can call her. Perhaps there's a message there.'

'At least I don't have to pay for it.'

'I don't have to do anything, buddy. I chose to. An important distinction. I am taking part in an act of commerce. Helping to keep the economy afloat in these troubled times.'

'The Chancellor of the Exchequer should send you a wee note of thanks.'

'Or at the very least a tax rebate.'

'You pay tax?'

Kenny held his hand up. The pad of his thumb and his index finger barely touching.

Ray drained his glass and returned to the bar. The barmaid actually sighed.

'Customers get in the way of a hard day's work, don't you think?' Ray asked her.

She smiled an apology as if feeling a pang of conscience. She raised an eyebrow and pursed her lips. 'Same again?'

'You can read me like a book, sweetheart.'

She leaned over the bar, giving him a look down her cleavage. Her breasts were so far apart and her top so low and loose he could almost see down to her navel.

'Can I get you anything else...?' she asked. The space she left at the end of her sentence a request for his name.

'A pair of dark glasses?' he said.

She completely misread him and gave a little toss of her hair as if to say, *You'll have to try harder than that, mister*.

She served the drinks. He paid and carried them over to the table.

'I think I preferred it when she was playing hard to get,' he said to Kenny.

'You just can't get the staff,' Kenny replied, reaching for his fresh glass. Ray was only aware of part of his various enterprises, had no idea he was the owner of The Blue Owl.

'What kind of name is that, anyway? The Blue Fucking Owl?' asked Ray.

'I like it,' argued Kenny. 'Makes me want to stay up all night and play jazz.'

'Is that a euphemism?'

Kenny pushed back into the cushion of the chair, enjoyed the whisky that glowed in his system and they settled into silence. Sometimes you just wanted the presence of a friend without having to fill their ears with the minutiae of your day. And sometimes you want to tell them everything.

He leaned forward in his chair and told Ray the lot: his memory of that night, his life with Aunt Vi and Uncle Colin, the letters. He spoke without emotion, relaying the facts, allowing them the freedom of the atmosphere.

After speaking, drained like an anorexic after a feast, Kenny sat back in his chair and cleared his throat. To get the words out was enough. He didn't need to know what solution Ray might suggest.

'So,' said Ray with a grin, 'a man saves your life and you've got to listen to his whole freakin' life story, jeez.' He grinned. Grew serious. 'What now?'

'I find the fucker who killed my mother.' His phone beeped. A pause. 'Right after I answer this text.'

11

It was the next morning and Alexis still hadn't answered any of his texts. He woke with the light thrusting in under his eyelids and a mouth as dry as a sandpit. He opened his eyes and squinted. It wasn't like him to leave the curtains open. He had another look at his phone. Still no answer. Then he assessed his physical condition. Apart from the dry mouth, he felt fine. He was fortunate this was as bad as a hangover ever got for him. He threw his mobile on the bed and turned his mind to a different form of drink – coffee.

He stretched and then lifted his feet off the bed and on to the floor. Looking at the foot of the bed, he could see that his clothes were in a pile. Struggling to remember even taking them off and uncaring that people in the tenement flat opposite might be able to see him, he walked naked into his kitchen.

'Aww, bless.' Ray was standing with his back to the window with a glass of water in his hand and looking at Kenny's morning semi-erection as if it was the saddest thing he'd ever seen. 'I didn't know you cared.'

Kenny sat on a breakfast stool. 'It's big enough for me.' He flipped Ray the finger. 'You... you stayed over?' He looked around himself. 'Yes, I'm home. This is my place. What time is it?'

'You're not much of a boozer, Kenny. You were snoring in the taxi. I almost had to carry you up the stairs. I threw you on your bed and left you to it. To my everlasting regret,' – he made a face

57

– 'you managed to take your own clothes off.' He took a long, slow drink from his glass. 'I slept in your spare room. And it's now...' – he looked at his wristwatch – '...eight-fifteen.'

'Coffee?'

'Aye.'

'What does the day hold for Mr Detective Extraordinaire?'

'Kenny, I can't hold a conversation with a naked man. Go put something on for fuck's sake and I'll make us some breakfast.'

'Coffee,' said Kenny. 'Only want coffee.' He stood up and walked out of the room, scratching his arse. He returned moments later wearing jogging pants and a T-shirt and holding his phone.

Ray was pouring milk into a couple of steaming mugs. He looked over his shoulder when he heard Kenny walk back in. He shuddered. 'Burned into my memory, mate.'

'That's handy. You can wank off to it every morning.'

'Tell me why I'm not locking you up right now?'

'You want to see just how low you can go?'

Ray opened a drawer, picked out a spoon and stirred the coffee. 'What do you take in yours again? Ricin?'

Kenny reached past him and picked up a mug. He took a sip and groaned with pleasure. Then he studied his phone.

'I should just text her again,' he said to himself. Then to McBain: 'How come you don't have a hangover? And talking about locking people up, do you not have work to go to today?'

Ray nodded. 'I don't have a hangover because I didn't drink that much. You had a good start on me if I remember correctly. And before I go I wanted to talk to you.'

Kenny was back on the stool, slumped over the breakfast bar. He took another sip, swallowed and nodded once. 'Right.'

'Your dad's name was Peter, right?'

'Right,' Kenny said, sitting up.

'While you were' – Ray waved a hand in the direction of the bedroom – 'working on your morning stiffy, I was making a few phone calls.'

'You were? Why?' Kenny's face was expressionless.

'I am a detective, Kenny, it's what I do.'

'In this instance, why?' Kenny asked. He could hear the anger in his voice and it surprised him. He felt the air between them shift and the energy shrink. He didn't want Ray to know anything about his father. Didn't want him to know too much about his family for that matter and this realisation shocked him. What was it, shame? He was what he was. Why was it suddenly an issue? Why couldn't he care less what his friend thought about him and then worry about the impression knowledge of his family might make?

'Fine.' Ray gave a shrug that would be the envy of any car salesman in Paris. 'Just trying to help.' He drained what was left of his cup and picked his own phone from a pocket. He was fond of telling anyone who would listen that this was a proper phone. All it did was make calls. He managed texts at a push. He scrolled down a few numbers on his contacts.

'I'll just get a taxi...'

'Okay,' said Kenny, giving himself a shake. 'Sorry. What do you know?'

'Kenny, this is obviously new and very raw. You need time to make your own enquiries...'

'Oh for fuck's sake, McBain, can it. If you've got something to tell me, tell me.'

'Seeing you asked so nicely...' Ray moved to the other seat at the breakfast bar and leaned against it. 'Your dad disappeared in the early-Nineties, right?'

Kenny nodded.

'Glasgow might be a big place, Kenny, but it's a small city. The cops know most of the bad guys. So I called a couple of colleagues to see who might remember a case where a woman committed suicide and the husband disappeared.'

Again Kenny nodded. He'd always wondered about that. The police would have been suspicious about his father. A woman dies, seemingly by her own hand, and her husband vanishes shortly after.

There must have been some sort of investigation. 'And...?'

'I've been given the name of a retired cop, lives out in Shawlands. Name of Harry Fyfe. Seems he was heavily involved in organised crime in those days. And if anyone heard any rumours of what might have happened it would be him. A bottle of Glenlivet is all that's required to dislodge a few memories apparently.'

'So we're going to see him right now?' Kenny stood up.

Ray pushed him back down. 'You're going nowhere, pal.' His eyebrows were close to his hairline. 'You any idea what damage you could cause me if you went there?'

They had an agreement that their professional lives would never cross. This had never been articulated, but understood from the start. Suddenly, Kenny didn't care.

'I need to speak to the guy, McBain. I need to...'

'You need to take a breath and think about this.' Ray took a breath himself as if struggling to contain his irritation. 'Cops are gossips, Kenny. None more so than retired cops. He'll be on the phone two minutes after we're out that door. When he finds out that no one knows who the fuck you are...'

'On this occasion, I have to...'

'Kenny, you need to think about this. He'll know as soon as you walk in that door that you are not a policeman.'

'That's shite. A cheap brown suit, a blue tie and...'

'Let me put this another way. You're not fucking going. You want the information; you have to trust me to get it for you.' Ray was loud, on his feet and thrusting his index finger in Kenny's face.

12

The house number was 32 and advertised by the burnished brass numbers on the door. The porch provided welcome shelter from the rain as he waited to be welcomed in to the house. He shook the raindrops from his umbrella; each drop formed like its own perfect universe on the waterproof surface before being thrust back into the air.

The door opened and a middle-aged man stood before him. He was tall, with a bristle of thick white hair that was sticking out as if he had a Van de Graaff generator in his pocket. He was wearing a pair of brown trousers and Kenny could see his legs were so thin they could have doubled as pipe-cleaners. As a contrast to the width of his legs, he looked like he was hiding a medicine ball under the front of his cardigan.

The man's eyes were bright with curiosity and the skin of his face was tight over his bones as if it had been shrink-wrapped. He was clean-shaven and pock-marked.

'You'll be Ray McBain?'

'You'll be Harry Fyfe,' Kenny said and held up the bottle of whisky by the neck.

'Ach, you didn't need to,' Harry said, his face a tragic comedy of thirst and denial. 'But it would be rude not to.' His face broke into a grin. 'Come in, son, come in.'

Harry guided him in to the front room, pointed him in the direction of a seat and said he'd be back in a minute.

While the older man was out of the room, Kenny had a good look around. Every surface was so shiny he felt he could eat off it. The thick pile of the carpet had track marks from the hoover. There was one photograph on the mantelpiece. It was in a glass frame and showed a smiling couple on holiday. The man was a slightly younger Harry and Kenny guessed this was his wife.

'Right.' Harry walked back in with a pair of crystal whisky glasses and the now open bottle. 'Somewhere in the world it's 7pm.' He poured, his eyes gleaming to the promise of the liquid falling into the glass.

He handed Kenny a glass and sat down. 'How long have you been in the polis?'

'Oh, about...' – Kenny recalled what he knew about Ray's career – '...twelve years.' He took a sip and hoped this was the right answer.

'What division you in?'

'Serious crime unit...'

'Do you know Gavin Wilson? He was a rookie when I retired. Seems he's headed for big things.'

Kenny nodded and hmm'd and oh'd for a few minutes more as Harry talked about people he knew who were still in the force. Kenny tried to be as non-committal as he could. He didn't want to be caught up in a conversation about who knew who or who worked where, and the more Harry talked the more he was convinced he was going to trip himself up. He loosened his collar. He was beginning to regret his impulse about ignoring Ray's demand that he leave this interview to him.

The name and the fact that Harry lived in Shawlands had been enough information for Kenny to track him down. Kenny O'Neill knew people with a wide set of skills. Once the address was found and a number obtained, a phone call to Harry and an over-the-phone introduction was enough to be given the green light to come knocking.

'Listen, Harry, I'm sorry to be rude but can I ask you–'

'You in a hurry, son?' Harry asked.

'No it's just...' Kenny sighed. He'd miscalculated. The old fella was going to realise he was not who he said he was. 'I have an attachment to this case.' In Kenny's experience the best lies were the ones that stuck more closely to the truth so he took a small gamble. 'This is a kind of favour I'm doing for my best mate. His mum and dad are both dead...'

'No need to explain yourself, son,' said Harry. 'I understand.' He smiled and his eyes shone a whisky glow. He toasted Kenny. 'You're only an alcoholic when you want to stop and realise you can't.' He made a face of certainty. A challenge to Kenny to refute him. 'I could stop tomorrow. If I wanted.'

Kenny looked over at the photograph. As soon as the words were out of his mouth he regretted them. 'That your wife?'

Harry nodded. He stretched his mouth into the slip of a smile. He could only hold it for a moment. His eyes filled. 'She hated my job. The long hours. How obsessed I became. She made endless plans about how we would fill our time when I retired. She even went to computer classes so she could get a computer and research holiday hotspots.' He coughed, swallowed, but despite his best efforts to choke back his emotions a tear strayed and slid down his face. 'She called it the interweb.' His laugh was a short, sharp bark, like a warning of barely suppressed pain. 'All those years together and me moaning about queues at the airport.' With long fingers he twisted his wedding ring round and round. 'Stupid bastard. Why didn't I go on just one of those fucking planes?'

He sobbed and leaning forward, hid his face in his hands.

Kenny didn't know what to do. He shifted forwards in his seat as if to offer comfort. He wondered about offering the man a glass of water. He settled for doing nothing.

'Sorry,' Harry whispered. 'It's not that long since.'

'What happened?' asked Kenny after he swallowed back his own reaction. He was wishing he was anywhere but in that chair and surprised by how moved he was by the older man's grief.

'Heart attack.' He wiped at his cheek with the back of his hand. 'I thought that was just a man's disease. What do I know?'

Feeling awkward and ill-equipped to deal with this situation and regretting his impulse to visit, Kenny stood up. 'I really should...'

'Nonsense, son.' Harry drained his glass before continuing. 'She's been in her grave for ten months. Most of the time I'm fine and then...' – a smile – '...it all comes back. You were just the poor sap who happened to be here.' He laughed and this time his laugh had real humour in it and Kenny caught a glimpse of the cop. The man who dealt with all kinds of people and all kinds of events; wielding his humour like it was a baton against the dark thoughts that visit in the chill of a weak morning.

'Do you remember the case I was asking about on the phone?' Kenny dived in.

'Like it was yesterday, son,' Harry answered and stared out of the window and down through the years. 'The woman died from an overdose. Can't remember the pills but they were washed down with booze. This is Glasgow, after all.' Harry's voice strengthened. He was on safer, more familiar ground here.

'I remember thinking there was something funny about it all.'

'You do? How?' Kenny's stomach churned.

'You get a feel for people, you know?'

Kenny nodded.

'Her sister pestered us with phone calls and letters. She refused to believe her wee sister had topped herself. A nice house, a man that loved her and a beautiful wee boy. That's what she kept saying. Her sister had everything to live for so why kill herself?' Harry shrugged as if sloughing off the worst the world could offer, knowing that his respite was only temporary. 'The Fiscal ruled that it was suicide. What could you say to that?' Harry leaned back in his chair. 'But then the husband vanished... and the rumours started.'

'Rumours?' Kenny's heart surged at his ribs.

'Aye. The allegations were that the father was abusing the boy... the mother found out and unable to deal with it, swallowed–'

'No fucking way.' Kenny jumped to his feet. 'No way Peter O'Neill was abusing his boy.'

Harry stood up and took a step nearer Kenny. His eyebrows were raised. His eyes focused, sharp and peering into his.

'You're a wee bit too emotionally involved in this story, son. Exactly who was Peter O'Neill to you?'

'Who started these allegations? Who made up horrible fucking lies like that?' Kenny sprayed saliva with the words, such was his anger.

'Again, son. Who exactly was Peter O'Neill to you?' Harry narrowed his eyes.

Kenny turned away from him and forced calm into his centre. He sought the same place his mind went when he was in danger, when he knew he had to be at his best. This man might be a drunk, he might be retired and suffering from the passing of his wife, but he was still a cop. And his eyes were boring into him, demanding his story.

Without knowing what was going to leave his mouth Kenny began to speak, trusting that his brain would find an answer to appease Harry Fyfe.

'Sorry.' He turned back to face him. To distract the older man from his reaction he needed to come up with something good. 'I know Peter's son. Very well.' His expression was an apology while his mind searched for a plausible excuse.

'Oh,' said Harry and offered a smile of understanding. 'You see so much in my job you realise it doesn't matter if someone's light in their loafers. Live and let live, that's what I say.'

Fuck, thought Kenny. The eejit still talks like he's in the job and he thinks he's telling him that they, he and McBain, were a gay couple.

'Don't worry.' Harry patted him on the shoulder. 'Cops are the worst gossips imaginable, but you're secret's safe with me.' He paused. 'Unless of course you are out and proud?'

Kenny forced a grin thinking, what the fuck do you say? McBain was going to kill him. Then the funnier side of the situation bubbled up into laughter. Just how far could he take this?

Sanity won over and he said, 'You're the only person who knows, Harry. I'll trust your judgement on this.' He sat back down again. Harry took the opportunity while he was on his feet to top up his glass. He sipped and, bending his knees with effort, he also sat down.

'I often wondered about Peter O'Neill's son over the years. Kids are the innocent victims in the crap that adults throw into the world.' He paused and peered into Kenny's face. 'How's he keeping?'

'He's good.' Kenny felt odd talking about himself in the third person.

'Boys need their dad.' Harry sipped and stared out of the window. 'Sometimes they build their father into some kind of hero when he's not there to add a dose of reality. I've heard rumours over the years.' His face assumed a doleful expression. 'From what I hear, you are on the straight and narrow. You've a good reputation, Ray, why are you...? Must make things awkward for you being a cop?'

Oh my God, thought Kenny. This is going from bad to worse. Harry was making some dangerous connections. Answer a question with a question.

'I don't know too much about Peter,' said Kenny. 'His son doesn't say too much about his father. What can you tell me about him?'

Harry made a small face of surprise. 'Peter was, I guess you could call it, an "enforcer". He worked with one of the Glasgow crimelords. Met him a few times. A personable guy. Popular with the ladies.' He looked at Kenny, who began to feel very warm. Harry had clearly lost none of the skills that made him a good cop. His gaze penetrated. 'Same build as you. Shorter. Different colouring. But that was the thing with some of these bad guys... as you know... they might work on the different side of the law but some of them could be good company over a pint. Not that you'd like to bump into Peter O'Neill in a dark alley.

'Anyway,' he sighed, 'Peter disappeared and the rumours started.' He made a face of apology. 'Someone kills themselves and people search for a reason. And the reason has to be almost as bad as the suicide, doesn't it?'

'Did you ever get to the source of the rumours?'

'Nah. Although I remember the sister's husband was a bit vocal.'

'Colin?' asked Kenny.

'Was that his name? I remember him vaguely. He was an accountant. A proper accountant. There were suspicions about his connections with the crime factions in the city but nothing was ever uncovered. In the end we discounted him. We put any suspicions down to the fact Peter was his brother-in-law, kept an eye on him from time to time and let it go at that.'

Kenny's phone buzzed as a message came through. He ignored it.

'Ach, it's good to talk about the old times. Sometimes I think it's all I've got.' He looked in the direction of Kenny's pocket. 'You want to get that?'

'Nah,' said Kenny, feeling his heart charge at the thought it might be Alexis. 'But I do have to move on.' He got to his feet and Harry walked with him to the door. As they shook hands Harry said, 'Next time you need to share a wee bottle of whisky, feel free to stop by.'

'I will, Harry, I will.' To his surprise, Kenny felt that he meant it. He'd enjoyed the man's company. 'Oh, before I go...' It had suddenly occurred to him that McBain might visit the man at the end of his shift. And then he'd be in the shit. '...Kenny O'Neill is an impatient guy. He might turn up here pretending to be me before the end of the day. If you could just humour him?'

Harry's eyebrows dipped. 'Impersonating a policeman is a serious offence.' Then he grinned and winked. 'But in this instance, Kenny, I'll let it pass.'

Kenny turned and took a couple of steps up the path. He stopped. Harry just called him Kenny. He turned to see Harry still standing at the door.

'You knew all along?'

Harry was so pleased with himself he was rocking on his heels. He nodded.

'How?'

'I haven't lost it after all these years, eh?'

'What gave me away?'

'I knew. Just let's leave it at that, son.'

'And when Ray McBain comes visiting?'

'You were never here.'

'And the gay couple thing?'

Harry laughed and rocked back on his heels. 'You should have seen your face. I was just yanking your chain, son.'

Kenny shrugged it off with a smile. He'd earned it. 'What about the rest of your story?'

'Don't worry, Kenny. You don't joke about with stuff like that.'

13

Kenny steered the car off the A84 at the Kingshouse Hotel and passed an old signpost that looked like it might have guided Queen Victoria herself down this road. In one direction it arrowed the miles for Crianlarich and Oban, in the other it pointed towards 'Rob Roy's Grave'.

Alexis squealed from the passenger seat.

'It's soooo romantic, Kenny.' Her head swivelled from side to side as she processed the scenery. 'It's gorgeous.' She squeezed out the word gorgeous as if it hurt her to say it.

It was now three weeks after Alexis had suffered at the hands of her assailant. For the first few of those she had ignored Kenny's calls. He had persisted and eventually she agreed to meet him. She refused to talk about the incident, however. She insisted she had put it behind her and told Kenny he must too. She also declined to explain why she hadn't taken any of his calls and he put this down to the fact that he had been with her shortly after. He reasoned that this must have built an association with the rape and that she couldn't bear to be reminded of it. This logic collapsed when eventually she answered when he rang. Two visits later and he told her they were going away for the weekend and that she would be paid for her time.

'Isn't it just beautiful?' She was leaning forward in her seat. Her eyes were wide, her mouth open. 'I've been in Scotland for six years now and haven't been out of the city.' She playfully punched Kenny's arm. 'How could you not tell me there was so much beauty out here?'

'We're kind of famous for it.' Kenny gave the shrug of the inured. Which he wasn't. He always felt a soothing, a loosening of dark energy whenever he was in sight of the Scottish hills.

'Famous for what?' Alexis grinned. 'Not talking?'

'The beauty of our countryside, of course. As for talking, you've been in Glasgow for six years – how can you accuse us of not talking? We're like the most verbose citizens in the country.'

Kenny looked in the mirror. The small, blue Toyota was still there. He was just being paranoid. No one would be after them. And if they were, they would surely choose something more exciting than a Toyota Yaris.

'It's the hills, the colours, the light...' She stopped as if running out of words. 'Man, you guys are so lucky.'

The road took them through the village of Balquhidder and past the MacGregor Murray Mausoleum. They caught a glimpse of its dark stone, crow-stepped gables and buttresses as the car passed the road-end. Alexis demanded to know what it was. 'It's too small for a church. Not enough windows for a house. What could it be?'

Kenny worked through his memory of his last visit here. He was eleven. His dad was keen to give him lessons about the folk heroes of Scotland and it was never enough to read from a book, he had to bring him to the actual place. First, there had been the Wallace Monument in Stirling and then they came here.

He remembered being curious about this building and his father being anxious to get to the church where Rob Roy himself was buried.

'The local landowners built this in the early 1820s,' Kenny said.

'The wealthy build a tomb like this to honour their dead,' said Alexis, 'while the poor peasants probably lived ten to a room in a tiny hovel.'

'Couldn't have put it better myself.'

'They had a good sense of the dramatic,' Alexis said as she took in the narrow tree-lined avenue and the impressive doors.

The road curved into the village proper and set back from the road on the left was the kirkyard and the ruins of the old church where Rob Roy MacGregor lay with his wife and two of his sons. Standing there with his father was a poignant moment for him now. Then, it was mostly boring, with Kenny suffering through his father's enthusiasm. His dad explained it in terms of a cowboy and Indian movie. The costumes were different, swap the bow and arrow for a claymore, the locals were the poor, set-upon wild natives and the Duke of Montrose was the baddy.

In the teenage parlance of modern times he might have said, *Yeah, right, whatever*. But nobody talked to Peter O'Neill like that. Not even his son.

The road carried them through the village and then to the three-storey baronial style building that would be their home for the next two nights.

'They put a hotel way out here?' asked Alexis, clapping her hands as the gravel crunched under the car tyres.

'An award-winning hotel,' said Kenny, examining the view from his wing mirror. No blue Toyota. No more paranoia.

'Do you bring all your lady friends here?'

'Only the ones that deserve it,' said Kenny, who'd never passed through its doors before. He'd researched the area while wondering how to investigate the truth behind his mother's death. Running through the reels of his history, most of the events that came to him involved his father. He'd remembered the time at Rob Roy's grave, looked it up in the web and spotted an advert for the Moniack Mhor Hotel, which was perched next to a beautiful loch.

He needed time out. So did Alexis. A phone call later and the weekend was booked.

Their room was sumptuous. Designed for a lover's retreat with silks and deep velour, the bed was a giant centrepiece to the room. Alexis touched everything in the room, giving off a series of oohs and aahs and wows.

She stood before Kenny, stretched up and kissed him.

'I hope you have plenty of energy.'

'We'll just need to wait and see,' said Kenny with a grin.

'Sit.' Alexis put a hand on his shoulder and prompted him to sit on the bed. She kneeled before him and, working at his belt and zip, freed him from his trousers.

'Somebody's ready,' Alexis giggled while taking a grip of his shaft. Kenny moaned in anticipation and then lost himself to the throb and pulse of his pleasure.

• • •

Later, Alexis looked down at Kenny stretched out naked on the bed. She ran her hand from his left nipple, past his navel and a feather touch on his thigh. 'Now that we've got that out of the way, I fancy a bath. Care to join me?'

'Love to.'

She leaped from the bed and skipped over to the en-suite bathroom. She opened the door and squealed. 'Oh my god, we have twin baths. How cool is that?' She did the quick clapping thing again and Kenny groaned. When did that action become so popular?

Feeling zoned out, post-orgasmic relaxed, Kenny took the four steps to the bathroom to examine the baths. They sat in the middle of the large, white walled room on their pedestals, side by side. Alexis already had the water running and was pouring scented bath oils into the water.

'Excellent,' said Kenny. He turned back into the bedroom, rummaged in his luggage and produced a bottle of red wine. 'This should add the finishing touch.' He brandished the bottle at Alexis.

She ran towards him and gave him a hug. 'What did I do to deserve you?'

'You cleared my cheques.'

'Oh, shove off,' she smiled and swiped at his shoulder. Alexis rarely swore. 'You know what I mean. Why are you so nice to me?'

'There is no why, there is only do.'

'You stole that from Yoda.'

'And how much better it sounds with the alteration.'

'Any other *Star Wars* wisdom you'd like to impart?' Alexis asked and sat on the side of the bath, completely unmindful of her nudity. Kenny appreciated her with a smile.

'Size matters not.' He opened his arms. 'Judge me by my size, do you? For the Force is my ally.'

'Oh and the force stirs within you,' Alexis laughed as Kenny began to stiffen again. 'Quick, in the bath. A woman needs a rest.'

Kenny stepped into the bath, turned off the tap and sank in to the perfumed water with a long sigh. He slipped completely under and surfaced. Alexis leaned forward and planted a kiss on his forehead.

'What was that for?'

'There is no what, there is only do.'

Kenny made a face. 'That doesn't quite work.'

'Sue me.' Alexis kissed him again, poured them both a glass of wine and stepped into her own bath after handing Kenny a glass.

They each lay in silence, wary of speech in case it spoiled the moment. Closing his eyes, Kenny gave in to the heat and the caress of the water. His breath slowed, his mind sank and rose and dipped again. He drifted over the last few weeks, Alexis' assault, the two young men with road-rage, McBain and Harry Fyfe.

The information he received from Harry was replicated when Ray went to visit and Harry was true to his word; nothing was mentioned of Kenny's visit. Since then Kenny had done nothing more. He knew his next step was to question Uncle Colin and so far the man had been avoiding him. Whenever Kenny called the house he wasn't in and when he visited he was out.

Monday. He'd collar the man on Monday. There was only so long he could allow the man to avoid him. If that was what he was doing.

• • •

After bathtime they dried each other off and then reclined on the bed. A kiss from Alexis led to the inevitable response and they made love again. Then they both slept.

Kenny woke with a start, realising his stomach was grumbling. He stirred Alexis and they both dressed for dinner. Fortunately, Alexis was not one of those women who took an age over getting ready. If anything, Kenny was the slower.

In the dining room, they were the last to be seated and were placed by a window. Being late spring, light remained and painted the tip of the hills opposite a delicate pink. The waters of the loch were motionless, as if covered in a sheet of ice.

Alexis studied the view for a long moment and turned to Kenny. 'This is good for the soul, no?'

Kenny smiled in answer and studied the menu. The waiter approached after a decent time had elapsed. Kenny ordered the lamb and Alexis the monkfish.

'Why did you never marry?' Alexis asked while they waited for the food.

'I prefer my transactions to be more open,' Kenny answered. He and Alexis never spoke about these things, and normally he would have backed off from this type of conversation with a smile, but on this evening he was more relaxed than he had been in a long time.

'If you don't mind me saying so, Kenny, what you just said is complete b.s.'

Kenny laughed. This woman could say almost anything to him and he'd be fine with it.

'I'll tell you if you tell me how you came to sell your body,' Kenny said.

Alexis looked into the distance. 'I like men. I like sex. I ran out of work. I kind of... slipped into it.'

Kenny wondered how much was being left unsaid. He opened his mouth to speak but a waiter appeared at his side with their food.

While they ate their meals the conversation moved on to safer ground. Kenny talked about his family visit nearby. Kenny talked and Alexis listened. Occasionally he would try to steer the conversation back to her, but she carefully deflected each of his questions with a question of her own.

Once the meal was over Alexis touched each corner of her mouth with her linen napkin and took a sip of wine.

'Kenny, darling,' she said ensuring she had his attention.

'Mmmm?'

'I have a proposition for you.'

14

Mason Budge liked the small, blue Toyota. It was reliable, barely noticeable and with this version being a 1.4 diesel engine it could go fast enough for most of the driving he needed to do.

It was effectively anonymous, just like him.

He'd followed the whore down to this godforsaken part of the country. Hills and heather, he thought, who fucking needs them? Give him the cold, wet, grey city streets and lines of street lamps any day of the week. He looked at the clock on the dashboard of the car, from there to the weakening light in the sky and shuddered at the thought of the darkness to come.

His boss didn't know where he was. If he did, he would freak, quickly guess at his reasons and then fire him. Mason shrugged. He could get a new boss any time. People with his particular talents were few and far between in a small country like this. A few phone calls and he would be back in work in jig time.

Another thing to like about this country was the cute phrases they came up with. He admired inventiveness with language.

He hadn't realised that this road was effectively a dead-end and when the car he was following had driven up the road to the hotel he had stopped himself just in time from following them.

The man presented an interesting challenge. Mason watched him as he carried the whore's overnight bag to the hotel door. He was a handsome man and fit, and he walked with an assurance that could only come from knowing how to look after himself. Mason could recognise a fighter from any distance. Men who were less sure of themselves often worked a swagger; a loud sort of body language that shouted, *Don't mess with me*. Those kind of guys were easy targets to a man like Budge. No, this fellow had something else, something that only another fighter would recognise. This was a man not to trifle with and for that reason Mason was desperate to have a go. He then spent a very pleasant thirty minutes thinking up ways to hurt them both. Other people daydreamed about winning the lottery, he loved to pass the time thinking up ways to hurt and humiliate. He would tie him up and rape her. No. That was too straightforward. He could tie her up and rape him.

What was this man's angle with this woman, anyway? He had looks and, judging by the car and clothes, he had money. Why would he need to pay for it? Maybe his wife didn't understand him; his mother hated him. Maybe he had all the social skills of a shrub.

Everyone had a reason, right?

Except him. He had the loving parents and the two-point-four siblings growing up. His gramps, however, read him like a one-page advert; got it right when he paid him – yes, paid him – twenty thousand bucks to leave town. Surely, his life savings. He looked him in the eye and said, 'Some people are just born bad, little buddy, and you are one of 'em.'

Born bad. He liked that. The old fella's way with words had earned him a stay of execution. He had the notion of killing the old fucker there and then and then finishing off the rest of the family. Doing a Columbine on their asses. He could have and often thought he should have. Ducks in a shooting gallery. Fish in a barrel. And it would have taken as much effort but that kind of action was so over and too short on the career trail for his liking. Most of those dumbasses shot themselves once they got the hurting out of their system. He had much more in the way of pain to be doling out.

He thought back to the man with the whore and shrugged a *whatever*. He had given up on trying to understand the motivation men had for the things they did. He had come across many crazies in his time and taking a prostitute out for an overnight at a country hotel ranked pretty low in his weird-o-meter.

They'd be up in their room right now screwing their asses off while he was sat in this shitty little car holding his dick. His boss was to blame. He shouldn't have asked him to 'punish' the woman in such a way. Ever since his time with the whore, he couldn't get her out of his mind. The defiance, the hate, the will to live in her eyes and the feel of her body under him were an intoxicating mix.

He felt his groin stir, closed his eyes, pressed down on his erection with the heel of his hand and replayed the attack in his mind. He grew even harder and groaned. What he would give right now to plunge deep inside her. He gave himself a mental shake, he would have her again. And again. Soon. Some things were better if the anticipation was allowed to build.

15

Kenny woke early in the pitch black and reached for Alexis. She mumbled and turned over, facing away from him. He spooned into her, pushing his arousal against the silk of her bare backside, hoping she would take the hint. She mumbled again and burrowed deeper under the quilt.

He smiled. Thought how this was like being married. He didn't mind. The girl needed her sleep.

Turning over onto his back, Kenny realised he was wide awake. Because of the blackout curtains he couldn't judge what time it was so he stretched across to the bedside cabinet and pressed a key on his phone. His phone lit up to show it was six-thirty. Like that was a surprise. He closed his eyes and judged if he could get back to sleep. Nope. That wasn't going to work. Wide. Awake. His running gear was in his luggage. He'd put that on and go for a jog along the side of the loch. That would beat his usual background of Glasgow's streets. Then by the time he returned maybe Alexis would be up for some more. He grinned.

The receptionist offered a smile behind a yawn when he went downstairs.

'Been a long night?' Kenny asked, his eyes automatically going for the badge. '…Davie.' Davie's face was lined and long, his hair grey and short and his eyes sparked with good humour.

'That's me just started for the day, sir,' Davie answered. 'People are beginning to stir. We have a few fishermen staying over and they'll be hoping to catch a couple of hours on the loch.'

'Never did get the fishing thing,' said Kenny as he stretched out his left calf.

'Never did get the running thing,' said Davie with a grin.

'Yeah,' said Kenny, feeling himself respond to the man's good humour with a grin of his own.

'Did you sleep well, sir?'

'Very well,' answered Kenny, resisting the comment about not much sleep being had. His grin amped up a few notches. Davie raised his eyebrows and smiled.

'Romance is good for the soul, is it not?'

'Is it that obvious?'

'If you don't mind me saying, sir, it's written all over you.'

'Do you share the love of a good woman, Davie?'

'Married ten years. Started late. And been wondering every day since why I waited so long.'

'Right,' said Kenny, feeling his grin fade. This was a conversation he didn't want to go any further. Next Davie would be asking him when he was getting married and if they had any plans for kids. Jeez, it was just gone six o'clock and his life story was up for grabs. 'Man, it's too early and I'm too sober for this conversation to go any further.' He turned and walked towards the door. Realising he had been a little short with Davie, he turned back and offered the man a wave.

'You have a good day.'

As the words issued from his mouth, Kenny was thinking, Holy fuck, O'Neill, you have a night of passion and you come over all American.

• • •

'Smirr' was the Scottish word for the constant, light rain that coated his skin within seconds. As he stretched, his even breathing was like a whisper in his ear. He ran on the spot, looking around himself.

80

The sky was overcast and mist hung above the waters of the loch, stretching up the wall of the far hills. The world was in soft focus; picture-postcard perfect and Kenny had rarely felt so alive.

He stretched some more by the hotel door. He looked along the building. Everything was clean and precise, understated and classy, from the wood used for the door to the urns of fresh flowers placed along the wall. Good choice, mate, he congratulated himself and then set off for his run.

He reached the bottom of the hotel road and looked left and right. Left took him back along the loch towards Balquhidder; right took him God knows where. He turned left, thinking it would be nice to stand once again in the places his father took him all those years ago.

As he ran he thought about Alexis. She'd still be snuffling in her sleep, pleased to get the bed to herself. He recognised that their relationship was not the norm. He also recognised that his feelings for her were too strong and that they were not reciprocated. What did Alexis see in him? A punter who didn't repulse her? A set of male genitalia with a wallet?

The previous night over dinner she attempted to take their relationship on to a different level altogether. Kenny grinned when he remembered his response.

'Let me get this right. You want me to become your pimp?'

'God, that is such a horrible word,' replied Alexis.

'But it's the right word and the answer is no.'

'It's not the right word. After that...' – her face twisted as she remembered the attack – '...evil prick had his way with me I just to feel that I need someone to protect my interests.'

'So what happens between us? I like the fact that...'

'You looking for some free booty, Mr O'Neill?' Alexis grinned.

'That's the point... I like to know that I can call you when I feel the urge, hand over the cash and we can...'

'That won't change, Kenny.'

'But do I get mates' rates?'

'Mates' rates? This is a new one on me.' Alexis paused and took a sip of her wine.

'It means... never mind what it means, I don't like it, Alexis.'

'Okay, Kenny, let's go over it one more time. You value the service I provide, yes?'

'Yes,' said Kenny and looked into Alexis' eyes, thinking she had never looked so beautiful.

'Do you agree that other men might also value such a service?'

'Yes.'

'Do you not also agree that this sort of service keeps sex for sale off the streets and makes it much more...' – she considered the right word – '...palatable?'

'Yes.'

'Do you not also agree that if I were to take on a stable of girls like myself and the service was marketed in the right way that it could make a lot of money?'

'Yes.'

'And as the manager of such a service would you not also be in a position to make a lot of money?'

'Yes, but...'

'Whenever I hear someone say the words "Yes, but" I know they think I am right but they just don't want to face it.'

'Not if it comes with the size of the but I have.'

'Oh, I dunno, Kenny.' Alexis' smile sent a flicker of pleasure straight to Kenny's penis. 'Your butt is just the right size.'

'Anyway,' – Kenny fought down his answering smile – 'you couldn't describe me as a man who was shy of making a few pounds, nor one who is shy of the legal process in doing so. However, I do have some scruples. I don't deal in human misery; drugs and pros- titution are definite no-no's.'

'Well, good for you, Kenny.' Alexis sat upright in her chair. 'We all need to draw the line somewhere.'

'Don't get sniffy with me, Alexis. I just–'

'You are just a hypocrite, Kenny.' She leant forward in her chair, nostrils flaring. 'Ignore your emotional needs by paying for sex if that's what does it for you, but don't pretend you are not part of the problem...'

'Wait a wee minute here.' Kenny always believed the best form of defence was attack. Whether that was in a physical fight or verbal one it didn't matter. 'Why this? Why now? Is this something to do with the man that attacked you? Aren't you really just looking to take advantage of my muscle?'

'Aren't you just looking to take advantage of the honeypot between my legs? We both have something the other wants.'

'I'm confused,' said Kenny. 'Where is this argument going?'

'Hopefully to a resolution that benefits us both,' Alexis said and leaned forward on to her elbows.

'Can we sleep on it?' Kenny asked. 'My gut reaction is no, but I need to think through the implications.'

Alexis took a deep breath. Swallowed as if forcing herself to lighten up. Kenny read something else tightening her fine features. Was it fear? Was there something she was hiding from him?

This question came back to him as he ran. How long had he been meeting Alexis... and why had she come up with this now? Surely there was a link to the man who attacked her.

He got his guy to rape me.

The text: *Lesson learned?*

Kenny had tried on several occasions to dig into the facts of those statements and gotten nowhere. Alexis wasn't being totally up front with him and he had to find out the truth before they took things any further.

There was also the matter of his mother's death. He had achieved nothing there either. Harry Fyfe had produced a little background knowledge but nothing more. As soon as this weekend was over he needed to get back on the case.

The road took a dip and then a small climb. Kenny enjoyed the variation and stretched out his legs, pushing up the work levels. Another bend and he came across a car parked in a passing spot. He tutted. Not the done thing in these small roads. This was a single-track road. The passing places were there so cars could pull over and let cars coming in the opposite direction drive past. If some numpty parked there, it could cause a problem. Must be a tourist, he thought.

It was a blue car. He ran closer. A blue Toyota Yaris. He reduced his speed to a walk. When he arrived the day before he was worried that just such a car was following him. Could it be the same car? Surely there were loads of these cars on the roads, but two of them down such a quiet road in the space of a few hours? Must be the same one.

The windows were slightly steamed up, suggesting that whoever was it in it had been there for some time. He didn't believe in coincidences. He'd have to check this out.

He could see a man-sized shape through the window. The driver's seat had been reclined all the way back. The driver had his head facing away from him and looked as if he was fast asleep.

Kenny knocked on the window.

The head turned round and faced him. The man sat up, pushed open the car door and stepped out on to the road.

'Don't think you should be parking there, mate,' said Kenny, aiming for a friendly tone. 'Could cause an accident.'

The man stretched extravagantly. Yawned. And stretched some more. He was wearing jeans and a checked shirt. Around five feet ten and slim. The man rubbed his eyes and peered at Kenny.

'And you are?' he asked with a smile.

'Just a concerned punter,' answered Kenny, not completely taken in by the smile. 'You really shouldn't park in these spaces. If two cars came along here at the same time, there would be nowhere for them to go.'

'You're right, dude,' the other man said, rubbing his head. 'I got lost late last night and wasn't sure where else to go.'

'American?' asked Kenny.

'Canadian,' the man replied while still smiling.

'Sorry. You must get that a lot.'

'More than I care to mention, fella. But no harm done, huh?' He looked down at Kenny's bare legs and his running gear. 'You out for a little light exercise?'

'Yeah,' answered Kenny, kicking his legs out to keep them warm and then changed the subject. 'Didn't you realise that there was a hotel just down the road?' Kenny gestured behind him with his thumb.

'They're full, man. I arrived fairly late yesterday. Just a spur-of-the-moment thing. Thought I would get in some fishing.' He looked over his shoulder at the loch. Kenny followed his line of vision to see just through the trees and ten yards down the lochside that there was a small beach. A couple of men were already thigh deep in the water, their lines cast.

'You going far?' the man asked.

'Nah,' answered Kenny. 'Another half hour.' He gave each leg a little kick, took a deep breath and turned away. He waved over his shoulder at the tourist. Paused, smiled and said, 'Have a nice day.'

He was still chuckling to himself five minutes later.

Ten minutes later he arrived in Balquhidder and thought again about the tourist guy. Pretty nondescript. He'd have trouble picking him out of a police line-up.

16

Mason Budge pursed his lips as he considered the sport of fishing. The nearest he wanted to come to a fish was when it was served up with a nice garlic sauce. The thought of standing in cold water up to his balls for hours on end just did not appeal.

Placing his hands on his lower back he arched out his spine. And groaned. Jeez, it was great to get out of that car. What a horrible night. He hated the dark out here in the country and because it had been a cloudy night it had gotten *really* dark. He shuddered. Man, the countryside was messed up. Nature could go and fuck itself for all he cared. All those noises. All those critters scrabbling about in the dirt; heavens only knew what diseases they could pass on.

If you asked him, that was where AIDS came from right there. Some fucker went camping and caught it and then infected the rest of the world. Gay plague, my ass, he thought and grinned at his unintentional joke. Them right-wing scientists couldn't work out where the disease came from and thought, I know, I hate gays, let's blame them.

As for those midges. Man, it was a wonder anyone stayed outside the cities in this country. Nasty little fuckers. He had gone for a little walk before dark, going for a little recon, and got bitten on every available piece of skin. He'd raced back to the car and blessed its airtight seals for the rest of the night.

It was the army he turned to when his gramps' money ran out. He thought about going back for more but realised that was a waste of time. Best to find a way to hurt people and get paid for it. The Canadian army welcomed him with open arms and then when it realised he had a knack for it they moved him to Special Ops and from there to NATO's peacekeeping corps. Peacekeeping, my ass.

He had a ball.

At first.

Before Bosnia, he could pretty much take on anything; after a week in a basement waiting out a sniper, with a dead colleague at his side, he developed issues.

Budge looked back down the road at the runner. Good set of shoulders on him and an easy stride pattern that was eating up the road. What a dick, thought Budge. Who could be bothered? The army tried to beat a love of exercise into him. Didn't work.

Fortunately, he was naturally fit. A few press-ups and sit-ups here and there was enough for him. Also, his job was physical. Beating up people on a regular basis tended to keep him healthy and strong, he thought with a grin.

He sat back in the car, turned on the engine and wondered how far on the runner was. Thought about the shape of him as he vanished into the distance. They were of a similar height and weight. A thought occurred to him. Might be interesting to find out if they were the same size all over.

No point in coming all the way out here without having a little fun now, was there?

17

Kenny loved the sensation of having an endless source of energy in his thighs. That's what keeping fit did for him. A night of no-conscience shagging, followed by a deep sleep, followed by a run: life just didn't get any better. He gave a wee skip when he reached the red telephone box at the village hall – laughed at himself – and considered going on till the A84. He could feel the power in his legs, the evenness of his breathing and the hormones feeding his system. Felt like he could go on forever.

Then he thought about Alexis lying in the hotel bed, the softness of her skin and her words hot in his ear last night urging him on to bigger effort. He felt a stirring. Stopped and turned. He could go for a run any morning.

Back at the hotel, a wink to Davie behind the reception desk and he was up the stairs to his room three at a time. He opened the door and slid in. The curtains were still shut but enough light came in the door behind him to see that an Alexis-shaped bump still warmed the sheets.

He considered jumping in beside her. Right, and a smelly, sweaty body was going to receive a welcome. He shucked off his clothes and walked over to the bathroom. The shower was hot and brisk. His groin tingling with anticipation as he soaped himself clean of his efforts.

A quick rub-down with a towel and he was ready.

He lifted up the quilt and slid in behind Alexis. She made a happy little mewling sound as he put an arm round her.

A moan as he slid deep inside her.

'O'Neill,' she said with a husky voice, 'you're an animal.'

Kenny felt his breath shorten as he moved in and out. The feeling was delicious. He savoured her heat and wetness as he slowed down his movements. He groaned. She was so wet. She was always quick to respond to him, but not this quick.

'Mmm, yes, Kenny. This is so nice.'

Kenny closed his eyes and stopped moving. He didn't want to come just yet.

Alexis had a chuckle in her voice. 'You'd think once in the morning would be enough for you.'

Her words didn't register for a moment as he began to slowly move.

Then he stopped.

'What do you mean, "once in the morning"?'

Alexis laughed and he could hear her head move on the pillow as she turned to face him. 'You animal.' She laughed again. 'You just had your way with me minutes ago.'

Kenny sat up. 'What do you mean, "minutes ago"?' He reached across her to the bedroom lamp. 'I'm just back from a run. You sure you weren't dreaming about me? Again.'

'Again, my backside,' Alexis said and pushed at his chest. Her smile faltered on her face as she read the look on his face. 'Kenny O'Neill, you are a horror.' From her expression she expected him to admit he was teasing her. 'Stop kidding me on.'

'I'm not kidding, Alexis. Look.' He pointed to his running gear in a damp slump by the bathroom door. He gripped her arm, suddenly anxious. 'Tell me. Did you think you had sex with me already this morning, or were you dreaming?'

Alexis was staring at his running clothes as she tried to work out just what had happened.

'I can still feel you. Inside me,' she said. 'I was still half asleep. At the start. It wasn't a dream.' Her head moved slightly. 'And where did those flowers come from?'

'What...?' Kenny followed her line of sight and saw a large bunch of flowers on the floor by the door. 'Where the fuck did they come from?'

'Oh my god. Ohmyfuckinggod.' Alexis brought her knees up to her chest, her face tight with horror. 'Someone came in here and...'

'Alexis.' Kenny reached for her.

She jumped up as if burned. 'Get your fucking hands off me.' She stood, her hands over her breasts. 'What the fuck is going on?'

Her face stretched in horror as her mind replayed recent events. 'You... he... someone was behind me. He just slid in a little...' Her eyes filled with tears. 'Didn't last long. I thought... Kenny, what happened?'

'Fucked if I know,' said Kenny, grabbing his jeans. 'But I'm about to find out.'

He dressed in record time and ran down to the reception. Davie looked up from his computer terminal. He instantly read the anger on Kenny's face.

'Has something gone wrong, sir?'

'Apart from your guests, has anyone else come in the hotel this morning?'

'Just the usual deliveries, sir. Oh, and did madam like the flowers you ordered for her?'

'What flowers?'

'There was a man. He... he... he turned up not long after you went out for your run. Said he was making a delivery. Asked for the room number for the couple...'

'Did you not think it was a bit fucking unusual for a flower delivery at six-thirty on a Sunday morning?'

'I... eh... is something wrong with the flowers, sir?'

'It's more with the delivery!' Kenny shouted. He paused and his head shot round to the front door. He had seen those flowers before. He walked out the door, noticed one of the urns was empty.

Davie appeared at his shoulder.

'Ooh.' He blanched.

Kenny brushed past him and ran back up to the room. Alexis was dressed and was throwing her things back into her overnight bag.

'Take me home, Kenny. Take me home now.'

'Alexis, what the fuck is going on?'

She had been crying, her eyes were puffy and her bottom lip was trembling.

'Alexis.' Kenny tried to force some composure into his voice. 'Tell me what happened. Tell me everything.'

'I... I was half asleep, you know, and then... you...' – disgust framed her face –'...whoever the fuck it was slid across the bed. He... fucked me. I fell asleep again and next thing I know you... you were inside me and...' Her face lengthened in grief. 'I've been... again.' She tore at her clothes. 'I need a shower. I need to clean myself. I need...'

Kenny strode over to her and gripped her arms, thinking about the guy in the Blue Yaris.

'Can you describe him?'

'One, I don't have eyes in the back of my head. And two, even if I did the room was dark.' Alexis fought to get her arms free from Kenny. Such was the force of her movement that when Kenny let go her fist connected with his cheekbone.

He rubbed at it. 'Fuck.'

'Wish I could do that to the bastard who...' Alexis turned and started to unbutton her cardigan as she walked towards the bathroom. 'I need to shower.'

'No.' Kenny caught up with her. 'Did the guy...?' He made a face.

'Yes, he came, Kenny, but his junk will be mixed up with yours and besides...'

'On this occasion you are not a hooker,' said Kenny, knowing where she was going with this. 'You're here with your boyfriend and you've been violated. The police have to listen to you.'

'You think I'm going to the police?' Alexis was leaning forward, one arm out of her sleeve. 'I'll deal with this in my own way.' She stood in front of a mirror and put her arm back in the sleeve. 'Occupational hazard, don't you know.' Her eyes were full of loathing. Whether for herself, or for the man who had done this to her, Kenny had no idea.

'But the man, whoever he was, had no idea you were a hooker...' He tailed off as the implications of what she said hit home. 'You know this man?'

'I told you before, Kenny. It was dark. It was just another cock.' She spat the words out.

That part of his ego that was always wondering how Alexis felt about him got its answer. He was just another cock. Just another customer. He put it to the side for the moment. There was much more important issues at play here than his male pride.

This was no accident, he was sure of it, and if Alexis didn't know who had raped her, she knew why.

'What aren't you telling me, Alexis?'

'Fuck you, O'Neill.'

'You either know this guy, or you know why you were targeted. C'mon, tell me.' Kenny only realised that he was gripping her arms again when she shrugged him off. He automatically moved back out of her reach in case another fist connected with his face.

'Take me home, Kenny. Please,' said Alexis as she slumped to the floor on her knees.

There was a knock at the door and Davie's face appeared. Then he stepped into the room, tugging at his sleeves and all but shrinking with every step he took. 'I'm sorry, Mr and Mrs O'Neill, the hotel management would like to know what they can do to...' He tailed off as he wondered what exactly had gone on and how on earth they could compensate. 'There will of course be no charge for your stay and I have written down the number of the local police station...'

'There will be no police.' Alexis managed to get back to her feet, stepped forward and pulled the paper from the man's hand. 'Nothing happened...' – she looked at his badge and offered him a thousand-watt smile – '…Davie.' Davie almost buckled at the knees. 'There is no need either to tear up our bill, we are happy to pay.'

'Are we fuck,' roared Kenny. 'This fuckwit gave a bogus flower delivery man our room number and...'

'Kenny,' Alexis said firmly, 'if you want this relationship to continue, you will do as I say.' She squared her shoulders and turned to face Davie. 'We have to go back to Glasgow. A business emergency of sorts. Please prepare our bill.' Again with the smile and Davie was mallow.

'Yes, of course, Mrs O'Neill.' With a furtive look at Kenny, Davie fled the room.

'If you think...' Kenny began.

'Kenny, I'm not arguing with you,' said Alexis, her face showing all the expression of a mime's mask. 'We are leaving now and we will speak of this no more.'

'Yeah, that'll be fucking right,' he replied. Alexis raised her eyebrows, but her eyes shone with tears betraying the fact that her hard-fought control was moments away from being lost again. Kenny swallowed what he was going to say next and thought, give it a couple of days and if she doesn't explain what the fuck is going on, there will be no deal.

They gathered their belongings and flung them without any care in their respective bags. Alexis left the room before Kenny was finished packing. His eyes followed her out of the room and he read fragile defiance in every step she took. What strength it took to do so he had no idea, but he had never admired anyone more than he did in that moment.

At reception Kenny ignored the middle-aged couple who were about to step up to the desk.

'Davie,' Kenny said and nodded to the side.

Davie excused himself with the couple and walked to the side of the desk. He stepped to where he might have with a 'normal' customer, took one look at Kenny's face and took a step back.

'Describe the flower guy,' Kenny said. It was not a request.

'He was about your height.' Davie screwed up his face as he thought. 'Lean. A bit of muscle on him. Cropped hair, army style.'

'Face, race, colouring?'

'White, average,' Davie said hesitantly. 'You know, to be honest, if I had to pick him out of a police line-up I don't think I could.'

Kenny said nothing. He had thought exactly the same thing.

He looked at Davie, who seemed to shrink under his gaze. He threw a card at him. 'Anything else occurs to you, you phone me, okay?'

'Okay, sir. I'll do that.' The relief that his ordeal by Kenny was almost over was palpable.

'As for your bill,' said Kenny, 'you can shove it up your arse.'

The male customer at the far side of the desk opened his mouth as if to complain at Kenny's language. At the intake of his breath Kenny turned to face him. Reading Kenny's face, the man stopped as if the words were stuck in his throat like a bone.

18

Kenny needed to kick ass. He sent a text to his cousin, Ian.

You want to meet down the gym?

Half an hour later he got a reply.

Busy, dude. Got me some chill-out stuff, if you know what I mean. Another time?

Kenny did know what he meant. Other than alcohol he had never been tempted by drugs. He was too afraid of losing control. With alcohol he knew where he stood, but with drugs there was always a chance they contained an unknown substance. Fuck that for a carry on. Mug's game. However, on this occasion he could almost see the attraction. Wouldn't it be nice to just give up his worries to the weed for a few hours?

Nah.

The worries would still be there when the shit wore off.

He considered his options. There was the drive around town until a road-rager ran into him option. Or he could go down to The Hut. This was actually a hut – well, two or three large huts nailed together and just this side of health and safety safe. It was called King's Gym, although everyone who used it preferred 'The Hut' and it was a Mixed Martial Arts gym where some of his bouncers trained. Monday night was a free night. Guys often turned up to see if there was someone available to spar.

An hour later he was in his shorts and vest and a guy just shy of seven feet tall was rubbing his face in the mat. He reached back for a pressure point but the other man – 'Shug' was the only word to be issued from his thick, rubber hose lips before the sparring began – managed to move out of reach.

Kenny shifted. Brought his hips up and his head down at the same time. Managed to move onto his back, but it was only a moment's respite before Shug's forearm was across his throat and Kenny was wondering about the wisdom of this visit. His skills weren't suitable for this kind of fighting. Once it got down on the ground he lacked the moves to get himself free from his opponent if he was pinned.

A grappler he was not.

Shug kept his centre of gravity low and his weight over Kenny's chest. His vision started to spark. It was only a wee sparring match. He should tap out, but he was fucked if he was giving in. His breathing, already laboured before he got into this position, was getting shorter. He couldn't fill his lungs. His feet scrabbled for purchase on the mat. He punched at Shug's kidney area and it had all the effect of hitting the man with a bath sponge.

A tap on the floor and it would be all over.

Wasn't going to happen.

There was always a way, his old master told him. Before his oxygen supply failed he had to find one.

An escape, he had to find an escape. He had to create space. A move popped into his head and he reached under Shug's stomach with his left arm and brought his right leg up. He grabbed his foot and twisted his hip and as he twisted his hip he brought his knee up. He pushed back, brought the other knee up and he was now safe in the butterfly guard.

Shug grinned and nodded. 'Nice.'

The bell rang and the match was over. Kenny hid his relief. He wasn't sure he could have stood any more of Shug's treatment.

At the showers, the gym owner, Matt, was standing with a towel round his waist talking to another man. He started this place in the Seventies to try and keep the young away from gangs. He didn't look old enough to have had such a social conscience all those years ago. Think unlined face, bald head, cauliflower ears and shoulders as wide as the backseat of a car.

Matty the Hut was his nickname. But only used behind his back. Despite being in his early sixties, he regularly took to the mat and beat men half his age.

'Wee Shug nearly had you there, Kenny,' the older man grinned. 'There is such a thing as matching up height and weight, you know.'

Wee Shug. That happy Scots tendency towards irony.

'Wouldn't like to meet his bigger cousin.' He made a face to emphasise the effort he had just put in. 'Mind you, where's the fun in a good match?' Kenny laughed. 'Don't want things too easy, do you?' Now that the fight was over he was exhilarated. Just what the doctor ordered.

'You look like a man who's found some resolution,' said Matt. For an old bruiser he had a decent vocabulary on him.

'Never fails,' said Kenny.

'Do you know...?' Matt turned to the side and indicated the man he had been talking to.

'Hey, Liam,' Kenny said.

Liam Devlin, Glasgow councillor, nodded.

'Fuck's sake, O'Neill, do you know everybody?' asked Matt.

'Only the important people, eh Kenny?' Liam smiled. This was the first time Kenny had ever seen the man without a shirt and tie on. Until now, if anyone asked, Kenny would have said he slept with his suit on and he simply eased off the knot of his tie a little before jumping under the quilt.

First time he'd seen him naked.

Who knew, he thought. Under that pudgy face and M&S suit was a well-muscled torso. Legs that would look okay behind some chicken wire mind you, but he had done a fair bit of upper-body work.

Kenny smiled at both men and walked through to the showers.

Afterwards, he sought Matt out. A lot of people came through the doors of this place. The MMA community was a large one. In the main they were a good bunch but some of them got to like the power that came with strength and an ability to use it. Some of them mixed in the wrong circles. Circles where Kenny had a few contacts.

Information was important to him and Matt might let slip something that he didn't realise was of any importance. Ergo, a good man to be on talking terms with. Which was why he occasionally made a charitable contribution.

Matt was ringside, talking a pair of teenagers through some grappling moves.

'Couldn't you have been here earlier when Wee Shug was driving my head through the mat?' Kenny asked.

'Ach, you were fine, man,' said Matt, keeping his eyes on the boys. 'Buy you a coffee?'

'Sure,' he said to Kenny. 'Right, guys,' he addressed the boys. 'I'll be back in five minutes. Take turns at being the one mounted, eh?'

The boys made a face and said in concert, 'Mounted, ewww.'

The coffee machine was a couple of bucket chairs down from the ladies' changing room. Which was new since his last visit.

'You going P.C. on us, Matt?'

'Got to, Kenny. Or the bastards will close me down. Besides, the lassies are getting pretty good at this stuff now.'

'The usual?' Kenny put some coins in the machine without waiting for an answer and it produced a couple of white coffees with an apologetic effort of foam on top. He sipped at it. Hot and tasted as if someone had mixed the contents of an ashtray into the coffee granules.

In the pause before the conversation started, Kenny looked afresh at the older man. How long had he been coming here, and how little did he know about the man? Pathetic. For someone whose 'thing' was information he'd slipped up here. As far as he knew, Matt had no family and devoted his life to the gym. And that was it.

'How long you known Liam Devlin?' asked Matt.

'Long enough to know he's a man who can get things done,' Kenny answered, surprised by the question.

'Okay.' Matt nodded slowly as he considered something.

'Why do you ask?'

'The usual,' Matt answered. 'Money...'

'Hey, you know I'll...'

'I cannae always come to you, Kenny. Don't think I don't appreciate everything you've done for the club...'

'It's not always community spirit that motivates me, Matt. Take those clapped out heaters you had in here last winter. It'll be nice to train during a cold snap without freezing my balls off.'

'Ah,' Matt laughed. 'Might have guessed it was more than altruism at play the way you insisted on how the money should be spent.'

'What do you need it for now?'

'New mats, repairs on the roof, need to replace some of the... Christ...' He paused. 'I could go on for some time.'

'So where does Devlin come in?'

'He's been training here for over six months now–'

'First time I've seen him,' Kenny interrupted.

'Aye well, he comes in at odd times. Anyway, he was in the fast lane to a heart attack. We got him fit and now he wants to help.' Matt shrugged. 'Didn't want to pin my hopes on a wide-boy.'

'Liam Devlin, a wide-boy?' Kenny asked.

'That's maybe understating some of the stuff I've heard, Kenny. Not a nice man to get on the wrong side of.'

Kenny made a face of disbelief. 'Aye, he might manage to get your car impounded.'

'Naw, Kenny,' argued Matt. 'From what I hear he's in to some heavy duty stuff.'

Kenny exhaled loudly through pursed lips. 'Nah, he's a pussycat. Believe me, if Devlin was into dodgy stuff, I'd know about it.'

'Okay, Kenny, okay.' Matt looked unconvinced. 'Maybe I could trust him with some funding ventures then. Eh?' Kenny nodded. Matt nodded and smiled and patted Kenny on the knee.

'Hey, it's good to see you. Keeping your nose clean?'

'Squeaky.' Kenny paused. He'd not articulated to himself what he wanted to ask Matt about. 'Know that programme on the Beeb where famous people try to find out where they came from?'

'Aye,' said Matt, '*Who Do You Think You Are?*'

'Aye,' said Kenny. 'Well, I thought I'd look into it myself.'

'Ah shit, and there's me left my genealogy degree at home today. How the fuck am I supposed to help you with that?' Matt asked.

A loud squeal sounded from where they'd left the boys sparring.

'Hey, don't you two be killing each other over there,' Matt shouted in their direction.

'Ear to the ground, Matt,' Kenny said and judging that the coffee would be cool enough to drink now, he took a sip. He made a face. It tasted even worse second mouthful round. 'You're a man with his ear to the ground.'

'Aye, only when he's got the knee of a twenty-stone bruiser pinning him there.'

'My dad's name was, or is – I don't know if he's alive or dead – Peter O'Neill and...' Something in Matt's expression made him stop speaking.

'Pete O'Neill's your old man?' asked Matt with a stunned look. Then something else flitted across his face before the look of surprise returned. 'Fuck me.'

'You knew him?' Kenny's heart pounded.

'Man, he was quite the character. Knew him? Everybody knew Pete.' He examined Kenny's face for a second. A second that lengthened into a minute. 'Fuck me, I don't know how it didn't occur to me before now. You're his spit.'

'How well did you know him, Matt?'

'Well enough to know that the BBC would only film a toned-down version of his life,' Matt said and shook his head again. 'Jee-sus. How come it didn't occur to me already? You are so like him.' He slapped his forehead. 'And then there's the name. Man, I'm losing it.'

Loud swearing boomed from where the boys were training. Sounded like they were about to take it to another level.

Matt stood up and craned his neck to see what was going on.

'What can you tell me about him, Matt?'

More swearing and the sound of bone on bone.

'Aww, fuck lads,' Matt shouted. 'Kenny, I'll need to stop these two from killing each other.' He moved away at a half-run. 'I've got your number,' he shouted over his shoulder. 'I'll give you a call, aye?'

19

'How's your mum?' Kenny was on hands-free, driving past Bellahouston Park. He was on his way to a meet with Dimitri of the Manners, as he called him, and thought he should check in with his cousin. As he pressed speed-dial for the number it occurred to him that he couldn't remember the last time he and his cousin met face to face. Their entire relationship was conducted by text and telephone call.

'She's... fine... dandy,' answered Ian with a why-the-fuck-are-you-asking? tone.

'Jesus, she'd have to O.D. in front of you for you to realise there was something wrong.'

'Harsh, m'man. I love my mother.' Ian sounded as if he was in the middle of a smoke.

'Has she said anything about the letters?'

'The letters?' There was now an urgency in Ian's voice and a sound as if he had just sat up straight. 'That's right. The letters. I totally forgot. What did you learn?'

What did he learn, thought Kenny. His father abandoned him when he needed him most. His father tried to explain this by saying he was in trouble and running away had saved Kenny's life. And Aunt Vi was convinced his mother hadn't committed suicide but was instead murdered. Ian spent most of his energy keeping his brain free from pain and stuck in a fog – could he handle any of that?

'My dad has a new family. I don't know where they are.'

'Did he say why he did a runner?'

'Couldn't face your dad's sour puss any longer.'

'Harsh, m'man. I love my father.' Ian chuckled. 'But he does suffer from a serious case of the miseries.'

'You should put some of your junk in his yoghurt.' They both laughed at the thought of Ian's dad being a stoner. Once they recovered Kenny asked, 'What do you remember of those days, Ian?'

'Aww, man, I have enough trouble trying to remember where I left my cigarette lighter.' He paused, sounded as if he was stifling a cough and then he could fight it no longer. He barked like an Alsatian warning off a burglar.

'Je-sus, Ian, that stuff will kill you.'

'Least of my worries, dude. Anyways, where was I? Trying to remember...'

Kenny clicked his tongue. 'If it doesn't come to you straight away it's not going to, Ian. It's not like your aunt kills herself and your uncle disappears every fucking day of the week.'

'Chill, dude... lemme give this some thought. You know the...'

'Aw fuck off, Ian.' Kenny hung up. He took a deep breath, regretting his irritation. The poor guy couldn't help it; God knows what his combat injuries and heroin combo had done to him.

The car stereo was on a local radio station and playing the latest single from an all-girl pop band. Band, my arse, he thought and muted the sound. When he was younger the word 'band' suggested an ability to play some instruments. These days it meant a talent for simpering in front of a camera wearing nothing but some sparkle and a smile.

Jeez, listen to you, Old Man Noah.

He felt at a loss. What should he do? The situation with Alexis hadn't been resolved yet and he was nowhere nearer finding out the truth of his mother's death. That she had died of an overdose was a clear and accepted fact. If, as his Aunt Vi suggested, she was murdered then somebody had forced the pills down her throat.

Such was his horror at this thought, he braked. And the driver behind him stepped on his horn. Kenny waved an apology over his shoulder.

Fuck.

How would you feel? Somebody forcing drugs down your throat. The panic and terror of knowing you were about to die. Did she pray for her husband to come home early that night? How much of a fight did she put up? Why didn't he hear anything?

Why didn't he fucking hear anything?

He felt his eyes sting and blinked in surprise. If anyone had asked him how he felt about his mother's death until now he would have shrugged and said, *Ancient history*. And yet here he was making like a guest on Oprah.

He had to find out what happened.

He thought about his father's letters. His father said he left to protect him. Who was he protecting him from? Find that out and you have your murderer. Simple.

How angry would he have to be to target someone in this way? The letters talked about an accident and the death of a woman and a child. His mother was repayment for the woman. He would have been collateral damage for the child had his father not done his vanishing act.

Your run-of-the-mill revenge-driven psycho would have taken out the father and the child as well, surely? It takes one sick fuck to do the wife and leave the father to worry about himself and the son. That could be a strong piece of torture right there, but it would only work if your long-term plan was to take them both out after a suitable period of being worried into a living grave.

It takes a certain mindset to kill a young woman in such a way. An individual capable of such an act wouldn't give up on the rest of his revenge so easily. Why did he stop there?

The building he was aiming for loomed on the road ahead. Wondering how he had managed to arrive at his destination safely, Kenny swooped into the car park and chose a parking bay. He pointed his car towards the exit as was his habit. You never knew when a quick getaway might be required.

In the bar of the hotel, Dimitri was wearing his usual suit-and-tie combo and he looked over Kenny's T-shirt and jeans outfit with an expression of disapproval. Kenny hid a smile. He had chosen his clothes carefully to piss the man off. The two men ordered soft drinks. They were both driving. Such is the new Glasgow. Aye, right.

They sat at a table in the corner of the room.

'What was so fucking urgent, Dimitri?' Kenny asked.

Dimitri attempted a huff at Kenny's tone and then gave in. 'I have some stuff you might be interested in.'

'What, no preamble? No pleasant chat before we get to the meat of the meeting?'

'You appear to be a man in a hurry, Mr O'Neill. I'm adjusting my approach to suit yours.'

'It's Kenny, remember? What kind of stuff?' Kenny sat down at a table beside him. The table was dotted with beer mats and ring circles.

'Hugely desirable, symbols of affluence, works of...'

'Dimitri, what happened to adjusting your approach to mine? Save me the spiel and give me the detail.'

'Designer gear. High end. The real deal. Didn't even get as far as the lorry, fell off the container ship.'

'Price?'

Dimitri gave him a figure. Kenny halved it. Dimitri made a face and went back to his original figure.

'Dimitri, haven't you guessed I'm not in the mood? You're here because I'm your best bet to get this stuff moved on before it's last season's and therefore worthless. Spare us both the dance and agree my price and then I can get the fuck out of here.'

Dimitri's face displayed his owner's internal journey as he mentally fought with Kenny's assertion. Then his bulldog features settled into an expression of acceptance.

'Fine.'

He sounded like a teenager who'd just been sent to his room. He leaned forward on the table, his elbow planted like a prop and his fingers leaving indents in the putty of his face.

'What did you do before you got into this racket?' Kenny asked.

'I.T.' Dimitri made a face.

'Couldn't you hack it?'

'Oh, very funny. Haven't heard that before,' said Dimitri while loosening the knot on his tie.

'There must have been easier ways to earn your living while still attached to your motherboard.'

'There was and I did.' Dimitri frowned. 'Before I was caught and locked up.'

'Tell me more?'

'Condition of my parole is that I don't own a computer or have access to the internet.'

'That must be like telling a food addict to step away from the pies.'

'True.' Dimitri laughed and for the first time since they had met Kenny got a glimpse into the real man.

'How did you get caught?'

'By thinking I was smarter than anyone else.' Dimitri's face grew red. He scratched at his forehead. 'If you don't mind, I'd rather we change the subject. Where do you want me to send the goods?'

They arranged a time and place.

Kenny thought about Dimitri and how he might be of more help to him. The guy was embarrassed at the mere mention of his capture. This meant he had some professional pride. Take this into conjunction with the fact he was shit as a face-to-face merchant, Dimitri really should get another job. Kenny told him as much.

'Thanks, mate,' Dimitri said. 'None taken.'

'Your parole people...' Kenny thought out loud. 'If you were to be given a desk and a computer with a cheeky wee internet connection, how would they know?'

Dimitri shrugged. 'Knowing my luck they'd find out. I'm not

going back to jail, man. I have a wife and two teenage daughters to take care of.'

'How do they think you're making a living right now?'

'They couldn't care less, so long as it doesn't involve a computer.'

'How can anyone work nowadays without a computer?'

'You don't.'

Kenny gave this some thought. 'True.' He did have a laptop but he didn't commit anything from his business onto it.

'What did you do? Steal millions? Hack into the US defence system?'

Dimitri shook his head.

'If it wasn't for money or violence, that leaves a woman?' Kenny surmised.

Dimitri relaxed back into his chair and looked at Kenny's glass. 'If I'm going to tell you this properly, you're going to need a refill.'

Kenny looked at his watch. He didn't have to be anywhere. 'Get me a coffee, will you?'

Dimitri attracted the presence of a waiter and the drinks were ordered and quickly supplied. All the while Dimitri sat in his chair wearing more faces than the town clock. One moment he looked resigned; the next depressed; then anger, then uncertainty. Then back to resigned.

'I'm really shite at this, aren't I?'

'Aye.' Kenny nodded. 'You're a nice guy, Dimitri. What made you try for a life of crime?'

'There was this guy in the jail...'

'Guys in jail are full of piss and wind, Dimitri.'

'Anyway,' – Dimitri took a sip of his coffee – 'my entrance to a life of crime was all for the love of a beautiful woman.'

'Good start, D. There might even be a movie in here.'

'Shut the fuck up, Kenny, and let me tell it.'

Kenny, impressed with the assertive side of Dimitri, did as he was told and shut the fuck up.

'Her name was Elizabeth. Gorgeous woman. Sexiest woman I've

ever met.' His eyes all but glazed over at the thought of her. 'What did she see in me? Bald, overweight, hairy like a chimp.'

'Don't tell me... you've a nine-inch tongue and you can breathe through your ears?'

Dimitri stuck his tongue out and grinned. 'Anyway, we had an affair. I swear to God I've never been unfaithful before, but this woman... out of my league. It was like Man United playing Stranraer. Whatever she saw in me, she saw in me. I wasn't complaining.' His eyes drifted away from Kenny and into the past. 'Long story short. We were going to run away together. She booked a room in one of the Hiltons in London. From there we were going to jump on a plane and go to Spain.'

He sipped from his cup and swallowed like it pained him. 'She wasn't at the hotel. Nor did she arrive the next day. I got a text – a fucking text – to say that she couldn't go through with it. Too many people would get hurt.' He spread his arms wide. 'What's a guy to do? I made a fool of myself with this girl. I was humiliated. I needed to say something, do something, yeah? But first I had to find her. She wasn't answering her phone. So I got this not-so-clever idea of hacking into the hotel computer.' He made a cheeky wee face. 'It was SO easy. But there was nothing under her booking that I didn't already know... her email, mobile number, address. Just then it occurred to me that there must have been loads of couples staying in that hotel that weekend who weren't with who they were supposed to be.

'It was just a harmless prank, right? I emailed everyone staying at the hotel that weekend and thanked them for their custom. Offered them all a free weekend if they re-booked within six months. I was just messing around, man.

'During my trial, the papers reported that as a result of my email fourteen married couples split up. The wives or husbands who hadn't been there, for whatever reason, intercepted the email and found out their partners had been doing the dirty on them.'

Kenny laughed. 'Oh man, that is brilliant. Wouldn't it have been great to see their faces?'

'Who cheats and leaves a joint email address? Fucking idiots. My guess is they wanted to get caught. In any case, the hotel group got so many complaints they ran the diagnostics and found my IP address. I got eighteen months and lost my job.' He squeezed his cheeks into a smile. 'At least the wife took me back.'

'And now you need to pay her back by earning some good money?'

Dimitri nodded.

'How much you been earning in your new life of crime?'

'Fifteen, give or take.'

'Pathetic.' *Fifteen thousand.*

Dimitri nodded.

Kenny shook his head. 'You need a change in career. You need to use your skills and I'm the man to help you.' Kenny looked into his eyes. 'How are you at serving beer?'

'Eh?'

'Bar Manager is the front, but you'll spend most of your time in the office on the computer doing special tasks for me. How does thirty thou a year sound?' He would be a manager in one of Kenny's bars. Which one, he wasn't quite sure yet, but that would be the front. His real job would be in computers. It was about time Kenny went digital. Better records meant work analysed and lessons learned. Lessons learned meant more money. 'But first...'

Dimitri opened his mouth. A sound like the chirp of a bird sounded. He coughed. 'Aye?' was all he could muster.

'Got a pen?'

A nod.

'Write this down...' Kenny waited for Dimitri to locate a spare piece of paper in his filofax, while inwardly groaning – a fucking filofax. Then he gave Dimitri a name and a date.

'He's my father. He disappeared eighteen years ago and you're going to help me find him.'

20

Mason Budge was wearing a grey suit, white shirt and black shoes. He looked like any other prosperous young man walking his way through this part of the city. Tilting his neck, Mason extended his view up the height of the buildings that surrounded him. Red sandstone cut in ornate shapes, large windows giving way to high ceilings.

The people who built Glasgow must have made shitloads of money back in the day, he thought. Sugar, cotton, slaves and a serious lack of conscience had contributed to the city's wealth in those times. You do what you know until you know better, Mason had once heard some uppity black woman say on TV.

What if you never learn to know what 'better' looks like, he grinned to himself.

A tall woman, bobbed-blonde in tight jeans walking towards him read the smile and thought it was aimed at her. She smiled back.

Mason sent his eyes on the slow slide down her body. He liked what he saw. Her jeans looked expensive and didn't appear like they had much trouble containing the curves. Up close, her skin was lined and her eyes heavily made-up. Didn't bother him; he liked older women. He winked and walked past her. As he did so he drawled, 'Made my day, darling.'

He caught the woman's answering blush and delighted smile. Nice to be nice, Mason thought, but it wouldn't do to dally with the locals. Especially not when he was trying to be all invisible and stuff. Making like a ninja cowboy.

Walking backwards for a few steps he checked out the woman from behind. Nice ass, he thought. He stopped and caught up with her. He could have some fun with this one. Fuck with her mind. He had the time and he wasn't so close to his destination that two and two would later add up to a police witness.

'Hi,' she breathed. Pleased and wary at the same time.

'What say you and me have a party?'

'Ehm, I'm sorry,' she said pushing a strand of hair behind an ear. 'You're being very forward, son.'

Mason smiled his best smile. Up close, she wasn't half bad. Once you got past the loose skin on her neck.

'Don't you know young men nowadays got a thing about older women? Milfs, we call 'em.'

She crossed her arms and looked up and down the street; obviously, she wasn't quite ready to trust him. Mason followed her line of sight. Nobody was paying any attention whatsoever. He could pull this woman into the doorway behind her and no one would see a thing.

'Milf?' the woman asked, her smile growing warmer as she looked him up and down, liking what she saw and flattered that someone so much younger than her would pay her any attention. Mason hooked his wallet out of his pocket and, as he spoke, he pulled out some notes.

'Mother I'd Like to Fuck,' he explained and counted out some money, ignoring her indignant gasp. 'Fifty do for a blowjob?'

'I'm a grandmother now, son, and I'd still be way too much work for your scrawny wee arse.' She put both hands on his chest and pushed him away. 'Away and have a wank.' She turned and walked away so fast her high heels were clicking up a storm on the stone.

Mason chuckled at her spirit. He could have had a lot of fun with this one. Shame he was on the clock. Places to be and all that.

Things to do.

People to kill.

21

By the time Kenny had talked things through with Dimitri he had six missed calls on his mobile. One was from a number he didn't recognise, four were from Alexis and one from Ian. On dialling his answering service a voice told him he had four messages and he guessed they would all be from Alexis.

He should call them both but couldn't be arsed talking to either. His head was full of the plans he had for Dimitri. This man could be a real big help to him. The idea to have him do a search for his father hadn't even been in his thoughts when he began to outline what he was looking for. Then it just came pouring out.

'The human mind is a funny thing,' he said out loud as he sparked the ignition. Enjoying the purr of the engine, and thinking of whom he needed to phone – the delay before the inevitable – he sat back in the chair and exhaled. Kenny believed in getting the difficult jobs out of the way first, and then he could get on with having a good time without the distraction of worry.

Alexis could wait; she'd only be looking for an answer from her prospective pimp. Wearing a grimace, he dialled Ian's number. It went straight to answerphone.

'Ian, it's me. Gimme a call.'

With a different grimace he tried Alexis. She answered straightaway. Kenny couldn't make out much of what she was saying given the fact she was hysterical.

'You're what?' Kenny asked, his stomach churning in reaction to her distress. 'Babe, you're going to have to calm down. I can't understand a word.' The signal faded and her voice came through in snatches, as if a violent wind had torn every other word from her mouth. Then the signal was gone.

What the fuck?

What should he do? Part of her anxiety had transmitted to him. Something had gone terribly wrong. He put the car in gear and made for the car park exit. So lost was he in thought that he missed the halting wave offered to him from his newest employee.

Kenny hit the M8 into the city centre. He sent a prayer of thanks to the traffic gods that the Kingston Bridge was quiet and he was soon heading through the city centre towards the Merchant City.

The build-up of traffic was his first warning. The next was the blue flashing lights. Like every one ever caught up in a worrying scenario, he just *knew* that the lights were flashing from the home he was headed towards.

Alexis' street was blocked off. Police cars and police officers were everywhere. Kenny gripped the steering wheel tighter. There wouldn't be this much of a police presence if for a call out to a beaten prostitute. Somebody had to have died here.

He took the detour offered by the uniformed guys and took a left and another left, knowing it would bring him back in to Alexis' street from another angle. It was also blocked off. From here he could see an ambulance parked at an angle facing in to Alexis' front door. A paramedic in his green all-in-one uniform was talking to a guy in a suit. He recognised the guy. It was Ray McBain.

He found a space outside a café further down the street. Then he picked his phone from his pocket and sent a text.

Big favour. Meet me outside the café round the corner. Right now. Then as an afterthought he added, *Please.*

Fuck off. Very busy, read the almost instant reply.

Kenny raged. Realised he was overreacting, but still called Ray a prick. He forced himself to calm down. Demanding anything of

Ray McBain was only going to seriously piss the man off.

A flash of insight shot into his brain. He had been talking to Alexis, what, thirty minutes ago? From the look of the set-up outside her flat the emergency services had been there for longer than that. So whoever had died, and a murder was almost certainly what had happened here, it wasn't Alexis.

So who was it?

He thumbed the keyboard on his phone and sent another text.

Big favour. Before you go back to the office to do your typing thing. Come and speak to me. Will make it worth your while.

No tongues, was the reply. Kenny grinned. McBain might be a mate but he was a typical cop. All he was interested in was information.

McBain kept him waiting for over an hour, during which time Kenny continuously dialled Alexis. No reply.

'Help you?' McBain asked when he opened the passenger door and sat down. It was now dark and the streetlight offered a red tinge to his face.

'Someone was murdered here, yeah?'

Ray just looked at him. Made a face. 'And I should tell you before the next of kin knows, why?'

'Which flat was it?'

'What am I, your bitch?'

'Ray,' – Kenny waved a slow-down motion – 'this isn't idle curiosity. A friend of mine lives in that building. What number flat was it?'

Ray relented when he saw how worried Kenny was. '12B.'

Kenny sat back in his chair and exhaled sharply. That was Alexis' flat.

'Emergency services got a call about an hour ago from a neighbour. She said there was some thumping noises and a loud scream.' Ray looked at his friend, not sure if he should be concerned on his behalf. 'It wasn't pretty, mate.'

'Do you have an ID on the dead woman? Do you know yet who

she is... was?' Kenny had already reasoned that it couldn't be Alexis, but he had to be sure.

'Unusually for a woman, she had very little in her handbag. No bank or credit cards...'

'Ray, do you know who she was?' Kenny's heart was thumping. He wiped his palms dry on his thighs.

'No. Not yet. But we know the flat is owned by a private landlord. As most of them are in these parts.' He looked up at the buildings around him as if their owners' names were going to flash from the windows.

'You have a name for the landlord?' Kenny asked, wondering if Alexis had set up some form of property firm and then rented a flat out to herself.

'Some faceless corporation,' Ray answered. 'We've yet to run down the facts on that.'

Kenny paused, almost afraid to ask. 'What can you tell me about the dead woman?'

Ray chewed on the inside of his cheek as if wondering just what to say. 'Describe your friend.'

'Long blonde hair...'

Ray nodded.

Kenny's gut churned.

'Hard to judge given that she was lying down, but I'd say about five feet-ish. Not the tallest?'

Kenny leaned his head against the headrest and closed his eyes. 'Good, good...' It wasn't her. Alexis was tall for a woman. Five ten.

'Glad I cleared that up for you,' Ray said. 'Now how about you explain why I am sitting in your car right now? What's going on, Kenny?'

'Do you not need to go back to...?'

'Kenny, what's going on? What do you know?'

'I'll drop you off at your car?' Kenny fired the ignition.

'O'Neill, if you don't tell me why you've just dragged me away from a fucking murder investigation, I'll do you with wasting police time.'

'Okay, okay, keep your hair on, big guy,' Kenny said and shut down the engine. 'I don't know who the dead girl might be. But that flat is where my girlfriend stayed... or worked out of.'

'What do you mean... worked out of?'

Kenny made a face.

'Oh. Right. *Worked* out of.' The penny dropped with McBain.

'Yeah. She's a prostitute... my friend is a prostitute. The girl you found might also be...'

'And this wasn't just a trick turned sour, judging by the amount of concern you are showing?'

Kenny nodded. 'She asked me if I could go into business with her. She was high class, but she still needed a strong arm around the place in case... you know.' It was pointless to point out what 'in case' might refer to.

'Did your friend need protection from punters or something more...' – Ray searched for the right word – '...organised?'

Kenny nodded. 'She won't tell me who, but some Mr Big has been trying to keep her for himself.'

Ray stared ahead, working on a theory; processing all of the information. Kenny watched him and thought that his friend suddenly looked tired. No, not tired; his features suggested a mix of frustration, disgust and bone-weariness.

Kenny looked at the curve of the steering wheel, the dash and his hands. Everything wore a flash of red. Like the car had its own personal wee sunset. He leaned forward and looked up. A street sign on the wall above spelled out the word *Parking* in neon crimson. Kenny wondered what that colour might be called in a decorator's chart – murderous red?

Ray shook his head, slow and measured. His eyes looked as if they were unable to contain everything they had witnessed.

'Do you think it was like a shared flat for some working girls? Or do you think your friend actually stayed there?'

Kenny considered how tidy the place had been. How it had been missing the clutter that people bring into their lives. He offered, 'Shared.'

'Now, having heard about the girls' working life, that would be my guess too.' He paused and turned to face Kenny. 'So where is she?'

'Don't know.'

'Don't fuck with me, Kenny. This girl could be a sole witness to a murder or even the murderer herself.'

Kenny snorted.

'Where is she?'

'I swear to God,' Kenny said, 'I don't know. I've been calling her...'

'Did you have an appointment with your friend?'

'No.'

'How did you know to come over here? And don't tell me you were in the area.'

Kenny paused. Spoke. 'I was in the area?' He needed a little time while he tried to organise his thoughts. Ray was too smart. He needed his help, but just how much should he tell him?

'I don't fuck about when it's murder, Kenny. You've got to tell me everything you know and tell me now.'

'My friend's name is Alexis Bouvoir, she's Swiss-Italian...'

'Real name or stage name?'

'Fucked if I know,' Kenny shrugged. 'It's all I've ever known her by. Never even thought for a minute it could be a false name.' And that is why, he added silently, I'm not a cop. 'She called me this afternoon. I had four missed calls from her...'

'We'll need her phone number and access to any messages.'

'I can do that,' said Kenny while wondering how he could keep his name out of this investigation. 'I'll sign whatever you need me to sign to get a hold of my phone records.'

They sat in silence for a few minutes.

'Let me get this from the top,' Ray began. 'Working girls sharing a flat for business purposes. Some Mr Big wants them to work for him. Your friend reneges on the deal, or refuses to make a deal in the first place. She comes to you... and the next thing one of her friends winds up with her throat cut.'

'All of the above.'

'Sounds like a severe warning. Was your... was Alexis there when it happened?'

'Not sure, but judging by her distress over the phone she is both aware of the death and aware of... the violence involved.'

More silence.

Ray spoke first. 'You never get used to it – violent death. Some guys try to see the body like a slab of meat. It just...' He paused, working his jaw and then sighed for what felt to Kenny like a minute. It was if all his worries about the world were leaving him in a long, dark exhalation. 'It's like... it's like...'

'Hey.' Kenny gripped his shoulder and gave him a little shake. What the fuck he was doing? He had no idea but he hoped it suggested at least an offer of support.

'The poor girl,' Ray said. 'She looked so young. Nobody should die like that. Regardless of their occupation. At times like these I'm ashamed of my gender. It's like we're at war...' His face was twisted, wreathed in shadow. 'We... men... are in a forever war and women and children are nothing but collateral damage.'

22

'Hey cuz, how's it hangin'?'

'What the fuck do you want, Ian?' snapped Kenny while he negotiated a roundabout with his mobile trapped between his ear and his shoulder. When people pulled him up on this habit, his answer was that Bluetooth headsets made you look like a wanker and he'd rather pay the fine thankyouverymuch.

'You fuckin' phoned me, mate,' replied Ian.

'Oh,' said Kenny, remembering. 'So I did. Sorry, buddy.'

'Aye, so you should be...' Ian tailed off. 'You in the car? You're not hands-free, are you? Don't come crying to me when you break your back in a car crash, mate.'

'Why don't I save us both the hassle and hang up then, eh?'

'Well, I'd certainly feel better about it,' Ian said.

'Fuck off, Ian. For a dope-head you're very law-abiding all of a–'

'Hanging up, Kenny. Catch you later, bye.'

The phone went dead. 'Bastard.' He picked it from his shoulder and ended the call. The prick had a point, he supposed. He'd thought for a second the call had been Alexis.

Still no word from her.

How must she be feeling? She'd be in a state.

He was working himself into a frenzy. Where the fuck was she? If he had a 'normal' girlfriend, the most he would 'normally' have to worry about was her getting lost between the hairdresser and the nail salon. This is what happens when you get in tow with a working girl, O'Neill. There is a downside to that uncomplicated sex thing.

His sat-nav announced, 'You have arrived.' He was home.

He parked and wondered how he had made it home without causing a ten-car pile-up on the Clydeside Expressway. He could barely remember the last twenty minutes' driving.

A young couple walked past the controlled entrance to the foyer of his building. They were a typical young Glasgow couple living in this part of the city. Collar to toe in designer gear. Surprisingly for any part of the city, they were both stick-thin. Give them time, Kenny thought. Her hair was brown and straightened to a hair-advert sheen. His head was shaved and his face looked like he'd glued some iron fillings on to it.

They had been arguing. The man was staring ahead of him, giving nothing back while she tried her best to puncture his ear-drums with her voice.

Kenny got out of his car and locked it with his remote. As he walked past them the woman was completely uncaring of his presence and continued to shout.

'You're a liar, Davie. I saw you looking at that woman. Your eyes were locked onto her tits, Davie.'

Davie had clearly given up trying to defend himself and sought release in a Zen-like countenance and a pace that was carefully judged to give her a more than a little trouble in her high heels.

Inside his flat, Kenny made straight for the espresso pot. Coffee made, he took a seat on his sofa, picked up the TV remote and aimlessly clicked through some channels.

He didn't want to watch celebrities, singing, dancing, dancing on ice, birdwatching, pretending to be down-and-outs or pretending to have a life so he switched it back off. He kicked off his shoes and lay back on the sofa. He looked around himself at his flat that managed to be both clean and untidy at the same time. Several times each day he told himself he should take more care of his home. Several times a day he told himself to get real. Some boys' toys, a sofa, a bed, kitchen and toilet – what more did he need? Every now and again he'd buy some flowers from a supermarket and put them on display. After a couple of months he'd notice they'd dried out to husks and should be replaced.

He sat forward, elbows on his knees. Where the hell was Alexis and what the fuck was going on?

He thought about the dead girl and what McBain told him about her death. Her throat had been cut. It takes a particular kind of killer to do something like that. If it was a professional job, a silencer and a shot to the brain would have done the job. This was a man who enjoyed his work.

Kenny took a sip from his espresso. He wondered if it was the guy in the Toyota. He tried to bring his image to mind and couldn't. He could state colouring, approximate height and build, but his facial features were a blur.

Toyota man had raped Alexis twice now. He had no evidence to suggest both events had been carried out by the same man, but something told him this was the case. The first time was his 'job'. The second time, no message was delivered. If Alexis hadn't jokingly called Kenny an animal or if he had just got ready for breakfast after his shower, neither of them would have realised that anything untoward had happened.

The man had a taste for Alexis, Kenny thought. The visit to the hotel room was for his own sick pleasure: nothing to do with his work. He was messing with them both. And if this was the same guy who murdered the girl in the flat, he was someone to be very wary of.

Kenny tried to picture him again. He shook his head with frustration. It was like trying to catch your reflection on a plate of brushed steel. Enough was showing to suggest a face, but not enough detail to indicate who the face belonged to.

And he'd spoken to the evil fucker. If only he'd known. Kenny clenched a fist. He knew fighters and in retrospect this man was definitely a fighter, but he could take him. Easy.

He stood up, walked through to the toilet for a piss. When he was mid-stream he heard his mobile phone ring. He dribbled down his trouser leg as he rushed to finish and zip himself up.

'Hello?' he said.

'Izzat Kenny O'Neill?'

Kenny couldn't recognise the voice.

'Aye. Who's this?'

'It's' – cough – 'Mark Donaldson. You told my brother Calum he should call you when he was looking for some work.'

Kenny screwed his forehead up in thought. Mark? Calum?

'We're the' – cough – 'road-ragers you came across... you crocked my brother's knee.'

'Oh. Right. How is the knee?'

'Aye, no bad, mate,' said Mark, becoming more confident. 'Turns out it was just badly bruised. The ligament–'

'I told Calum to call me.'

'Well... I thought that... he's the quiet one and–'

'I've got your number now, Mark. So if I have anything, I'll get in touch, awright?'

'Yeah, that's cool, Kenny, cos we can do anything you need. Bouncer–'

'Hanging up now, Mark.'

'Right. Okay. Bye.'

Despite himself, Kenny realised a grin was stretching his face. Mark could be annoying but he liked his energy.

He was about to put the phone in his pocket when a ping signalled the arrival of a text. Alexis. His stomach twisted and he read the message. It was a short series of numbers and letters with a space in the middle. Thinking how odd it was, he read it out loud. What the fuck did it mean? He read it out again. It was a postcode.

23

The M74 looped ahead of him in the gloom. Even at this time of night the main route from the west of Scotland down into England was busy. Plenty of buses, trucks and even caravans. Kenny guessed that most of them would be either going on holiday or carrying out some form of work duties. Not too many of them would be on a mission of mercy to save a prostitute.

Something to be said for living a vanilla lifestyle.

He studied each of his mirrors and tried to work out if any of the cars behind him had been there for any part of his journey. He had deliberately varied his speed over the last thirty miles – driving at eighty miles an hour, reducing to half that and speeding up again to see if any cars stayed with him. None had that he could see. He had paid particular attention to Toyotas.

Although, if it was Yaris guy, he'd know that he had been spotted the last time and would change to a different make and model.

You're a killer for hire and you drive a modest car. Why? You want to blend in; you don't want to be spotted. Perhaps the thrill of killing is such that material possessions mean next to fuck-all for such a man.

Kenny liked cars, but he didn't like attracting attention, which was why he went for the Ford. It has all the toys he wants, a ride that's baby-butt smooth and it blends in.

He looked at the more affordable cars around him. Fords, Vauxhalls, Renaults and so on. Nothing stood out. Nothing shouted,

Hey, I'm harbouring a psycho. And nothing looked like it had been on him for any length of time.

He checked his sat-nav. Only twenty-two miles to go. It indicated that he should be leaving at the next exit. Doing as he was told, he was soon on a twisting country road. Sometime later he read a road sign with the legend *Welcome to Sanquhar*.

He wasn't sure even how to pronounce it. Where the fuck was he? Even in the fading light he could see that this was, or had been, a prosperous town. Large sandstone houses, a row of shops, then as he stopped at the traffic lights he spotted a sign on a building that said it was the oldest post office in the world; with a date of 1712.

The sat-nav urged him forwards and the road narrowed where a very old building edged into the road. As he waited for the oncoming car to pass, he looked at the architecture of the building. The outside stairway leading to the first floor, and the turret, dredged up a word from Scottish history lessons: Tolbooth. These buildings were centuries old and served multiple purposes – town halls, courts and debtor's prisons. And, if the locals cared enough to preserve them in modern times, they were often some form of museum.

He drove past and he was pointed to the next on the right. From there, a left and the computer voice he had nicknamed Morag issued welcome news: 'You have arrived.' Every time he heard that from Morag, it tickled him. Sometimes he even felt like applauding, but tonight he was too distracted and anxious.

It was dark now and the streetlights stretched ahead of him for a few hundred yards. He had the postcode, but which house? He slowed to a crawl and as the car inched forward he looked into the houses either side of him for inspiration.

A horn tooted behind him. Short, sharp. He pulled over and offered a wave of apology to the driver behind. He was rewarded with a look of fury, a jaw that was working on a mouthful of curses and a hand motion that suggested his hand was never far away from his genitals.

Kenny shook his head. Over-reacting much? 'Who's the wanker?'

he mouthed back.

He parked and reached for his phone. No more messages. The signal was weak, He called Alexis. No answer. He sent her a text – *I'm here* – and waited. No answer.

He got out of the car and locked it. Perhaps he'd now be better off on foot. If Alexis was looking out for him, she'd spot him out of a window and come and get him. He walked along one side of the street and back down the other, getting nothing but a few curtain movements and an indignant stare from one householder. Kenny waved at him, thinking, if you leave your curtains open I'm going to look in. Another hand signal in response. This time it was a vigorous 'Up Yours'.

The houses all looked alike. Terraced villas built from red sandstone. Low walls hemmed in small gardens in front with shrubs and planters in such abundance that it suggested that everyone was trying to outdo their neighbour. Or going for some Town in Bloom award.

He stood with his hands on his hips. He was getting pissed off and was about to start knocking on doors. But what would he ask everyone? Excuse me, you harbouring a prostitute whose friend has just been murdered?

Back in the car, his phone was showing no bars and there was still no message from Alexis.

He exhaled. Fuck. Where was she? He looked out of his car at the houses around him, praying for inspiration. He looked at the clock on his dashboard. No way could he go knocking on doors at eleven o'clock at night. The only news being delivered at this time would be bad news. People would have heart attacks up and down the postcode and they'd remember him for years to come.

A curtain twitched. Did they make any other movement? In that particular window a large red candle warmed the sill; its flame dancing to the tune of the house's internal breeze.

Who puts a large red candle in their window with the curtains all but shut behind it?

Kenny slapped his forehead. What an idiot. He was at the door double-quick. He knocked and was all but pulled through it before the sound reached his ear.

'I thought you were going to be sat in that car all night,' a woman's voice whispered in the dark of the hallway. She had a Scottish accent.

'Where's Alexis?'

'Ssshh,' he was told. 'In here.' A door was pushed open.

His senses told him he was in no danger so he walked through the door into a living room. It held the standard sofa, two armchairs and TV, along with a running motif of teddy bears. They were in cloth, china and in pictures everywhere his eyes moved.

'Have a seat,' he was told, so, swallowing his impatience, he moved to an armchair and sat down and looked at the person who'd brought him in to their home.

His immediate impression was: short, with hair, and enough attitude for a family of neds. Even in her heels she would be lucky if she hit five feet. And the way she was standing before him with her hands on her hips, Kenny was sure she was more than a match for him verbally.

Her face was lined but lively – late-fifties or early-sixties? – and surrounded by a mass of black hair – a wig? – that added six inches to her height and reached well past her shoulders. She was dressed like a caricature of a character from an Eighties American soap opera. Shoulder pads, short tight skirt and knee length boots. Everything with a touch of pink.

Was she for real, he wondered, and one look at the focus that pierced him from her heavily made-up eyes told him that she was.

'Alexis is sleeping,' she said, arranging herself on the armchair opposite him. 'She's been through a lot.' The way she said those last two words it was like she was blaming Kenny.

'I'd like to talk to her.'

'Not a chance, buddy. She needs a good rest before she thinks about what she's going to do next.'

'Listen, missus, I appreciate you helping her out and everything, but I've driven a long way to talk to her and that's what I'm going to do.' Kenny stood up.

'Oh, sit on your arse. You don't intimidate me.'

'Look...'

'Sit.'

'But...'

She pointed to the chair.

He sat down.

'Excellent.' Her smile was genuine. 'So you'll be Kenny.'

'Aye,' he replied. He didn't know what to make of her; he'd never met anyone quite so unaffected by him. There was no bluster, no hidden tremble, nothing. He was a bug; she was the shoe. 'And you are?'

'You can call me Diana.' She crossed her slim legs, pulled some hair behind her ear, cocked her head to the side and gave a little smile. 'I've always liked that name.'

Je-sus, Kenny thought, she's flirting with me. He looked at her heavily made-up face; he'd initially thought she was in her late-fifties now he was revising that up to mid-seventies. She was mutton cryogenically frozen, dressed as a Dallas makeover lamb,

Whatever she was, he felt himself drawn to her.

'And Alexis came to you because?'

'I'm her mother.' This was said with pride, worry and a slight uplift to her eyebrows.

Kenny opened his mouth to speak. Nothing came out. He couldn't have been more surprised if she'd asserted she was a vampire and *Twilight* was based on her life story. Did she know what her daughter did for a living? Did she really know why she had fled the city?

'I know everything, Kenny. My daughter keeps no secrets from me.'

The question must have been written all over his face. 'You sure about that?'

'She's a working girl and you're one of her... nice clients.'

'Right,' Kenny said. What else could he say? 'I... she told me she was Italian-Swiss.'

'Her father is,' Diana smiled and looked up at the ceiling as if she could see through it and into the bedroom above, where her daughter lay sleeping. 'Her mother is as Scottish as you are.'

'Do you know what happened in Glasgow today?'

Diana nodded and bit her lip and for the first time Kenny read fear in her expression.

'Do you have any idea who this monster is?' she asked him, leaning forward in her chair.

'I don't. No. But as soon as I find out I'll deal with him.'

Diana sat back in her chair. She looked at Kenny. She scanned the room and then her eyes stared into his as if she was measuring him for a lobotomy.

'Will you be able to do the necessary?' she eventually asked.

The necessary? Kenny made a face.

'Don't be naïve, son. I know you skirt outside the law. I can tell looking at you that you're a man of violence. Will you be able to take this evil man on and make sure he never harms another person?' Her expression was dark, her nostrils flared with the need to see her daughter safe.

'Yes,' Kenny replied and meant it. He's never hid from a fight and had started more than a few, but his actions had never led to another man's life being taken. This man, however, had him worried. His actions were disturbing and in his viscera Kenny knew that there would be a reckoning and only one of them would walk away. 'I'll do what it takes to protect my friends.'

Diana laughed loudly, throwing her head back like a pantomime villain. 'A *friend*, bless you, son.'

'What's so funny?' Kenny found himself irritated by her response.

'You, ya numpty. Her friend. Alexis is a stunningly beautiful woman. You've a penis and a pulse. You no more want to be her friend than I want to get my nipples pierced.' She shuddered. 'You want to possess her. You want to have her hang off your arm so that all your tiny-dicked pals will be jealous.'

'That's harsh and unfair,' said Kenny. 'I've driven all the way to this bumfuck of a place to help her, so don't tell me...'

'Oh, don't get your gusset all twisted, son. I'm just messing with you,' She laughed again. Then she studied him again. 'I get it.' She paused. 'You're in love with her.'

'I... I... eh.' Kenny was at a serious loss at what to say. This woman could tie him up in verbal knots.

'Ach, I shouldn't be surprised. They all are.' She chewed on the inside of her lip. 'Whisky?'

'Eh...'

'Here's the deal, Kenny me lad. If you want to help my daughter, you'll let her sleep tonight and find somewhere to keep her safe in the morning. In the meantime, you're welcome to the couch and a wee drop of the hard stuff. I'll throw in the banter as an added bonus.'

'How could I refuse such a generous offer?' Kenny felt himself match her smile.

'Where do you think Alexis got all that charm from?'

'Were you on the game as well?'

'Cheeky monkey,' Diana laughed. 'Fair enough question, I suppose.' She stood up and walked out of the door. She returned moments later carrying a bottle of Glenmorangie and two glasses. 'In answer to your frankly impertinent question,' – grin – 'no, I wasn't on the game, but I am a wee bit... unconventional, you might say. So my daughter felt able to fill me in on her career choice.'

'And where do you get your conventions from?'

'My mother died when I was a child. My father was a touring actor and over the years I had many mothers from a variety of walks of life.' The emphasis she placed on the word 'variety' suggested to Kenny that her mothers could have been anything from teachers to whores. Diana poured them both a generous measure. 'I learned not to judge.'

'Nice house,' said Kenny, taking the offered glass.

'Liar.' Diana sat back down. 'All these fucking teddy bears do my head in.'

Kenny must have looked mystified, for Diana went straight into an explanation. 'Mad psycho attacks daughter and kills her friend. Do you think she'd be daft enough to risk him following her when she goes to pay her old mother a visit? The house belongs to a friend.' She made a dismissive noise as she eyed up a line of ceramic teddy bears on the mantelpiece. 'A very sad friend.'

For a time they sat in companionable silence, both of them sipping their whisky and each of them lost in thought.

Diana drained her glass and walked out of the room. Kenny heard her go upstairs, rummage in a cupboard and then come back down again. She was holding a quilt and a pillow when she walked back in the room. Kenny could just about make out the peak of her hair over the height of the bedding.

'God.' She let it all fall to the floor. 'Nearly bloody killed myself coming back down those stairs.' She blew some hair out of her mouth and stood before him with her hands on her hips. 'Right, don't even think of trying to sneak into her room in the middle of the night. I'm a mother, I know all these tricks. Besides,' she laughed. 'I slipped her some antihistamine instead of paracetomol. Used to knock her out for days when she was a wee girl.'

She turned as if to walk out of the room and then turned back. Her expression was a study in fear and an acknowledgement of her weakness in the face of the threat to her daughter. For the first time, Kenny thought that despite the make-up and the clothes, Diana looked like what she was: an old woman.

'You'll keep my daughter safe, won't you, son?' she asked.

24

Kenny was blessed with an ability to sleep anywhere, any time. His cousin Ian used to joke that if he was hanging off the edge of a cliff he would take time out for a catnap before trying to save himself.

This was a talent he put to good use as soon as Diana's feet hit the bottom of the stairs. He was frustrated about not getting a chance to speak to Alexis, but her mother was not someone you could easily defy.

He pulled his mobile phone from his pocket. Searched for recent numbers and sent a text with the postcode and house number and then kicked off his shoes and slumped into the chair.

It felt like only minutes since he closed his eyes when he opened them to find Alexis curled up on the chair opposite him.

'Hi,' she said softly.

Kenny groaned and stretched. 'Who are you?' he asked while looking out of one eye. 'And what have you done with the nice lady who was talking to me last night?'

'She's something, isn't she?' Alexis left her seat to come over to sit on Kenny's knee. She placed her head on his shoulder. 'Thanks for coming. I had no idea what to do.' Her voice was small like a child's.

'Want to talk about it?'

'My knight in shining armour,' Alexis said and sat up. Even shadowed with grief and weak with fear, Kenny thought she looked gorgeous. 'Coffee?' she said.

'You sure you're up to it?'

Alexis placed a hand on his shoulder and gave him a weak push. 'I'm sick with worry, Kenny not paralysed.' She stood up and took a hold of his hand. 'C'mon through to the kitchen.'

The kitchen was larger than the narrow hallway leading to it suggested it might be. Big enough to have a panoramic window above the sink, all the usual cupboards – in a fetching pink pine – and all the usual electrics. In the middle of the floor sat a circular pine table. Diana sat in one of the four chairs in front of a pot of coffee. She looked once again like just she'd come out of hair and make-up department at Weird Old Ladies R Us.

'Coffee?' she asked in the same tone she'd offered a whisky with the night before. Kenny nodded and slumped into a chair. Alexis sat beside him and poured drinks for them both into a pair of matching teddy bear mugs.

Diana grimaced. 'See what I mean? These bears are getting on my tits.'

'Mother!' Alexis admonished.

Diana exhaled. 'Right, like he's never heard the word "tits" before.'

'I'm certain he's heard it, but not from the mouth of an old lady.'

'Oh.' Diana held a hand over her heart. 'How careless the young are. I'll "old lady" you, missy. I could show you and your young man a thing or two.'

'My mother' – Alexis turned to Kenny – 'hit her peak in the Eighties and decided to take up permanent residence there.'

'Is that code for my mum's an out-of-touch old slapper?'

Looking at the faces of the two women, Kenny could see that this was a well-worn argument that would re-surface whenever there were tensions in either of their lives.

'It certainly wasn't easy bringing my friends home from school to be faced with...' – Alexis held her hand out towards her mother and moved it up and down – '...that.'

'Ladies.' Kenny thought he should interrupt before it became even more personal. 'This is all very Jerry Springer, but there's no cameras here and I'm sure we have more pressing matters in mind.

Like, who the psycho killer is? Why he's after you and how we are going to find him?'

'I like him, Alexis,' Diana smiled and patted his hand. 'But Kenny, you have a lot to learn about mothers and daughters. That was just how we say good morning.'

'In that case I hope to God I never see you fight.'

'Can I get you some breakfast, Kenny? Some toast, perhaps?'

'She makes it seem like you have a choice, Kenny. It's either toast or toast, I'm afraid,' said Alexis.

'I don't want anything, thank you Diana, apart from being told what the hell is going on here.' He turned to face Alexis. 'Do you still want me to be your business partner?'

Alexis nodded, her movement quick but sure.

'In that case I need to get up to speed with whatever the hell is going on.'

'In that case I need some whisky in my coffee. Mother?'

'You want to pickle your liver at seven in the morning, you do it yourself.'

'Oh for chrissakes, where's the bottle?'

Diana told her; Alexis fetched it and poured a generous measure into her black coffee. She took a small sip, shuddered and then took some more. She offered her mug in a salute. 'Here's to Scots courage. Why's it always Dutch, eh?'

Kenny allowed her to settle before telling her story. He knew that to press her at this point would only delay her even more.

'I was in the Merchant City flat. The one you...' She gave Kenny a meaningful look. 'I was finished for the afternoon and one of the girls... Cora...' Alexis choked on the word. She coughed and dabbed at her eye. 'Cora had booked the flat for the evening and she was about to...' She couldn't speak anymore and leaning forward, head in her hands, hair obscuring her face, she began to sob.

Diana stood up from her chair and moved round to hug her daughter. After a couple of minutes of Kenny feeling as useless as tooth floss in a nursing home the women separated and Alexis appeared ready to resume her story.

'Where was I? Cora... I can barely mention her name without seeing her like that...' Alexis screwed her eyes shut. 'He... pulled the knife across her throat like... she was nothing. Nothing.'

'Was it the same man who attacked you?' Kenny asked.

Alexis nodded.

'You're sure?'

'No doubt.'

'So who is he?'

'I don't know his name, but he was sent by my old boss with the warning.'

'Why did you need to be warned?'

Alexis took a sip from her drink. 'That is the question...'

'Alex,' warned Diana, 'time to stop dithering. Tell the man.'

'Right, Mum. Give me a minute. This isn't easy.'

'I'll tell you what's not easy. Being in labour for fourteen hours and then seeing your beautiful daughter throwing herself away for a man.'

'God, Mother. Every time you get annoyed with me you throw that in my face. I was in love, for fuck's sake. Have you never been in love?'

'Will the pair of you stop it?' Kenny interrupted. 'You're doing my head in.'

'My daughter was a market trader, Kenny. Working for an investment bank. She was one of the best traders in the city.'

'Mother...'

'Her so-called husband was a waster...'

Kenny was stunned and tried to hide it. Of course she had a history, it just wasn't something you asked your favourite prostitute about.

'He was an addict, Kenny.' Alexis took over from her mother with a look. 'Gambling, cocaine, alcohol... you name it, he scored it. He got into some serious problems. I tried to bail him out... and a series of bad choices led to him taking a nosedive into the

134

Thames and me fleeing London to escape.'

'Except that kind of life follows you, Kenny,' Diana butted in. 'Alexis was given to a local bigshot as payment of a debt...'

'I feel that debt has been repaid with interest and I want my independence,' Alexis said, putting steel in her posture and determination in her voice.

'And lemme guess, Mr Bigshot doesn't agree?' asked Kenny.

'Give that man a prize,' said Diana. 'Or at the very least a fresh cup of coffee?'

Kenny smiled at her attempt to add some levity to the conversation and nodded.

'Bloody hell,' he said, 'it's like a TV drama.' He paused in thought. 'Who's Mr Bigshot?'

'You don't want to know.'

'Yes I do.'

'You don't, trust me,' said Alexis, her eyes heavy with warning. 'If I told you his name, neither of us would be alive this time next week.'

'Sounds like a man with a lot to hide,' said Kenny.

'Kenny, don't, please.'

'A man with a lot to hide can be bargained with.'

'Not this guy, Kenny. He won't risk the world knowing his secrets.'

'So he's a real bigshot? A prominent citizen? Have I met him?

'Kenny. I've said enough. Please stop asking me.' She leaned towards him and took a grip of his hand. 'I couldn't bear it if something happened to you as well.'

'Who else has been hurt?' Kenny asked. 'Apart from Cora and yourself?'

'That's the first time they've gone after one of my friends.'

'So,' said Kenny thinking aloud, 'they'll kill your friends, but they want to keep you alive.'

'She's the asset they don't want to lose, Kenny,' said Diana, making a face.

'I could do without the sarcasm, Mother.'

'It wasn't sarcasm, sweetheart. It was pride. What mother

wouldn't choose such a career path for her daughter?' Diana tossed her hair. Her words were flippant, but her expression was tight with self-loathing. She wasn't having a go at her daughter; she was blaming herself. Somewhere along the line she had failed her child and she couldn't bear it.

'Enough, ladies. Do I have to put one of you on the naughty step?'

'Oh, that would be nice,' said Diana. 'Will you spank me as well?'

'Oh, Mother,' said Alexis wearily. 'Do you ever turn it off?'

'When they nail my coffin shut, darling,' Diana replied and took a swig from her coffee.

Kenny felt a dull ache in his abdomen and pressure on his bladder and realised he hadn't used the toilet since he arrived the previous evening. He stood up. 'The toilet?'

'Up the stairs,' both women answered in unison. 'Second door on the left.'

Once inside the toilet he was not surprised to see that the teddy bear theme continued, albeit in a more relaxed manner. A toilet roll was sat on the top of the cistern with a pink crocheted cover on it and part of the design was a small blue bear.

The sink, bath and toilet were all white, the carpet was a dark pink, as were the curtains and the huge fluffy towels strategically positioned here and there. Everywhere Kenny looked in the small room there were feminine touches; lace, ribbon, powder puffs, perfume and soaps. So much so that as he unzipped and pulled his trousers down he felt that he should be covering his genitals, in no way should he touch them and that as soon as he was finished he should set about the room with a scrubbing brush to erase any sign that a man had even been here.

He gave vent to his relief with a soft 'Aaaah' when his bowels and bladder emptied. This feel-good factor even extended to him humming a tune.

A noise made him stop. A knocking noise. Could someone be at the door? He wiped himself clean and thought about the text he sent the previous night. It was to Mark Donaldson and simply gave his whereabouts and the line, *A protection job. Interested?*

It was really a test. He didn't think he needed them to help out, but it would see how keen they were for some work if they dropped everything and drove down.

He heard footsteps, the creak of the door and the rumble of a male voice. Kenny could almost picture Mark trying to act like he was here to protect the President. He'd be all bluster and self-importance. Calum would be standing to the side and slightly behind him, looking more the part.

Thinking he'd better get downstairs and introduce everyone, Kenny quickly pulled up his trousers and ran his hands under the tap. As he was drying off with one of the softest towels he'd ever held in his hands he heard another voice. Alexis. Even from where he was Kenny could tell it held a note of panic. Then there was a muffled scream, a clicking sound and a thud as if someone had fallen to the floor.

What the fuck...?

He opened the door and ran across the small landing to the top of the stairs. His senses screamed danger. From his position he could see that the front door was open, light leaked into the hallway. At the bottom of the stairs he could see a pair of small feet clad in purple leather.

Without thinking he bounded down the stairs, leaping the last three to land near a body. It was Diana. She was on her back, eyes closed, mouth open and her long wig askew.

'Diana, Diana,' Kenny shouted and knelt at her side. There was a wound on the upper right section of her chest. Blood flooded into the carpet beneath her. Where was...? He looked up and down the line of the hall into the kitchen. 'Alexis,' he shouted. 'Alexis.'

He heard someone behind him. He turned in time to catch a single blow from something hard and metallic on the side of his head.

'Alexis,' he mumbled and fell to the floor beside the supine form of Diana.

All went black.

25

He didn't know where he was or what he was dreaming about but his head hurt like a bastard and some eejit was saying his name over and over again.

'Kenny,' it said. 'Kenny. Wake up, will ye?'

'Leave me alone,' he mumbled. 'Can't you see I'm in agony here?'

A hand pushed at his shoulder, the voice louder, more urgent. 'Kenny, you really need to wake up, mate.'

Two things struck him then. One, he wasn't sleeping, his head really was this sore; and two, he had been unconscious on the floor beside a dead woman.

With one hand at the side of his head, he tried to push himself off the floor with the other before he realised he was holding something. Something heavy. He lifted it to his eyes and tried to force them open.

'Kenny, where did you get the gun?'

He managed to open his eyes; took in the gun and the speaker at the same time.

'Mark?' he said.

'No. I'm Calum. Mark's chasing some guy down the street.'

'Wha...?'

'Here...' Calum held out a hand. 'Let me help you up.'

Kenny's legs felt as if his muscles had been replaced with sponge. His head spun as he got to his feet and he leaned against Calum.

'Is she...?' He pointed at the body at his feet and then Alexis popped into his head. 'Is there anyone else here? A young woman?'

Calum shook his head. 'Just you and...'

'What happened? What did you see?'

'Shouldn't we phone an ambulance?' Calum asked while kneeling down beside Diana. He felt at her neck.

'Is she...?' Kenny's gut scored acid. He was almost too scared to ask.

'I can feel something,' said Calum. 'I'm no expert but–'

Just then the door opened. A large figure blocked out the light. Kenny forced himself to look through the pain.

'Put the gun down, mate. It's me, Mark.'

'We really need to phone an ambulance,' said Calum. 'This woman could die if we–'

'Before we phone anybody, is it just us three in this house?'

'Aye,' said Calum. He turned to Mark. 'Did he get away?'

Mark nodded, disgusted at himself. 'Got in a car and drove off.'

'Was he on his own?' Kenny asked.

A nod.

'You sure it's just us here? You checked every room?' Kenny asked, looking down at the gun that was in his hand. It was heavy. How did it get there? He felt his knees give and Calum steadied him before he fell down again. Taking his weight, Calum shifted him round to the foot of the stairs and guided him to have a seat.

'Is she dead?' asked Mark. He leaned forward and peered down at Diana. He looked to Kenny like a small boy who had just discovered the corpse of a dog. All that was missing was a stick for him to poke her with.

'Mark,' said Kenny, 'get me a glass of water, please. Calum, from the top tell me what happened.'

'You don't know?' Calum screwed his face up.

'I was kinda out of it, mate. On account of someone tried to crush my skull with a... ' – he held the gun up – '... whatever it is.'

'So you didn't shoot the old dear?' asked Mark, returning with a teddy bear mug filled with water.

Kenny took a sip. 'What did the text say?'

'Protection job,' said Calum.

'Right,' said Kenny after another sip. 'I'm hardly going to kill someone I'm trying to protect. Which reminds me, are you sure there's no one else here?'

'Should there be?' asked Mark.

'Mark, could you do a tour of the place and Calum tell me what the fuck happened.'

'Okay,' Calum said as he watched Mark bound up the stairs. 'We got your text last night. Wondered at first if you were serious...' He paused. 'It was a bit cryptic, like. So we decided it was a test. Left straightaway and we've been outside the house since two o'clock this morning.' He looked a little shame-faced as he described what happened next. 'We kinda fell asleep... and when we woke up we saw this guy walking out of the front door and down the path. He left the door open so we legged it over here and found you and...' His voice tailed off. He coughed. '...And the old lady lying there. Mark took off after the man and I tried to wake you up.' He shrugged. 'Then you woke up.'

Kenny drained the mug. He felt more alert now, but his headache was still intense. He fingered the lump pulsing on the side of his head. About big enough for an egg, he thought.

Mark ran back down the stairs. 'Nobody here but us chickens,' he said.

'Mark, could you rake through the kitchen drawers and see if you could find me some painkillers?'

'Do I have to do everything?' Mark looked at Calum.

'I'll go,' said Calum, shaking his head.

Kenny stood up. 'Feeling a little better now,' he said and moved round to kneel beside Diana. He felt for a pulse on the side of her neck. Nothing. He leaned forward and placed his ear just before her mouth. Nothing. He put his fingers on the side of his own neck, found his pulse point and transferred that brief experience to Diana's skin.

It was cool to the touch, but a vein rose against his fingers. It was weak.

'Did you make much noise chasing after the shooter?'

'Fuck me.' Mark's mouth hung open. 'I was chasing a killer down the street?'

'Stay with me, Mark. We don't have much time. I need to judge if an ambulance, or worse, the police, are on their way.'

'Jesus. I don't know what I would have done if I caught up with him.'

Calum arrived with a packet in his hand and more water. He popped a couple of pills from the packet and handed them to Kenny.

'Thanks, Calum. Did you get a good look at the shooter?'

Mark was striding up and down. Agitated. The reality of the situation was pushing at his mind. 'I could have got killed. What the fuck is going on here?'

'Explanations later, Mark. We need to stay focused; get help for Diana and then get the fuck out of here.'

'We need to phone the police.'

'We'll do that once we're on our way,' Kenny answered.

'But we can't do that,' said Mark. 'We'll be aiding and abetting and other such shit.'

'We'll be giving ourselves space to find the bastard that did this,' said Kenny. 'Don't fucking argue with me, Mark. My head is too fucking sore. I've lost my girlfriend and her mother's at death's door. I'm not in the mood.'

Calum stared at him as if making a decision. His brow furrowed. In his expression Kenny could read his thoughts: if we step over this line, we don't go back.

Mark was hoping from one foot to the other whispering 'Holy fuck' over and over.

'Right,' said Calum, 'the sooner we get out of here, the sooner we can get this old lady some help.'

Kenny nodded, liking what he was hearing. This lad had promise.

'Right, Mark,' Kenny said, taking charge and beginning to feel almost like himself, 'you go to the bathroom and wipe down every surface you think I might have touched.'

'But...'

'Mark, just fucking do it,' said Calum. He looked at Kenny. 'Where else were you?'

'Kitchen. Living room.' Kenny appraised Calum. A cool head, and quick actions in a crisis, he could use someone like this. 'You take the kitchen. I sat at the table for a wee while. Drank from a mug.'

As Calum and Mark set about removing all traces of his presence, Kenny did the same in the living room, but not until he had made Diana a little more comfortable. Picking up the quilt and pillow she had given him the previous night, Kenny did his best for her. She gave off a little moan as he lifted her head to place the pillow below it. He felt a hot rush of relief. It sounded like the old bird had some life left in her.

Moments later they were in their cars and headed back out of the town towards the M74 and Glasgow. Kenny judged that he wasn't quite safe enough to drive so he asked Calum to drive for him, for no other reason than he needed to think and he couldn't while Mark was chirping in his ear all the way back up to the city.

In the car he prompted Calum to phone emergency services. 'Say there was a gunshot, the gun man is gone and there's an old woman hurt.'

Calum dialled and did as he was told. The operator tried to get more information from him. Calum looked across at Kenny and forced his voice up a pitch. 'Listen, missus, I'm only sixteen and I'm worried about my gran, so stop asking me questions and get the polis and the paramedics here pronto, will ye?' He closed the connection and turned to Kenny. 'Let's get back to the city and find us a madman.'

26

Back in Glasgow, Kenny brought the two young men up to his flat. He left them in the living room and went into his kitchen for some more painkillers and something he could use to make a cold compress.

Some paracetamol dissolving in his stomach and a pack of frozen peas wrapped in a tea-towel against his head, he returned to his guests. Mark was standing by the window taking everything in and Calum was sitting on the sofa, straight-backed, both feet on the floor.

At the window Mark was looking up and down the street. 'Hey, you can pure see in to folk's bedrooms at the other side of the street. D'ye ever catch anybody shagging, Kenny?'

'Your knee okay, then?' Kenny asked Calum, pointedly ignoring Mark.

Calum nodded.

'Man, this place is so cool,' said Mark. 'When I get my act together I'm going to get me some of this.' As he spoke, his eyes coasted around the room, taking in the electronics and the expensive furniture. 'You're a lucky man, m'man.'

'Luck has fuck-all to do with it, m'man. Turn it down a notch, will you, Mark?' Kenny asked, making a face. He recognised his irritability and chewed it down. Sometimes the man's energy was too much for him. He sat opposite Calum and looked from one to the other. They were so different. The one chunkier and lively, the other leaner and steadier.

What was he going to do with them? He thought back to the moment when he sent Mark the text: what was he thinking about? At that point he hadn't thought beyond having some back-up. He didn't think he really needed it, but some sixth sense had prompted him. Good job he had sent the text. If he hadn't, he might well be warming a cell in Dumfriesshire that very morning as a suspect of an attempted murder.

Diana. He wondered how she was.

Alexis. Where the fuck was she?

One thing was for sure, she hadn't been taken by the shooter. Mark reported that he jumped into a car on his own. So where had she gone? He was beginning to regret coming back up to Glasgow. He was disorientated; hadn't been thinking straight. Mind you, he'd been thinking straight enough to remove all trace of himself, and then he'd abandoned Alexis. What a colossal prick. Not his brightest moment.

All he could see was that he needed to get the hell out of there before the police arrived. The shooter and his boss were in Glasgow, so that was where he needed to be. But only Alexis knew who the boss-man was, and she had vanished.

Mark walked across the room and sat beside his brother. He picked up a remote.

'You got Sky Sports on this thing?' he asked as he pointed it at the receiver.

'No,' said Kenny. 'Put on a news channel, will you?'

'The *news*?' said Mark in a dismissive tone.

'In case the shooting we've just come from has reached the media,' Calum explained.

'Oh, right.' Mark's eyebrows all but merged with his hairline. 'Fuck me, we could be on the telly.'

What was he going to do with these two, Kenny thought again to himself. Calum returned his gaze, nothing showing on his face, looking as if one word was enough for him to spring into action, but until then energy would be conserved. Mark leaned forward, elbows on his knees, rocking in position, his face and body charged with the possibilities of this new connection with Kenny. All action; little thought.

The news channels were full of the latest natural disaster. Black heads bobbing in floodwater. Naked children without the energy to swat flies away from their faces. The Westerner raped their lands for centuries, moved out and they continued to pay the price.

He fired up his laptop. Opened the BBC website and looked for West of Scotland news. There was nothing. Not yet anyway, but he was sure it would make the news. Thankfully, guns were rare in this part of the world and therefore newsworthy when used. The fact that an old woman was shot should get everyone clutching at their breasts in panic.

'Hungry?' he asked them.

'Thought you'd never ask, mate,' Mark grinned. 'I'm hank marvin.'

Calum nodded.

Kenny considered what might be in his fridge and freezer and nodded. The staple of the Scottish male was waiting for his hand to put it together. 'Bacon rolls do you?'

'Champion.'

'Thanks.'

Fifteen minutes later they had each munched their way through two bacon rolls and two cups of coffee. Kenny felt a little nauseous, but he knew he needed some fuel in his body or he would collapse. He forced the food down with a grimace while skimming through the various news channels. Nothing.

'So,' he said, thinking out loud, 'I'm in the loo. Diana answers the door. She gets shot. Alexis will be next but I disturb the killer by running down the stairs. He hides from me. Alexis runs – where to? Only place could be the back door.' He faced Calum. 'Was the back door open when you cleaned down the kitchen?'

'The door was closed, but I didn't check if it was locked.'

Kenny tried to recall the view from the kitchen window. He got an image of a well-maintained garden. Some trees and bushes. Could there have been a hut?

'I need to find out how Diana is,' Kenny said.

'Want me to be the grandson again?' asked Calum.

'Good idea.' Kenny returned to the search engine. Mumbled, 'Hospitals in Dumfriesshire,' as he typed. Got a hit, dialled a number. Handed the phone to Calum.

'An old woman was brought in this morning with a gunshot. Can you tell me how she is?' Same voice, same note of concern. 'No one's been brought in? Who am I? I'm her grandson, Davie.' A pause. He looked over at Kenny.

Kenny heard the electronic crackle of a male voice coming down the telephone line.

'This is not a prank, mate,' said Calum. 'I saw her body. The blood was all over the place. I'm no telling you where I am.' He hung up.

'What the fuck was that about?' asked Kenny.

Calum was wearing a grim smile. 'They've had no gunshot wounds today. In fact the receptionist can't remember the last time they did have to treat a gunshot wound. He was going to call the police on me for wasting his time.'

Kenny pulled up a mental image of Diana the last time he'd seen her. The wound was in the upper part of her chest. With luck it would have missed all of her vitals and exited the other side. If so, she'd be in a lot of pain, would possibly need a blood transfusion, but her life wouldn't be in danger.

Could Alexis have doubled back and taken both her and her mother somewhere safe? Man, he couldn't think straight. That bump to the head was causing him serious trouble.

He leaned back on the sofa, let the leather comfort his aching muscles and closed his eyes. How tired was he. He felt the pull of sleep and fought it. Not yet. There was work to do.

'Describe the shooter.'

'Kinda ordinary,' Mark shrugged.

'Slim with a hint of muscle,' said Calum. 'About five ten. Short dark hair. Walked like he knew how to take care of himself.'

It was the same guy. Kenny was sure of it. Hired muscle. But who was he working for? He needed to get out onto the streets, speak to some undesirables, find out who this guy was. Glasgow was a small city. Someone was bound to know.

He closed his eyes. So tired. The knock to the head must have taken more out of him than he realised. Five minutes. He could sleep for five minutes.

'Shouldn't we get you checked out for concussion?' asked Calum.

'I'm bloody fine,' Kenny replied, sitting up straight. 'Totally fine. Nothing that a few hours kip wouldn't cure.' He'd suffered through the symptoms of a simple concussion several times before. The doctors would just take a note of his vitals and leave him in a cubicle for a couple of hours before coming back to check on him again.

He made a mental inventory of his body and his reactions. Nausea, tired and irritable. Confused thinking, initially; that had made him leave without finding Alexis. Apart from that he was fine. He just couldn't afford to take another one to the head for a few more days.

He closed his eyes.

Five minutes. All he needed was five minutes.

His phone rang. Anxiously, he read the display. Disappointed, he answered.

'Ian, what is it?'

His cousin's voice sobered him instantly.

'It's Mum,' Ian said.

27

Corridors. Kenny hated corridors. He hated the way his footsteps echoed along them, the linoleum they used for the floors and the inevitable grey paint on the walls.

For most people corridors were a sheltered link from one room to another. A way of moving from A to B. To Kenny, they signalled an institution. Miserable places where the needs of the helpless were met by the uncaring. He'd been in a couple as a boy. When his dad disappeared, he was taken to an orphanage before his Aunt Vi claimed him. It took her six months to satisfy the bureaucrats; six months in which he needed the love and support of those closest to him but received nothing but lukewarm food, cold sheets and a cool disinterest. Then when the hormones, assisted by a gutful of anger, surged through his body, a number of misdemeanours got him locked up in a borstal.

When Kenny arrived in such a place, bursting with acne and attitude, the term borstal had officially been replaced with 'Youth Custody Centre'. His time had been brief and vital, but the education he received there was not the one intended by the authorities. He learned when to blend in, when to make use of his natural aggression and how to hide the evidence of nocturnal masturbation. This was expressly forbidden and to the young Kenny it was bizarre that the guards would check their beds each morning for stiff sheets.

He also observed that in the main the boys around him were stupid, lacking in education and minus the drive to do anything about it. He vowed that he would do what he needed to do, but that he'd never get caught again.

When his sentence was over, there was Aunt Vi at the end of a corridor, ready to pat his shoulder, offer advice and the shelter of her home.

This time the corridor was in a hospital and again, Aunt Vi waited at the far end, but now he was the visitor. She'd suffered from a massive stroke, Ian told him.

She was in the High Dependency Unit in Southern General Hospital. This was situated on the far side of the River Clyde and would take him twenty minutes, traffic-dependent. Visiting time began at 2:30pm, which had given him a couple of hours to sleep.

Not that he could.

He'd sent the brothers packing and lay down on his bed. His mind wouldn't allow him rest. It jumped from one worry to the next. Aunt Vi, Alexis and Diana. His father. He'd promised himself he'd find out the truth of his past, but the danger that Alexis was in had thrown all of that from his mind.

His stomach twisted and his jaw ached with it all. When he was a teenager and in this much turmoil he'd simply find a car and take a joyride or he'd find a boy bigger than him and challenge him to a fight.

He was beyond all that now, wasn't he? But if a certain sick fuck had been in front of him right then he'd have taken take great joy in jumping on his head until grey matter leaked out of his ears.

His heels thunked on the concrete-grey, linoleum-clad floor as he walked down the corridor to where his aunt was being looked after. He approached a desk and several tired faces turned to address him. He gave his aunt's name. A nurse stood up and walked over to the desk. Her uniform struggled to contain her, buttons threatened to pop from chin to knee.

'You'll be Kenny,' she said, her face warmed through with concern. 'She's had a hard time. Don't expect too much, son.'

Son. She looked younger than he was.

She pointed where the corridor split in two. He was to go to the right. 'Room Four,' she said.

The door had a glass panel, through it he could see his uncle in a chair by the bed. Vi was out of his line of sight. Colin was leaning forward, one hand reaching across the bed, his full attention on the bed's occupant. To Kenny, he looked smaller and thinner, his face slack with worry and the sudden onslaught of age.

Kenny took a deep breath and replayed the nurse's words.

Don't expect too much.

He set his features and walked in to the room. His Uncle Colin looked up at him, his face registering nothing by way of a reaction to Kenny's appearance. It was like he had left the room minutes ago on an errand and simply returned.

'I sent Ian home,' Colin said, his eyes back on his wife. 'He's been here all night. Needs to get some sleep.'

'How is she?' Kenny asked, finally turning his attention to his aunt.

Shock stole a gasp from his lungs. He closed his mouth and set a smile on it. When had he seen her last, he tried to recall. It was only a matter of weeks ago. The difference was incredible. If Colin's pain hadn't been so evident, he would have thought he was bent over the wrong woman.

Her body had shrunk, barely causing a ripple on the sheets that covered the low-lying line of her limbs. Her head and shoulders were held up by a small tower of pillows, her face twisted to the side. Her bottom lip had worked its way to the left, a swollen lump. One eye was closed and the left eye seemed to have grown to dominate the space all but vacated by the other. This eye fixed on him as he moved closer to the bed.

'You been in the wars, Aunt Vi?' he asked. It felt like his voice was loud and harsh in the confined space.

He could tell that she was fighting to respond to his question but whatever her brain demanded of her body nothing happened; the signals blocked and incapable of reaching muscle. Her eye seemed to grow larger in her urgency to communicate with him.

'You alright, Colin?' Kenny asked, keeping his smile loaded and locked on his aunt.

'Just feckin' dandy,' said Colin.

The eye moved to Colin's face. Even now, Vi was working to keep the peace between them.

'You want a break? Want to go for a coffee or something and I'll keep her company?'

Colin said nothing. Simply sat where he was, gripping his wife's lifeless hand in the great wedges of skin, bone and muscle that were his. He opened his mouth as if to speak and closed it again. He was so tired he was beyond making a decision.

Kenny studied his uncle – the brown Marks and Spencer cardigan, the jut of his Adam's apple, the grey stubble and the throb of defeat in his eyes. If Vi didn't recover from this, he expected the next phone call from Ian might be to say that his Uncle Colin had driven headfirst into a tree.

'Uncle Colin, take a break. I'll sit with Vi for ten minutes.' As he spoke, Kenny moved towards the seat his uncle was crouched in, his actions telling the older man that he'd not take a refusal. Without taking his eyes from his wife, Colin got to his feet as if it was a monumental effort to reach his full height.

'See you in a minute, love,' he said and gave his wife's hand a little shake then, without a glance at his nephew, he left the room.

Kenny was used to his uncle's gruff treatment of him and on this occasion brushed it off like lint from cloth. Sitting down, he adopted his uncle's posture and gripped Vi's hand in both of his. Her focus was completely on him now, her stare unwavering. So much so he wondered if she had lost the ability to blink.

'You're in the best place, eh?' he said, completely at a loss. It was apparent that his aunt was able to understand what he was saying;

he just didn't know what he should say other than a stream of inanities. A sentence about the weather edged towards his tongue but was blocked off by his refusal to issue the words.

'They ran out of grapes down at the gift shop.' He smiled and held his hands out. 'Sorry. Oh and the Lucozade was also gone.' He laughed. It always seemed as a child that when he was forced to visit relatives in the hospital that everyone came supplied with Lucozade and grapes. Like they were on some universal prescription.

He looked at the living petrification that the stroke had visited upon his aunt. How quickly the human body could be turned off. This was not his aunt. She was in there somewhere and all that was required was some arcane science to bring her back to the surface.

Holding her hand was giving him an anchor of sorts, her skin as dry as cotton, the bones so light he fancied that it was nothing but slender straws held together by muscle. He leaned forward and pressed his lips against her skin. Emotion clogged his chest, restricted his breathing. Tears stung his eyes.

'You've got to get better, Aunt Vi,' he whispered onto the back of a hand as ineffective as a glove. 'Who else have I got?' He fought for some control. This wasn't fair. She could understand everything and he shouldn't be putting her under any pressure.

He lifted his head to see a tear squeeze from the corner of her eyelid. He reached for it and wiped it dry. Smiled ruefully. 'If only I could return you to you so easily.'

A memory breached. One of the few times he could actually remember his mother and his aunt together. He must have been about five or six. He'd fallen off his bike and his knee was a patch of gravel and torn skin. His howls could have woken the catatonic.

Mum and Aunt Vi came rushing to his rescue and between them they carried him into the kitchen. Once there, they sat him on the table. The very table he found his mother slumped over all those years later. As he sobbed, snot bubbled out his right nostril. His chest heaved and he tried to tell the women what had happened.

'A dog...' – sob – '...ran out...' – sob.

His mum pressed his head to her chest and issued words of calm and soothing while Aunt Vi picked at the stones that had been pushed through his skin. When he wouldn't calm down, his mother lost patience.

'What's all the crying for?' she said. 'Big boys don't cry.'

'Don't you do that, Vicky. Don't be pressing that rubbish onto him. If little boys were allowed to cry, maybe they'd grow up to be real men and able to deal with emotional stuff.'

Through his sobs, Kenny watched his mother study his aunt as if she'd just dropped in from a far-flung corner of the Earth. Eventually her need to be dominant in her own home surfaced.

'Don't you tell me how to raise my son, Vi.'

His aunt shrugged, made a face at Kenny as if to say, *Sorry son, but I tried*, and without a word went back to cleaning the wound. Once she was finished she applied some disinfectant with the warning that it might sting. Then she moved out of the way to allow his mother the elbow-room to add a large brown sticking plaster.

That was his aunt, Kenny thought. Ahead of her time. Issuing advice long before the experts thought of it.

'You know I've never said this, Aunt Vi. And it's a disgrace that it had to wait until now, but I was very lucky to have you.' He bit his lip and closed his eyes tight, trying to hold back the emotion that threatened to surface. 'You were... are a better mum than I deserved.'

The door opened and the nurse he spoke to earlier bustled in. As she walked, her thighs rubbed together, making more sound than the tread of her feet.

'Your aunt needs her rest, son,' she said. The nurse looked at him, her mouth bunched tight like a knot at the end of a child's balloon. Her expression an offer of sympathy and apology.

'Right. Of course. ' He stood up and dried his face with his sleeve. 'I'll go find my uncle.'

• • •

He found his uncle in the hospital cafeteria sitting at a table on his own, a full mug of coffee in his hand. He was staring at the mug as if he needed instructions to tell him how to get the drink into his stomach.

Kenny joined the queue of people waiting to be served and looked around. The room was a long rectangle, painted hospital-blue with tables lined up along each wall like beds in a ward. By way of offering an atmosphere, the hospital authorities had placed a wooden trellis between tables. Each trellis supported the weight of an artificial plant. Given that official visiting times were over, most of the people at the tables were in uniform. Kenny made a face at the thought of spending his breaks from work in such a place.

The woman behind the counter offered him a smile at odds with the cool of the room.

'What can I get you, love?' she asked.

'A mochaccino?'

'What's that, love? One of them fancy coffees?' She laughed. 'That's a new one. Wait till I tell the lassies.'

'White coffee will do,' Kenny grinned, responding to her good cheer.

'What about some munchies to go with it? You're way too skinny, son. How about a nice wee muffin?' She pointed at a basket that held some mass-produced bakery goods.

'No, thanks,' Kenny said. 'I've had my chemicals for the day.'

'Don't tell me,' she said, adopting an expression meant to convey grief, 'you're on a diet?'

'You got it,' he replied. 'I've lost twenty stones in the last twelve months.'

She paused in the act of pouring his coffee. 'Don't tell me. Gastric bypass? Everybody's doing it these days. Here's a wee trick for you, son.' She leaned forward and held a hand to the side of her face. 'Pop some chocolate cake in the liquidiser. It's genius.'

Kenny laughed, shook his head and walked over to join his uncle. The older man didn't move his eyes from the top of his mug.

'You left her on her own?' His voice was a low rumble.

'The nurse told me to leave the room,' bristled Kenny. 'What was I to do? Tell her to go fuck herself?' Kenny closed his eyes and listed the reasons why what he had just said was inappropriate. Then he listed the reasons why he was justified. It was a pretty even list.

'Always were one with the smart mouth,' said Colin. 'Always knew more than everybody else.'

'What did I ever do to you, Uncle Colin?' Kenny asked, tired of the tension that was always between them. 'Why could I never please you?'

Colin looked at him, the line of his mouth twisted as if he had just drunk something sour. 'You were your father's son.'

'Great. Wonderful.' Kenny clapped his hands. 'Your wife is seriously ill. The gloves are off. C'mon, tell me more. What else have you been burning to say to me all these years?'

Colin's eyes bore into Kenny's. They burned with the need to offload. Words piled up behind them and then faded into the mists of the unspoken. Words without a voice; sound stolen from them, perhaps by an old promise. Colin returned to his drink. 'Nothing,' he said. 'I have nothing to say to you.'

'Well guess what, *Uncle* Colin,' Kenny said, 'I have plenty to say to you.' He didn't know what prompted him to offload in such a way. Blame the concussion, blame his fatigue, he didn't really give a toss who to blame, he just needed to get the words out and he didn't much care that the man was worried sick about his wife. 'That woman up those stairs is worth twenty of you. Thirty. Why she stuck around a miserable old cunt like you I'll never know.' He paused, searching to see if his words were reaching through. 'You do nothing but complain. How long have you two been married? Twenty-odd years? Fuck me. Folk get less for murder and that's what it would feel like being married to you. Murder.'

Kenny leaned back in his chair, disgusted with himself. What was he achieving here? Nothing. This was like pulling the legs off a defenceless spider. He took a sip of his coffee and swallowed. 'I was just a boy. My mum died. My dad vanished and you turned on me.'

'I never raised a hand to you.' Colin roused himself. 'God knows I should have. You might have turned out better.'

'You didn't need to lay a hand on me. Sticks and stones, Uncle Colin. That's the lie that every adult passes to children, but every child knows the truth of it. Long after the bruises have faded, the petty insults, the sting of the sarcasm carries on burrowing under the skin.' Kenny pushed the coffee mug out of reach. He couldn't bear the taste of it. 'You had the chance to do some good. The chance to offer a little kindness to a wee boy whose whole world had been ripped apart. But you chose to give in to your petty jealousy and to make that wee boy's life a misery.'

'Jealousy?' Colin laughed harshly. 'You haven't a fucking clue, boy. What did I have to be jealous of a wee skelf like you?'

'I was my father's son,' Kenny said and watched the other man's expression. 'You and him were friends, were you not?'

At least that was the family legend. They had been inseparable from school, went in to the same line of work and met the Collins sisters. Got one each, got married and had a child each. Then the timing belt snapped in that particular engine and it all fell apart.

'Then my mum died.' Kenny spoke the words out loud, not sure where he was going with them. The idea pressed at his mind, looking for articulation but remained just beyond him, like a note of currency blown just out of his reach by a stiff breeze.

'Your mum was worth ten of him. Twenty,' Colin said.

The breeze fell and the note landed in his hand.

'You married the wrong sister.' The words were out of Kenny's mouth before the thought was fully formed.

'What are you talking about?' asked Colin, and Kenny could tell he had something.

'You fell for my mum. Except she was in love with my dad and you got Vi by default.'

'Rubbish,' said Colin. 'Total rubbish.' His expression was dark and twisted.

'That's why you've been a complete tosser to your wife all these years...'

'Fucking nonsense.' Colin stood up.

'That's why you couldn't bear the sight of me,' Kenny stood up. The two men stood face to face. His uncle trembled with the force of his anger.

'And that's why you've got it in for me,' said Kenny, aware that a he was spraying saliva as he spoke.

'I've had enough of this.' Colin turned and walked out of the room.

'Come back here,' Kenny raised his voice. Every head in the room turned to see what was going on. Kenny followed his uncle out of the cafeteria and caught up with him outside. He raced ahead of him and barred his path.

'What aren't you telling me, Uncle?' Kenny demanded.

'There you go again, Kenny,' said Colin, refusing to bow under Kenny's anger. 'Thinking you know everything.' His smile was one of triumph. 'You know nothing. You can only guess at the truth.'

'I know this much.' Kenny allowed free rein to his imagination and threw a wildcard into the conversation. 'My mother didn't commit suicide. She was murdered and maybe you had a hand in staging it to look like she had.'

Colin slapped him. Hard. Kenny's ears rang with it.

'Whatever hole you crawled out of, away you go back into it,' said Colin.

'Hoy!' A passing male nurse stopped and challenged them. 'What the hell's going on here?'

'Nothing, mate,' Kenny rubbed at his face. 'A family misunderstanding.'

'Family, my arse,' said Colin. 'The day my wife brought you into my home was the worst day of my life.' He spat on the ground. 'Now, I'm off to spend time with my sick wife. You're no longer welcome.' His expression was carved from rock. 'Just like your father. Thieves and whores. That's all you're good for.'

28

He knew where his aunt and uncle kept a spare key to their front door. His Uncle Colin was a sucker for those wee shopping magazines that fell out of every Sunday newspaper. The ones that most people threw in the trash. He was always buying stuff from them and one particular item was a false rock with a secret compartment large enough for a key that would sit on the back step.

Kenny bent down to pick the rock up and when he straightened up his head spun. He breathed deep, blinked hard. Fuck. Still with the concussion. He should really be tucked up in bed but he couldn't allow himself any rest. He had no idea how long Colin would remain at the hospital.

Nor had he any idea what he was looking for, but he couldn't shake the feeling that his uncle knew more than he was letting on.

Once inside he paused in the hallway. The house really hadn't changed much since that day his aunt brought him back from the children's home. He looked to the left and the door into the living room. He could remember his uncle standing there that day as if barring him from entering the room. A look on his face that could sour wine. Oh, he'd put on an act for his wife, but Kenny was a good reader of people and he knew from the first false 'Welcome home, kiddo' that his uncle would rather he find a bus to run under.

The colours used in the decor hadn't changed much either. Magnolia paint over woodchip. The cheap bastard. Here and there his aunt had dressed it up with a female touch, but was clearly hampered by her husband's control over the family purse.

He quickly reviewed what he knew of the house. If his uncle was going to hide something of value only to him, where would he put it? The rooms everyone used could be discounted. The only places he and Ian hadn't been allowed to roam as boys were the master bedroom, the loft and the garden shed.

The master bedroom could also be ruled out. The old fucker wasn't daft enough to hide stuff where his wife might find it. Which left the loft and the shed as likely possibilities. He walked to the kitchen and looked in the drawers near the back door, found the back door key and a longer key that could only be for something like a shed.

Walking down the neat path, past the carefully planted borders he was aware of someone's eyes on him. He turned and looked into the windows of the neighbours. Shit. He'd been spotted. It was old Kate Ford next door, one hand pulling back the net curtain with the other offering a wave. She paused in her wave and made a sign for him to wait.

Seconds later she was out of the door and hobbling on arthritic legs to a position just over the waist-high fence from him. She didn't move as fast or as much as she used to, but her need for information would have propelled her into place even if she were to use her very last charge of energy.

'Kenny, son,' she breathed, one hand gripping her cardigan closed over her chest. 'How's your auntie?'

'She's in a bad way, Mrs Ford.'

'It's terrible, son, just terrible.' As she spoke her expression was six parts sympathy and six parts excitement. She had something to talk about. Something she could be an authority on for the rest of the neighbourhood gossips. 'Just terrible. One minute happy as Larry, the next you're paralysed and in the hospital.'

'She's in the best place though, eh?' Kenny mentally shook himself for making the conversation last one second longer than it needed to. What he really wanted to say to the old biddy was, *Fuck off back into your hovel.* Instead he fixed his smile in place and played the role of concerned relative.

'How's your Uncle Colin?'

'He's not taken it so well,' Kenny replied while wondering how he was going to explain why he was going in to the garden shed.

'And how are you, son?' she asked. Her tone suggested this was more than a polite enquiry. 'Haven't seen you round here for ages. Then it's twice in the one week…' A carefully judged pause that she expected him to fill.

'Oh,' he said, putting a hand to his head. 'A wee spot of rain.' He looked up to the sky and the light covering of cloud, hoping he could convince the old woman against all the evidence. 'Think we're in for a downpour.'

'You think, son?' Mrs Ford scanned the sky, looking more worried about the possibility of rain than she had about the health of her neighbour. 'I'd better be getting back in. It's my lumbago.' She turned and evidenced even more speed than when she arrived at the fence she returned to her house. And her vigil by the window.

Inside the shed Kenny was faced with the usual array of garden implements and a few more besides: a lawnmower with a bright orange lid, electric hedge-trimmer, shovel, weeding tools, bags of compost and stacks of pots. Everything was neatly in place with barely a speck of dirt. If the garden hadn't looked so well maintained, he'd have thought that these tools were never used.

He looked up at the higher shelves and spotted a couple of tins. He pulled them down one by one, but they contained nothing but nails and screws and screwdrivers. There was nothing here that suggested evidence of a dodgy past.

He left the shed and locked it. As he walked down the garden and towards the back door he saw Mrs Ford at her window. She was scanning the sky for evidence of rain. Kenny gave her a cheeky wave. Back in the kitchen he put everything exactly where it had been. There was no real need for such subterfuge because as sure as

Mrs Ford got her blue rinse every fourth pension day, when she saw Uncle Colin return she'd be over to tell him that Kenny had been here, as fast as her arthritic wee legs could carry her.

Next stop, the loft.

Standing in the upstairs landing he stretched up with his left hand and touched the ceiling. All it needed was a wee jump and a push and he could open the hatch.

He and Ian had been barred from entry as teenagers. Which of course meant that as soon as Uncle Colin was out of the house they would be clambering inside for a rummage.

Kenny jumped and with both hands pushed at the attic's hatch. This was enough to dislodge it and give him room. His next tactic was to jump and grab hold of the rim. From there it was an easy pull for a man of his strength to get his chest up through the space and from there a lean forward, a twist and he could sit on the ledge. His vision melted, his stomach churned. He paused to allow his breathing to return to normal. This head injury was having more effect that he thought it might. Normally he would be completely unaffected by such a manoeuvre.

He knew there was a cord just by his right hand to switch on a bare lightbulb, but he didn't need it. There was enough daylight coming in from the two small windows positioned either side of the eaves. He turned his head left and right and viewed the narrow space. It was just as he remembered: full of old toys, clothes and books. The hoardings of a couple who believed everything could be recycled within the extended family and then never bothered to do it.

He pulled his legs under him and stood. He sneezed and banged his head. He groaned. Just what he needed, more brain damage. He crouched and waited for his eyes to adjust to the gloom.

The air was dry, full of dust and smelled of things left untouched for decades. Three suitcases sat just ahead of him. He snapped open the locks of the top one and recoiled at the sudden noise. Inside was a neat collection of knitted children's clothes. In the weak light he could see that they were mainly blue or cream. They'd have been Ian's then.

He worked his way carefully through each of the suitcases. More clothing. Nothing of interest. Next was a parade of boxes, all of them would have been brightly coloured at one point and advertising the wares within. One read *Kellogs*, another *Tetley*. They were closed with brown tape. He picked the Kellogs box and carefully peeled back the tape to reveal a pile of comics. There were copies of *Victor* and *Roy of the Rovers*. *The Beano* and *The Dandy*. Could be worth a few pounds, Kenny thought, if his uncle could be bothered to get off his fat arse and sell them.

He held one up to his face and smelled the paper. He smiled. Memories of rainy Sundays. He and Ian on their bunk beds, shouting out story lines, wondering if the writers of the comics knew any other German than *Achtung* or *Mein Gott in Himmel*.

He closed the boxes up with care. This was no time to be sentimental. He needed to find evidence of his uncle's duplicity, not hop down the tracks of memory lane.

Working his way down the loft and back up the other side he found more of the same; clothes, toys, books. He was replacing one large box when he spotted the edge of something sticking out from under a thick layer of loft insulation. He pulled out a small wooden box. The outside surfaces displayed the black and white checked board of a chess set. He turned the box every which way and could see that it was hinged. He remembered having one of these as a kid. Inside his box each half held a piece of foam with two rows of holes, each just big enough to take a piece of the set.

Blowing some dust from the surface, he opened it up. A piece of paper fell out. No, not a piece of paper: a photograph. He picked up the photo and with more care opened the box wide. It held a number of photographs. Checking his feet he walked closer to the skylight. The photos were bleached of most of their colour in the gloom, but he could clearly make out the people in them.

Ian in his pram. Ian in his baby-walker. Ian kicking his first football. Kenny felt an old envy return. His aunt and uncle doted on their son and despite Vi's best intentions and the gentle nature of her son, Kenny often felt excluded.

There were some adults in the photos as well. His Aunt Vi looking glamourous in some Seventies gear. Kenny nodded in appreciation. She was a good-looking woman. Then he spotted one where she was with another woman. Kenny looked closer. This woman could have been Vi's twin. Her beauty shone through the aged and dull quality of the photograph. His mother.

He swallowed with the missing of her. Her lack, a squeeze of his heart, a tightness in his throat. If only. How might his life have been different if she had survived? If his father had stayed around. He closed his eyes against the emotion and damped it down. What was the use of crying over the loss now? He'd cried enough for two people those first few weeks in the orphanage.

Looking at the photo again, he searched her face as if it might offer up a clue. Did you really kill yourself, or were you 'helped' to do so? He didn't remember her being this attractive. She was his mother; he was a just a boy and you don't look at your mum in that way, except through the eyes of others.

He turned the photo over, looking for a date. Nothing. He contemplated keeping it. Would Colin even notice? The fact that the box wore a heavy layer of dust suggested it had been a while since anyone had been here.

There were some more photographs under that one. He plucked at one and held it up to the light. This one had a chunk torn off it. To be accurate a section had been torn off each side of the photo. Kenny could see it had once been of two couples standing side by side, but one half of each couple had been removed leaving two people standing there. His mum and his Uncle Colin.

Kenny could guess who had been torn away. The person who'd vandalised the scene hadn't been too careful. Down the length of Colin's thigh a dress jutted out; a dress he recognised from another photo as worn by his Aunt Vi.

The tear left his mum slightly apart from his Uncle Colin but the illusion might have been enough to satisfy the imaginings of a spurned lover. However, in his workings of the scene there was one other thing that Colin could not have erased. An arm and a hand was draped over his mum's shoulder. The hand that curved round the shape of her shoulder, pulling her close, wore a large ring. A ring that Kenny remembered very well. Anybody that hurts me and mine, Kenny could hear him say while he jokingly brandished a fist in his face, gets this. It was a large, gold sovereign ring. His dad called it his knuckle-duster.

29

Kenny replaced everything carefully as it had been. Except for the photo. He pocketed that. Then he walked over to the exit, sat on the edge of the hatch, took one look around and then swung himself out and down onto the landing below.

Once safely on the ground, he pulled a chair from Ian's old bedroom, positioned it below the hatch, stood on it and stretched up so that he could close the lid properly. Then he reconsidered. Uncle Colin was under a great degree of stress at the moment. People make mistakes when they are stressed. So he reached up and knocked the lid slightly out of place. When he returned from the hospital Colin was bound to notice that someone had been up here. Mrs Ford was bound to tell him that Kenny had stopped by. He'd put it all together and spell out trouble.

All in all a good day's work, Kenny thought, wiping the dust from his hands on the back of his jeans.

In the car, Kenny reached for his phone. No messages. Without thinking, he dialled Alexis. No answer. Something about that whole situation was troubling him and he couldn't think what. Why did she seek him out and then ignore him? Unless she had no way now of contacting him.

Then there was Diana. An old woman gets shot and doesn't get admitted to hospital. Strange.

But then perhaps not. The shooter had tracked them down to Sanquhar; he'd easily find them in a hospital and finish the job.

Perhaps Alexis could have doubled back and with all of the different contacts she has, found someone to take care of Diana without raising suspicion.

Which raised another question. How had the shooter tracked them down to Sanquhar? Kenny shrugged. Probably with ease. None of them had training in subterfuge. A different model of car and staying well back from Kenny on his drive down the M74 and he wouldn't have had much difficulty.

This was doing his head in. He couldn't think straight. He pulled the photo out from his pocket and studied it some more. A detail he had missed in his earlier viewing now presented itself. Colin was standing fairly close to his mum. His right hand was missing, presumably it was across Vi's back. His mum wasn't standing quite close enough to Colin to allow symmetry in the pose. Nonetheless, he still had reached over with his left hand to hold Kenny's mother's elbow.

She was standing facing whoever was taking the photo, but with her weight against the man who'd been removed. Her chin was down, tucked into her scarf and her eyes looked as if they'd been trailing up from the hand at her elbow. As if she hadn't wanted to be so obvious as to shrug her arm out of his grip, but still managed to get off a warning glance.

A glance that said, *Leave me alone.*

What had he here: proof? But proof of what? Colin was in this up to his skinny neck and Kenny had to find out how.

His cousin, Ian. Would he know anything? Nah. Kenny dismissed that question instantly. Ian was clueless. In his own wee world most of the time. Feckless on weed.

He thumbed out a text to him.

Been to see Vi. She's in best place. Keep your pecker up, dude.

Kenny put the phone in his breast pocket and drummed his fingers on the steering wheel. What now?

Alexis had disappeared. Would she be daft enough to come back to Glasgow? Had she taken on the threats and come back to

Mr Bigshot with an apology and a willingness to work off her debt once again?

He wouldn't expect so but nothing about that situation would surprise him. Whatever was going on with her, she needed to know that he was there for her. He clicked out another text.

Call me. Let me know if u r ok.

He fired up the engine and drove off. Minutes later he was on the Clydeside Expressway and almost home. Perchance to sleep.

Once inside he checked his emails. Nothing. He checked the news channels. Still no news of an old lady being shot.

Leaning back into the cushion of his sofa he struggled to keep his eyes open. Everything was frustrating him. He couldn't find Alexis and he was nowhere nearer finding his father.

His uncle's voice sounded in his mind just as he was drifting off.

Thieves and whores.

All he was good for was thieves and whores. Kenny surfaced from sleep. The old wanker had a point. You had to work to your strengths. Most of his contacts were thieves or whores. He should get in touch with them and see what he could dig up.

He dialled Dimitri.

'Hello?'

'Dimitri, it's Kenny.'

'Hey, Kenny. Whassup?'

'What, has everyone been taken over by an American?'

'Sorry, bud. Been catching up on *The Wire*.'

'Just don't be calling me no motherfucker,' said Kenny with a grin. Then serious. Time for chit-chat with the staff was kept to a minimum. 'How are you getting on with that job I gave you?'

'Oh right.' Dimitri paused. 'Just, like, well on account of it being the weekend...'

'Sorry,' said Kenny. He should have known that Dimitri was a 9 to 5'er. 'It slipped my mind. Normal people rest on the Sabbath, eh?' He thought for a minute. 'What day is it?'

'It's Saturday, Kenny... you sound like you've taken a knock to the head. Maybe you need to be taking it easy.'

'Nah.' Kenny rubbed at his eyes. 'I'm fine. Totally fine.'

'You're the boss,' said Dimitri. 'And first thing Monday you'll have my undivided.'

'Yeah,' said Kenny. He hung up and mumbled, 'Over and out, muthafugga.'

He dumped his mobile on the coffee table and trudged through to the bedroom. Kicking off his shoes, he fell onto the surface of the bed. The linen of the pillow was cool against his skin. He burrowed down, savouring the softness and comfort. Just a few hours. A wee drop of sleep and he'd be dandy.

He considered taking off his clothes and slipping under the quilt. He thought about it some more, doing nothing. Couldn't be arsed.

His phone rang. He ignored it. The tune continued. He moaned; why the hell did he leave it in the living room? He sat up. Whoever was calling him wouldn't give up. He sank back into the pillow. His answering service would kick in; if his caller was keen they could leave a message.

That it might be Alexis niggled at him. He got up and walked back into the living room. Just when he reached for the phone it stopped ringing.

'Bastard,' he shouted. He looked at his missed calls. Didn't recognise the number. He went back to bed carrying the phone with him. Just as his head pushed into the pillow it began to ring again. It was from the same number as moments ago.

'S'Kenny,' he said.

'What the fuck are you doing snooping around my house?' his Uncle Colin demanded.

'Eh?' Hoping for Alexis, Kenny was taken aback by the aggression in the voice of his caller.

'Don't come the innocent with me, Kenny. Mrs Ford was practically on her knees with desperation to tell me that you were raking through my garden shed.'

'Oh, that.' No mention of the lift hatch being slightly askew. He couldn't have noticed that yet. Kenny decided to say nothing about it. Let that be a wee surprise for him later.

'So what were you looking for?'

'Your lawnmower,' said Kenny. 'I have a problem with my grass.'

'Given that you live three floors up it would have to be a fucking miracle that you were having with your grass.'

'Why don't you fuck off, *Uncle* Colin? I'm not in the mood.'

'What were you after, Kenny?'

'Evidence that you have something to do with my mother's death.'

'Oh get over yourself, you halfwit. It was a suicide. It was a long time ago and we've all moved on.'

'You'd think so, wouldn't you?' asked Kenny.

'What do you mean by that?'

'Just the other day. Talking with my Aunt Vi...'

'You leave your Aunt Vi out of this.'

'Talking with my Aunt Vi, just the other day when she voiced her opinion that her sister, my mother, didn't commit suicide. That she was in fact murdered and her...'

'Kenny, I'm warning you. Stay away from Vi.'

'Where is he, Colin? Where's my dad?'

'Oh, how the fuck should I know? I haven't seen hide nor hair of him for eighteen years.'

'But you were his bestest friend once.'

'I haven't seen him, Kenny.'

'Before he stole Vicky off you.'

'Yeah, whatever. And then he abandons his only son. Is that really the kind of father you want to find, Kenny?'

'How angry were you when Vicky went for Pete? Angry enough to set him up...'

'Kenny,' – Colin's voice was quiet; and his tone suggested he was using every last piece of patience he could access – 'let it go.'

There was something about his tone. A quaver of worry. Was it there from his fear of what might happen to Vi? Or did he really have something to hide?

Kenny decided to change tactics. Keep the old man guessing. Sighed. 'From your knowledge of him, Uncle Colin, where would he go?'

'How the hell should I know?'

'You were mates once. He must have talked about dreams, ambitions, places he'd love to go visit.'

Colin was silent for a long moment. 'He did talk about Canada once.'

30

Mason Budge was sitting in an office. It was a fairly generic space – long wooden desk, leather swivel chair and filing cabinets. Along the wall-length window stretched a sofa. A tall plant offered some colour into the drab. A framed poster hung on the wall behind him. *Teamwork Makes the Dream Work*, it proudly stated. It made him laugh; corporate shit, but it added to the overall image he was looking to present.

He looked out of the window to the river beyond. The mighty Clyde. Source of a nation's wealth and the inspiration for many a song. Today the Clyde was a solid line of grey, calm as a pond reflecting a monotone sky. In Mason's opinion, Glasgow could do grey like nowhere else.

Still, the people were nice. Nice and talkative given the right inspiration. Just as well he had a knack to inspire.

He surveyed the items on his desk. A phone. A computer. A blotting pad. Who the heck needs a blotting pad these days? He picked the phone up, dialled an extension.

'Yes, Mr Brown?' a voice answered. He'd gone for a *Reservoir Dogs*-theme with that particular name.

'Send her in,' he ordered.

A knock at the door and a woman walked in. She was slim, dressed in a navy trouser suit, long blonde hair and a determined set to her full lips. She crossed the room until she was standing in front of him and then she slapped him.

'Owww.' He held his face and grinned. That was so hot. 'What was that for?'

'If you ever so much as touch me again, I swear I will kill you. The idea was that I acted like you had raped me. I managed to act it so well because you completely and utterly repel me. You got into that bed and...' – she shuddered – '...squeezed my breast. I should have kicked you in the balls, you weirdo.'

Mason simply smiled. Then he pointed to the sofa. 'Why don't you take a weight off?'

'No, thanks. I won't be staying long.'

'You sure I can't tempt you with a coffee?'

'You can't tempt me with anything.'

'Why so adversarial, honey? We have an agreement.' He pointed to the poster. 'We're a team now.'

'Only until I have my money and then I never ever want to see you again.' She stood before him with her arms crossed, one foot tapping on the thick pile of the carpet. Mason felt himself get the horn. This woman. It was her coldness that attracted him. He knew what she was. He recognised it in himself and had never seen it in a woman until her. Her complete lack of thought for anyone else. The way she could adopt a persona to suit whatever her situation was. She could be the coquette, the vulnerable, the damaged, the tease and then shuck it off like it was yesterday's underwear.

'Have you fallen for him?' Mason asked. He loved to piss people off. In his view confrontation got him the most out of others.

'Don't be so naive, Mr Brown, or Budge, or whatever the hell your name is today. He's a job. A mark. Nothing more, nothing less.'

'Call me Mason. I like to think we're friends.' He scratched his groin and grinned at the disgust on her face. 'As for your mark. I'm pleased with your response. I wouldn't like to think you were going native on us.'

'Couldn't we have done this over the phone like we normally do?'

'Then how could we judge if you were telling the truth?'

'We?'

'I will be reporting back to the boss.'

'Tell him he has nothing to concern himself with.'

'How would you describe your job's state of mind?'

'Driven. Determined.' She paused. 'Disorientated.'

'How neat. Answered with alliteration.' He cocked his head to the side. 'How's your mother?' He made quotation marks with his fingers when he said the word 'mother'.

'Back in residence at the nursing home.'

'Wherever did you find her? She performed her part beautifully. The fake blood was amazing. You sure you're fully aware of what's at stake here?'

'Yes. You release me from my contract and I can get out of this stinkhole once and for all.'

'You're ready for the next part of the job, Alexis?'

'He's mine, Mason. Ready for the plucking.'

31

Kenny couldn't sleep.

Whenever he closed his eyes, events of the last few days lit up in his brain like a movie. Aunt Vi in the hospital. Alexis' mother lying in a pool of blood. The blow to the back of his head. The photos in the attic of the house he spent his childhood in.

The letters from his father.

Uncle Colin's evasions. His suggestion that his father might have gone to Canada. An attempt at misdirection if he had ever heard one.

He thought about the letters. Recalled the words on the page. Exhaled through his teeth. He had another family. He had been discarded and replaced as easily as someone might change their clothes.

Two months ago, if anyone had bothered to ask him about his parents, he would have answered with a blank stare and a what-can-you-do? shrug, yet here he was mooning like someone about to write a misery memoir. Fuck me, give yourself a shake, O'Neill.

He rose from the bed and walked into the living room. His skin prickled with the cold. He wrapped the soft throw from the sofa around his shoulders and sat down.

Flicking through the TV channels he found nothing of interest. By habit he scrolled along to the sex chat shows. Women pretending to copulate with fresh air did nothing for him, but the glimpse of a few naked breasts always cheered him up.

The regulatory fake blonde was lying back, wearing nothing but a thong. Her large breasts were lying plump to either side of her ribs. She thrust her groin at the screen, her eyes a mix of fake desire and boredom.

Kenny lay back on the sofa and considered masturbating. It might help him get back to sleep. Pathetic. Couldn't remember ever feeling so lonely.

'Alexis, where the hell are you?' His voice was low and lacked any energy and sounded like the voice of a wraith in the early morning darkness. He pressed *Select* on his remote and read the time. 5:17. Too early to get up and too late to get any worthwhile sleep. If he lay down and slept, his brain would just wake him at his usual slot.

He walked through to the kitchen and made himself a coffee. Then he returned to his place on the sofa and the view of the joyless breasts.

• • •

Next morning, he was the first person at the gym. Matty the Hut had just unlocked the door and switched on the lights when Kenny strode over from his car.

'It's like that, is it?' Matt asked him.

Kenny simply grunted and walked past on the way to the changing room. He felt the need for a burn this morning and after a five-minute warm-up on the recline bike he attacked the weights. Arms, chest and shoulders duly aching, he sought the release of a shower.

'Need that?' asked Matt when Kenny stuck his head in the gym office after he had dried off and dressed.

Despite himself Kenny managed a smile.

'Something eating your gusset?' Matt asked as he twisted away from his computer screen. Kenny entered the office and sat on the only other chair in the room. 'Room' was a bit of an exaggeration. Walk-in cupboard would have been more accurate. A desk that any self-respecting child would have turned their nose down at sat under the window. The only other pieces of furniture in the room were the two red plastic chairs that looked like they'd been rescued from a skip and a chest-high filing cabinet in local authority grey.

'You were talking to me about my dad the last time I was here.'

'Yeah,' Matt grinned. 'Before the two wee tossers in the cage tried to kill each other.'

'How well did you know him?'

Matt scratched the skin at the side of his right eye. He looked tired and Kenny got a glimpse that he might not be the only one with troubles.

'Your dad was Mr Charisma, Kenny. You get that off him...'

'Fuck me,' said Kenny. 'A compliment from Matty the Hut.'

'Shut it,' Matt grinned and then sobered. 'What do you remember of him?'

Kenny shrugged. 'Lots. Nothing. Lots of nothing. Him and Mum used to argue all the time. She always ended up giving in to him...' He tailed off as he remembered the night he found his mother dead.

As if he could read his mind, Matt asked, 'It was you that found her, eh?'

Kenny nodded and felt his eyes sting.

Matt stared into his eyes for a long moment. 'You never allowed yourself to grieve, did you?'

Kenny coughed. Swallowed. Managed a smile. 'I grieved by breaking a few noses.'

Matt looked at him, his eyes swimming with empathy. It was almost more than Kenny could take. He stared out of the window, seeing nothing. Swallowed again. He couldn't allow himself to let go. Felt that he might never stop.

'So tell me about my dad.'

Matt opened his mouth to speak.

A knock sounded at the door. Both men swung their heads round. It was Liam Devlin.

'Okay, boys?'

Kenny could see the warmth leaking from Matt's eyes.

'Morning, Mr Devlin,' said Matt. 'A wee bit early for you today?'

'You know how it is. The world waits for no man and in the meantime his gut spreads.' As he said this Liam held his shrinking belly with both hands. He was clearly looking for a compliment. Kenny wasn't for giving him one.

'Civic receptions and corporate freebies will do that to a man.'

'Everything okay, Kenny?'

'It was until we were rudely interrupted.'

'I'm very sorry,' said Liam as his eyes showed that he was anything but. Devlin was a man in a hurry. He looked at Matt. 'You were going to set me up with a new exercise programme, Matt?'

'Yes, I was, Liam.' Matt stood up and from the top drawer of the cabinet pulled a piece of card. He checked the name at the top. 'This is yours.'

Liam took it from him and scanned it quickly. 'This exercise here. Dumb-bell flies. What's that again?'

'It's where you...' As he spoke Matt brought his arms up in a slow flying motion.

Suddenly Kenny felt he had to be elsewhere. He stood up.

'I'll catch you later,' he said to Matt and stepped from the room. Matt followed him out.

'Look, Kenny, just wait...'

'I'm sorry,' Liam said and this time he did seem so. 'I shouldn't have... I was just keen to...'

'Don't sweat it, guys,' said Kenny, shouldering his training bag and walking towards the exit. 'I've got stuff I need to do.'

'Well, anytime you want a...' Matt tailed off before he could say the word that most west of Scotland males were in terror of: talk.

Just as he reached the door, Kenny heard Liam Devlin's voice calling him.

'Keep meaning to say to you, Kenny, but do you remember Tommy Hunt?'

'Should I?'

'He was the businessman at that reception at Malmaison a year or so ago. The older guy who you tried to steal his date from. The beautiful blonde girl.'

Kenny stopped walking as if he'd walked into a wall. Liam might have inadvertently given him an idea. The beautiful blonde could only be one person. And Tommy Hunt could well be the Mr Big who was threatening Alexis. 'What about him?'

'He was asking after you the other day.'

Kenny turned. 'How would he know to ask after me?'

'He was on the phone to me as soon as that reception was over demanding to know who the wee wanker was that tried to steal his escort. He paid good money for her that night. Didn't take kindly to you chatting her up.'

'Aye, well,' Kenny said, 'serves him right for being so old.' He chewed on his lip. 'Why now? Why was he asking about me now?'

'We had another do at Malmaison. It reminded him of you. Said he admired your balls. Very few people stand up to Tommy Hunt, Kenny.'

'Needs to put himself about a little more.'

'He asked me what line of work you were in.'

'And you said?'

'This and that. Mostly that.' Liam chuckled. 'But I'm sure you and he could... come to some sort of profitable agreement.'

Kenny nodded. This was the Liam Devlin he had come to know and admire. The man who brought people together. People who could help him and each other earn lots of money.

'And he asked to meet me?'

'He even suggested a time and place.'

32

The time and place were the very next day. Lunch, where else but Malmaison? Kenny needed to do his research. He had his suspicions about this guy and felt that this would give him the opportunity to work a face-to-face meeting and see what his gut told him.

Kenny was a man who believed in gut instinct, although his recent form wasn't going to win him any prizes. So, on this occasion he would find out as much as he could about the man before he met him.

He phoned his I.T. sleuth.

'Whassup?'

'Dimitri, if you insist on talking to me like that I may have to sack you.'

'Aww, boss, it's how all the young trendies are talking.'

'Aye and it's sad when middle-aged men try to copy it. Anyway, I'm not on the phone to talk about language. You got anything for me?'

'Early days, Kenny,' said Dimitri. 'Let's not get too excited. I've only been working for you for...' – Kenny heard a sound like the rustle of cloth as if Dimitri was holding his phone away from his ear – 'officially, it's now three hours.'

'So do I have three hours' worth of Dimitri?'

Dimitri sighed. 'Okay. Here's what we've got so far. Not a lot. There's some good search places on the web...'

'The web?' asked Kenny. 'Surely it wouldn't be so straightforward?'

'You've got to discount the obvious and the easy first. There's a great site called 192.com and the voters' roll is online too. Lots of material there. We could do with a likely location and a name though. Can't imagine that someone who's managed to stay hidden for eighteen years is going to keep his original one.'

Kenny allowed his thoughts to take sound. 'What do we know of him? He's a patriot. My uncle said he dreamed about going to Canada. Canada, my hairy hole. When I was a kid he was forever taking me round the cliché Scottish tourist stops. It's a wonder he didn't tattoo a tartan on my legs.' As he spoke, Kenny thought about his uncle's answer and wondered if the man was trying to give him some misdirection. And if so, why?

'Good,' said Dimitri. 'That gives me something to go on.' He stopped talking and Kenny could hear the sound of chewing. Teeth on pencil. 'What about a name? How close would he stick to his own name?'

'If it were me, I'd keep my first name. Would make it easier to live the lie.'

'What about a surname?'

'My mum's maiden name was Marshall. You could try that.'

'Cool,' said Dimitri. 'I'll see what I can do with that.'

'Nobody says "cool" anymore,' said Kenny, wondering when he'd become such a language pedant. 'Oh, I have another guy I want you to look into. This one has a name and can you do this first, please?'

Sigh. 'Okay.'

'His name is Tommy Hunt. Reputable businessman. I want you to dig up some dirt on this guy for tomorrow morning.'

'No rush, then?' asked Dimitri.

• • •

Later that day, while some cop series blared across his TV, Kenny caught up with his cousin by text.

how's your ma?

hangin in there. Asking 4 u. Wants to c u, was the instant reply.

will try and pop in 2morrow

do better than try dude. Thinks she's dyin

He sat up in his chair sharply.

what does doctor say?

doc says she recovering well. She's convinced she's going to die

That wasn't like his Aunt Vi. She was a glass-full-to-the-brim kind of woman.

you worried about her? Kenny asked.

nah. Doc seems to know his stuff. Blame an old woman's imagination

Ok. Thanks. Take it easy, dude

jeez, he's turning yank!!!!

if I was I'd be saying 'love you' man. instead here's a great big fuck you muthafucka

Kenny felt the warmth of a smile as he pressed send. Over the years, as the adults swooped in and leaped out of his life, Ian had been a constant. They rarely met in person these days, which was in truth the way Ian preferred it. He had enough pride not to want his wee cousin to see him in thrall to the dragon or the weed or whatever substance he was currently ingesting.

• • •

The best sleep he'd had in an age, a three-mile jog, a shower and Kenny was ready to face a new day. As his lunch appointment with Tommy Hunt drew closer he couldn't help but be buoyed by a sense of optimism. His Aunt Vi had passed the worst. He was looking for his father and he would find him. Alexis was the only smudge on his hopefulness, but he was convinced she was alive and well. She was just hiding. The fact that her mother's death by shooting hadn't been reported anywhere in the Scottish media suggested that she somehow had the wherewithal to deal with such a tricky situation.

In the spare bedroom that acted as his wardrobe, Kenny examined his clothes. He was highly aware that most of what he did was based an illusion. People in his experience were too quick to base their instincts on what they saw. A certain look. A presentation of confidence. The right words delivered with certainty. All of this gave him an edge and this edge was completed by the correct clothing.

Along the wall on his right were suits, trousers and jackets. He picked an expensive suit. Designer names did nothing for him but he enjoyed the cut of a nice piece of cloth.

A suit would be needed for an old stager like Hunt. He picked a dark brown one that said the wearer was conventional but liked his own sense of style. Under this he chose a white shirt but neglected the barrage of ties to his far left. Hunt would expect a suit and tie. A suit showed that he was respectful and the missing tie would suggest that he was his own man.

Or not.

He dressed and then checked his appearance in the full-length mirror behind the door.

Yeah. He would do.

In the car, he called Dimitri.

'Morning, boss,' said Dimitri.

'What you got?'

'What, no small talk? No how was your evening? How's the wife and kids?'

'How's the wife and kids?'

'A royal pain in my arse. Every single one of them. Don't have daughters, Kenny. Or if you do, say goodbye to a long comfortable shit in the morning. My God. You have to wait, like, hours to get in and as soon as you've bared your backside, the door's knocking and someone else is–'

'Dimitri, have I ever given you the impression that I give a fuck about any of this stuff? Forgive my momentary weakness. I'll get back to my original question. What you got?'

Dimitri didn't bother to hide the chuckle in his voice. 'I was only messing with you, Kenny. What have I got? On your father: nothing, nada, zip. On Tommy Hunt... now there's an interesting man.'

'How so?'

'Came from money. Money of a dubious source, I might add.'

'How so?'

'Nothing certain, just a few comments in the articles I read that suggested Daddy's riches weren't completely kosher. Hints that he was in bed with the Campbells' – Kenny knew that the Campbells were a notorious Glasgow crime family in the Sixties and Seventies – 'but nothing was ever proven. Anywho, Tom takes his father's millions and instead of whoring it up, he makes more millions. North Sea oil. Engineering. Seems something horrible happened in his early-thirties and he handled his grief by throwing himself into business.'

'You got anything on the "something horrible"?'

'Still working on that, boss.'

'Right. Go back to the search for my old man, will you? And keep me posted as soon as you find something.'

Next he phoned Liam Devlin. The older man answered his phone with a curt, 'Devlin.'

'It's Kenny. Just wanted a quick word.'

'Sprint.' Liam chuckled.

'Jings, I'd better find someone with some needle and thread on account of my split sides here, Liam.'

'You need to have a wee laugh, Kenny.'

'Yeah. Whatever. You coming to this meeting today?'

'No,' said Devlin. 'I have other stuff on. Besides the man prefers you two to meet on your own.'

'Any ideas why he wants a meet?'

'Just what I said the other day. He admires someone with balls and he thinks you and he could work together.'

'Tell me something about him. I need to get more of a handle on who I'm dealing with here.'

'He's a successful guy. Took Daddy's millions and made more–'

'Tell me something I'm not going to read on a business pamphlet. That first time I met him you said he was a dangerous man to get on the wrong side of.' This was less of a statement than it was a question.

'He was accused of bribery in the late-Seventies. He wanted a contract that some local jobsworth put the scuppers on. Before the case went to trial, the jobsworth recanted his evidence and took up a job in a Caribbean tax haven. Six months later his house was broken into and he was murdered. The thieves stole a TV.'

'Proves nothing.'

'Exactly. Think Teflon. Nothing sticks. There was also a family tragedy in the –oh... lemme think – late-Eighties or early-Nineties. His wife and daughter died.'

'What?' Kenny's attention was gripped. There were parallels here with his own story.

'A big broom and an even bigger rug was found to hide it all under. He never talks about it, but it seems to have spurred him on to even bigger success. The view is he has nothing in his life but work. And that's why he lets nothing and no one get in his way.'

• • •

Kenny found a parking space just round the corner from Malmaison in Blytheswood Square. As was his wont, he was early. He couldn't find a space where he could watch people entering and leaving the hotel, which was also a habit. In the usual circumstances it was because he wanted to make sure there were no plainclothes policemen loitering with intent to slap some handcuffs on him. Today he would have liked to get a measure of the man he was about to meet, but Glasgow's perennial problem of parking spaces got in his way.

He wasn't happy. By the time they were sat down together, the other man's mask would be firmly in place. His game face would be in play and he would be a little more difficult to read. He would have preferred some time to watch the man when he had no idea he was being observed. There was certainly something more to this man than successful businessman and darling of the Entrepreneurial Exchange.

33

The bar in the hotel was large, bright and airy and filled with the low hum of chatter. There were a few people dotted about the room in pairs. All of them in business dress.

Although he was ten minutes early, he could see Hunt sitting in the furthest corner of the room with his back to the wall. All the better to observe everyone who came and went. Kenny smiled to himself; he could get to like him.

As he made the long walk towards his lunch companion he tried to take a measure of the man. While Kenny walked, Hunt was mouthing into his mobile phone. His face was tanned and lean. Lines bunched at the side of his eyes and across his forehead. He was wearing a dark suit, with blue shirt and gold-coloured tie, and he sat in the large leather chair like it was a throne.

Kenny sat in the chair directly in front of him and waited for an acknowledgement, but Hunt was deep in conversation. He didn't so much as look at him. Kenny swallowed his irritation and chewed on the inside of his lip. He needed to stay calm but so far he was being treated like he was insignificant.

A waiter appeared at Kenny's side. He was a short, chunky guy with a nose almost as wide as his face. Kenny took the measure of the glass in front of Hunt and asked for a mineral water. Hunt smiled at the waiter, apologised to whoever was on the phone with him, and said, 'Could you get me another one, thank you?'

Very fucking good, thought Kenny.

Then he breathed deep and slow as it occurred to him that this was all part of the dance. He leaned back on his chair, rested his right ankle on his left knee and placed his hands on his lap as if he was waiting for his favourite uncle to tell him one of his loved anecdotes.

Hunt ended his call and stood up with his hand outstretched. Kenny had no option but to stand as well. He hated the fact that already Tommy Hunt was dictating the tune.

'Thanks for coming today, Kenny. I appreciate your time.' His grip was strong. Kenny gave it an extra squeeze.

'When Liam told me you wanted to meet, I was intrigued.'

'Okay. Here's the deal. You come and work for me. 100k a year, basic. Nothing outside the law and we both make a lot of money.'

Kenny was used to all kinds of tactics but this was as brutally frank an opening as he'd ever come across.

'Excuse me?'

'No funny stuff. I know how you make your money and I think that if your energy was deflected onto legal activities, with me by your side, it could be every bit as rewarding.'

'By "rewarding", you mean great wodges of cash in a Swiss bank vault?'

'You'll be making so much money you won't have to worry about hiding it from the tax man. Or cleaning it through a collection of cash businesses.' Certainty shone from the man's eyes like a torch and Kenny wanted to dim it with a bucket of ice water.

'You think you know a lot about me.'

'I have my methods.'

'And your great wodges of cash in a Swiss bank vault.'

A shrug of those finely-tailored shoulders. 'Perhaps.'

'What exactly would I be doing for you?'

'You'd be my number one.'

Whatever the fuck that means, thought Kenny. 'I don't work for anyone but myself, Tommy.'

'Yes, you're your own man. And look where that's got you.'

'What the fuck is that supposed to mean?'

'Please don't use profanities when you're talking with me, Kenny. English is a pretty expansive language. I'm sure you could find other words that would work just as well.' Hunt's eyebrows were raised and he looked over at Kenny as though he was the headmaster and Kenny was the recalcitrant child.

'I have a vocabulary as expansive as anyone I know, Tom, and I'll tell you something for nothing. There are times when you can't beat a good loud "fuck".'

'Well, in that case, this meeting is over,' Hunt said and stood up. Just at that point the waiter arrived with two bottles of mineral water and glasses on a tray. He looked from one man to the other, waiting for some form of cue.

Kenny ignored the waiter. 'You're kidding me on?'

'I rarely make jokes, Mr O'Neill.'

'Oh sit down, man. You didn't set up this meeting just to walk out after two minutes.'

'It often takes less than that to make an opinion.'

'You knew what I was like before we came here. This is all just part of your act, Mr Hunt. So why don't you sit down and we can get on with the conversation?'

'I'll... eh...' – the waiter made a face that suggested he wished invisibility was one of his life gifts – '...just leave... this...' He leaned forward and placed the tray on the table and turned away, his shoulders up around his ears.

'Did you ever meet my father?' asked Kenny.

'What?' Hunt made a face. He was clearly wrong-footed by the question.

'Peter O'Neill. Did you know him?'

'You're the first person I've ever met with that surname.' Tommy Hunt said and scratched at the side of his face.

Fuck me, thought Kenny, if that wasn't an obvious tell. He stared into Hunt's eyes. He tried to read the man's thoughts. What was going on in his head?

'Did you really think you could work with me?' Kenny asked.

Hunt sat back down. 'You understand this is like turning down Alan Sugar. Nobody walks away from *The Apprentice*.'

'If I remember correctly, you turned me down because I wouldn't modify my language.' Kenny stopped as a thought occurred to him. 'Why now? You met me more than a year ago.'

'We had an opening. My main man decided he could do better on his own.'

'What about Alexis? You seen her recently?' Kenny liked to throw in a question from left field.

Hunt scratched at his face again. 'Alexis who?' And Kenny was thinking, how bad a liar is this guy?

Kenny heard the loud click of high heels as they approached their corner. Both men had been so caught up in their conversation they hadn't noticed anyone drawing near. They both turned at the same time.

'Did I hear someone mention my name?' Alexis asked with a small smile and that tilt of the head that Kenny loved.

34

Kenny turned on to Argyle Street. Headed north on the Clydeside Expressway and from there the Clyde Tunnel and onwards to the hospital.

Uncle Colin was standing outside the room talking to a doctor and gave Kenny a look as he walked up.

'Don't start,' Kenny said in a voice that brooked no argument and pushed past him and into the bedroom. His Aunt Vi was sitting up in the bed and was almost unrecognisable from the woman he had last seen lying there. Until she smiled and only half of her face moved. Her hair had been washed and brushed, her eye make-up applied and she was wearing a pink cardigan over her shoulders.

'Grrreat to see you, son,' she slurred. Her left hand was curled like a claw on her lap and her right hand was holding a handkerchief, which she moved to wipe some saliva from her chin. The effort was slow and clearly took some effort, but Kenny knew that his fastidious aunt would be mortified that she was spilling fluid from her mouth in that way.

Whatever smile was missing from her mouth was leaking out of her eyes.

'Wow, look at you,' said Kenny, stretching over to kiss her cheek. 'You'll be out of that bed in no time doing Zumba down at the community centre.'

'Don't sink so,' she answered and then made a strange noise that Kenny realised was a chuckle.

The door opened behind him and Kenny heard someone enter the room.

'Thought I told you I don't want you here,' his Uncle Colin said.

Kenny looked at his uncle. 'I think your wants are relegated to the bottom of the pile for now, don't you?'

'Ah... but...' Colin blustered.

'Grow up, Colin,' Kenny said to his uncle and turned back to his aunt. For her sake, that was as harsh as he was prepared to be, but if Colin wanted to start something he would be happy to take him outside and convince him that was how things had to be.

He was lucky he was showing so much restraint after what had happened this lunchtime.

When Alexis turned up, Tommy Hunt had looked so smug it was all Kenny could do not to re-arrange his teeth.

'What the fuck is going on here?' Kenny demanded.

Alexis looked at him as if afraid to speak and then a look clouded her eyes that was unreadable. She had her hair pulled back into a ponytail and she was wearing jeans, a T-shirt and a dress jacket. Clothes that Kenny had never seen her wearing. It was as if she had borrowed them from someone.

Hunt stood up and moved towards her, placing a hand on her elbow. The old stag claiming the hind.

'I think you should apologise to the lady for your language, Kenny.'

'I think the young lady should explain what the fuck is going on.'

'I'm sorry, Kenny...' Alexis moved closer to Hunt as if under his protection. 'I just haven't had a chance to...'

'I was worried you were dead, Alexis.'

'Oh, c'mon, really. That's a bit dramatic, Kenny,' said Hunt in a voice that Kenny thought took patronising to a whole new level of irritant.

'Butt out, old man.' He turned to Alexis. 'A phone call. All it would have taken was a phone call. I think I'm owed that at least.'

'I've never been spoken to...' Hunt was pushing his face into

Kenny's and it was only with an act of supreme will that Kenny didn't crash his forehead onto the bridge of the older man's nose.

'Are you fucking deaf? I told you to butt out.'

'I invited you here to talk business. Then I was planning to spend an afternoon with my young friend here. If you're going to be so rude you can...'

'Alexis, what's going on?' Kenny stepped back and to the side. If Hunt touched him he, couldn't be responsible for his actions.

'I'm working, Kenny,' she said and studied the floor.

Kenny opened his mouth and nothing came out. He looked from one to the other. Alexis couldn't meet his gaze and Hunt was trying to stare him out like he was the alpha dog.

'Is it him, Alexis? Is it?' Kenny moved back towards Tommy. Hunt could be Mr Big. It all pointed to him. Kenny's face so close that all he needed to do was stick out his tongue an inch to touch the other man's face. 'If it's him, tell me cos I'm just looking for an excuse.'

Kenny felt her hand on his arm.

'I swear I didn't know you'd be here,' Alexis said. In her agitation, some of her hair had become loose from the ponytail and was partly obscuring her left eye. 'I needed to get back to work and this is my first...'

'I could have helped you. I could give you money,' Kenny said. 'You don't need to...' He broke off. The thought of this old man's flabby arse working above her was almost more than he could take. She was his now, didn't she see that? He didn't realise he was holding her arm until Hunt grabbed at his.

'Oww, Kenny. You're hurting me.' Alexis whimpered.

'I think you should leave the young woman alone, Kenny. And if you ever think you're going to get work from me, you're sadly mistaken. In fact, consider yourself unemployable in this city.'

'What's your game, mate?' Kenny demanded. He thrust his hands in his pockets, ashamed that he'd hurt Alexis. 'I get it. You watch me working and becoming more legit, more successful and more of a threat. You think you can show the young pup a thing or two. You contact my woman and employ her as your whore in front of my eyes. Is that your message? You're bigger than me? You've got more money than me? Is that it?' Kenny was shouting and he didn't care. He could see that people around them were watching. A waiter and another man were walking towards them. Kenny ignored them.

'You know what, old man?' He straightened an index finger and prodded Hunt's chest. 'I'm on to you and your demonstration. This is nothing but a pissing contest. We should just pull out our dicks right here and now and see who's is the biggest and just get it over with. Why don't we just do that?'

'Oh for goodness sake, grow up,' said Hunt. 'You'll embarrass the young lady.'

'It's nothing the young lady hasn't seen before,' said Kenny. 'In fact, why doesn't she just get on her knees right now and give me her special.' Kenny was beyond sense. He wanted to hurt her.

Alexis' mouth was open in disbelief. She crossed her arms and looked as if she was ready to give Kenny a blast.

'You bastard,' she said. 'You utter...'

'Sir, we're going to have to ask you to leave,' the man in the suit said who'd just arrived with the waiter. 'Or we'll have to call the police.'

'Oh for fuck's sake,' said Kenny. Too loudly. Heads turned in their direction from all around the room.

'Sir, if you don't leave now, I'm going to have to call the police,' the manager said. He raised an arm as if he was about to grab him. Kenny gave him a look that could pierce muscle tissue. He dropped it but held his gaze.

'I think you should just go, mate,' the waiter said in a low quiet voice that suggested he'd met a few nutters in his time and knew just how to deal with them.

Kenny looked at Alexis. Then at Tommy Hunt.

'You're welcome to each other,' he said and walked away.

• • •

So wrapped up in his anger was he that barely registered when his Uncle Colin was speaking to him. His aunt's good eye was fixed on him.

'If you're going to visit, at least say something,' Colin said.

Kenny looked at him in response. Considered an apology. Rejected the idea. 'I've had a difficult morning,' he said.

'Yeah. Welcome to our world, Kenny,' Colin mumbled.

'Why don't... you... leave me... and Kenny... to talk.' Vi managed to say.

'You sure, sweetheart?' Colin held his wife's hand and shot Kenny some ice with his eyes. 'You spoil him, you know?'

'He'ssistersson.' The sentence slipped out of her mouth as if in one long drawn-out sibilant syllable. He's my sister's son.

Colin looked across his wife's slim form at Kenny. Whenever his eyes met Kenny, they were full of resentment, disappointment, anger and any other number of emotions he hadn't the skill to articulate. His wife was ill and he was at a loss without her. Kenny was the fall guy. Or maybe something else. And he was happy to bear that particular burden.

His uncle's expression softened as he looked into his wife's eyes. His smile all but collapsing in on itself; his eyes begging her to get better. Colin was just holding it together and witnessing this made Kenny feel almost sorry for the man.

Once Colin left the room, Kenny moved closer. He sat on a chair and leaned forward with his elbows on the bed. He held his aunt's small frozen hand in his great mitts.

'Wanted to talk before I die,' said Vi.

'Nonsense,' said Kenny. 'The doctors are saying you're on the mend, Aunt Vi.' He looked into her eyes and he was a small boy again and dependent on this woman for shelter and safety. She was the one person who asked for nothing but his presence. How could he cope without her?

'What do the doctors know?' Again with the half-smile. 'Eejits, the lot of them.'

'You need to stop talking about dying, Aunt Vi, and concentrate on getting better.'

Vi made a dismissive sound. 'I feel stronger, son,' she said. 'Though I can't help but feel I'm only leaving here in a wooden box.'

'Vi,' said Kenny. 'Don't. Please?'

'Listen. Don't talk.' She paused and allowed her head to sink back into the pillows. She closed her eyes and Kenny could read just how much of an effort this all was.

'I need to confess. This has bothered me all these years,' she said and her eyes begged forgiveness.

'Vi, stop it. You've nothing to confess. Stop it.' Kenny didn't want her to continue. He had the certain feeling whatever she was going to say was going to change his view of her forever. And he couldn't deal with that.

'I need to and you need to know the truth.' She stopped again and closed her eyes. She opened them again and wiped the excess saliva from her chin. 'I loved your mum.' Smile. A smile that lingered on her lips like a goodbye kiss. 'But I loved your father more.'

'Aunt Vi, I don't want to hear this,' Kenny said and sat back in his chair. He wanted to stand up and walk out, but his aunt's need to offload had him glued to his seat.

'Your mum's death. My fault. If I hadn't loved your dad...' She tailed off and a fat tear gathered in the lower lid of her left eye before beginning a slow glide down her cheek. 'I had him first, you know. But then once Pete caught sight of my lovely sister, he went off me. Like I was last year's fashion. I'm so ashamed but I hated my sister. Hated her.'

Kenny wanted to interrupt her; wanted the words to stop flowing but he was caught up in her story and, despite everything, he needed to know.

'I looked after you like my penance. Colin was also my penance. He knew I loved Pete. Knew he was second-best but he stayed with me.' She hiccupped a sob. 'Don't know what I did to deserve that man.'

Her good hand waved to the side. 'Glass?'

Kenny spotted a tall glass of water with a bendy straw in it. He held it so his aunt could take a sip.

'Thanks, son.' She looked into Kenny's eyes. Searching. 'You two boys. So different. Yet the same father.'

What? Kenny was suddenly lost. What was she telling him?

'Once your dad had something, he no longer wanted it. My sister. Now his wife. No appeal. So I made him work for me. Gave a little. Withdrew. Became a real little tease until he began an affair with me. I even went through a phase of trying to bring your mum and Colin together so I could have Pete for myself. Didn't work.'

Kenny didn't want to, but he couldn't deny the truth in his aunt's tone. He thought once again about the photo he found in the loft. He had looked at it so much it was a fixture in his mind. He had read it all wrong. Colin's efforts to get close to his mother were not some sad bastard's attempt at un-reconciled affection. They were an offer of support.

'Ian was born...'

'Aunt Vi, please...'

'I wasn't sure whose he was. Neither was Colin. I'm sure that's why Ian's turned out the...' She sobbed. Remorse flowing from her in waves.

Kenny wanted to take her hand and soothe her, but he couldn't move. He tried to access the adult inside, tried to reason that mistakes were not the reserve of the few, but the small boy who was in permanent residence couldn't help but be disappointed that his aunt was human after all. Why should she be the one forced to wear such a heavy expectation, he asked himself. He was unable to answer, only knowing that this was the case.

She was the one adult who had always been there with an ear, a cup of tea and an 'Aww, son' expression. She had been sitting on a pedestal his whole life. The fall from such grace would be hard and painful.

'Then you were born.' Sigh. 'You were perfect. All the mothers used to coo over your pram. All but ignored poor wee Ian.' She took another sip and waved away the glass. Kenny placed it back on the table. Vi fell silent. Retreated to memory and the respite of a brief silence. But her need to issue the words was relentless and she returned to her story.

'Pete had what he wanted now. You. And as your mum gave birth to you, she was part of the deal. I was distraught. Once he made up his mind, he looked at me as if I was shit under his fingernail.' The tears began again. 'God. If only I could have my time again.' She closed her eyes. Her face grew flush. She grimaced. Her forehead was beaded with sweat.

'Hot. Too hot,' she moaned.

'What's wrong, Auntie?' Kenny felt a flush of panic. 'You need a nurse? More water?'

Vi's face twisted. Her back arched. A whelp of pain like from a whipped dog.

'I'm going for a nurse.' Kenny stood up. Vi grabbed his hand.

'Got to finish. My fault.' She groaned. Her arm twitched. 'That poor woman.' She cried out loud and the machine linked to her gave a loud warning noise.

'Vi, you need to stop talking,' Kenny stood up. 'I'm going for a nurse.'

'No. Don't.' Her hand gripped Kenny's. 'I need to tell you everything. It was me. It was all my fault. They killed the wrong woman.'

35

A group of nurses rushed into the room like a well-drilled team, purpose etched on each of their faces. One took Kenny by the arm and guided him from the room while talking to him in a calm and authoritative voice.

'You have to leave Vi with us for the moment. Stay outside and we'll keep you informed.'

Outside the room and there was no sign of Colin.

A nurse was at a computer screen in the Nursing Station ahead. She lifted her head from the screen as Kenny approached.

'Did my Uncle Colin say where...?'

'Yeah, he wanted a coffee and a cigarette.' She offered a smile of apology. 'Said he'd be back in fifteen.'

Kenny walked over to the door of his aunt's bedroom. The curtain was drawn round the bed and he couldn't see what was happening. He turned and leaned against the wall, thinking furiously. She was going to be alright, wasn't she? The nursing staff seemed to be incredibly efficient. Surely they'll do just what was needed.

His stomach churned. She wasn't in danger, was she? He remembered her words as he entered her room and her certainty that the only way she was going to leave the hospital was in a box.

And what the fuck was that all about? *They killed the wrong woman.* What the hell did she mean by that? Kenny rested his head again the wall as if the structure would give him some level of control over his thoughts. Like it could stop his head from spinning like a drunk's. He needed to get a better handle on all of this before he lost it.

He looked down the passageway at the doors that he expected his Uncle Colin to walk through at any minute. They stayed resolutely shut. Should he stay and tell Colin what had happened, or should he leg it while the coast was clear? Whichever action he took, he was sure that Colin would find some way to blame him for what had happened. And he couldn't handle a more agitated Colin at the moment.

Nor could he leave him to find out by himself. Should he walk over to the canteen or should he wait for him to return?

His phone buzzed against his hip and he pulled it from his pocket. He had three texts. The first was from Dimitri. It read,

Just an update with nothing to report.

The next was from Alexis.

I need to explain. Call me.

Yeah, he thought and you can fuck right off.

The last one read, *Kenny, I'm so sorry. I had no idea you would be with my client. Please give me the chance to explain. A x*

And again, thought Kenny, kiss or no kiss: fuck off.

The doors squeaked open and Kenny swung his head round.

'Very good,' Colin said. 'I leave you to keep her company and you can't even stomach more than ten minutes.'

Kenny walked towards him, his hand raised in a conciliatory manner. 'Uncle Colin, you need to come and have a seat.' Kenny wasn't sure whether it was his tone that worked or the use of the title but his uncle did exactly what Kenny said.

Colin sat on the edge of a bucket seat and Kenny could see his Adam's apple bob up and down in his throat as he swallowed. 'What is it? What's happened?'

Kenny ran his hand through his hair. 'I'm not sure. Vi went a wee bit funny. The alarms went off and all these nurses ran in the room...'

Colin stood up and sprinted to his wife's door. Just as he reached for the handle, the door opened and the team of nurses filed out.

Seeing Colin, the more senior nurse approached him and placed an arm round his shoulder. 'Your wife gave us a wee fright there, Colin. We don't know for sure but it looked and felt like a heart attack. Some tests will let us know for sure...'

'Is she...?' Colin stumbled over the word.

'Good God, man, no.' The nurse chuckled as if the thought was bizarre. 'That wee woman's a survivor. It'll take more than a stroke and a heart attack to get her.' As the nurse was talking she was guiding Colin back to his seat. 'She's out of danger now and sleeping. You need to give her some time to rest. Okay?'

Colin nodded.

'You should probably go home and we'll keep you posted. You're no use to her here at the moment.' The nurse looked over at Kenny. 'You going to keep him company?'

Colin shook his head. 'Don't need company.' He coughed as if the act gave him strength. 'Especially not his sort of company. I'll be fine.'

Kenny gave the nurse a what-can-you-do? look and said to no one in particular, 'Right, then. I'm off.'

In the car park he fired up the engine, pulled off the handbrake and got ready to drive off when his phone rang.

'Hello?' he said.

'I didn't think you would answer,' Alexis said.

'If I had bothered to look at the display, I wouldn't have.'

'Is everything okay? You sound–'

'What? Angry? Let down? Left out like the only circumcised dick on the nudist beach?'

'Oh man. That was funny...'

'I'm not in the mood for laughing.'

'...when you threatened to pull your dick out in that restaurant, I thought...' Alexis laughed and Kenny felt himself respond to the sound of it. Chewed on his answering smile.

'Yeah, whatever. If you're done laughing, I have stuff to do.' He cut the connection, annoyed that he had reacted to her laughter.

It rang back immediately. He considered letting it go to his answering service. Despite himself, he picked up.

'Kenny, please,' Alexis said before he could speak. 'I owe you an explanation. Let me–'

'That was my mistake, Alexis. Thinking you owed me anything. You owe me nothing. I owe you nothing. You're a whore. I'm your client. End of. Now you may have nothing better to do than wait for wankers with a full wallet and a hard-on to call, but I have real work to do.'

'You sanctimonious arse.'

'Goodbye.' Even as he hung up, he was enjoying the way Alexis said the word 'arse'. Her accent made it seem more like a term of endearment than an insult.

Hell. Was he being too harsh, he asked himself. He mentally shrugged, decided he was happy if he was and, putting his car in gear, he drove off.

As he drove he considered his next step. Still no closer to finding his father; Alexis had seriously pissed him off; Vi's health issues and her strange admission. Admissions. Were they the imaginings of a woman in pain? The issue of a fevered mind?

Kenny was used to dealing with people and it was a fact of life – one that should be taught right after the sperm meets egg – that People Lie. But Vi's words had a strong ring of truth. In any case, why would you make all of that stuff up?

As he headed back across town, he spotted a large supermarket. A five-minute detour and armed with a bottle of malt whisky he was on his way to visit one of the few people he knew who'd been around at the same time as his father.

Harry Fyfe opened his door with a broad smile and a warm 'In you come, son.'

The thick hall carpet had the expected track marks from a hoover, and a row of jackets and hats hung like a display on the wall behind the door.

Kenny followed Harry into his living room and sat on the same seat as last time.

'So, your pal Ray McBain popped by the other day,' said Harry as he poured each of them a generous measure. He winked. 'I didn't let on that you'd been by.'

'Cheers, Harry. I appreciate it.'

Harry held his glass up. 'It's 7pm somewhere in the world, right?' As he drank he closed his eyes. 'Aaaah. Boy, did that hit the spot.'

Kenny took a sip from his more as an effort in community than any real thirst.

'So,' – Harry leaned forward in his chair – 'you're not here to feed my habit, Kenny. What do you need?'

'God, you're a cheap date, Harry,' Kenny said and grinned. Then he allowed his expression to fold into worry. 'It's just... you're one of the few people who knew my family and...' He paused. 'My Aunt Vi took me in after Mum died and my dad disappeared. She's the one adult who didn't let me down.' He looked up into Harry's eyes. 'She's dying, Harry.'

'Ach, son. Life's a bastard, eh?' He lifted one foot so that it was resting on the other knee. 'What's wrong?'

'She had a stroke last week. This week, well, today she's had a heart attack.'

Harry looked through Kenny into his own memory. He sniffed, twisted his mouth as if suppressing emotion and exhaled. 'That's rotten, son. Pure rotten. What's the prognosis?'

'They don't know for sure. But one on top of the other can't be good.' Kenny took another sip. He was actually confident that his aunt would recover but it wouldn't do any harm to engage Harry's sympathy.

Harry sucked at his teeth and looked at Kenny for a long moment. 'I didn't know your Aunt Vi well, Kenny. But the fact she took you in the way she did suggests she's a good woman.'

'Were you ever aware of any relationships she might have had other than my uncle?'

Harry looked confused. 'Strange question. What's brought that on?'

'She did.' Kenny made a face. 'It was like her deathbed confession.

Please forgive me, I have sinned and had an affair with your dad.'

Harry slumped back into his chair. He whistled. 'D'ye know, nothing surprises me anymore. Families, eh? And they do say it's the quiet ones you have to watch out for.'

'She also said something even more strange. Apart from my cousin might be my brother. She said it was her fault and that they killed the wrong woman.'

'Je-sus. That's strange right enough. Any idea what she's talking about?'

'Nope. Haven't a clue. I was hoping you might be able to shed some light.'

Harry shrugged. Looked to the side. 'What do I remember of your Aunt Vi? They probably went out in a foursome with your mum and dad. Vi was like a toned-down version of your mum. You could tell they were sisters but the same features on your mum had more of a glamour on them.' Harry thought some more with the help of a generous slug of whisky. 'Nah. Can't remember much else. Sorry, son.'

It was pretty much what Kenny expected but he hid his disappointment behind a rueful grin.

'She was persistent, right enough, on the phone when your mum died. Demanding an investigation. Trying to make sure we didn't put it down to a suicide.' Harry scratched at the side of his face as he studied Kenny some more. 'You don't look so good, young man. Not been sleeping?'

'You could say that.'

'Up shagging all night or is this all getting to you?'

Kenny made an och-you-know face. 'If I tell you, I have to kill you.'

'There's a reason that sayings become popular, Kenny. Because of the truth we all see in them. And here's an expression for you. Let sleeping dogs lie.'

Kenny shrugged.

'Jings. Get me,' said Harry. 'Getting all philosophical on one large whisky.'

'You do have something, Harry, but there's something about this. I can't let it go.' He told Harry about his father's letters.

After he had finished talking, Harry demonstrated that, once a cop always a cop.

'A mother and child died. Your dad said it was an accident. No one believes him.' Harry chewed on the inside of his mouth and creased his eyes in thought. 'Can't remember any tragedies around that same time...' Another sip. 'Leave it with me. I'll see what I can dig up, eh?' He seemed to become more alert at the thought of having something to do. He nodded. 'Leave it with me, Kenny.'

'Sorry to change the subject on you, but what do you know about Tommy Hunt?'

'Nothing more than what I read in the papers. Made a lot of money. I seem to remember something about – oh, what was it? – it was a Sunday paper special. Successful Scots and all that. He came from a moneyed background and made shitloads more rather than sitting back and...' He shot forward. 'If I remember rightly, they made a big deal about his motivation to work harder. His wife died and then he spent all of his energy in making his business a success.' Harry's eyes had a strong light in them now. 'You're not thinking what I'm thinking?'

'Might be.'

'You'd need to find out when Hunt's wife died. And how she died.' Harry rubbed his hands together. 'God, I miss this stuff.' He suddenly had more energy than at any time since Kenny first met him.

'What about my dad, Harry? Can you remember any conversations you might have had with him that could give a clue as to where he might have gone?'

'He was a good talker, I'll give you that, Kenny. Full of the blethers.' Harry stopped speaking for a moment as he sought information in his memory cells. 'Thing is I cannae remember what I had for breakfast but I can remember whole conversations and interviews I had years ago with convicts.' He held a hand up. 'Sorry, Kenny. Don't want to be calling your old man names.'

'Don't apologise, Harry. That's what he was. A convict.'

'Actually he wasn't. He was never tried and convicted for anything. Too smart. Just like yourself.' Harry wore a wicked grin. 'Maybe he got out of the life in the nick of time. Before his luck ran out.' Harry slapped a hand down on his thigh. His voice loud. 'Anyway. Conversations with Pete O'Neill.' A pause. 'Partick Thistle. He talked a lot about games down at Firhill. Said he would hate to take the lazy way out and follow Celtic or Rangers. I remember he talked about one holiday he was planning for you and your mum. He was going to take you to Edinburgh to take in the castle and the Tattoo. He could never understand why any Scot would want to go abroad when we had all this on our doorstep.'

'That's pretty much the impression I have of him too, Harry. Did he ever tell you about the women in his life?'

'Not really. He was quite discreet that way. Some men delight in giving you a stroke-by-stroke account of their love affairs. To be fair, Pete acted like he was above all that. He definitely had an eye for the ladies. He was just more... aye, "discreet" is a good word to use.' Harry whistled. 'So he had an affair with your Aunt Vi?'

'Apparently.'

'Cannae see why the woman would make up something like that. Did your uncle know about it?'

'Why?'

'That could provide some motivation. Colin finds out his wife is shagging his mate. He sets Pete up. Bish, bash, bosh.'

'Nah. I can't see it. Colin's your archetypal accountant. He's all about the numbers.'

'Here's another saying for you, Kenny. Still waters run deep.'

36

Mason Budge had a diamond-edged hard-on. He could punch through glass with this one.

His heart started beating like a drill when the text came through and it felt like every drop of blood in his body surged straight to his dick.

It was from the boss. It read,

Disappointed!!! She's not done her job yet. Make sure she does. Do whatever it takes.

Carte blanche, that's what that text gave him. Permission to do whatever the fuck he liked. He felt like getting out a pen and drawing up a list. The thought of that pussy wrapped round his shaft was almost enough to make him swoon. He gripped his phallus and shut his eyes. Savoured the thrill.

Exhaled slowly in an attempt to make his heartbeat calm down.

Not yet. Some restraint was called for. If he let himself go completely she wouldn't be in a fit state to do the job the boss wanted. Fun could be had though. Just enough fist and cock to get the message across and then, when the job was finally done, he could allow himself to really let go.

37

Kenny left ten minutes later with Harry's promise ringing in his ears. He would scour his mind for memories of that time and see if he could remember anything about a woman and her child dying in an accident.

So lost was he in thought it was a wonder of absent-minded driving that he made it back to his flat without getting into an accident. He found a parking space on his road and reaching for his phone he dialled Dimitri. It was time for some different thinking on this one.

'Dimitri and O'Neill. Finding people is our speciality. How can I help you?'

'Except you couldn't find your way out of a garden shed with a key, an axe and a map, mate.'

'Och, just having a wee laugh, boss,' said Dimitri.

'Not in a laughing mood, mate. Got anything?'

'Sorry. It's like he vanished into thin air, boss. Generally if someone really doesn't want to be found it's nigh on impossible to find them.'

'I don't do impossible, Dimitri. There's always a way.'

'Mmmm. Any ideas, Mr Positivity?'

'You know those milk cartons you see in American TV with the faces of missing people on them?'

'Oh. Right,' said Dimitri thinking out loud. 'That could work. Do you have an up-to-date photo?'

Kenny had scanned the photo of his dad into his computer. He reached over to his laptop, opened up his email, attached the photo and sent it to Dimitri.

'No, but you're the computer whizz. I've just sent you a photograph. Get yourself some of that face-ageing software and do a mock-up of what he might look like now.'

'You going for blanket coverage of Scotland with your milk?'

Kenny thought for a minute. 'No. I'm going to draw up a list. No. You're going to draw up a list. Historical tourist spots on the west coast and central Scotland and then find out the milk producers in the regions concerned and appeal to their better nature. Failing that we'll spill some cash their way.'

'How much you willing to spend?'

'Let's wait and see if it's possible first. Then we'll talk money.'

Something caught his eye as he was talking and he looked up. Someone was bundled up and sitting at the communal entrance to his flat. They hadn't been there when he parked. Better not be one of the local druggies or he'd kick their arse.

A head lifted from the collection of dark clothing. He could make out blood and bruising. The right eye was swollen shut and entire left side of the face was a lumpen mess. The person had long dirty hair that might have been blonde. They turned and looked down the street as if waiting for someone. Or possibly hiding from someone. The face stopped its traverse of the street when they saw Kenny's car. He could make out that it was a girl now and the person met his gaze with their one good eye and then looked away as if they had recognised him.

That small movement was enough for Kenny to work out who it was.

'Dimitri, need to go.'

He was out of the car and on his knees in front of the damaged woman.

'Alexis,' he said. 'What the fuck...?'

'Just take me inside, Kenny. Please?' The words were hard to make out as they stumbled from the face that Kenny used to know so well.

'Inside? You need to get to a hospital, like now.'

'No. No hospital.' Alexis grabbed his jacket, her one open eye desperate with the need to get her message across. 'No. Please. No hospital. That will get the police involved.' She shook her head, now mute.

'What bastard did this?' Kenny was filled with rage. It was so hot it almost blinded him. He didn't need to ask, he knew who it was. Mr Bigshot and his enforcer guy. If Kenny ever got his hands on either of them...

'Inside, Kenny. Please?'

She was almost weightless in Kenny's arms as he climbed the stairs to his flat. She was wordless as he filled his bath and then carefully undressed her. When he pulled off her jeans he saw the blood and bite marks on her inner thighs and his anger took on new levels.

'I think you should get a tetanus shot,' he said. She didn't respond to his suggestion. It was as if all of her strength was being used to keep the air flowing in and out of her lungs. 'Did you hear me?' he said again. 'Human bites are worse than dog bites. You need a doctor to stop any infection.'

'He bit me?' she asked in a whisper. 'Everything so sore... didn't notice...' Eyes half-closed with pain and loathing, she turned to him. 'No doctor. I can't...' She began to sob.

'Okay. Okay,' he said, stroking her head. 'No doctor.'

She was in her bra and pants now. Her flesh was mottled down one side. One bruise settling into another. Kenny didn't know how to touch her without causing her more pain. Neither did he know if he should remove her underwear. She was doing nothing for herself and he didn't think she would be comfortable being naked before a man after what she had just gone through.

'In you go,' he said, thinking that she might make the decision for him. She did and stepped in to the water just as she was. As the hot water touched the more tender parts she inhaled with a sharp hiss. First she went down on to her knees and then she eased on to her backside, twisting so that each leg was placed in front of her. Then she pulled her knees up to her chest and focussed on the shiny metal of the taps as if looking anywhere else was going to hurt her eyes.

Kenny picked up a sponge and flushed it with water, dabbed some soap on it and then began to slowly wash her back. In and out of the water he pushed the sponge and then allowed the water to pour down the bruised landscape of her back. Each of her vertebrae jutted out from her skin like an accusation. *You are a man*, they said. You are guilty by association. He kept his movement even, suspecting that the rhythm he created was more soothing for him than it was for her.

'You in a lot of pain?' he asked and then cursed himself as an ass. Of course she was in a lot of pain. His knees creaked as he stood up. 'I'll get you some painkillers.'

In the kitchen he found a small white packet that he kept for emergencies. Usually these emergencies were for his own broken bones and sprained joints after a training bout down at The Hut. He never imagined it would be put to use like this.

With a glass of water in his hand along with two tablets, he returned to the bathroom. Alexis was sitting in exactly the same place he had left her.

'Here you go,' he said and handed them to her. As if they had performed this action a thousand times, she kept her focus on the tap and held a hand out for the tablets. Once they were in her mouth she took the glass and, tipping it to her mouth, she swallowed.

'Whenever I take these, I sleep for hours,' Kenny said. 'So let's get you out of there and dried and into a nice warm bed.' Listen to yourself, O'Neill. As if a pill and a pillow is going to make everything better.

Like a child might, she did as he suggested and stepped from the water. She stood in the middle of the floor waiting for him to dry her off.

'I'll need to...' He unfastened her bra and then pulled down her soaking panties. As he did so he averted his eyes. Alexis was past caring. Then he picked a large white towel from the pile in the corner and rubbed her dry. He draped the towel over her shoulders and ran into his dressing room. There he found a large grey T-shirt and a pair of white briefs. She needed to feel kind of decent again, he suspected and these would have to do.

Once she was dried and dressed, after a fashion, he held her hand and walked her through to his bedroom. He pulled the quilt back from the bed and guided her towards it. She climbed in, laid her head on the pillow and waited for Kenny to pull the cover over her.

Kenny looked down at her, at the mess of her face and the numbness in her expression. It made him think of Vi. He'd left her not long ago looking much the same, minus the bruising.

'Sorry, Kenny,' Alexis slurred.

'No need to apologise,' Kenny said.

Alexis grabbed his hand and held on with surprising strength. 'I have no choice. So sorry.' Her one good eye begged him to believe her. She struggled up onto her elbows. 'I need to talk to you. There's things I need to tell...'

'Don't you worry, sweetheart,' he said, all of his earlier frustrations about her completely forgiven. Whatever she needed to tell him could wait until she was a little better. 'You're safe here. Just get some rest.'

'Sorry. Need to...' She slurred again and closed her eyes. Her grip loosened and Kenny allowed her hand to fall onto the bed.

How could someone do this, he asked himself. How could a man do this to a woman? He'd hurt plenty of men in his time and he was aching to hurt one particular man. If only he knew who he was and how to find him.

Although Kenny had hurt many men in his time, he had never killed anyone. He couldn't promise that wasn't about to change.

• • •

In the living room, Kenny walked from the window to the door countless times. He needed to do something. He needed to find out who this bastard was and explain how women should be treated. There was a nice quiet spot up in the Campsie Hills where no one would be able to hear screaming. Or there was a particularly dark basement in one of the pubs he owned where no one would interrupt him.

He needed to find this fucker so badly his jaw hurt. But he wasn't going to find anyone stuck inside the flat. He picked out a number on his mobile and dialled. It was answered immediately.

'Hey boss. You needing some work done?'

'Mark, are you and your brother free right now?'

'Yup.'

'You know where I live. Be here asap.'

Half an hour of more pacing, with the odd visit to stand at his bedroom door and gaze over the supine form in his bed, and his doorbell rang.

He answered it and allowed Mark and Calum in.

Mark was bouncing on his toes. Calum performed the usual sombre contrast to his brother.

'What's the job, Kenny?' asked Mark. 'Anybody needing a doin'?'

Calum looked to the ceiling in frustration. 'Chill, brother.'

'If anybody's needing a doin' I'll be the one to do it,' said Kenny. 'I need you two to stay here and look after someone special.'

'Okay, man.' Mark nodded his head like he was trying to beat the world record for nods per second. 'There's a burd?'

'Yes, Mark. There's a woman. She's in my bedroom and she's hurt...'

'This got anything to do with that woman down in that place...'

'Mark, give it a rest. Let the man talk, for fuck's sake,' said Calum.

Kenny managed a smile at Calum. 'All you need to know is that you've to let no one in or out of this flat until I come back. Understood?'

Both men nodded. Kenny had one last look in at his bedroom

and quietly closed the door. In his bathroom he picked up Alexis' clothes and her handbag. He carried everything through to his kitchen and, out of sight of the two guys, he went through all of her belongings. There was nothing of any real interest apart from a large group of house keys and her mobile. He pocketed the keys. Her phone was still switched on so he scrolled through it, not sure exactly what he was looking for.

The text inbox was empty, as was the sent items box. Unusual, he thought. How many people are so careful with their mobile phones? They only time he emptied his phone folders was when they were full.

Her contacts were similarly sparse. Mostly initials. He read his. K.O. and looked for Tommy Hunt's and was disappointed. There were only two names not initialised. Cora and Jo. The first name rang a faint bell of recognition. Cora. Could that have been the name of the girl who was murdered in Alexis' flat?

Jo's number was highlighted. Might as well press *Call*.

It was answered after four rings. A voice giggled. A note of happiness that was aimed at someone on her side of the phone. 'Alexis, how are you, sweetheart?'

Kenny read the voice for any sound of concern before he spoke. There was none.

'Sorry, Jo. This is Kenny. I'm a friend of Alexis.'

'Ohmygod,' Jo breathed. 'Is she okay?'

'She is now,' said Kenny. 'But one of her clients has hit her rather badly.'

'Ohmygod,' Jo repeated, sounding close to tears. 'I told her she was too good for this game. Is she okay? Did she...?'

'I don't think anything's broken, Jo, but she won't let me call the police or take her to a doctor.' He wondered how much to tell her. If she was part of the same group as Alexis, she would have contact with the bastard who did this.

'Do you know the flat in the Merchant City where Alexis sometimes works out of?'

'Never been there, but I know of it.'

Smart girl, thought Kenny, she was being cautious in her response.

'Jo, I'm going to trust you.' *I'm desperate and running out of options*, he might have added. 'I'm...' – he paused for dramatic effect and allowed his voice to crack a little – '...in love with Alexis. I was trying to get her out of the game when this happened.'

'Right...'

Kenny tried to judge from that one syllable if she was falling for his Richard Gere in *Pretty Woman* act. 'Jo. I need your help. I need to find out who did this to her and I need to make him suffer.'

'Now you're singing my song, mate,' said Jo. 'How soon can you get there?' She paused. 'You got a key?'

'I'll be there in half an hour.'

'Cool. Bring a bottle of gin. And thirty quid.'

'Thirty quid?'

'Or fifty. A blow for thirty. A full shag is fifty. Bareback and it's a hundred. Might as well earn some money while I'm at it. Time is money, mister.'

• • •

In his car and passing through familiar streets clogged with the usual number of cars and his phone rang again.

'Harry Fyfe here, Kenny. Got a minute?'

'I'm all ears, old man.' Kenny was surprised by the feeling of warmth he had for the old cop.

'I'll "old man" you. And I hope you're not driving?'

'Don't worry. The pigs won't stop me, I'm hands-free.'

'Aw son, you're not one of those wankers who wears one of those ear-pieces like it's a status symbol, are you?'

Kenny grinned. 'What you wanting, you old fucker?'

'Right. Aye. The banter's fine, but. Got to thinking about the murder of a woman and child before your mum killed herself and I don't know why it didn't come into my head straight away.'

'Yeah?' Kenny's stomach twisted.

'This one was high profile at the time, but the reason I haven't said anything was because it was a young mother who was killed. No child.'

'Horrible as that is, Harry, it doesn't stand out in terms of what we are looking for.'

'True. True.' Two syllables and he sounded really disappointed.

'Tell me the rest,' said Kenny. Less from curiosity than a need to make Harry feel useful.

'It's probably nothing that will help you, but you never know. The papers were full of it for weeks. Such a tragedy...'

Kenny had arrived outside Alexis' flat in the Merchant City and he was wishing Harry would get on with it.

'...the woman didn't die with her son. She was killed by him. With a gun.'

'A gun?' Gun crime was still relatively uncommon in Scotland but it was even rarer in those days.

'It gets worse. The boy was only ten or eleven and he thought the gun was a toy.'

38

With thoughts of such a horrible event filling his mind, Kenny locked his car and walked to the entrance of the flat. How would that boy have felt after he shot his mother? No amount of reassurance would ever allow the boy to reconcile himself with his actions. He wondered where he might be now, how he had turned out. He'd be about the same age as Kenny.

Whatever the situation was with this poor boy, it had no reflection on his. The letters from his father mentioned the death of a mother and son. He'd finished the call with Harry and asked him to keep drilling his memory bank.

His musings were interrupted by a voice at his ear.

'Yeah, these are, like, keys. K.E.Y.S. and they open doors.'

Kenny turned to his left to see a small pale face squinting at him. She must have been under five feet, her long dark hair tied back in a ponytail, teeth stained with nicotine and the skin around her eyes had more lines than a plate of spaghetti.

'You Kenny?'

'Jo, I presume?'

'At your service.' She bobbed up and down and flicked a smile at him. Her hands were in the pocket of her puffed jacket, which along with the hair and minus the lines on her face made her look like a schoolgirl. The words *Must have had a hard paper round* ran through his mind. 'Look, I've been thinking I was a wee bit hasty agreeing to meet you in the flat...' She looked past him, eyes roving up and down the street. 'Would you mind buying me a coffee somewhere first? There's been a lot of weird shit going on around here recently and I don't want to end up in a bodybag.'

'None taken,' said Kenny.

'Yeah, you don't look like a killer, but I like the whole breathing thing so much I don't want to take any chances.'

'Where do you suggest?'

'You're paying,' – she flicked the smile again and Kenny could see that a month of long lie-ins and a detox later she could be very attractive – 'so you decide.'

Kenny shrugged, put the keys back in his pocket and began walking. Jo kept up with his pace, her heels clicking a staccato on the pavement. They walked for about five minutes before Jo tried to begin a conversation.

'You, like, the strong silent type then?' Jo asked.

'You, like, the short yappy type then?'

'Better than being a miserable bastard.'

Kenny laughed. 'Sorry. I've a lot on my mind.' He had reached his target. He stopped walking and pushed open a glass door, allowing Jo to walk in first.

She held a hand to her heart as she walked past him. 'My,' – she pretended to swoon – 'a gentleman.'

'Aye. Something like that,' said Kenny as he joined her in the small café. The room was lined with tables just large enough to take two chairs, and a glass-fronted cooling cabinet displayed a bounty of cakes and pastries. The tables were almost all occupied, which Kenny took as a good sign.

Kenny picked a table at the back of the café. Jo complained.

'Awww. I like to sit near the window so I can see everybody walking past.'

Kenny ignored her and sat down. 'I decide, right?'

Jo sat down and looked to the ceiling, playing at being in a huff.

'I'll have a latte,' she said. 'With cinnamon syrup.' Then she began to sing to the song playing in the background. It was an old Sinatra number.

'Want anything to eat?' Kenny asked.

Jo continued to mouth the words to the song until the chorus ended. 'Ohmygod,' she said, 'I have such a sweet tooth.' She stood up again. 'Let me go over to the cabinet and pick something.' She walked over to the display and bent over towards it, keeping up a monologue to no one in particular. 'Oh, that carrot cake looks lovely. Oh, and the doughnuts. And look at the size of those empire biscuits. Aye but, I always have a weakness for a nice big slice of Victoria sponge.'

She returned to her seat with an apologetic expression. 'Apart from having a sweet tooth, I have a terrible habit of having a motor-mouth when I'm nervous. Other than that,' she grinned, 'I have no vices.'

A waitress who looked like she had her own personal feeder waddled over to take their order.

'Somebody ate all the pies,' Jo whispered. 'Or should we change that for croissants seeing we're in the Merchant City?'

'Help you?' the waitress asked, her face wearing a faint blush, suggesting that she heard Jo's comment. She was large, but in proportion. Kenny could definitely see a waist.

Like all thin people, Jo had no idea of the offence she had just caused. 'You look like you enjoy your scran, babes. What would you suggest?'

'Ten years of an eating disorder and a copy of *How to Win Friends and Influence People*?' the waitress replied with an I-dare-you-to-complain smile.

Kenny laughed. So did Jo.

'Nice one, babes. I asked for that,' Jo said. 'Now that we're best pals, I'll have a giant chunk of Viccy sponge and a latte. The strong silent one over there will have a black coffee.'

Kenny raised an eyebrow in question.

Jo shrugged. 'You have black coffee written all over your face, babes.'

Kenny nodded at the waitress. 'That'll do nicely,' he said.

'Right.' Jo leaned forward on the table. Her eyes betrayed her concern. 'How's Alexis?'

'Not good. She's had a real beating this time.'

'This time?' Jo's eyebrows were almost as high as her hairline. 'I thought Alexis was too good for that. You saying she's been beat up before?'

'She didn't tell you?'

'How did you get my number again?'

'On Alexis' phone.'

Jo made a face. 'I didn't think she'd kept my number.' She fidgeted in her pocket and pulled out a packet of cigarettes. 'This smoking ban's a pile of shite, by the way.' She opened the packet, sniffed at the neat row of cigarette tips and then closed it again. 'That'll have to do.' Smile. 'No, she didn't tell me. We had a wee fall-out some time ago. But I was the first street-worker Alexis met when she came up to Glasgow. I gave her some tips. Taught her the lie of the land.' Jo looked towards the window and then back to Kenny. 'So. She kept my number?' She made another face. 'I feel bad. I gave her such a hard time the last time we spoke.'

'Why? What did you say?'

'She forgot where she came from. Was becoming too big for her Kurt Geigers.'

'Eh?'

'Designer boots. And she looked down her nose at me.' Jo chewed on the inside of her lip, her eyes leaking a light and being filled with a sense of judgement in which she found herself lacking. 'There's nothing like someone telling you an uncomfortable truth to make you hate yourself.'

'She was trying to set up on her own?'

'That was the line she gave me last time too.'

'You didn't believe her?'

The waitress arrived with a tray and the conversation stopped. It didn't resume until they had been served. Jo took a sip of her drink. When she lifted her head up she had a milk moustache. She made no attempt to wipe it off.

'Alexis was always making plans. She hated her pimp, said she was determined to buy herself out of her contract and go back to London.'

'She's going to London?'

Jo reached across and patted the back of Kenny's hand. 'Poor sap,' she said. 'And here's you thinking you were getting her out of the game.' Jo cut through her sponge with the side of her fork and spoke with her mouth full. 'A word to the less than wise. Alexis whatever her name is – and I speak as a friend – is one woman who loves her job. Drop her anywhere in the world and she'd find a man, fuck him and then bleed him dry.'

'No. Don't believe you,' said Kenny, shaking his head. This didn't square with the woman he knew. And fell in love with.

Jo reached across the table and slapped him on the face.

'Oww,' said Kenny, more from the reflex that any actual pain.

'Sorry, but that's for your own good. Wake the fuck up, mate. You seem a nice guy. You're good-looking. Why not get yourself a nice–'

'Look. Can we get back to finding out who might have attacked Alexis?'

'Sorry. Jeez, I keep saying sorry.' Jo coughed. 'You're right.' Pause. 'Sorry.' Smile.

'Tell me about this pimp she hated.'

'That's the thing. None of us girls ever met him. He had a buddy though. A Yank, or he might have been Canadian.' She screwed up her face. 'He is one sick bastard. He never hurt me, like. Knew better.' She put on what she thought was her tough face but it only made her look young and vulnerable. 'You know, I've never met a nasty Canadian. The nicest peeps in the world. Apart from this guy. If he is Canadian, that is. Anyway, his name is Mason Budge. What the fuck kinda name is that? He must've made it up.'

'Describe him.'

'Kinda non-descript kinda guy. Lean. Looks like he knows how to handle himself. Same height as you, mibbe? Or just a wee bit shorter. Cropped dark hair.' She took a sip from her coffee and acknowledged the waitress, who had returned with the bill. 'Gorgeous cake this, hen. Did you make it?'

'No,' the waitress replied, clearly still unsure how to take Jo.

'And where might I find this Mason guy?'

'Oh, you don't find Mason. He finds you.' Jo shivered. 'And you pray that you've got a can of mace on quick-draw if he does.'

'There's always a way,' Kenny said, more to himself. 'Do you know if he works exclusively for this pimp guy or if he does other work?'

Jo shrugged. 'Haven't a clue.'

'What about the pimp? Any ideas who he might be?'

'None whatsoever.'

'Alexis never gave you any hints?'

'Just that he had layers of people between him and the less savoury side of his work. She called him Teflon Guy.'

'Ever heard of Tommy Hunt?'

Jo shook her head. 'Should I?'

Kenny stood up and pulled his wallet out of his pocket. He counted out four tenners and threw them on the table. 'That's for your time. Thanks.'

'Hey,' said Jo, making a sad face. 'You never got to try out the Jo Jo special.'

'Another time, eh?'

'Too bad, babes, I would have rocked your world.'

• • •

Back at his flat and Alexis was still sleeping. He fed the guys some notes and asked them to stay on standby.

His mind reeling with all of the recent events in his life and the information provided by Jo, he went into his spare bedroom, stripped and slipped under the covers. So, according to Jo, he was kidding himself on. Alexis would only ever see him as a hard cock with a wallet.

The curtains remained open all night and all night he studied the stipple on the ceiling and how the moon shadowed the bulb and slender pendant of the light fighting.

The shape stretched like a warning across the ceiling in the shape of a giant noose.

39

He woke early and automatically reached for his mobile. And then checked himself. The person he'd normally be looking for was in his bed, while here he was in the spare. The light from his phone showed that the time was six fifteen.

Feeling pressure on his bladder he walked through to his bathroom and did the necessary. Over the drum of his piss on the toilet water he could hear voices. He paused before he pulled the flush to listen. The voices were coming from the living room.

Planting his feet with care he walked over to the living room door and looked in. His TV was flickering light into the room and with the help of this he could see the small shape curled up on his sofa, wrapped up in a quilt.

Alexis lifted her head, spotted him and cleared her throat. Even in the dark he could read the discolouring on the pearl of her face.

'You coming in?'

'I'm naked,' Kenny said, pointing out the obvious.

Alexis shrugged. 'And it's chilly. Come here and keep me company.'

He walked over. She lifted the quilt up and he slipped in behind her.

'Mmmm,' she said. 'Nice to have you nearby.'

Kenny slipped a hand over her stomach and studied the TV.

'What you watching?'

'No idea,' said Alexis. 'The voices were just company.'

'Why are we whispering?' asked Kenny.

He could feel her answering shrug. 'It just seems suitable for this time of day. Most of the world is asleep.' She moved her bum back towards him, pressing against him. To Kenny it felt like a movement a girlfriend might make for heat and comfort, nonetheless her backside was pressing against his penis and the inevitable happened.

Alexis stretched back and grabbed his solid shaft. She stroked it slowly. Kenny groaned.

'You want me to...'

Kenny savoured the feel of it for a moment before answering. 'No, it's fine.'

'You might be saying so, but little Kenny's telling me something different.' He could hear the smile in her voice. And, surprisingly, the longing.

'S'okay, let's just lie here and enjoy the company and the cuddle.'

Alexis released her grip, twisted round towards him and allowed her head to fall onto his chest. 'Thanks for looking after me, Kenny. You have no idea how much I appreciate it.'

'Welcome.'

They settled into silence, soothed by the smooth tones of the news presenters. A world in distress flitted across their screen and neither of them registered any of it.

Kenny considered telling her that he had met with Jo the day before but something held him back. Jo's words hadn't stopped running through his mind all night. Alexis loved her job. In order to gain Jo's sympathy, he had pretended he was in love with Alexis and told her his aim was to take her out of the business.

It was only now with Alexis in his arms that he realised that this ambition wasn't too far from the truth.

Alexis was probably used to her punters falling in love with her. This time might be unusual because he had all his own teeth and didn't need to resort to Viagra. But it was never going to happen, was it?

'What are you thinking, sweetheart?' Alexis asked and Kenny felt a stab… of what… disappointment? Loneliness? That was a question any 'normal' girlfriend might have asked her man.

'Nothing, babes. Get some sleep.' He pulled a hand from behind the quilt and began to gently stroke Alexis' forehead – the undamaged side – and from this angle and with the help of the light from the TV, he could see down the swell of her cheek, to the bump of her lips and to where the light dropped off the curve of her chin.

As he stroked he could hear her breath settle, slow and lengthen. He kept going until he was certain she was sleeping and then with the voices in the background an indistinct hum he felt himself follow her into sleep.

• • •

He wasn't aware of any dreams. He felt her weight rest on his hips, her wetness surrounding his hard flesh and his breathing harsh with pleasure. The feeling grew in his thighs, his buttocks, his gut. He felt his balls so tight they ached; his cock so hard…

'Fuck. This is…'

'Shhh,' Alexis leaned over him, her lips light against his ear. She leaned forward further and Kenny felt the trail of her hair over his forehead before her breast was offered to his mouth. He took it in and nibbled at her nipple while her hips continued their rhythm.

'Stop… before…' He didn't want the feeling to end. But Alexis, reading the speed of his breathing, increased her rhythm and before Kenny knew it he was shouting his climax into the warmed air above them.

Alexis fell into his chest as if felled.

Kenny cleared her hair from his face and shifted his weight so that they were side by side. Alexis curled into him and Kenny exhaled.

'That was…' he said and stopped. It felt crass to try and offer a category. In any case, ten out of ten didn't quite cut it. He turned his head and kissed her forehead, tasting her sweat.

'Love you,' he said and the words were out before he could even identify the thought. His chest was tight with it. He could no more hold the words back than he could stop his heart from taking its next beat.

Alexis pushed up until she was leaning on an elbow. Her expression shifted from one emotion to another. As soon as Kenny gave one a name it was replaced by another; surprise, joy, fear and finally she settled on sorrow.

'You can't love me, Kenny. I'm flawed. I'm not good enough for you.' A tear gathered on her eyelid before sliding down the side of her nose.

'Do I not get to decide?'

She turned in to his side, hiding her face behind her hair. 'Don't,' she whispered.

Words crammed his thoughts but none found their way from between teeth and tongue. His throat tightened.

'Don't,' she said again but this time her voice had an edge.

'I… I… don't know where that came from...'

'You were grateful. A fantastic shag and you were grateful.'

Kenny retreated. Allowed his head to fall back onto a cushion. 'Right,' he said. 'And what a shag it was.' He laughed and found the noise was tinged with relief. Alexis was giving him a get-out clause and he accepted it gratefully.

'Fancy a cuppa?' he asked.

'Thought you'd never ask,' she said and sat up as if lighter. The crisis had passed and they could both now relax. Their relationship had threatened to shift, but was now back onto familiar ground. Client and customer. Victim and protector. Love was a dangerous element to add to the mix and Kenny was forever grateful to Alexis for allowing the moment to slip by. A storm reduced to a breeze by a simple lack of attention.

Who was he kidding, thought Kenny as he walked into the kitchen and filled the kettle. 'Love' was a word that, once said, could never be revoked. In his experience it brought a cost. He would just have to wait and see what that cost might be.

Minutes later he brought a pair of mugs back into the living room. Alexis made herself comfortable before reaching out with both hands for the drink. Her eyes unable to meet his.

And so it begins, thought Kenny, the quiet erosion of whatever bond they had built up. He did not accept this feeling with regret, but more with relief. He may have acknowledged his feelings for her but just as easily as the words slipped from his mouth he could dampen them down. He'd done it before. He couldn't afford to fall in love.

He sat beside her, claimed back part of the quilt with a grin to her mock complaint and sat down to face the television. How many couples, how many families, across the world allowed their emotions to re-group behind the blaze and blur of a TV screen?

Except this TV was clear and strong and showing an image of a face he recognised. He tuned in to the voice of the presenter.

'After the tragic death of another addict, will Josephine Connelly's overdose be the one that finally gets the authorities hunting down this recent batch of fatal heroin?'

Could it have been just the previous day when he'd sat across a table from that very same woman? The photograph was an old one and her face at that point in her life was lightened by a life well lived. Whatever poor choices she was about to make, or be forced into, had yet to show their disturbance on her face.

This was too much of a coincidence. He spoke to her yesterday and just hours later she was dead? Was it the money he gave her? Enough for one more fix. Or did something more sinister happen to her?

Alexis' head swung round. 'Did you know her?'

'No.' Kenny said, fixing his gaze on her, not quite understanding why he decided to lie. 'Did you?'

Alexis turned back to study the TV. Swallowed. 'Never seen her before in my life.'

40

Kenny showered, dressed and made them both a breakfast of bacon, sausage and eggs. Alexis made a face when he put the plate in front of her.

'Coffee will do, please Kenny.'

'Nope. Your body needs fuel. Eat up.'

Whatever her complaint was, she finished the plateful before Kenny. Noticing this, he said, 'I thought you didn't want any.'

'Who am I to argue? Besides, you do have a point.' She worked a smile into her swollen face.

Kenny winced on her behalf. 'Still sore?'

'I'll survive.'

Something in her tone suggested she'd been through worse. Kenny nodded as if to say he wasn't surprised. Sipping at his coffee, he stared into her eyes. Was she any different since he stated his undying love? He felt a cringe sour his mouth and curl his toes. Fucking idiot.

'What?' she challenged.

'There's so much about you I don't know.'

'Believe me, it's best it stays that way.'

'Who for? You or me?'

She inclined her head and offered a smile. This was a look that worked well when her face was of normal dimensions. It didn't have quite the same impact when she was so bruised and swollen. Nor was he feeling quite so enamoured of her. Was this because he said the L-word? His natural state was to be on his own, so his head was taking corrective action.

'You should get some ice on that,' Kenny said, more for a way to cover his confusion than out of any concern. His feelings were all over the place. One minute he wanted to take her away and live on a Highland croft, the next... well, what did he want?

'Will I ever get to know the real Alexis?'

'Be careful what you wish for, Kenny.'

'What's that supposed to mean?' Kenny was surprised at the strength of his irritation.

Alexis rubbed her eyes. 'Not now, Kenny. I'm tired.'

'Right enough.' Kenny stood up and walked out of the room. He came back in with his gym bag. 'I need some head space.' Alexis was on her feet and in front of him with surprising haste.

'You can't leave me here on my own,' she said with large eyes and one hand on his chest.

'S'okay. No one can hurt you here.'

'You sure about that?' Her eyes were huge, her hand trembling on his chest like a trapped bird.

'Hey, babes,' – he brought her head into his chest – 'nobody, but nobody, can hurt you here.' He held her head in both hands and gently lifted it into view. He kissed her, feeling only tenderness. He would kill to protect this woman.

'Don't leave me, Kenny. I'm begging you.'

Kenny chewed on that for a moment.

'I need...'

'Please?'

Guilt scored a line across his gut.

'I'll get the guys to sit outside the door?'

'What, Trill and Coma-boy?' she snorted. 'Useful as a chocolate teapot, those boys. One's hyperactive and the other one has all the personality of a lettuce.' She made a face. 'I need you, Kenny. I only feel safe with you.'

'Okay. Okay,' he said as she buried her head into his chest again.

A muffled, 'Thank you.'

• • •

A few days later, they were on the sofa. Alexis had her head on his lap and was sleeping. From there he could see that the swelling had reduced a good deal and the bruises were shifting colours. She didn't look quite so freaky as she did when she first turned up on his doorstep.

Kenny had been online and ordered a delivery of groceries, he'd also visited every website he knew and he was now about to crawl up the wall with boredom and forced inactivity. He couldn't take much more of this. He needed to do something. He needed some exercise. He needed to find the fucker who hurt Alexis.

He phoned his cousin.

'Ian. How's your mum?'

'Awright, mate. Getting there.'

'I can just see that on her medical report. That'll help the docs get her back on her feet.'

'Sarcasm is the lowest, mate.'

'It's either that or I pull you through the phone lines and bitch-slap you until you give me some real information.'

'In periods of tension I always recommend some exercise. Or a wee session of self-love, Kenny. You clearly are in need of one. Or both.'

'Meanwhile, I know nothing about Aunt Vi.'

'She's... they're not quite sure yet. She's stabilised a little, but she's not totally out of danger. On several monitors and drips. The doctors just need time.'

'Thank you. Was that so hard?'

'Oh, and my old man never wants to see you again.' There was a smile in Ian's voice as he spoke this often-used phrase.

'Thanks, buddy,' Kenny said. His voice softened. 'You needing anything?'

'Apart from a healthy mum and some fresh weed? Nah, I'm good, mate.'

Next on his call list was Dimitri. The older man answered his phone after three rings.

'Investigations R US, how can I serve you today?'

'What's happening, Dimitri? Found anything? *Done* anything?'

'Morning, Kenny. I'm just about to send you an email. It's a mock-up of what your father might look like now.'

Kenny's laptop pinged. He opened the email and the attachment. A picture bloomed onto the screen.

'Looks a bit...'

'Like you,' Dimitri finished.

'Plastic, I was about to say. But yes, he is my old man.' It was in the broad forehead, the cant of the eyes, the line of the nose. No one could doubt he and Kenny were related. Would this be how his father had aged? Early-fifties wasn't old nowadays, he could still be fit and strong. Hair rusted grey, skin weathered into fine lines.

Might he have changed over the years? Would he still be the man the boy knew? Loud, charismatic and wearing a fuck-you confidence like a suit of armour.

'Looks good, Dimitri. Forget the milk cartons. I have another idea. Get a hold of the local newspapers in tourist country. Run an advert. Offer a reward for information.'

'We need to give them an interesting reason in the blurb.'

'How about a Canadian relative died without issue and after making lots of money? Make sure you say there's a house on the edge of a lake.'

'Why?'

'The romance of it.'

'Why, will your old man fall for it?'

'My old man will completely ignore it. I'm targeting his neighbours. They'll think they're doing him a favour,' Kenny paused while the idea took hold. 'And we'll offer a reward for information that leads to a meeting with him. £5,000. Not too much or we attract the wrong sort of attention, but enough to prod someone from being vaguely curious into activity.'

'Oh man, you're worth the watching.'

'And get a pay-as-you-go phone from the supermarket and use that as a contact number for the advert.'

'Kenny?'

'What?'

Dimitri giggled. 'I am so loving working with you.'

Kenny cut the connection and continued to stare at the photo as if it could provide all the answers.

Alexis was at his shoulder. 'What you up to?'

'Nothing.'

'Doesn't look like... hey, is that you been made to look older?'

'Yeah, cos I'm that fucking bored.'

Alexis nudged his shoulder with a fist. 'Nobody's forcing you to...'

'Sorry.' Kenny immediately regretted his irritable response. 'It's meant to be my father.'

Alexis sat down beside him. 'Oh,' she breathed. 'You never talk about him.'

'That's cos he doesn't deserve the title of father anymore.'

'Sadly, you're not the only one who can claim that.'

'Tell me about yours.'

Alexis looked to the side, considered her words. 'Distant. Busy. Excelled at making money so he spent all of his time doing it... and see how nicely you shift the focus of the conversation from you to me.' She smiled. 'You know about mine. Your turn.'

Kenny closed the lid of his computer and turned so that he was facing Alexis. 'When he was here, he was the big man, your typical alpha male. Then my mum died. Apparently by her own hand and my dad disappeared. I was twelve.'

'That's awful.' She stroked his face and he shrugged it off. Something about the action appeared contrived, as if she'd learned how to console someone from reading a pamphlet. 'What's wrong?' she asked. 'Did I offend you?'

Did she? He hadn't quite articulated to himself why he had reacted in such a way.

'I just don't like sympathy,' he said. 'Managed fine on my own all these years.'

Alexis shifted back in her seat, creating inches of space. 'I understand.' She looked wounded and Kenny re-claimed the space she offered between them.

'God, I'm such an arse,' he said while holding her. 'I've been on my own so long I don't know how to act when I'm with someone.' And there you go again with the contradictions, he thought to himself.

'Look,' he said, standing up. 'I'm going stir crazy. I really need to get some exercise. I could just go for a jog round the block a few times?'

Alexis stood up too. Her head reached the middle of his chest. She bit her lip as if coming to a decision. 'Yeah, you're right. I can't keep a big man like you cooped up in here for too long. You go have a run. Go to the gym. I'll manage.'

'I'll phone the guys to come and watch over you.'

'Oh, please. I'm safer on my own.'

Kenny reached for his phone and thumbed out a text. *I'll tell them to stay in the car and park at the entrance to the flat.*

She smiled and placed a hand on his thigh. High up on his thigh. Her thumb stretched to lightly rub at the swell of his right testicle. He felt the familiar jolt of pleasure. Blood surged to his groin.

'I could just wait for a few minutes,' he grinned.

She withdrew. 'Nah. Get to the gym. But leave some energy for me later, eh?' Her smile was almost enough to drive Kenny to take her there and then.

He drove to the gym, but once there he sat in the car park. Now that he was in position, the thought of changing, working, showering and dressing was a task requiring the dedication he didn't possess.

What the hell was happening with his life? His aunt was near death, his cousin an addict, his girlfriend was a battered prostitute and his father remained invisible. It was too much. He could almost understand why some people sold out and vanished.

A knock at the window disrupted his thoughts. He turned about to give whoever it was a mouthful of fucks.

'Oh, it's you, Liam,' he acknowledged his friend. Then motioned him into the car.

Liam opened the door and slid into the seat. 'You alright, mate? You don't look so good.'

'Ah, Liam. What I wouldn't give for a flight ticket and a villa in Spain right now.'

'I've a flat in Rothesay. How does that sound?' Liam offered. 'Doesn't quite have the ring of Valencia, but it's yours if you want it.'

'Nah, you're okay, mate.' Kenny offered a smile. 'Don't bother with me. I'm just feeling sorry for myself.'

'Needing to offload?'

'Fuck off, Liam. I'm Scottish and therefore way too sober to be talking about feelings for chrissake.'

'Oh, go on. Subvert the national cliché. Tell me what's on your mind.'

'Here's the short version...' And ten minutes later Kenny was still talking. He told him everything, simply stating the facts without gilding them with emotion or judgement. There was silence in the car when he eventually stopped, disrupted only by a bleep from Liam's phone. He apologised, looked at the screen and tapped out a very quick response.

'Fuck me,' said Liam. 'You don't have your troubles to seek.'

'Or much of a solution.'

'So, this prostitute... she's the one you met with Tommy Hunt the other day?'

'Yup.'

Liam laughed. 'What I would have given to have been there. I heard you put him in his place.'

'Yeah, I doubt he's been spoken to like that since he was in his nappies.' Kenny chuckled.

Liam punched him on the knee. 'You're a mad bastard, O'Neill.' He paused. 'Seriously. If you want my place in Rothesay for a week or so, it's yours. We only use it for the odd weekend.'

'Thanks, buddy. I'll give it some thought,' Kenny said, but his face said it wasn't going to happen.

'Yeah,' said Liam slowly. 'You won't. Anyway, your problems will still be here when you get back.'

'And I wouldn't want to be too far away if Aunt Vi took a turn for the worse.'

'You know what they say, Kenny: the best way to get past something is to go through it.'

'Yeah, thanks for that, Mr Homespun Wisdom.'

'Just call me homey for short.'

Kenny laughed. 'Anyway, fuck off. I've a workout to get through.'

By the time Kenny had finished his session at The Hut, dusk was falling. He exited the gym door with a sense of satisfaction that had been missing the last few days. He felt alive, relaxed and ready to take on anything life vomited into his path.

The car park was a large rectangle, lit by street lamps and shared with a DIY outlet at the far end of the rectangle. There weren't many cars nearby. Monday nights at this time of year were never popular for gym-bunnies or DIY enthusiasts. A crushed can of cola was at his feet and he kicked it across the park. The can echoed its ring around the space.

His hair was damp but he was warm in the early evening chill. He carried his bag in one hand and his jacket in the other. The streets around him were quiet. All the people who worked in the nearby offices and shops would be home eating their dinner. It was only ne'er-do-wells like himself who were out and about.

Walking to his car, he studied a couple of other cars parked next to him. Top of the range Ford and a VW Golf. Boy-racers' cars. Wankers. The urban landscape was full of young lads driving their souped-up people-pleasers, trying to impress their pals and young girls with their wheels. Must waste a shitload of petrol, going round in circles too fast.

He laughed at himself. That sounded like something his Uncle Colin might say. He reached the can again and gave it another kick. He was looking forward to getting back to the flat and finishing off his workout on top of Alexis.

Something sounded just behind him. Another gym member going to his car, he thought. Or not. A warning signalled in a deep part of his brain. Instinct made him turn and duck. It wasn't quite enough. A blow from a blunt weapon caught him on the side of the head. He stumbled. Don't fall, he told himself. Fall and you're done.

'What the...'

His sight was blurred. He could make out the wide shoulders of a grey figure above him and brought up his arm in a defensive move. Something flashed. Connected. He heard a loud snap. Screamed. The pain in his arm was incredible. His vision flared and sharpened to the view of his arm dangling at a strange angle before another blow to his temple and the light caved to a pinprick. And died.

41

Mason Budge was thinking that if he had a Facebook page he'd be making an entry around now that would read, '**Mason Budge** wonders if life could get any better!' He might even add another couple of exclamation marks to that.

All of his plans for the boss were coming along nicely. He had Kenny O'Neill on the rack and he'd even managed to give his girlfriend a real good time. Now if he could manage to get the lovely Kenny into the same prone position he wouldn't rule out giving him exactly the same treatment.

Fist and cock could be an even more potent mix when used on a man. And let's face it, the sexual rush – and jeez, was it a rush – came from the power, not the body he was fucking.

Yes. The bold Kenny wouldn't be quite so fucking confident if that were to happen to him. He should speak to the boss and see if he could make that part of the plan.

He picked his phone from his breast pocket and dialled a number.

'Yes?' was the terse, frightened answer. There was still a note of defiance though and Budge loved a little bit of defiance. Made him horny as all hell.

'Alexis, babycakes,' he said. 'Walk to the window and look down onto the street.' He waited a moment and then spotted her pale face leaning out from behind a curtain. He could see her spot him and then look up the street at a car parked at the entrance to the flat. Nice, thought Budge. That was an interesting glance. Told him exactly where he should be looking. He took a step closer to the car and made out the form of two young men in the front seats. He nodded to himself, this could get interesting. A nice little diversion could be in order. The guys looked barely out of their teens; he could take them out as easily and with as much emotion as he might trim a nail. And where's the fun in that?

'You can't be here, Budge. Kenny will be back any second.' Her voice was sharp, distant. To see her mouth move and the words come from the small machine in his hand gave him a buzz.

'Say something else, Alexis.'

'What are you on, you madman? Go away. Kenny can't see you.' She ducked behind the curtain as if the sight of him was too much.

'Correct,' he said. 'Kenny can't see me.'

'Right.' Alexis paused as if trying to gauge his meaning. 'So why the hell are you standing across from his building?'

'Aww, you know. I was passing. Thought I should say hi to my favourite girl.'

Her breath was ragged. Her fear reached him through the phone, warming his heart. 'Please, Budge. I've done everything you asked. I'm doing everything you ask.'

'So what's fresh, what's new?'

'Kenny's not in. He's gone out to the gym. But he will be back shortly. So piss off and leave me alone.'

'Such a potty mouth on such a beautiful young lady. I should come up there and wash your mouth out with my cock.'

'I have a knife, you bastard. And I will use it.'

Mason loved the way her accent sounded on the word bastard. 'Alexis, don't be so harsh. We really could be such good friends.'

'Apart from trying to torture me, what the hell do you want?'

'To remind you that you are not to let O'Neill out of your sight.' He paused to let that one drive home. 'He's not exactly in view at the moment, is he?'

'I'm sorry... he... he's not the kind of man to sit around playing nurse.'

'Well, you need to be a little more convincing then, don't you? Perhaps I should come up there and reapply some bruising?'

A whimper then she collected herself. 'I told you I have a knife. And I will use it.'

'Sure you will, babes.' He laughed. Revelling in the moment. 'Anywho, do you have anything interesting to report?'

'He's been a bit preoccupied with his sick aunt at the moment to be doing much.'

'What about his father?'

Alexis said nothing. Crossed her arms. Silence sang in his ear.

Budge added a quiet note of promised violence to his tone. 'What about his father?'

42

'So, let's go over this again, Mr O'Neill. You were walking to your car?'

'Oh fuck off, McBain, and don't look so fucking pleased with yourself.'

'Well, it's not everyday that Kenny O'Neill gets mugged. And watch your mouth.' Ray turned and smiled at a nurse who had just pulled aside the curtain that offered a modicum of privacy to the Accident and Emergency cubicle they were resident in.

She was tall and, judging by the look on Ray McBain's face, had a waist to hip ratio that was very pleasing. Her hair was thick auburn and she had large brown eyes that were looking at McBain as if to say, *You really should leave now.*

'It's okay, nurse. He's kind of a friend.'

'Didn't you get lucky?' she said to Kenny while striding over to the bed. Her shoes squeaked on the floor.

Ray laughed his big warm boom and said, 'When I die, I'm coming back as a doctor.'

'McBain, shut it. I'm in pain here, in case you haven't noticed. Do your hunting for babes in your own time.'

'I'm flattered,' said the nurse, batting her eyelids in an exaggerated manner. She was on the near side of forty and clearly looked after herself. 'It's been a long time since someone called me a babe.'

'What's wrong with my friend…' – McBain paused – '…babe?'

The nurse dismissed him with a snort, but her eyes were shining with a suppressed smile.

She turned to Kenny. 'Mr O'Neill, you have concussion so we need to keep you here for a wee while for observation. You have also broken your radius and ulna.' She turned to Ray. 'For the medically challenged, that's your forearm.' Back to Kenny. 'The good news is that it was a clean snap. No surgical intervention required. A few weeks in a plaster cast and you'll be right as rain.' Smile. She turned to include Ray in the conversation. 'Just don't be letting any daft friends graffiti the plaster.'

'Awww, miss,' said Ray. 'I've been practising drawing big willies for just this occasion.'

'Can't imagine that would be from real life,' she said.

'Ouch.' Ray grinned.

'For crying out loud, guys,' said Kenny. 'Man in pain here. Can we flirt on our own time, please?'

'Don't be such a whiner, O'Neill,' laughed Ray.

'Someone will be along shortly to apply a cast to your arm. And by "shortly" I mean anytime within the next twenty-four hours,' the nurse said and looked at Ray. 'I finish at ten.' With that, she left the cubicle as briskly as she'd entered.

'So,' said Ray, trying to hide a smug expression, 'what do you remember?'

'I remember coming out of the gym.' Kenny paused. 'Do you think she was joking when she said twenty-four hours? And by the way, if you don't wait here until ten, I'm calling Pitt Street to tell everybody that you're gay.'

'So's your face,' Ray said. 'Twenty-four hours?' He looked around himself at the pale, blue empty walls and the cream floor-length curtains. He shuddered.

'Yeah, lucky me,' said Kenny, reading his movement. 'I came out the gym. I remember walking towards the car. I heard something. My spidey senses were a wee bit slow; I knew something was up but I didn't react fast enough.' Kenny was disgusted with himself. 'I spun and ducked but it wasn't enough. The bastard caught me on the side of the head. I tried to protect myself...' He looked down at his arm. He mentally replayed his actions. 'My arm was... and then he caught me on the head again. After that, I have no idea.'

'Your wallet is still in your pocket,' said Ray. 'I checked. It has some money and a few credit and bank cards. And your phone is still in your jacket, so if someone was trying to mug you, they must have been disturbed before they could complete the theft.'

'How much money?'

'Sixty quid. In tens.'

Kenny nodded. That was just as he remembered. 'Are there any closed circuit cameras around there?' asked Kenny.

'Nope.'

'How did you get to hear about it?' By 'you' he meant the police.

'A passing good Samaritan. He didn't hang around to see if there was any reward.'

'You hear the phone call?'

Ray shook a no. 'Apparently it was a male voice. Said there was a man lying unconscious in the car park and we should get an ambulance down there asap.'

'Nothing remarkable about the caller?' Kenny asked.

'Jeez,' said Ray. 'Who's the polis here?' Pause. 'Afraid not. Typical west of Scotland accent. Male.'

Kenny slumped back onto his pillow, his face scrunched in pain.

'Want me to get the nurse back for you?' asked Ray.

'For you, or for me?'

'Don't be crass,' said Ray. 'I wouldn't let my libido get in the way of your health.' He creased his face in sympathy. 'You do look like you could take some pain relief, mate.'

Kenny breathed deeply, forced himself to relax and rode the next wave of pain. Whatever they had given him when he first arrived was wearing off and he needed more, but he wanted to keep his thoughts free and run through events leading up to his attack. A fresh set of drugs and he would remember nothing.

He went through the whole course of events again. Leaving the gym door. Walking towards the car. Kicking the can. The sound of someone approaching.

There were three strikes with a blunt weapon. Two to the head. One to the arm.

He thought some more about the gym. The place was well known locally. Well known as a place where some of the toughest bouncers in Glasgow trained. Either it was someone who didn't know the area and he was in the wrong place at the wrong time, or it was...

Kenny sat up sharply. 'I think I was targeted.'

'What makes you say that?' Ray had too much respect for Kenny's experience and hunches to dismiss them.

'The gym. Only a crazy person would attack someone who just left that gym. It's well respected as a place where some top fighters train. And nobody is going to mess with Matty the Hut.'

'Aye,' Ray nodded his head, 'unless Matty the Hut – sounds like a charmer, by the way – was in on it?'

Kenny snorted. 'Hasn't got a bad bone in his body, that man. Besides, he's a mate and I've donated loads of cash to his charity work. So he's hardly going to bash the golden goose.'

McBain winced. 'There goes a mangled metaphor. What about a passing opportunist?'

'No.' Kenny was firm on that. 'If you're an opportunist mugger then you pick someone small and vulnerable; someone who looks like prey.'

'Again. Good point.' You'd have to be drug-addled to think Kenny looked anything remotely like a victim.

'Also there was something about the way he attacked me. Once to the head and I was stunned. Unable to defend myself. My arm was out at the side when his weapon hit it. It wasn't a defensive injury... it was calculated.' He paused while the implications of this worked through his mind. 'The fucker was deliberately trying to break my arm.'

43

It was the small hours of the morning before Kenny was allowed to leave the hospital. First he called Alexis to let her know he was safe. The next thing was to call Calum and Mark. As he dialled the number he realised that Ray had in fact disappeared close to the ten o'clock mark. Right after the nurse administered some pain relief. Lucky bastard.

Mark answered and he asked him to stay on site and for Calum to come and pick him up in the car.

'Oh man,' said Mark, 'it's my car; can I no come and pick you up?'

'I have a sore head, Mark,' said Kenny. 'I need someone who hoards words like a miser stores coin.'

'Eh?' asked Mark.

'You talk too much,' replied Kenny. Now was not the time to be sparing anyone's feelings. 'Sore head. I need silence.'

When Calum arrived, Kenny opened the car door and sat in the passenger seat with a relieved sigh, delighted to be leaving the hospital.

'Where to, boss?' asked Calum and Kenny could have hugged him. No questions, no chat, just a simple request for information.

'I need to eat something full of fat and calories,' Kenny thought out loud. 'A supermarket's probably the easiest place to get a cooked breakfast, without thinking too much. Find me a supermarket.'

'Okay, boss.' Calum put the car in gear and drove off. Within fifteen minutes they were in a supermarket cafeteria. Calum was drinking a black coffee, five sugars. Kenny shook his head at that one, while he cut into a plate high with sausages, bacon, black pudding and a pair of fried eggs. Which was not easy with one good hand. He washed it down with a coffee of his own, sat back in his chair and exhaled.

'Right. I feel like a human being once again.'

Calum simply sipped at his mug.

'You can speak now and again, Calum.'

The younger man shrugged. 'Confucious said that gratuitous speech was the province of the foolish.'

Kenny laughed. 'That's what I get for taking on a philosophy student.' He reached across and patted Calum's meaty shoulder. 'You sure you and Mark are related?'

'That's what the grown-ups tell us,' he replied and twitched his face in a brief smile.

'I'm going to need a driver' – Kenny held up his plaster cast with his other hand – 'for a few weeks. You up for the job?'

Calum nodded. 'What about Mark?'

Kenny sucked on his bottom lip before answering. He did like the fella but only in small doses. A smile stretched his face as he imagined the complaints from Alexis when he set Mark as her protector. He needed to find out what the hell was going on and sitting in the flat with Alexis was going to get him nowhere.

There was also the issue of his father. He was still as determined to find the man, regardless of the mess his life was in.

He called Alexis.

'Babe.' She started crying almost immediately she heard his voice and his stomach lurched in response.

'Nothing else has happened, has it?' he asked.

'I need you here. Where the hell are you?'

'I've got stuff to do, so I'm going to send Mark up to sit with you...'

'The hell you are.' She recovered quickly, such was her irritation.

'He's a boring twat. I need you, Kenny. You need to be here.' There was a strong taste of panic in her voice.

'You need to be patient with me, Alexis. Let Mark in. Make him a coffee and I'll be there before you know it.' He cut the connection before she could complain any more.

Next he called Ray McBain.

'Meet me for a coffee?' he asked.

'Yeah, cos crime has paused for the day to allow me the chance of a cappuccino with my mate.'

'Sarcasm is the lowest,' said Kenny. Wondered where he'd heard that recently. Ian. Shit, he'd forgotten all about Vi. 'Have you got the time or not?'

A pause while Ray held his phone out in front of him to check the hour. Kenny wondered how everyone managed before this piece of technology took over lives.

'As luck would have it I'm out and about today. Meet me at eleven. Starbucks in Byres Road?'

While walking back to the car, stomach heavy with his breakfast, he called the next on his list of contacts.

'Good morning, Dimitri and O'Neill. Your problem is our problem. How can I help?'

'Dimitri, do you stay up all night to practise these greetings?'

'Yeah, and you're the only schmuck that phones. How sad is that?' Dimitri laughed.

'Okay,' said Kenny. He was resigned to Dimitri's permanent good mood. 'Enough of the jibber-jabber. Any news?'

'Yeah. There's a couple of newspapers ready to run with the ad. I've sent a pdf to you by email. Not had a chance to see it yet?'

'Not had a chance to do much, mate. Long story. Can't be arsed telling it.'

'Fine.' Dimitri brushed off Kenny's brusqueness. 'I have the pay-as-you-go phone we're using for any callers. You want to keep it?'

'Aye. I'll be by some time later on today; you can give it to me then.' He hung up and almost collided with a teenage girl pushing a pram. She was about five feet six, skinny as a pole-dancer's pole and dressed in a pair of jeans and a cropped T-shirt that displayed the ring through her belly-button.

'Sorry,' Kenny said.

The girl said nothing, simply looked at him through her fringe. The woman with her, possibly her mother, was dressed identically, but she had a good deal more flesh for her piercing to cling to. The mother, who was holding the hand of a small blonde boy, gave Kenny an appraising smile.

As the small family group walked on, the child made a break for independence. His grandmother shouted him back.

'Kai, ya wee bastard, come back here.'

Just before Kenny shut his car door he heard the girl remonstrate with her mother. 'Mum, I wish you wouldn't talk to him like that.'

'Well, he is a wee bastard, isn't he?'

'Oh my God,' the teenager said. 'You are unbelievable.' And stomped away from her mother to retrieve the boy.

Kenny looked at Calum. 'Well, that wee tableau didn't work out quite the way I expected.'

Calum raised an articulate eyebrow. 'Where to now?'

• • •

The Starbucks on Byres Road was right next to the Hillhead underground station. Calum stayed with the car while Kenny went off for his meeting. He walked in the shop and looked around for Ray. The room was small and dark and crowded with students. Some were hunched over books, others over laptops and some were hunched over each other.

He climbed the stairs at the back to find himself in a larger space with more light and some low sofas. Ray McBain sat at one with two large cups and a chocolate muffin on the table in front of him.

'I had to threaten someone with deportation to get this seat,' he said to Kenny. 'Hurry up and sit down before someone else claims it.'

Kenny sat down on the sofa beside Ray and, turning to face him, their knees brushed against each other.

'Cosy,' said Kenny. 'Good job I don't mind my personal space being violated.'

'How's the arm?' Ray asked as Kenny reached for his coffee mug.

'Oh, you know. Broken.' Kenny made a face. 'How's the nurse?'

'Oh, you know, glad she finally met a real man.'

'So she got to meet Little Ray, did she?'

'I like to call him Ray of Sunshine.' Ray grinned.

'There's an often-used line if ever I heard one.'

'And yet I never tire of using it.' Ray tore a piece of sponge from his muffin. 'So, that's the social niceties dealt with, what you wanting?'

'Did you ever get anyone for that prostitute that was killed in my "friend's" flat?'

Ray shook his head and sat forward. '*You* got any information on that?'

'Nope.' He paused, wondering just how much to tell Ray. He accepted that there always had to be a fair exchange but he wanted to find the crazy fucker who was hurting Alexis and deal with him on his own. Outside of legal constraints. 'My friend, the one who lived in that flat, is currently staying with me.'

'You need to bring her in, Kenny, she's a possible witness.'

'She wasn't there when it happened. Besides, she's terrified. This fucker has battered her twice already. If you force her to give a statement, she'll be on the next plane to whichever South American country speaks French.'

Ray chewed on another mouthful of muffin.

'Your body is a temple,' said Kenny.

'Temple of Doom,' replied Ray. 'Ah, the old jokes are the best. You think the beating you got the other night has anything to do with whatever is going on with your friend?'

Kenny shrugged. 'I wouldn't rule anything out.' Another sip of his coffee. 'What about that young pro that died the other night?'

Ray twisted his expression into a question mark.

'There was an overdose the other night from this strong batch of heroin that's apparently powdering our streets,' Kenny explained.

'You think that wasn't an overdose?'

'Her number was on Alexis' mobile. I called her behind Alexis' back. Went to meet her to see if she knew anything about the people Alexis was working for. That very night, she died.'

'Could be a coincidence?' As he said it Ray's expression matched Kenny's. Neither of them put too much stock in such things. Ray sat back in his seat and considered Kenny's comments. 'I think I might have a quiet word with the autopsy guys and see if there is anything out of the ordinary.' He twisted in his seat and his knee knocked against Kenny's again. He smiled and raised his eyebrows. 'We'll have to stop meeting like this.' He clasped his hands in front of his gut, noticed Kenny noticing the size of his gut. 'Shut it,' he said, 'I'll go jogging this weekend.'

'Aye, and then have a haggis supper to celebrate.'

'It's all about a balanced lifestyle, buddy.'

'So if you get any information that's contrary to the old junkie overdose story, you'll let me know?'

'If you get anything on the guy who's doing this, you'll let me know?'

Kenny nodded.

'Fucking liar,' said Ray. 'If you go after this guy on your own, I can't protect you from the law, Kenny.'

Kenny grimaced. Ray was far too clever at times.

'What about your dad?' Ray asked. 'You any closer to finding him?'

For the next few minutes Kenny filled Ray in on recent events. Minus any mention of Harry Fyfe. Once he'd finished talking, Ray looked at him, saying nothing, as if making his mind up about something.

'I know you went to see Harry Fyfe.'

Fucker. Kenny said nothing. What could he say?

'Trust is like your virginity, Kenny. You can only lose it once.'

Ray's expression was unreadable.

'Oh, can the lecture,' Kenny said, shifting in his seat. He looked at his mug and the coffee stains that ringed the inside. He wondered at the timeline between rings. Two minutes between that mouthful and the next one. He looked back at Ray.

'Let me help you out here, Kenny,' Ray said. 'You say to me, "I'm sorry, Ray, it will never happen again."'

'Right.' Kenny loosened his tie a little. 'Sorry.'

'And the rest, Kenny?'

'Fuck off, ya prick. I said I was sorry.'

Ray grinned. 'Man, I'm having a good couple of days. I get to see Kenny O'Neill beaten up and then I get to make him squirm.'

'Want another coffee?' Kenny asked, trying to change the subject.

'And don't change the subject,' said Ray, punching his good arm.

'Hey, mate, I'm under a lot of pressure here.'

'This thing... this advert in the papers with your dad's photo in it. You think it will work?'

'It's got to,' Kenny replied. 'If someone doesn't want to be found, it can be nigh on impossible to find them.'

'Are you not worried that it could all go horribly wrong?'

'Well, if it turns out my dad's an arse then I'll just not see him again, but I've got to try, Ray.'

'That's not what I mean, Kenny.' Ray paused for a couple of beats. 'In the letters, your dad said that he had to disappear to keep you safe. What if bringing him back into your life resurrects all that bad stuff that made him vanish in the first place?'

'Well, for one... no, because who holds a grudge for over eighteen years? And for two, I'm a big boy. I can look after myself.'

Ray thought about that for a moment before replying. 'One, you forget I'm a policeman and believe me people can hold a grudge for a lifetime. And for two...' he looked at Kenny's arm – 'Right now you're a wee bit disabled.'

44

When Kenny returned to the flat, Mark's face was so bright it looked like he'd been slapped around the room. Desperate to leave. Alexis simply sat on the sofa, feet under her, arms crossed and her view locked on to the TV.

'Good. Great. You're here,' said Mark, looking from Kenny to Alexis. He made a face to Kenny as if to say, *I tried, I really tried.*

'Yeah, I'm here and you can go. Calum's waiting in the car for you,' Kenny said while handing Mark some cash. 'Let me walk you out.'

They walked in silence to the front door. Kenny opened it and as Mark brushed past him on the way out he said quietly, 'Man, she might be a stunner, but she's hard work.'

'You didn't argue?'

'She uses too many big words, boss. I don't know if she's talking about the weather or if she's insulting me.'

'Thanks anyway, Mark.' Kenny patted his shoulder. 'I appreciate your help.'

Mark brightened as if he had expected Kenny to kick his arse on the way out. 'Nae bother, boss. Any time.'

Alexis was standing by the living room door, arms crossed, expression a mix of concern and irritation.

'The arm?' she asked as if afraid to.

'Broken.' Kenny replied as he walked towards her.

'I know that, you idiot.' She stretched on to her tip-toes and kissed his cheek. 'Are you okay? And don't go all macho on me.'

'I've had worse,' Kenny said and sat down on the sofa. He opened the box he'd picked up from Dimitri that contained his new mobile. He emptied out all of the different elements in the package, inserted the phone's sim card and then plugged the phone in for a charge. And was more than pleased that he'd managed to do it all with just one hand. While he was carrying out these actions, Alexis maintained her silence.

Then he opened his laptop, signed in to his email account and downloaded the advert that Dimitri had organised.

'Do you think it will work?' asked Alexis.

Kenny put his hand across her shoulder and drew her closer. 'God, I hope so. Don't know what I'll do if it doesn't.'

Alexis reached up and kissed his cheek. 'I hope so too, honey.'

And again Kenny thought this was a moment that ordinary people might share. If only they were just like everybody else. He returned her kiss, pressing his lips against the cool silk of her cheek for a few moments. He felt the side of her face push against his lips as she smiled.

'So what's the plan again?'

'We have the advert. We offer a reward for information. People phone it' – Kenny picked up the phone and showed it to her as if he was acting in a TV ad – 'and hey presto, my father is found.'

'You do look alike.' She gazed at the photo. 'I can see where you got your beautiful eyes.'

'Flatterer.'

'I never just flatter, Kenny. If I don't see it, I don't say it.'

'Even if you are with some old fart who doesn't know a clitoris from an elbow?'

Alexis stiffened. 'Please don't talk about my work, Kenny. It makes me feel uncomfortable.'

'Sorry, babes. I didn't mean to...'

Alexis shifted closer to him. 'S'okay. I'm... I just... this is just so not like me. I'm usually confident and know exactly what I want. I hate feeling so needy.'

'Hey, honey. No worries,' said Kenny and kissed her forehead. He understood her frustrations. 'We'll get you through this, okay?'

Smile. 'Okay.'

'Things are on course as far as finding my father. Now I just need to find out who has been bashing you about and teach them a lesson.'

Alexis reached over and stroked his hand just at the edge of his plaster cast. 'Are you really in the right shape to be teaching that kind of lesson?'

Kenny snorted. 'I've fought with worse than this.'

'Please, Kenny. Be careful.' Alexis' face was tight with worry. 'If something happened to you...' A tear shone on her cheek. Kenny wiped it away with the back of his hand. He held her face in both hands and kissed her slowly on the lips. His chest tight with emotion.

'You want to...?' Alexis asked with a small smile.

'Hell, yes,' said Kenny, picking her up and carrying her into the bedroom.

Afterwards, they lay side by side, both of them staring at the ceiling, waiting for their pulses and breathing to slow.

'Well, aren't we the married couple?' laughed Alexis. 'We made it through to the bedroom before tearing each other's clothes off.'

'Yeah,' said Kenny with a voice that suggested he was on the edge of sleep. 'That was nice.'

'Nice?' said Alexis as she propped herself up on an elbow. 'I think I'm much better than nice.'

'Och, you know what I mean,' said Kenny. 'Anyway, "nice" is a word that has a bad press. There's nothing boring or dull about nice. Life would be a lot better if we all had more access to nice.'

'That you finished your little discourse?'

'Aye,' Kenny laughed. 'After our next session we will discuss the etymology of the word "interesting".'

Alexis turned on her side, her back to Kenny inviting him to spoon into her. He placed his good arm under the pillow Alexis had her head on and his broken arm he kept outside the covers but draped over her side.

'God didn't think much about lovers cuddling up when he designed the whole arm thing, did he?' Kenny asked as he lined his stomach against her back, genitals against her soft buttocks and knees into the back of her knees. Every part of the front of his body was in contact with her. He closed his eyes and savoured the moment.

'Jesus, Kenny,' said Alexis. 'You getting horny again?'

'Just ignore me,' he grinned into her hair, grinding his growing penis against the swell of her.

'I'm so sorry, Kenny.' she said. 'I just don't have the same energy I usually have.'

'Don't worry, babes.' Kenny willed his erection into softness and allowed himself to slump back into the near-sleep he was enjoying moments before. 'Just chalk it up to one more injury we have to do to this guy Mason Budge.'

'What?' Alexis turned to face him.

'Mmm?' Kenny asked.

'Where did you hear that name?'

Her urgency pushed Kenny away from sleep. 'I... eh... did you not tell me?' Shit, he thought, he was still to tell Alexis about his meeting with Jo Connelly.

'No. How could I tell you when I didn't know his name?'

'And how do you now know that's his fucking name?'

'What? You're confusing me.' She sat up and twisted round on the bed so that she was facing him down on the pillow. 'What aren't you telling me, Kenny?'

'I've told you everything now, Alexis,' he answered. The quilt had slumped to crumple around her waist, exposing her breasts. Kenny stared. He could stare at their twin perfection for days.

'Stop looking at my tits.' Alexis pulled the quilt up to cover herself. Kenny pulled it back down, wearing a greedy grin.

'Gorgeous,' he said.

With a toss of her hair she gave up on trying to stop him staring.

'I'm up here, Kenny,' she said. 'What haven't you told me?'

'You know everything, Alexis.'

She started crying. 'My life's in danger, Kenny. Don't you think I deserve to know what's going on?'

'Don't cry, honey.' Kenny got up onto his knees and positioned himself in front of her. He pulled her head onto his shoulder. Like every other male, he couldn't take the sight and sound of a woman in tears. 'Of course you deserve to know...' He considered his words carefully. 'I found out the name of some of the girls who work out of the same area as you. I described the guy who followed us to Balquhidder, along with the North American accent, and they came up with the name of Mason Budge.'

Alexis was shivering in his arms. Kenny picked up the side of the quilt and tried to drape it around her shoulders.

'We need to know who this guy is. I need to know who his boss is and you have not exactly been forthcoming in giving me the information.'

'That's because the minute... no, the second, I tell you we are both dead.' Alexis lifted her head up, anger flashed in her eyes. 'I'm terrified for my life.' She jumped off the bed and with small quick steps started moving around the room, hunting for her clothes. She began wriggling into her trousers with one hand whilst holding her other arm across her breasts. Kenny climbed off the bed and unmindful of his nakedness walked towards her.

'Alexis, I'm just saying...'

'You're saying you don't trust me.' Her face was bright with fury.

'I'm saying you're not helping me very much.' Kenny replied. 'I had to hunt down these prostitutes to try and find this guy and then there's Jo Connolly.'

'Who?'

'Don't fucking lie to me, Alexis. I got her number from your mobile phone.'

'You did what? That's private information, you bastard.' She raised a hand as if she was going to slap him. He caught her wrist and his eyes flashed a warning.

'I got her number from your phone. I met her the other day. She gave me Budge's name and what do you know, she's dead soon after.'

She said nothing. Simply stared at him.

'And then I see her face on the telly and what do you say?' Kenny pretended to consider. 'Oh, yes. You said you had never seen her before in your life. What the fuck is going on, Alexis?'

'You can say what the hell you like.' Alexis now had a jumper on and was scouring the floor for her shoes. 'But you can say it to an empty room because I am out of here.' She stamped towards the living room.

'Don't be stupid,' Kenny said, following her. 'Where are you going to go?'

'Somewhere I won't be insulted.' She located her shoes at the side of the sofa and picked them up.

'Don't be stupid, Alexis. There's more at stake here than your pride.'

'Of course there is, you moron.' She swung round and faced him. 'These men have raped me, they've battered me and they're not going to stop until I'm selling blowjobs for a fiver down at the Buchanan Street bus station. So, if you're going to help me, help me, Kenny. Trust me. Don't accuse me of lying to you.'

Standing in front of him, her face pale with fear, her hair in damp strings around her forehead and her shoes in her hand, she had never looked so vulnerable. Kenny felt like a prick.

He exhaled, all fight left him.

'I said I would help you and I will help you.' He softened his voice and held his arms out. Her bottom lip trembled, she sighed. Once. Twice. And walked into his offered hug.

'Kenny, you've got to trust me. I'm terrified and you're all I've got.'

45

The long street stretched into silence. The rain was so light it seemed to suspend in the air as if asking for permission to fall. Sandstone tenements hung over him like guardians and cars lined the street bumper to bumper. The streets were switched to 'hush' before alarm clocks sounded throughout the city. This was Kenny's favourite time of day.

The only noise was the slap of his shoes on the road and his breath sounding an even rhythm. He couldn't understand why anyone would run at any other time.

Ahead he heard the high-pitched squeal and rattle of a shop-keeper's metal shutters being forced up. Then he saw an old man step out from the doorway and pick up a pile of newspapers.

'Morning,' he greeted Kenny as he straightened his back, his arms full of today's news.

Kenny nodded a reply and strode on. The old man glanced at his arm as if to ask whether he should be out running with such an obvious injury, but there was no way Kenny could sit on his arse any longer. Exercise was his drug. He clearly couldn't go to the gym and the rhythm of his running didn't cause any pain to his arm, so he'd laced up his shoes and gone out to pound the streets. Alexis had insisted she could cope without a babysitter if he was only gone for an hour, so he hadn't bothered to phone Mark. Let the boy have his beauty sleep, he sure as fuck needed it.

It had been a week since he bought the phone and posted the

advert and he'd heard nothing. Apart from a bunch of weirdos trying to earn a quick buck.

'That's my mate Danny,' a man with a soft Highland accent told him. 'He's living in Australia. What's the capital? Perth, aye, that's where you'll find him. Now, how do I get my money?'

'The money is paid for information leading to this man being found. If you just give me your address, I'll let you know how your information works out.'

'Aye, but you give me the money and then I'll give you the address,' the caller countered.

Kenny felt irritation sour his jaw. 'I need to check the validity of the information before I pay out.' In his mind he added, *you fuckwit*.

'Aye. Right,' the man said. 'Never thought of that.' The man spoke the address slowly as if reading it out, or making it up. Kenny pretended to write it down and then hung up.

One woman rang and asked him. 'How do I ken you're no going to keep the money for yoursel'?'

'It is my money,' he answered. 'So I would have nothing to gain by that.'

'I don't trust you people,' she said and then closed the connection. So far, he'd counted sixty-four calls and each one was stranger than the last.

One woman asked him for the real story. It was after ten o'clock, Kenny was sleepy after a session of lovemaking or he might have just hung up. His caller sounded fairly young and her words were clear and pronounced as if she was acting the part on behalf of someone else. Perhaps she was trying to disguise herself over the phone, he thought.

'The real story is as shown in the advert,' Kenny answered.

'I can sense there's more to this,' she said. 'Why don't you tell me the real story and I'll see if I can help you?'

Kenny moved the phone away from his face and read the display. The caller had hidden their number.

'The real story is in the advert,' Kenny insisted.

'In that case,' the woman said, 'I'll leave you in peace. I'm sorry to have disturbed you.'

'Wait,' said Kenny with urgency. Now that he was alert, this woman sounded saner than anyone else he'd spoken to over the last few days. 'The truth is kind of awkward. I need to find this man. He's family and that's all I want to say at this point.'

The woman said nothing. Kenny allowed the silence to fill his ear.

'Do you look like him?' she asked eventually.

'Sorry?' Kenny was completely taken aback.

'I'm not stupid, son,' she said. 'I can read between the lines. There's a lot of kids in the world looking for their fathers. Where do you live?'

'Glasgow. In the West End.' He wasn't sure why he answered so truthfully. It just felt like the right thing to do.

'Nice,' she said. 'Are you happy, son?'

Kenny felt his throat tighten at the sympathy from this stranger.

'Life has its moments.'

'You sound nice, son. I hope you find your father.'

She hung up.

That was two days ago and each time the phone rang he hoped it would be her again. Instinct told him that there was more to the call, but without a number or more of a conversation he had absolutely nothing to go on.

In the meantime he'd also been scouring his contacts for the whereabouts for a certain Mason Budge. Nobody knew nothing. There's a double negative for you, thought Kenny. Lots of people know something, they're just too scared to say anything.

He was also no nearer finding out who Budge's boss was. His favourite so far was Tommy Hunt and that was where he was headed this morning after he'd showered and changed. The man lived in a big house over in Pollokshields and he was going to get a flask of coffee, a bottle to piss in and sit and watch the man for as long as it took to find out what he was all about.

• • •

An hour later, he was sitting outside the man's house in Albert Drive. Looking around himself at the blonde, sandstone mansions that stretched along the street, Kenny wondered what the hell he was doing living in a tenement flat. This would be a much better way to spend his money.

Well, maybe not, he thought as he noted a female neighbour across the road walk towards a BMW 4x4 while studying his. In the crush of humanity that was his street, he had a certain amount of anonymity. Here, the yummy mummys would be discussing his every move after they had dropped off their spoiled brats at the nearest private school in their giant lumps of glossy metal.

You drive for twenty minutes a day, thought Kenny, why the hell do you need a machine the size of a house to do it in?

He returned his view to Hunt's home. The curtains were open at each of the windows, but he could see no movement beyond them. The garden was contained by a waist-high wall and pillars stood at either end of the gate into the short pebble-filled drive. The house itself had large windows and half a dozen steps up to a grand front door. To the side of the house was a double garage, in front of which rested a red Porsche and a silver Mercedes. The whole set-up was there to demonstrate wealth.

Above the bay window next to the front door Kenny spotted a small black box pinned to the sandstone that bore the legend, *Burglar Alarm.*

Hunt probably had another large house in the Trossachs for the weekends and a villa in Marbella that he saw once every four years when he convinced himself he needed a holiday. This was likely just a wee pied-à-terre where he could rest his head between business meetings.

Kenny poured a small espresso from his silver flask and sipped the warm, bitter fluid. He looked at the clock on his dashboard. Seven fifteen. He looked up and down the street. There was little traffic and most of the houses were starting to stir now. He wasn't comfortable here. Too visible. All it needed was some Neighbourhood

Watch fanny to note his registration number and he was in a file at the local police station. And these were all wealthy taxpayers – the local plod wouldn't ignore their complaints.

Praying that Tommy Hunt was an early riser, Kenny sipped at his cup and kept his eyes on the man's house.

Fifteen minutes later he had his reward. He heard the big door open, the thud of as it closed. Feet crunched across gravel and Hunt was reaching his car. There was no tell-tale set of bleeps before he shut the door. Unless the control box was further inside the house, Hunt hadn't set any alarm. Could the alarm box be a fake?

Hunt was wearing a grey, single-breasted suit with a white-shirt and blue-tie combo. How fucking boring is that, thought Kenny. White shirt, blue tie. Lots of cash, no imagination. Hunt shouldered his way out of his jacket, opened the back door and picked a coat hanger from the seat. No creases for our Tommy. Jacket duly cared for, Hunt sat in the driver's seat, fired up the engine and the Mercedes coasted up the short drive.

Luckily for Kenny, Hunt took a left so he didn't have to duck down to avoid being seen. He turned on his own ignition and slipped into the traffic a few cars behind.

As he drove he thought about Alexis and her face when he asked Mark to sit with her for the day. It was quite impressive the way a simple shift of the eyes and lift of the eyebrow could spell out the words, *You bastard*.

Calum had classes at university so Kenny was on his own. Which was fine. The pain had eased off considerably and he had the use of his fingers in that hand to help with the steering.

Keeping Hunt in his view, but staying two cars behind, Kenny followed the Mercedes to an industrial estate in Hillington. Large, long buildings with lurid signs squatted on each side of the road before Hunt took a left. Here was a row of office buildings, prim in trimmed grass. Hunt drove to the second one and slid into the parking space nearest the door. Kenny drove past, cut a u-turn and came back in time to see Hunt walk through a double glass door.

He kept on driving. Hunt was a grafter; chances are he would be there until six that evening, which gave him the whole day.

Worried that the curious neighbours might recognise his car from earlier, Kenny drove across to Dimitri's and borrowed his car.

'Morning, boss,' said Dimitri. He was at his desk, two blue folders in front of him and two books. One had a large oak tree on the cover and bore the title *People Finding*.

Kenny picked it up and read the back cover. 'Really?' he asked Dimitri.

'There's all different ways to skin the cat, boss.'

'Fair enough,' said Kenny. He reached forward and picked up one of the folders. He emptied the contents carefully on to the desk and examined the folder: blue plastic and containing a notepad and black pen.

'This will do nicely,' he said and tapped Dimitri on the head with it.

'No bother, boss,' Dimitri said, wearing an annoyed expression. 'Just you help yourself. What the feck do you need that for?'

Kenny tapped the side of his nose. 'I'm about to break into a man's house.'

'And you're going to what, knock him out with a sheet of blue plastic?'

Kenny winked. 'There are many ways to skin a cat, Dimitri.'

His next stop was to a double-glazing outlet he spotted on the way over to Dimitri's. Just in the front door was a stand with a display of brochures. He flicked through them deciding which was going to be best for his cover. He spotted one that was about alarm systems. Picked up half a dozen and placed them in his folder. As he was leaving, a young salesman approached him. He was wearing a white shirt and blue and red striped tie. The knot on his tie was smaller than the Adam's apple thrusting from the boy's throat like a mini-alp.

'You swallow a chunk of Toblerone, buddy?' Kenny asked.

The boy looked puzzled, decided it might be best to ignore the question and waded in. 'We have some special offers this week, sir. Four windows for the price of three and we'll throw in a door for only two hundred quid.'

'Nah, no thanks, buddy,' said Kenny. 'I live in caravan.' He walked away, chuckling at the salesman's confused expression.

When he arrived back at Tommy Hunt's house, instead of parking out front again, he swooped into the drive and took the space that Hunt had vacated earlier. Nothing attracts attention more than someone with body language that suggests they want to be invisible. Send out the message that you really don't care who sees you – that you belong – and you become as good as invisible.

Kenny carried the blue folder in front of him, making sure it was evident. He walked to the door and knocked on it. He waited. Then he knocked again. He stepped back and scratched his head, hoping this performance was enough for anybody who might be watching.

Scrunching over the gravel, he walked over to a window and peered in. Again he scratched his head.

Back to the door. He twisted the handle and pushed. It was locked and solid. Worth a try, he thought. You never knew when people might be careless.

He stepped back from the door and opened up his folder. He wrote on his paper, *Big fucking door*. Grinned at his wit and moved over to the window. He stared up at the alarm box and pretended to take more notes. Wrote, *Yeah right*.

Walking round the house, the rear presented him with some good news. The garden was fully enclosed and bordered with large trees. Nobody could see him.

He tried the back door. Just in case. It was locked, but on the ground beside it was a group of stones and a flowerpot bursting with blooms.

No, thought Kenny, it couldn't be that easy. He picked up the stones one by one, judging their weight. The third one was much lighter. He held it up to the light, twisted and turned it until a secret compartment opened. Inside was a nice shiny key.

What a stupid arse, thought Kenny. All that money and a security system a child could get through. He unlocked the door and stepped into a large kitchen. Cupboards washed in mint green lined the walls, flanking the usual white goods and in the middle of the floor sat a large pine table and six matching chairs.

For a single guy, the place was spotless. Rounding that piece of information up, Kenny was certain Hunt had a cleaner. Or even a pair of cleaners for a place as large as this. He sent a prayer to the god of house-breakers that today wasn't their day for a visit.

The kitchen led into a large wood-panelled hall with four doors leading off it. Two of the doors were closed. He peeked into the open room. It was a lounge, carpeted in a thick dark covering and bearing two giant, white leather sofas. A bay window looked out onto the street and he held back from entering in case he was visible to anyone passing. From this vantage point it didn't look like there was anything worth seeing anyway.

Another door led to a room at the back of the house. This room was smaller and large drapes minimised the light from the window. A bookcase sat against the far wall. Another wall was filled with a giant TV screen and in the middle of the floor, facing the screen sat a pair of leather lazy-boys.

So this was where Hunt would spend his spare time, Kenny reckoned. He sat on the nearest chair. Nice. Deeply comfortable. The arm held a cluster of remote controls. He switched on the TV first. Then he judged which one might be for the DVD player and pressed play. A blonde woman with unfeasibly large, naked breasts filled the screen. She moaned and held one of her breasts to her mouth and licked at her nipple. Kenny clicked on to the next scene. The same blonde had a man between her legs. He was shirtless but wearing a pair of jeans, and Kenny could see that she was wearing a pair of panties. The man arched his back as if he was in the throes of some deep and wonderful passion. Through three layers of clothing? This guy must have been locked in a cell for the last twenty years. For fuck's sake, thought Kenny. Even the man's porn stash was boring.

He stepped over to the bookcase to see if it gave him any other clues to the man who owned this house. There was a set of leather-bound encyclopaedias, which looked like they'd never been opened. Another row of spines displayed the names of sporting greats like Ali, Best and Schumacher.

On top rested the only two books that looked as if they might have actually been read. One was *Dreams of My Father* by Barack Obama. The other was *The Girl with the Dragon Tattoo*. There's a surprise, thought Kenny. Who hasn't read those two books? Not very original is our man Hunt.

Up a wide and easy oak staircase, Kenny arrived at landing with five doors leading off it. The first three doors were bedrooms, all well appointed, but looking as lived in as they might have done the minute the decorators tidied up after themselves.

Kenny looked behind paintings, opened drawers and looked under beds. He worked through Hunt's sock drawer and looked in the pockets of all his suits, hanging in a row in his wardrobe. Everything had its place and looked like it was rarely moved from it. He was struck by the thought that this wasn't a home. It was a beautifully set up waiting room. Kenny couldn't help but feel that if you were to find a way to remove Tommy Hunt from his work, the man would simply curl up into a ball and die.

The fourth door he opened led to a study. A wide desk with a small column of three drawers at the side. The first one Kenny tried was locked. So was the next. One by one he tried them all. Every one was locked. Old school, thought Kenny.

The drawers called to him. They must be hiding something worth checking out. Jimmying them open would be the work of seconds, but might be easily discovered.

Deciding the risk was worth it, Kenny ran back downstairs for something that might be useful. In a kitchen drawer he found a set of screwdrivers. He chose the longest, thinnest one and ran back up to the study.

An old mate had given him a lesson years ago and as he sat on the leather seat at the desk, he hoped that the lesson had stuck. His friend's words sounded in his ears.

'Actually all that needs to happen is if you put something thin enough in the lock and strike upward against the tumblers then when the tumblers go up and stay up it's much easier to open the lock then you think. The only thing that makes it tricky is applying torque to the hole right where the key usually enters. Torquing the outer hole allows the tumblers to stay up, and once the tumblers are jabbed up with your object they will stay in place and the inner lock mechanism will give way. That's basically...' his mate sniffed '...the secret.'

The top drawer on the right held a pile of business cards, a ruler, some small coins and an empty wallet. Next, he tried the top drawer on the left. Pulled out a black, leatherbound A4 notepad and black pen. Flicking through the pages, he stopped when he spotted his own name. Written beside it, in it has to be said a very neat script, was Liam Devlin's name and mobile number. Under that some bullet-points.

Streetwise.

Self-made.

Trains in mixed martial arts.

No wife or kids.

Mother dead. Suicide? Father disappeared. Wider family – Colin, Violet and cousin Ian.

Kenny read the list several times. The man had been doing his research in advance of his meeting with him. Why was Liam involved? Did Hunt get the information from him?

Something niggled. He read it again. The question mark after the word 'suicide'. What the hell was that about?

Not sure if he'd learned anything of importance, Kenny left the house, locked the back door and returned the key to its hiding place.

As he walked back to the front of the house, he heard someone walking across the gravel from the direction he was heading. He stopped. Looked back at the house. Did he have time to pluck out the key, get back in and hide? Not a chance.

He surveyed the garden. Was there a tree close enough for him to hide behind?

The footsteps were getting closer. He could hear a tune. The person was relaxed, humming a song. *It's Raining Men.* Sounded female. She rounded the corner. Brassy blonde hair piled on top of her head, dead-on five feet tall, blue pinny, black leggings. Her torso was solid and chunky like a postbox, her legs spindly like a heron's.

She stopped as soon as she saw him, hand over her heart. Kenny decided to brass it out. 'Who the hell are you?' he demanded.

'I'm Mr Hunt's housekeeper.' She recovered quickly. 'Who the hell are you?'

He held his blue folder in front of him, by way of explanation. 'Excellent,' he said and smiled like she was his favourite ever customer. He strode towards her. 'Keep Safe Alarms Ltd. I had an appointment with Mr Hunt.' He stood beside her. Opened his folder to let her see his scribbles, but not long enough for her to read them. 'But he didn't show, so I thought I'd take a look around, measure up the place. Look for weak points in his security system.'

'Weak points?' she asked incredulously. 'It's a pure wonder there's no a line of junkies like them army ants, punting every last piece of gear out his house.'

'Well, here's a leaflet, honey.' Kenny handed her one that he'd picked up from the double glazing shop earlier. 'I'll get my preliminary report to Mr Hunt by the end of the week.' He studied her face for a moment. She glowed under his scrutiny, like she rarely had men this interested.

'Are you ever in The Academy?'

'Me? No.' She pushed at her hair.

'I've not seen you on the dancefloor, shaking your stuff?'

'Well, I have been known to...'

'All woman,' said Kenny, walking past her towards his car. 'You have a good day, sweetheart.' Better not overdo it, he thought and dimmed his smile a little.

Last he saw her, she was standing at the corner of the house, her hip stuck out to the side like an invitation and her hand waving him away like he was a visiting dignitary.

• • •

As he drove back to Dimitri's, he reviewed the evidence. What had he learned? Next to nothing. What did he expect? A big sign somewhere saying that Tommy Hunt was a *Bad Man and Not to Be Trusted*?

Not going to happen.

He expected to find some clues though, not an absence of anything that most people would call a life. The whole building was beautifully sterile. What manner of man lives like that?

Then it occurred to him that something else was missing from the house. Photographs. He hadn't spotted one throughout the whole house. Hunt was supposedly a grieving husband and father yet there wasn't any visual reminders of those he had lost.

Was he so controlling of his feelings that he wouldn't allow himself a moment to reflect? Whatever the reason, it intrigued Kenny. It all pointed to a man who was emotionally bereft. Could a man like that run a business empire that included a stable of prostitutes?

Kenny drove back to his flat deep in thought. Managed to find a parking space about a hundred yards from his door and still working his thoughts for clues as to the machinations of Tommy Hunt.

Having already been attacked in the last few days, he was on high alert for any danger so when a man barred his path he automatically adopted a pose that would give him the greatest range of possible movement.

'I'm sorry,' the man said. 'I didn't mean to startle you.'

Kenny relaxed a little at the apology and looked at the man in front of him. He was a trim, weather-beaten five ten or eleven. His hair was down to his shoulders and woven with grey stripes. He had a row of white, even teeth winking out from behind a full beard. The smile may have been full but the eyes were hesitant.

'Hello, Kenny,' the man said, hands buried deep in his pockets, displaying more than a hint of nerves. 'It's me. Dad.'

46

Mason watched O'Neill as he strode out for his morning jog and thought to himself, what a colossal waste of fucking time. Wouldn't catch him running unless his dick was tied to a galloping horse. He waited until the man returned and left again just ten minutes later, all showered and changed, bless him. Away he drove, searching for the proverbial needle.

Budge knew that O'Neill was hunting for him; he also knew that no one was about to spill. They knew better. He waited. Budge was good at waiting. One hour. Two hours.

It was approaching noon when he dialled a number on his mobile phone.

A voice answered fearfully. 'Hello?'

'Report,' he said.

'I have nothing for you,' Alexis said. She was controlling herself well but he could taste the fear in her voice.

'C'mon, sweetheart. Two minutes and I could be at your front door.'

'I have a friend with me,' she said. 'Now is not a good time.'

'It never is, babycakes. Nonetheless, I'm sure I could persuade you otherwise.'

'Please, Mason. You already know everything.'

'I very much doubt it. Where has your fella driven off to today?'

'He has a business meeting.'

'With whom?'

'I dunno. He doesn't spill out the entire contents of his life and diary to me,' Alexis whispered into her phone.

'Why not? I thought that was your fucking job, lady.'

Silence.

'Give me something else, no matter how trivial it might seem, Alexis, or I'll be up in that flat and showing you and your bouncer boy what a good time Budge-style looks like.'

'He had a phone call the other night. A woman. She asked if he looked like his father.'

'Mmmm, that's a great big so-fucking-what. I'm on my...'

'He was also talking about his family last night. His Aunt Vi. Said she had an affair with his father years ago...'

'On my way.'

'No. He also said that his aunt is seriously ill and she confessed that her son, Ian, might be his half-brother.'

'Interesting,' said Budge. 'Not sure what I can do with it, but yes... interesting.' He could work with that. He needed to keep O'Neill continuously on edge. Never letting him settle. One nightmare situation after the other. He'd need to pay little Aunt Vi another visit. The little typed note he left for her just after O'Neill's birthday set the whole thing off perfectly.

He paused in his thoughts as a familiar car drove by and parked further down the street. Without notice, he closed his phone and his conversation with Alexis.

He watched as the driver climbed out of his car and walked towards the entrance of his flat. A man approached the driver. An older man. There was something familiar about him. The two men spoke. The older man held out a hand. O'Neill refused it.

The clues all clanged together like a peal of church bells and Budge could only think of one word that appealed in this particular situation.

Bingo.

47

They were in a pub. The older man baulked at the idea of going for a coffee.

'What, are you a fucking poof?' was his reply when Kenny suggested it.

'This is twenty-first century Glasgow. Coffee is the new booze.' Kenny almost finished his sentence with the word 'Dad' but it froze on his tongue like a lump of phlegm.

'You're talking pish, son. Coffee will never replace booze in this city. Never.'

Kenny thought about it some and decided his father was correct. He was talking pish. They walked in silence towards the nearest bar, which took up a corner position at the end of the street. Kenny walked beside his father, his gaze fixed ahead of him, but from time to time he would turn and examine the older man and measure him against the memories he had stored. His mind was also racing, wondering what had eventually forced his father out of hiding. It must have been his advert, surely?

Peter O'Neill hadn't changed much. Apart from the woodsman look he was sporting, and a few lines, he looked pretty much the same man. Each time he looked up, his father was waiting for his glance and met it with a small smile. A smile that said, *I can take whatever you throw at me – I deserve it.*

When they reached the outside of the bar, Peter pushed the door open and, walking in first, he held it open for Kenny to follow.

'What do you want?'

'I'll have a bottle of Stella Artois,' Kenny replied.

'Christ, one of those wanky designer beers...'

'If you're here looking to mend bridges, let me give you a few hints...'

'Sorry,' Peter said. 'Please. Take a seat and I'll bring the drinks over.'

By habit, Kenny took a seat with a central position in the bar. He could see down each side of the room and he could see everyone who came in the door.

'Good seat,' said Peter when he returned with two bottles of Stella. Kenny raised an eyebrow.

'If you cannae beat them,' Peter said and raised his bottle in greeting. Kenny resisted the social urge to clink bottles and offer the universal 'Cheers'. It was going to take more of an effort than the simple purchase of the same beer to get Kenny on side.

They faced each other across the table. Neither man spoke for long moments, as if questions were coin and the recession was a long way from over.

Kenny looked around the pub. It was busy. Groups of young men, young women, couples clustered around the room. Each one of them appearing certain of their place in the world. The noise of the chatter was a brightness in the room. It held the humour that Glasgow was famous for.

'Anything you want to ask, go ahead.' Peter was the first to break, his expression a mixture of apology, regret and challenge. It said, *I have treated you badly, with the best of reasons.*

'How long have we got?' asked Kenny.

'Good question. I knew you'd turn out to be a smart kid.'

'Don't do that,' said Kenny. 'Don't act like you have any right to be proud of me.'

'We have as long as you like,' said Peter, sitting back in his chair, arms by his side. He was giving his son the view that he had nothing

271

to hide. 'When's closing time?' he asked with a smile.

'So, we're not talking the rest of my life then?'

Peter shook his head slowly. 'I have other responsibilities.'

'Why did you leave?' Emotions surged within Kenny. He wanted to stand up and run out. He wanted to take both bottles and break them over his father's head. He wanted to take his father's shirt and shake answers out of the man.

The twelve-year-old inside of him wanted to run into a corner and hide and cry until his eyes were bleeding. 'Do you have any idea what it's like to be twelve and abandoned by the two people...?' The rest of his sentence stuck in his throat and Kenny tried to wash it down with a slug of beer. He choked and his father was out of his seat and thumping him between the shoulder blades.

'Fuck off,' Kenny managed to say. 'Don't fucking touch me.' He pushed him away with his good arm.

'What happened?' Peter looked at his broken one.

All sorts of answers crowded for release, but with a huge measure of will Kenny fought them back. If he wanted answers, he was going to have to calm down.

'Long story,' was the reply he settled for. 'Your letter said you had to go. Want to tell me more about that?'

Peter shook his head. 'Can't. You can ask me about anything, but don't ask about that.'

'What about the birds and the bees? What about a lecture on the use of condoms and the one about avoiding dirty women? What about–'

'I sent you letters.'

'Fuck the letters. Aunt Vi only let me see them a couple of months ago. She was frightened the sight of them would send me off the deep end.'

'God, you are so like me, son...'

'Don't call me son.'

'I can take the anger. I want your anger.' Peter's eyes blazed. A tear sparkled on his cheek. 'I can take whatever you want to deal out to me. You want to go outside and give me a pasting?' He stood up. 'That's okay with me.'

'Sit on your arse,' said Kenny. 'Even with one broken arm I could break every bone in your body.' Kenny paused. 'Tempting, but ultimately pointless.'

'You're *that* good, are you?' Peter asked with a half-smile like he wanted to test his son.

'Aye,' said Kenny, not a trace of doubt on his face. Then he exhaled, his breath long and painful. 'What *can* you tell me?'

'I re-married. A girl...' A distant smile as his mind played an image of her. 'A woman called Kathy. Kathy Garrett. She called you the other night.'

Kenny nodded. Made sense.

'She said you sounded really nice. It was her who convinced me that I should come and see you.'

'Need much convincing?'

Peter reached into his back pocket and pulled out a wallet. He opened it up and plucked two weathered photographs from the inside. Placing them on the table between them he kept talking. 'Kathy knows the dangers of me coming here and still she sent me on my way. That's the measure of her. She's a good woman.' In the first photo the colours were washed out, faded onto the fingers of the man who was positioning it on the table for Kenny to see. It was him. He was about ten years old and on his hunkers behind a football, wearing a Partick Thistle strip.

The other photo was much more recent. It showed the grinning faces of a boy and a girl. Both blonde. The boy was missing one of his two front teeth and the girl was trying to prove that she had a bigger smile than her brother.

'Nick is twelve now. Loves Rangers, to my shame. Joy is thirteen going on thirty. Been here before, that one.' Peter swept the photos back into his wallet as if afraid Kenny would rip them up. 'They're my attempt to make things right in the world.'

'And yet here I sit, a reminder of everything you did wrong.'

'Don't you think I had sleepless nights? Worried about you end-lessly? I missed you like someone had torn out one of my lungs.'

'Words, Pete. Words.'

His father shrunk at the shortened version of his name. 'I expect it would be too much to use the word "Dad".' His voice wore a coating of acceptance.

Kenny didn't answer; he simply raised an eyebrow in a what-the-fuck-do-you-think? gesture.

Peter placed his hands on the table and squared his shoulders. He exhaled. Bit down on his top lip.

'After today I can't see you again.'

The finality of it scorched through Kenny's gut. He looked away, allowed it to sink in. Swallowed. His eyes stung. His chest tight-ened. He fought the emotion. He would not give in to it. He would not let this man see he was hurting. He felt, from the moment he sat down, that this was going to be a one-off meeting and having it spelt out so honestly was almost more than he could bear.

His father reached out a hand. Silently begging for a touch. His fingertips millimetres from his son's skin. His own eyes were spar-kling with tears. Kenny withdrew his hand from the table.

'I can't, son. I can't risk it. The one compensation through all of this has been knowing my absence kept you safe.'

Kenny laughed. The sound was a harsh note that clashed with the everyday laughter that bounced around the room. 'Aye. The letters. How much of that can you explain?'

'Just what I wrote. Any more would be too much.'

'Not good enough, old man.'

'Please don't ask any more of me, Kenny.'

'You missed me as if someone had torn out one of your lungs.' Kenny repeated his father's words in a camp voice. 'I deserve more than platitudes, you cunt. I was fucking twelve!' He stood up and rushed from the pub, almost knocking a guy over in his rush to get out. The man turned to face up to him, read the look on his face and backed down.

Outside, Kenny marched up and down the pavement like he was desperate to get away, but knowing he couldn't because the thing he was trying to get away from was straddling his back. His breathing was hard and fast. He fought for control. He needed more from his father, but he wasn't going to get it if he carried on like this.

He marched back into the bar and sat in front of his father as if he had only gone off to the toilet.

'Where are you living?' he asked.

'I can't tell you that.' Peter's eyes were heavy with regret.

'Can't or won't?'

Peter reached a decision. 'Balquhidder.'

Kenny shot back in his chair. 'You're fucking kidding me?'

'No. Why?'

'I was up there not long ago. At the hotel further down the glen.'

'What made you go there?' asked Pete, shaken that they'd been so close.

Kenny shrugged. 'Memories. You took me there when I was a kid.'

'So I did,' Peter said, his view lost in the past. 'How can I ever make this up to you, son?'

Kenny shook his head. 'You can't. Or you won't?'

Peter said nothing. He met his son's challenge face on, with no answer but a legion of *I'm sorry*'s and a mountain of regret.

'I feel like getting wrecked.' Kenny stood up and looked at the bottle of beer his father had barely touched. 'Want something stronger than that pish?'

'A wee malt whisky wouldn't go amiss,' Peter replied, his face transformed with the hope of a thaw in his son's attitude. Kenny read this and almost slapped him down again. Decided there was no point and walked over to the bar.

He returned with two double whiskies and a tumbler of ice and water.

'What do you do up in Balquhidder?' asked Kenny.

'I work for the Forestry Commission. Kathy's a teacher in the local school.' He pulled a glass nearer and tipped a small amount of water into it. 'I was a mess when we met. She cleaned me up and got me on the straight...' He stopped when he read Kenny's expression. 'You're not interested in all that stuff.'

'The weird thing is,' said Kenny, 'I could never forget your face. But Mum? She vanished. A few years later and I really couldn't remember what she looked like.' As soon as Kenny thought he had dealt with his anger, something occurred to him and it flared back up again. He wasn't going to hit the old bastard, but sure as fuck he was going to make him squirm. 'Did you replace Mum as easily as you replaced me?'

'It wasn't like that. You've got to understand...'

'I don't have to understand anything.'

'I loved your mum. Truth be told, I still do.' Peter's hands were wrapped round his glass.

'Is that why you had an affair with Aunt Vi?'

Peter paused the journey of his arm as he was bringing the glass to his mouth.

'And please don't do me the disservice of trying to lie to me,' said Kenny.

'You've not made any mistakes, Kenny? You've done nothing wrong in your whole fucking life?'

'You don't get to bat it back to me, Pete. You fucked up. You get to answer for it.'

'Naw,' said Peter. 'It doesn't work like that, son. You're an adult. You know how it works. I was a silly wee boy. Full of spunk and vinegar. The world was mine and I was going to take everything I could fit in my pockets. Yes, I made mistakes and yes I've been answering for them the last eighteen years and twenty-four days.'

Kenny was unmoved. 'You had an affair with your wife's sister. How easy does that kind of betrayal come to you, *Dad*?

Peter took the blow. Breathed deep as if taking it into his lungs.

He had a penance and he was going to accept every last drop of whatever Kenny was going to throw at him. 'I was young, I was stupid. I was a powerful guy in those days. People looked up to me and it all went to my head. I wasn't a nice man, Kenny. But I've learned from those mistakes...'

'Vi is convinced that Ian is your son.'

Peter's face betrayed that he had his own suspicions all along. He shook his head, looked like he wanted to find a bridge and jump off it.

'How much shit can one man shovel in his life?' Peter asked and looked deep into the amber of the whisky. 'Did Colin take it out on you?'

'He still doesn't know. I think he knows that you and Vi had an affair and he made me suffer plenty for that over the years. If he ever found out Ian was yours, it would send him off the deep end.'

'We were good mates once. Colin was a good guy. One of the best. How's your Aunt Vi?'

'Not good. In fact, she thinks she's dying.'

'What?' Peter shot forward in his seat.

Kenny filled him in on Vi's health situation.

'Where is she?' Peter asked.

'She's in the Royal. You're not going to visit her, are you?'

'Wouldn't be safe. If they ever found out that Vi and I were close...'

'Who the fuck are "they"?'

'Kenny, please trust me on this. I can't tell you.'

'So we just hide for the rest of our lives? That's your answer?'

'Aye.'

'I say we take them on. You and me. Fuck hiding. There was a horrible accident nearly twenty years ago. Move on, for fuck's sake.'

'These people don't move on, Kenny.'

'In that case we take the fight to them.'

Peter shook his head. 'I can't anymore. I've been out of the game for too long. And you...' – he looked at Kenny's broken arm – 'you've been taken off the board.'

Kenny took in his father's words. Something was going on. Something in the wider scheme of things. Words and ideas formed in his mind and vanished before he could grasp them. Images came into focus and as he reached for them they broke up like the reflection on a pool when grabbed for by a child's hand.

He bit his lip. If only he could figure this all out. He felt like he was standing in the middle of a motorway thick with fog. A step in any direction meant danger. Or it could take him to safety.

'What did happen to your arm?' Peter asked.

Kenny explained.

Peter nodded as he listened.

'Tell me about this woman, Alexis.'

Peter studied Kenny's face as he spoke.

'You in love with her?' Peter asked.

Kenny nodded.

Peter leaned forward on to the table his head in his hands. He groaned. 'Fuck.' He stood up, looked around him wildly.

'What's going on?' asked Kenny.

'Oh my God. I've got to go.' Peter hurried to the door. Kenny followed and caught him out on the street.

'Kenny, what have you done? You fucking idiot.' Peter was striding back and forward much like Kenny was minutes before. 'This is how they work. Fuck! I've got to get home. Make sure everyone is okay.' His eyes were wild with panic.

'Will you calm the fuck down and tell me what the hell is going on?'

'Everything. Us two here. The broken arm. The prostitute. It's all part of the plan, Kenny, and they've got us exactly where they want us.'

48

Mason Budge stood in the shadows and watched the two men walk to the corner. Nice, he thought. Everything was falling into place, just as the boss suggested it would. He was a very clever man, devious as all hell, but that made it such a pleasure to work with him.

He thought of the old woman in the hospital. She'd had her uses. The stroke and the heart attack thing was just a bonus, but she'd unwittingly played her part in the whole opera beautifully. Because that was what it was: an opera minus the music and the fat bastards in black.

Movement caught his eye and it was the whore running out of O'Neill's door.

'Hey,' he shouted, 'where the hell are you going?'

Alexis' head swung round. She spotted him and her face lengthened in alarm. Then she spun and ran in the opposite direction.

'Don't make me fucking run, woman,' he shouted. 'It will be worse for you when I eventually catch up with you.' Her answer to this threat was a panicked clatter of heels on pavement as she increased her speed.

Budge caught her without too much trouble. This meant he wasn't *too* annoyed with her.

'Where do you think you're going, young lady?' he asked, holding on to her arm.

'Let me go, Budge.' Her voice was shrill. 'I can't take any more of this.'

'Need I remind you of the deal you struck with the boss?'

'I don't care.' She tried to wriggle out of his grasp. 'I don't care.'

'Stop,' Budge shouted in her face. Cowed by this display of aggression, she stopped moving and hung her head.

'You love him, don't you?' Budge asked.

'Don't be stupid.' She flicked her hair back from her face and stared defiance into his.

'Whatever,' said Budge. 'Doesn't really matter. Despite you're pathetic efforts, the final pieces are now on the board.'

'Ho!' a deep voice shouted from further up the street. 'Let her go, ya wanker.' The drum of feet and a large, broad-shouldered youth was in his face. 'Ah said let her go, fuckface.'

'Mark,' said Alexis, 'just go. You don't know who you're dealing with.'

Mark grabbed her other arm. 'No. You're coming with me. The boss trusted me to look after you. And thanks, by the way, for running away. Makes me look like a total tosser.'

'Mark, please,' Alexis said, stepping closer to Budge. 'Just go.'

'Naw, I'm no going without you. So Mr...' – he looked Budge up and down, looking for a suitable epithet – '...Mr Bawjaws can go and fuck himself.'

'Go on,' Budge said and smiled. 'Make it interesting.'

Mark was bouncing on his toes, looking from Alexis to Budge. Ready to attack.

'Mason, I'll do whatever you want. Just let Mark go,' Alexis shouted, her face a picture of panic.

Budge could read the expression on the boy's face. He was wondering why the woman was acting so scared; looking at him and thinking there was nothing to be scared of. The boy's posture read of nothing but confidence. He was sure he could take Budge.

Budge was happy to disabuse him of that notion.

The boy lunged. Budge slipped to the side and avoided him

easily. As the body mass passed him, Budge brought up a knee and caught the boy in the gut. A fist to the cheek and the boy was on the ground. Breathing heavy. His face bright with surprise. And fury.

The boy jumped to his feet. 'I made that easy for you, ya cunt. Now I'm about to make it much, much harder.'

Budge was light on his feet, ready to move in either direction. He was enjoying himself. This was like a warm-up to the main event. Except the boy surprised him. He feinted to the left but before Budge could read what was happening, the boy was inside his defences and planted a hook on his chin. Budge had moved with the punch and this diffused much of the intent but it did hurt. He rubbed at his jaw.

'Not so cocky now, ya bastard,' said Mark.

Nobody hits Mason Budge. He couldn't remember the last time anyone had ever made contact with him. The fun had gone. It was time to put a stop to this.

Alexis read his expression and she was shouting in his ear, 'No, Budge, no. He's only a kid.'

With a flick of his arm, the knife released from its hiding place and was in his grip. He stepped up to the boy quicker than he could blink and punched the steel spike through his belly. He withdrew the blade in a tearing motion to the side. Minimum effort, maximum damage. The boy went down in stages, hands over his wound, face folded in surprise. Alexis was leaning over his body screaming for help. Budge leaned over and wiped the blade on the boy's jeans.

'Knife crime in this city is shocking,' Budge said. 'They really oughta do something about it.' He smiled large and said to no one in particular:

'Now for the main event.'

49

'Where the fuck did I park my car?' Peter stood in the middle of the street, craning his neck the length of it.

'You're not going anywhere until you tell me everything,' said Kenny, stepping in front of him.

Peter pushed him out of the way. 'If they see us together...' He walked away. Stopped as if walking into a wall. 'What am I saying? They'll have people on us right now.'

Kenny was at his side. 'What people? Where are they? Tell me and I'll deal with them.'

'Got to go. Got to get home. Why did I agree to come here? Must have been off my fucking head.'

'None taken,' said Kenny. 'Look...' He grabbed Peter's arm. 'I understand you think your kids are in danger. But we need to deal with this rationally. Running off half-cocked is just going to get everyone killed.'

'You have no idea.' Peter was breathing hot in his face. 'No fucking idea. These people are ruthless.'

'Give me an idea,' Kenny argued. 'Let me know what I'm dealing with.'

Peter gave Kenny a hard push in his chest. He fell back, stumbled and managed to right himself. His father was half-walking, half-running along the street. Kenny caught him easily. Peter swung round to push him away again. Kenny dodged the hands, stepped in close, positioned a foot, twisted a hip and his father was on the ground on his back.

'What the...?' Peter struggled to get back to his feet. Kenny stopped him with a foot on his chest. A passing couple changed their course and gave them a wide berth. The woman mumbled something about not being safe on the streets.

'You tell me what exactly what we're dealing with or so fucking help me, every time you try to stand up I'm going to knock you back down.'

Peter stopped struggling and managed to raise himself up on to his elbows. 'Don't be stupid, how am I going to tell you everything from here?'

'Make a start and if you're doing good I'll let you up on to your knees.'

Kenny's mobile began to ring furiously in his pocket. He pulled it out and read the caller. 'Alexis,' he said out loud. 'Well, she can just bloody wait.' He terminated the call. 'Start talking, old man.'

'The family owned a hotel near Queens Park. It was a modest wee place but it was like the head office of their kingdom. They dealt in illegal immigrants, drugs, prostitutes, re-selling stolen goods. You name it. It was sticking to their fingers.' He stopped. 'This really isn't comfy. Can I get up now?'

'You can go as far as your knees.'

Peter moved on to his knees and sat back on his heels. 'I really didn't give you enough of a spanking when you were wee, did I?' His face showed an uneven mix of pride at how his son was handling himself and frustration that he was no longer the one in the position of power.

'We made a lot of money. I made a lot of money. Your mum hated me working for them. That was about the only thing we argued about. Well,' – he looked at Kenny – 'apart from the time she found out I was having an affair with Vi.' He sighed. 'I don't know how that woman put up with me. She was a saint.'

'Yeah,' said Kenny. 'And it fucking killed her.'

'You're not for cutting me any slack, are you?'

'Get on with the story.'

'They were a devious bunch. Gifted at making money from any illegal source. Gifted at making people regret they'd ever met them. Their son was about my age. Maybe a wee bit older. He was always looking to test my loyalty and he thought a gun would be the ultimate test.' Peter was committed to the story, locked into the past. He was now sitting on the ground with his legs crossed. Kenny joined him. Several groups of tourists walked past and stared at them as if waiting for them to produce a mouth organ or a banjo. They all walked away disappointed. Kenny heard one American accent: 'Kinda disappointed with the street theatre, man.'

'I refused to use it,' continued Peter. 'Gimme a knuckleduster, a club, I'll break a few skulls. Guns are just heartless. Hate the fucking things.' He exhaled. 'The son wasn't pleased. He was worse than his old man. He swore if I wasn't with him, I was against him. He saw me out one night with Vi. He made a pass at her. She slapped him in front of a lot of people. Man, was he crushed.'

'Good for Vi,' Kenny said.

Peter laughed. 'Yup, our Vi was a feisty one in her youth.' His eyes took on a dream-like sheen. 'I used to wish I could take your mum and Vi away to, like, a kibbutz by the side of the Red Sea and we'd live as a threesome. Sharing everything.'

'Enough with the wet dreams, Pete. You'll give yourself a heart attack. Get on with the story.'

'So the son's mad. Fucking furious. He wants Vi taken down a peg or two. I tell him, he touches her again and I'll take his gun and shove it up his arse.' Exhale. 'Ah, the folly of youth. I was so pleased with myself in those days. I could take on the world. Despite the fact I was sleeping with both sisters, the girls were still in and out of each other's houses. One day a parcel arrives at ours. Vi was there watching you while me and your mum were at the pictures. Robin Hood, or some such shite. Anyway, Vi opens the parcel. And it's a gun and a wee box of bullets. She freaks. She knows exactly where it has come from. So she wraps it back up – tells me nothing about it – and the very next day she takes it to the mad son's house.'

Pete bit down on his lip. Chewed on some words and then resumed speaking. 'This is where it all gets a bit Hollywood tragic. This guy lives out in Shawlands with his wife and boy. The boy was a wee bit older than you. Spoiled rotten. Anyway, this day he was home from school and he answered the door. Vi gave him the parcel and said something like, give this toy back to your father. So apparently the boy thinks everything his father has belongs to him, opens the parcel, sees the gun and is jumping for joy, thinking this is such a cool toy. He goes in to the kitchen, aims it at his mother, trying to give her a wee fright. He doesn't know the gun is real. Or that it's loaded. He pulls the trigger.'

'Oh my God,' said Kenny.

'Aye. The mum dies. The wee fella is distraught. Can't speak. Can't say where he got the gun, except they all know it was sent to me. But the tragedy isn't quite over, because about a week after the funeral the boy hangs himself.'

'Holy fuck.' Kenny remembered the words of Harry Fyfe. The old guy was spot-on. The truth of this story could already have been his if he'd only listened. 'The family. Who were they?' asked Kenny.

'They were numb with grief. As you might imagine. Completely took their eye off the ball. Some other gangsters moved in. They lost nearly everything apart from the hotel. The parents sold up what possessions they had and moved to Spain. The son paid your mother a wee visit when you were out. Told her he was going to kill every last one of us. Gave her the pills and the drink and told her she could save everyone. The choice was hers.'

'You mean?'

Peter nodded his head, his movement going back up again almost too much for him. As if the weight of the memory was robbing him of strength. 'Matthew was more than happy to tell me all of this before he warned me out of town. You,' – Peter looked at Kenny – 'you were next. If I didn't leave and promise never to return, he was going to have you gang-raped and your throat cut in front of me.'

The two men sat in silence as the horrors of the past coalesced, shifted and worked into shadow around them. Kenny was almost robbed of the will to move as the facts and actions of the past piled one on top of the other in his mind.

Then he thought of events of the last few weeks and his father's assertions that everything that was happening was all part of the plan. It was all part of the slow-burn of revenge.

How much patience, how much energy does it take to hate for so long?

Something his father said earlier burrowed its way out of the morass of information.

'Matthew?' he asked. 'You're saying this guy's name is Matthew?' It's a common enough name in a city, but the coincidence of it was worming its way through his thoughts.

'Aye, Matthew King.'

Kenny repeated the name. Recognition a tantalising distant. 'Tell me more.'

'I don't know what he's in to these days. Haven't kept track.' A shrug. 'Apart from the hotel he used to hang out in an old gym. Well, calling it a gym was a bit of a cheek. It was a pair of long huts with some weights and mats inside.'

50

'You are fucking kidding me?' Kenny demanded and jumped to his feet.

'Why? What? Why are you so...?' Peter's expression widened in alarm. 'You know him, don't you? The fucker's worked his way into your life.'

'Matty the Hut.'

Kenny wanted to kick something. He wanted to tear Matthew King apart with his bare hands. He walked a pace. Spun. Took another step. Fury surged through him, threatened to blind him with its force.

'I need to get home,' said Peter. 'I couldn't bear it if...'

'No,' said Kenny. 'The time for running from this man is over. We deal with him now. Once and for all.' All the times he had met with King; all the conversations they had ran through his mind.

'I don't get it,' Kenny said. 'Why the broken arm? Why the thing with the prostitutes?' He had an image of Alexis' mother lying in a pool of blood. His thoughts ran into the wall of realisation. 'Fuck me, but he's a clever bastard.'

'What?'

Kenny told him about his mission of mercy down to Dumfriesshire. How there was a body but it never appeared in any news programme or the body didn't turn up in any hospital. 'The whole thing was staged.' His head turned this way and that.

'Why so elaborate? Why is he going to all these lengths? Why not just murder me?'

'Where's the fun in that?' Peter said. 'Nobody held a grudge like Matt King. And now he's waited eighteen years for this moment. You don't savour that and then end it in the flash of a gun.' Peter placed his hand on Kenny's shoulder as if willing him to calm down. 'He knows your weaknesses and your strengths. He knows you better than you know yourself.'

'Like hell he does.'

'Here's what he really wants: me. He thinks it was me who returned the gun. If it had gone back to the hotel that would have been manageable, but he thinks I was playing him at his own devious game by sending it to his home. Cos that's what he would do. The whole event with his son played out just the way he would have hoped one of his plans might have. That's why this is all so over the top.

'Here's what he was thinking.' Peter held up his hand and counted off his points on his fingers. 'He needs to manipulate you into looking for me. He knows you are the only one I would react to. But he also knows how capable you are of defending yourself so he needs to distract you on a couple of levels. He knows you have a weakness for hookers. In pops Alexis. He knows that you have a brain on you, so he needs to manipulate your emotions, keep the distractions piling up. So he puts this woman through all sorts of shit knowing you'll do your knight-on-a-white-horse thing and come to the rescue...'

'...and he's seen me fighting so he knows I need to be limited in some way to make me more manageable, but not so much that I can't get around.' Kenny exhaled, loud and sharp. 'There's people around who are *that* devious?'

'Oh, the Kings were masters at all this shit. You've just got to remember what he did to your poor mother.'

'My God,' said Kenny and shivered. 'I was upstairs sleeping. He could easily have done whatever he wanted with me. Mum knew that and saw she had no option. Save my life by killing herself.'

'Kenny, son.' Peter held him by the shoulders. 'I need to make sure the kids are safe.'

'They're only going to be safe if we end this now. Today.'

'But...'

'But nothing. Are you not fed up running?'

'Aye, but that's how clever he is, he knows how to threaten us with the loss of the things we care about.'

'Right. While you're still here, the kids are safe. The minute you go back home, he'll track you and find them. Then it's–'

'Jesus, you're right. If I go back home, I'll lead him straight to them.'

'So we stay. We find him and we finish this.'

Peter swallowed and nodded. And thought of something.

'King's been talking to you recently?'

'Shit. Yes. I was at a low point the other day. We chatted down at the gym. Can't remember what I told him, to be honest.'

'You didn't know about me at that point, so that's fine. What did you know?'

'Not hellish much...' Kenny grimaced. 'But I did tell him about Aunt Vi.'

'What about her?'

'How she was ill in hospital and how she was sure she was dying. Oh fuck...' – Kenny rubbed his face – 'And how she confessed to me that Ian was your son. If that's not enough, I also told him about Vi saying they killed the wrong woman.' Kenny stamped on the ground. 'Man, I've been so stupid.'

'That's where he's going next.'

They both said her name at the same time.

'Vi.'

51

In the car and they're driving across to the hospital. Kenny's phone rang three times. Each time he read the display and cut the connection. He couldn't deal with Alexis right now. She had a part to play in all this and he couldn't quite work out if she was as much of a victim as he was or if she was in any way complicit.

'It's the prostitute,' he told his father.

'Don't be too harsh on her,' said Peter. 'She would have had something that King could use against her.'

Kenny said nothing, simply focusing on the road ahead. They were hitting the last of the rush-hour traffic, but it all seemed to be heading in the same direction as they were.

He tucked the car in behind a 4x4 and then aimed at the slip-road for the Clyde Tunnel. He resisted the urge to drive too fast. It would draw the wrong attention and stop him from getting where he needed to be.

'Fucking put your foot down, Missus,' Kenny shouted at a car in front. 'Jeez, it's like they're out for a wee stroll. It's the fucking city. There's nothing to see.'

'God, I've not been through here in years,' said Peter as the car entered the tunnel and the strip of lights on the roof led them into a brief darkness.

'You were never tempted to come back to the big smoke?'

'Apart from a couple of times when you were a teenager, I avoided the place. Didn't want to give King and his clan an excuse.'

'You think we're facing more than King?'

'I'd be surprised if he was doing this all on his own. He's bound to have at least one sidekick. He'll not have too many. From what I understand he's gone for an air of respectability. It wouldn't do to be surrounded by a gang of thick-necked thugs.'

'His main weapon is a guy called Mason Budge. He's the guy who seems to enforce King's will and from what I hear he's created a real aura of fear about himself.'

'What kind of name is that? Mason Budge.'

The gates of the hospital were visible just ahead. The traffic lights were at red. Kenny drummed at the steering wheel.

'Is there anyone you could phone to warn?' asked Peter.

'Nah, Colin fucking hates me. Ian will be high on hash and if I tell the nurses a psychotic killer is about to turn up, they'll be waiting for me with a straitjacket.'

The light changed and they were through. The drove through the hospital grounds, Kenny anxious to drive faster but knowing the danger that might put them in. At last they arrived at the right part of the vast hospital grounds, found a parking space and ran into the building.

Colin was sitting in the waiting room round the corner from Vi's room. He was staring at the pages of a magazine, not seeing anything when Kenny and Peter appeared.

The urgency of their movement made him stand up.

'What are you doing here, Kenny?' he asked. 'And why are you bringing a...?' Colin looked at Peter and after a moment of confusion, recognition struck. 'Pete? What the...?'

'We can do the friends re-united thing in a moment. How's Vi?'

'What do you mean?' Colin looked from one to the other. 'He's no friend... what do you mean, how's Vi?'

'Who's with her?'

'I was until minutes ago. A doctor came in. Nice young guy. New...'

Kenny didn't wait until Colin finished; he turned and ran towards the room. He burst through the door to see a man in a white coat leaning over the bed. It took a moment for the sense of the scene to hit him. The man was holding a pillow over his aunt's face.

He roared and charged forward. The man stepped away from the bed, read Kenny's lunge and ran round the other side of the bed. The man was grinning and this infuriated Kenny. He heard Peter and Colin arrive just behind him.

Budge noted the numbers were no longer in his favour and he charged at Kenny. He didn't go for his head, or throat; he went for his arm. The cast took the blow, but the pain was immense. Kenny groaned. That moment was enough for Budge. He ran at Peter with his shoulder and thrust him against the wall and then easily stepped aside from Colin's clumsy attack. In a heartbeat, he was out the door and down the corridor and through the double doors.

Kenny recovered from the pain, stepped over his uncle, ran out of the room and looked down the corridor. Nothing.

'Nurse,' he shouted at the Station. 'Phone the police. Someone has just tried to murder my aunt.'

The nurse looked up from her paperwork, locked into stupidity by the apparent absurdity of Kenny's shouts.

'Now. Police. There's a murderer in this hospital.'

'Right, right.' The nurse picked up the phone in front of her and dialled a number.

'And get someone in here, pronto. Someone just tried to suffocate...'

'Kenny, Kenny,' he heard his uncle speak. 'It's okay.'

'I'm okay, son,' Vi's voice sounded just behind his uncle. Kenny turned and stepped back into the room. Vi was leaning back on her pillows, stretching her hand out to take his. 'You were just in time.' She then looked at Peter and the recognition was instant.

His father was standing in the middle of the room, looking bewildered. Three people he'd spent the last eighteen years hiding from were within touching distance and he didn't know quite where to put himself.

'Pete?' asked Vi in a shaky voice.

'Hello, Vi,' Peter said. 'Seems like you've been in the wars.' Peter didn't know where to look, or what to say. He stuffed his hands in his pockets and managed to look like a schoolboy in front of the headmaster's office, despite the grey in his long hair and his beard.

'Is it really you, Pete?'

'Aye,' he said. 'It's me.'

'Aye and you can bloody piss off again,' shouted Colin, '...back under the stone you crawled from.'

'Colin.' Vi reached out her hand for her husband's. 'We're all a lot older and a lot wiser than we were in those days.' She grabbed her husband's hand and held on tight. With this small gesture, she was telling him he had nothing to worry about. She was his. Completely.

'You're looking remarkably well for someone who's just had an attempt on their life, Aunt Vi,' said Kenny, moving closer to the bed and taking a hold of his aunt's other hand. He leaned forward and planted a kiss on the paper of her cheek.

'Goodness,' she cried. 'What's been happening to you?'

Kenny held up his arm. 'Och, you know. Walked into a door.'

'Aye, and if I'm not mistaken, that door just tried to murder my wife.'

'Colin, you can massage your male pride some other time, ya daft lump.'

'After all you've been through, darling,' said Colin.

'Aye, I've not had so much attention for years,' said Vi. She was smiling but Kenny could see it was through the strain of the last few moments. She felt that she had to hold it together for her husband.

'You're alright, Vi?' asked Peter. 'You don't need us to get a nurse for you?'

'Goodness, no,' said Vi. 'But a wee cup of tea after all that excitement would be worth it.' She looked at her husband. 'Darling, would you mind?'

Colin looked from his wife to Kenny and then to Peter.

'Please, Colin?'

'Aye. Okay,' said Colin. 'But you two can forget it if you think I'm getting you anything.' Pride restored in Colin Land, he left the room. Only then did Vi allow the trauma of what she'd just experienced to show. Her hand shook badly as she placed it in front of her mouth.

'Oh my God,' she said. 'That man was trying to kill me, wasn't he?'

'Yes, but you're safe now,' said Kenny.

She breathed deeply, exhaled slowly, closed her eyes. A tear squeezed out from behind one eyelid.

'It's okay, Vi,' said Peter. 'You're safe now.'

'I'm not worried about me,' she said and smiled through her tears. 'I've faced dying so much in the last few weeks it no longer scares me. It's you two I'm worried about.'

'Don't know what you're talking about, Aunt Vi,' Kenny laughed.

'Don't treat me like a fool, Kenny son,' she said, patting his hand. 'I remember those days all too vividly.' She looked at Peter. 'It's come back to bite us, hasn't it?'

Peter nodded.

Vi looked away from them both and out of the window at a sky dark with greys. Her eyes were haunted, chasing ghosts before her vision returned to the room and the two men. She looked from one to the other before settling on Peter.

'You have a family now?' she asked and judging by her expression it was a guess.

Peter nodded.

'Did you find happiness?' Vi asked and Kenny thought she'd never looked more at peace.

Again, Peter nodded.

'Good. I'm pleased,' she swallowed as if drawing steel to her spine. And again she looked at Kenny and back to Peter, her eyes full of tenderness. 'Because now I'm going to ask you to put everything you hold dear at risk, Peter, and end this. Once and for all.'

52

There were twelve, steep stone steps up to the hotel entrance. An ornate steel railing was positioned either side of the steps. That's to offer any drunks a wee hand as they leave the hotel bar, thought Kenny. Give themselves something to hold on to as they leave after they'd spent the last of their wages.

It was the kind of place, he thought, that should have had a sign above the door that read only those in the early stages of cirrhosis need walk through here. The hotel itself was part of a long row of sandstone tenement houses, bordering Queens Park and built by the Victorians.

They'd be birling in their graves, thought Kenny, when he walked up to the purple wooden door into the hotel, with his father by his side. In those days this would have been a hotel for middle-class families, taking time out from the strains of village life and seeking the bright lights of one of the biggest cities in the British Empire.

Nowadays it was nothing better than a doss-house for alcoholics and addicts reliant on the welfare system to give them a roof and a bed.

Before they walked in the door, Peter put a restraining hand on his son's arm.

'Are you prepared to do what we need to do in here?' he asked.

Kenny nodded. His face set on grim. He didn't have a weapon on him, but he knew how to kill a man with his bare hands. Fuck, he thought. How casually the thought worked through his mind, but he knew he had no other choice. A warning wouldn't work for this guy. Nor would a jail sentence; he'd simply pay someone else to carry on the vendetta for him. There was only one way this was going to end. Matty the Hut's funeral service.

'You?' he asked. 'You ever killed anyone?'

Peter stared at Kenny, emotion worked at the muscles along his jaw. 'I'd rather not answer that question, son.'

In through the door and a small desk, no wider than a child might sit at, acted as a reception area. Kenny doubted if it was ever manned. To the left of this, a set of double doors led into a room with the ambitious title above the door of *Lounge*. If ever anyone attempted to lounge beyond those doors, their wallet would be emptied and their teeth spread across the sticky, carpeted floor.

The walls around the room were panelled with Formica to the halfway point, where a cream paint took over. Here and there, sporting trophies were hung on the walls along with some sponsored adverts from brewers.

Only one other man was in the room. He was leaning against the bar, wearing black jeans, a black T-shirt and, in stark contrast with what you'd expect in a place like this, he was pink with health.

'Fuck me,' he said with a huge smile. 'If it isn't Peter O'Neill.'

'Matthew,' Peter nodded, moving closer to the man. Kenny looked at his father from the corner of his eyes and thought, yes, he looks ready.

'Kenny,' said Matthew. 'How's the arm?'

'Fuck you,' said Kenny.

'No need for profanity, son.'

'And yet again, fuck you.'

Matthew simply smiled. 'I take it you two have now been re-united? You can thank me for that, Peter.' A shadow flitted across his face. 'At least you have a son to be re-united with.'

'You expect sympathy? After everything you've done?' asked Peter.

'I expect nothing, Pete. I asked for loyalty from you all those years ago. Remember? I could have made you rich beyond your wildest. You were nothing,' he spat. 'I gave you prestige, money and you play a horrible–'

'What happened, Matt, was an accident. A tragic accident.' Peter's view was locked on King. Kenny stepped further into the room and looked around. There was just the one door. The only other way out was through the window. Slowly, so as not to alarm King, he walked away from the door and positioned himself so that he could see all of the occupants of the room and he'd notice as soon as anyone else entered. To disguise his movement, he picked up a beer mat from a table.

'Look, Pops,' Kenny said, 'Stella Artois. Those wanky beers get everywhere.'

King smiled at Kenny as if to say his attempt to wind him up was juvenile.

'No, Peter,' he said. 'Here's what happened, you devious fucker…' And for the first time since they entered the bar King displayed some real emotion. He recognised this and visibly restrained himself. 'You were afraid that by turning down my gun and that particular contract..' He faced Kenny. 'Sorry, how rude of me, Kenny. I should explain your dad did certain jobs for me. Where lessons needed to be learned.' Kenny looked at Peter, whose face was white, lips drawn tight and fists clenched by his side. 'Your dad was quite the nasty individual in those days, Kenny.'

'And what you need to know, Matt, is that particular apple didn't fall too far from the tree,' Kenny replied.

'Don't make me laugh,' said King. 'Sure you can fight, but you're a pussy. You couldn't really hurt someone if your life depended on it.'

With an effort, Kenny bit down on his response. This was not going to be about his ego. Let King carry on thinking whatever he wanted.

Satisfied he had Kenny in his pigeonhole, King turned to Peter.

'Giving my son the gun and letting him think it was a toy...' King shook his head. 'Tut, tut.' His face was twisted with something so complex that labels like hate were inadequate. He had spent almost two decades in a state somewhere beyond rage and only now was he close to the revenge he sought. 'I've spent so many days thinking of this moment. You, Kenny, you took such a long time to grow up. Life is full of frustrations, eh?' His grin was bright with an insane light. 'But you had to be of a certain position in life for my plan to work. Too young and I just couldn't rely on you reacting the way I wanted.' He clapped his hands. 'I should have been a film director. Or...' He paused. 'Imagine what I could do with something like *Big Brother*.'

'Cut the theatrics, Matt,' said Peter. 'You're not crazy. At least not in the accepted version of the word. What do you want? What is it going to take to make this all stop?'

'Your mum was a lovely woman, Kenny. You were up in your bed. Tucked up in your Action Man quilt. You should know how brave your mum was. She didn't want her son to die...'

'You bastard,' Peter lunged forward. Kenny held his hand out, grabbed his father's arm and restrained him. He knew King wanted to get them riled up. Angry men don't fight so well. While King continued to speak, Kenny studied him. He well knew that Matty the Hut could look after himself, but that didn't explain the man's confidence. He was in a bar on his own with two men he knew were more than capable of hurting him. What was the game plan? When were the paid mercenaries going to troop in?

King was still speaking. 'You want it to stop, Pete? You watch as your son hangs from a noose made from a selection of school clothes. Arrange that and then it can stop.' King turned to Kenny and clapped his hands. One, two, three times. 'Do you know every time I clap my hands, a child in Africa dies?' King chuckled. 'Bono is such a wanker.'

'Do you know, I think he is crazy, Dad,' Kenny deliberately used the title. He wanted King to worry that despite his best efforts the two men were reconciled. 'Carrying a vendetta for so long has got to twist a man.'

'I'll tell you what's twisted,' said King. 'You're thirty now and you've yet to have a proper relationship. You'd rather pay for it than earn it the hard way. Through love, respect and affection.'

Kenny laughed. 'Morality lessons from a man like you, King. You are fucking crazy.'

'How's your little whore?' King asked. 'Think her bodyguard is keeping her safe?'

'Cool. You got her.' Kenny feigned disinterest. 'Well, that's one less worry on my mind. Since I worked out your fucked-up little plan and her part in it, I've been wondering how to ditch her. I take it you got Mason Budge to do the needful?'

Kenny's use of the name surprised King. 'You are a resourceful lad.' To Peter. 'You should be proud of the boy. While you still have the time.'

'You have to go through me to hurt him,' said Peter.

King stepped away from the bar. 'Happy to.'

'Now wait a minute, children,' said Kenny. He was not keen for the action to start until he had a better idea of what King's game plan was. 'Step back from the nice man, Matt. Let's talk. Is there anyway we can sort this out without resorting to violence?'

'Told you he was a pussy,' said King. His arms and shoulders all but trembled with anticipation at the violence he planned. 'In case you hadn't realised I'm taking a biblical stance on all of this. Eye for an eye, wife and son for a wife and son. Or even...' –King's smile was as bright as a candle. He'd been waiting to reveal just how much he now knew – '...a wife, a lover and two sons.'

Peter and Kenny exchanged glances. King still didn't know seem to know about the family up in Balquidder. It needed to stay that way.

King clapped his hands. Once. Twice. Three times. 'Every time I clap my hands a child in Africa dies,' said King while making a face that said, *Who the fuck cares?*

That's it, thought Kenny. That's the signal.

He moved quickly to the door, which meant he was behind Peter, but that would have to be okay and just as he got into position to the side of the door a man walked in.

Budge.

'I hope you didn't start the party without me, Matthew,' Budge said. He was standing ready for everything, weight balanced perfectly on each foot. He was speaking to Peter's back and couldn't quite see King's face and missed any warning that he might have given.

Kenny knew there was no time for banter with this guy. Long and short of it, Budge was a killer.

Kenny attacked.

53

Kenny stepped to his right, took all of his weight on his left foot and kicked out. Budge spotted the movement and twisted to the side, but he was too slow. Kenny's foot lashed high, connected with his jaw.

'Fuck,' said Budge and fell back. He got up quickly, shook his head and rubbed his face. 'That's the second time today.'

Kenny wasn't thinking to add any more comments to the conversation. He attacked again. Budge blocked and came at Kenny with an attack of his own.

Caught Kenny in the gut. He bent over. Breath exploded from him. He had enough presence of mind to back off quickly to give him room to regroup. This was just an opening sally, but he was impressed. Budge would have been a difficult opponent if Kenny had two strong arms, but with one he was going to be a real challenge.

Kenny loved challenges.

Budge took up an old-time boxing stance. Shadow-boxed for a couple of blows. Showing off, wasting energy, thought Kenny. He took this time to check out how his father was doing with King.

They were toe to toe, slugging it out like old-timers in a Western movie. He couldn't see which of them had the upper hand, but they were each showing blood and some puffiness on their faces.

'Watch out, Dad,' said Kenny. 'He's been training down at the gym all these years. Thinks cage-fighting is going to give him an edge.'

Peter nodded, gave Kenny a quick wink and brought up an arm to block a punch.

'Man, this is so cute. Father and son together at last. How the kinfolks would be proud,' sang Budge. As he spoke, he stretched out his right arm to the side, giving his wrist a dramatic flick. Something slim and about longer than his forearm slid from his sleeve. Kenny recognised it as a police ASP baton. He assessed the strengths and weaknesses of this weapon in an instant. Budge could attack with it while staying outside Kenny's reach. If a weapon like this landed on muscle, it could likely cause cramps. If it landed on bone, it could break it; if it connected with the skull or neck with sufficient force, it could be fatal.

Weakness? If Kenny got inside its reach it would become ineffective.

Thinking, *You should have broken my leg, you fucker*, Kenny danced inside Budge's reach, punched with his good hand at Budge's gut, aiming for sufficient force for the blow to carry through to the spine. In the next second, he struck downwards with his plaster cast on Budge's forearm. The force was enough for Budge to lose his grip of the baton, but it was also enough to cause Kenny considerable pain.

He screamed.

His bones hadn't knitted well enough yet for such use. The pain almost blinded him. Fuck. He was sure he'd re-broken the bones.

He had enough presence of mind to kick Budge's baton out of reach.

Budge himself was breathing heavily, but Kenny was momentarily in too much pain to take advantage. He fought to zone it out and, holding his wounded limb close to his chest, he lashed out with another kick; catching Budge on the chin.

He crashed back onto a table with a loud grunt. Screamed, 'Fuck.' Budge was clearly not used to people fighting back.

Trying to keep track of Budge, Kenny turned to see how the other fight was progressing. King had his father in a headlock.

Peter's face was red with effort. He was twisting to try and land some blows on King's kidneys, but missing. If this kept up, Peter was going to run out of oxygen.

Kenny grabbed a tray from a table, knowing it wasn't heavy enough, but launched it like a Frisbee at King's head. He ducked and this was enough distraction for Peter to scramble free.

Movement at his side caused Kenny to twist in reflex. Budge had recovered in the split second he was distracted with his father. The twist wasn't enough and Budge caught him on the temple. His next punch caught him in the gut.

Budge jumped, brought up a knee into Kenny's chin. He was thrown back on to a table. He felt the corner of it stab between two ribs. Kenny struggled to get up. If he didn't get back on to his feet, he couldn't defend himself.

Budge came at him again. Kicks and punches rained down on him in a fury. Kenny managed to deflect some of them with his good arm, but the odd one caught his cast. Each time the pain was more blinding than the last. It was taking all of Kenny's will and strength to stay on his feet. Much more of this and he was a goner.

As if he recognised this, Budge's attack increased in speed. It was relentless. Blow. Defend. Punch. Swerve, twist, absorb.

Neither man spoke. It was all grunt, groan, attack and counter.

Kenny was all but on his knees. He dodged another blow, tripped over a broken table. Budge followed until Kenny lashed out. His foot caught Budge in the stomach. Hard. It felt good.

He needed a weapon. If he took much more of this beating, Budge was going to walk away with the prize. Kenny couldn't allow that to happen.

The broken table. A leg was hanging off. One end was rounded like a club, the other end was breaking off at a sharp angle. He stretched over, twisted the leg and pulled it off so that it was like a spike.

A woman's voice sounded shrill as a beacon in the fog of testosterone.

'Enough,' she shouted. 'Everybody stop.'

Kenny looked up.

It was Alexis. She was shaking with fear, but the gun in her hand was surprisingly steady. Her eyes were locked on Budge. A shadow moved from behind her, his face hot with the need for action.

'Calum?' asked Kenny, climbing to his feet. He looked beyond the boy for his brother.

'Budge got Mark,' said Alexis. 'Gutted him like a fish.'

'No,' said Kenny. 'No.' He closed his eyes. Poor kid. That one was on him. If he'd not given the boys the work, this wouldn't have happened. 'I'm so sorry, Calum.' He locked down on his grief. It couldn't be allowed to get in the way.

Calum edged into the room. His eyes were red, his face rigid, his need for action tight in every frame of his body. 'You,' he said to Budge. His voice was quiet and all the more disturbing for it.

'Aww man,' said Budge. 'That was your brother?' He smiled. 'Sorry for your loss, dude.'

Alexis put out a hand and stopped Calum from reacting. The young man quivered like a bull waiting to attack the red rag.

Kenny surveyed the room. Tables and chairs were tossed everywhere as if a hurricane had blasted the room. Just beyond Calum's reach he could see the baton on the floor. Kenny caught Calum's eye and looked pointedly at the weapon.

Peter and Matt were side by side at the bar, both breathing heavily, both bruised, but both looked able to keep going for as long as it took.

Peter took a step away from his opponent, his eye on him at all times, but now there was a gun in the room the dynamic had changed considerably.

Kenny doubted that Alexis had the will or the strength to do anything with the gun and he was sure that every man in the room was thinking the same thing.

'On your knees,' Alexis screamed at Budge and King.

'Now, darling,' said Budge, moving slowly as he spoke. 'You sure a pretty little thing like you should be holding a messy big gun like that?' His movements were barely perceptible, but they brought him closer to Alexis with each passing second.

'On your fucking knees,' Alexis shouted.

King shouted, 'Okay, woman. Okay.' And leaning forward, did just that. This movement was enough for Alexis to shift her vision for a second. That second was enough.

Kenny shouted a warning.

Budge rushed forward, grabbed the gun, twisted it out of Alexis' hands and slapped her down on to the floor.

'And now the fun begins,' Budge crowed. He lifted, sighted and shot Peter. He was blown against the bar and slumped to the floor in a heap. Kenny dived behind a table, but not before he saw Calum, stretch, roll and come up onto his feet with the baton on his grip.

Budge brought the gun round and sighted. Calum lashed down with the baton on Budge's wrist. He screamed. The gun dropped to the floor. Calum adjusted his footing and with a vicious back-stroke, caught Budge on the temple. With that power, Kenny hoped the bone would have crumbled, shards shooting inwards piercing through Budge's brain.

Budge crumbled to his knees and fell over. His body on top of the gun. Kenny handed the wooden spike to Alexis so he could pick up the gun. He leaned forward to push Budge out of the way. Budge was heavy. Kenny pushed some more.

Budge moved. But not in the direction Kenny was aiming for. He pushed himself back onto his knees with one hand. The other was holding the gun.

The black hole of the barrel was pointed at Kenny's heart.

Alexis screamed, 'No.' And lashed the spike round like it was on a tight spring into Budge's right eye.

Budge screamed and fell forward once again. The gun fell from his fingers and bounced on the carpet. Kenny and King both dived for it.

Kenny got there first. He curled his fingers round the grip and kicked King out of the way. He watched as Calum helped Alexis back onto her feet.

King was on his knees, staring at him, glee wild in his face. 'Go on, son. Put an end to this. Pull that wee thing. It's called a trigger.' He laughed. 'Look at you. You can't do it, you pussy.'

'Give it to me,' said Alexis, pushing the hair from her face. Her mouth set in a grim line. 'I can do it. I'll happily do it.'

Kenny held the gun before him. He pointed it at King's face.

He knew what he wanted to do.

He looked from King to Alexis and Calum. Out of the corner of his eye, he could see movement at the bar.

Peter groaned and struggled to his feet. His left shoulder was hanging too low and was a bloody mess, but he was steady on his feet as he approached his son.

He put a hand on Kenny's shoulder and said, 'No. Give it to me.'

Peter took the gun from Kenny's hand. 'Take your friends outside.'

King stayed on his knees, his face shifting from fear to joy to relief. 'Yes. You won't do it either. Put the gun down, Pete. Let's finish this the way we started. You and me. Toe to toe.'

Peter looked out of the room, through the window to the darkness beyond. 'Is that police sirens I can hear?' he asked. Then looked at King. 'I should just leave you for them.' Kenny could hear nothing.

'Do that,' said King. 'None of the dead can be blamed on me. Budge was his own man. You'll be lucky if I do any time. Meanwhile I'll be planning...'

'Aw for fuck's sake, shut up, King. If I give you any more time to talk, you'll be laughing like a pantomime villain,' Peter said and turned to Kenny. 'Take your friends and leave. This is my responsibility.'

Kenny read the determination and acceptance in his father's eyes. He knew what he needed to do to end this once and for all.

Kenny nodded, turned and, stepping over Budge's body, he left the room with Alexis and Calum, both of whom were silent in shock.

They walked out of the hotel and climbed down the stairs. Kenny looked around himself, confused at how the world hadn't changed. All he'd known for the last few minutes, hours – however long it lasted – was violence. It felt like the world was tricking him by displaying a semblance of calm.

'Kenny, I need to...' Alexis said at his side. She was shaking. Her arms wrapped around her waist.

He held a hand up. 'I'm not sure that I want to listen to whatever you have to say, Alexis.'

'Well...' She stood in front of him, her face white and dirt-streaked, her eyes shining with defiance. 'I had to do what I had to do. King had me. It started off–'

'Not interested.'

'It was a job. At first,' said Alexis. 'I'm not going to lie to you...'

Kenny's laugh was ironic.

'I'm finished lying...' She looked up at him, trying to read him. 'But then I fell for you. You made me feel–'

'Shut up, Alexis,' Kenny shouted. 'Just shut...' His words faded. He turned away, trying to shake the confusion from his thoughts. Even bloody and bruised, she looked gorgeous. Loveable. He wanted nothing more than to forgive her, take her in his arms and tell her that everything would be alright.

But it wouldn't. Ever.

'I'll understand if you don't ever want to see me again...'

'How perceptive of you.'

'I'll just...' she said. Then Kenny could hear her heels clip the pavement as she began to walk away. It was all he could do to stop himself from running after her and gathering her into his arms. Instead, he turned to speak to the young man at his side.

'You okay, Calum?'

'Aye,' he replied.

'Go after her, will you? Make sure she gets wherever she needs to?'

Kenny turned back to watch Calum run after Alexis and continued watching as he took up her pace and walked quietly beside her.

On the pavement outside the hotel he looked up at the building, wondering what was happening with his father and King. Were they fighting again? Had Peter taken King up with his offer to end it all with fists? Surely not, that would be suicide for Peter given how badly he was injured.

Kenny was about to walk back up the stairs when he heard it. The gunshots sounded like someone clapping.

Once.

Twice.

Three times.

54

They were all sitting round the kitchen table. Words bounced off words; laughter weaved itself around and through the syllables. Over Kathy's shoulder, through the window above a sink piled high with pots and pans, Kenny could see hills curving an outline against a bright sky.

Christmas dinner was pheasant, potatoes and carrots followed by a large helping of warm chocolate fudge cake.

'Not very festive.' Kathy leaned her head to the side in an apology. 'But the kids demand it at every family occasion.'

She was an intriguing blend of warmth and steel and Kenny took to her from the first instant they met. Kathy was a good ten years younger than Peter, trim yet curvy with an expressive face. He could see what his father saw in her and in the months since he had come to know her, he was grateful for the changes she had wrought in his father.

This was the third time Kenny had visited since the shooting and they were yet to talk about any of the events of that evening. Kenny looked at his father at the end of the table. His expression was trapped in a smile as he watched the antics of his two youngest. They bickered good-naturedly with each other; the boy aware of his superior size but giving in to his sister's sharper wit.

'Kenny, what do you think?' asked Joy, her bottom lip sticking out in a pretend huff.

'What you said,' Kenny replied.

'That's not fair, Kenny,' his brother replied. 'You weren't even listening.'

Kenny laughed, but realised what he was doing and sent the boy a silent apology. Each time he was here, he was tripping over the kid. He leaned against him as they watched TV. He asked him questions about life when he was a child. He pulled Kenny into his bedroom to share with him his latest obsession. It was like he was his hero; and Kenny O'Neill was fit to be nobody's icon. Now and again, he felt he overcompensated for this and made small decisions that favoured Joy.

'Leave Kenny alone, son,' said Kathy. 'He came away from the city for a wee bit of quiet. Not to hear a pair of teenagers argue about who can win in a fight between Spiderman and Batman.'

A chair squeaked against the floor as Peter pushed his chair back and stood up.

'Going for a walk,' he said. 'Want to come?' He looked at Kenny.

'Yes,' Joy jumped in. Kathy silenced her with a look.

'I'd love to,' said Kenny and walked to the back door.

'You'll need a coat, you two,' said Kathy. 'The sun might be shining, but it's really cold out there.'

'Quit nagging, woman,' Peter said in good humour.

'Well, don't come running to me,' – Kathy reached him at the door, pecked his cheek and patted his bum – 'when you're full of the cold and desperate for some paracetamol.'

The teenagers made a face at each other. 'Gross,' they said in unison, mocking the open affection between their parents.

'You two don't know how lucky you are,' said Kenny with a smile.

Peter looked at him, worried about Kenny's reaction.

'They know exactly how lucky they are, Kenny,' said Kathy and patted him on the shoulder. A short time ago Kenny would have shrugged off that arm and all but run screaming from the room.

• • •

Outside, the two men walked to the end of the path and took a right down the road that would take them further into the glen. The air was clear, silent and held frost in its grip. Kenny breathed in, felt the chill fill his nostrils before warming and the air filling his lungs.

They walked in silence for a few hundred yards. Reached the water's edge and stared across at the hills beyond.

Both had their hands in their pockets and their shoulders hunched against the cold.

'How's the big city?' asked Peter, bending down to pick up a small stone. He discarded it and picked up another.

'Busy.'

'Your Aunt Vi?' Peter's thumbs worked at the stone's surface, smoothing off any grains of sand or soil.

'She's back to normal. Full of vim and sparkle. Looking after the two men in her life.'

'You didn't tell Ian that Colin is not his father?'

'What's the point?' asked Kenny. 'Colin might not have provided the fertiliser, but in every other way, he's the father.'

'True,' Peter nodded. 'After everything... I just worry about secrets. They have an amazing power to destroy.' He turned to look at his son. 'What about Alexis?'

What about Alexis?

The last time he saw her, she was heading in a taxi for the airport – destination London. Her face pale behind the car window; her gaze fixed straight ahead.

'I think she really did love you, you know.'

Kenny shrugged. 'Too much happened.'

'Everybody deserves a second chance, son...' He paused. His larynx jumped in his throat as he was suddenly taken with emotion. 'I'm grateful for mine.'

'Ach well,' said Kenny. 'You come out the other end of an evening like that and it tends to give you a fresh perspective.' Kenny then gave voice to the question that had been haunting him since that evening just a few short months ago. 'Do you ever regret it?'

'Killing King?' Peter asked. He threw the stone up into the air and caught it in the palm of his hand. 'Every day I thank God for those two kids and you. Do I regret it? Not for a second.'

Kenny read the truth in the words, but he also read the changes in his father. They'd only been together for a few short hours before the gun went off, but that was enough to see that since then his father was in some ways diminished. He still held a strength in his stance and a shine in his eye, but it was all somehow less. You don't kill a man and walk away unmarked.

He'd asked himself many times since that night if he could have pulled the trigger.

Dreams about that night visited him with alarming regularity, except he held the gun. His finger pulled back the trigger. But each time he was pulled from his dream before the bullet left the gun.

Could he have killed Matt? He'd rather not have to answer that question.

Peter crouched, whipped his arm back and sent the stone skimming across the water. It bounced four times before it lost momentum and vanished beneath the mirrored surface.

'I never quite got the hang of that,' said Kenny, bracing himself against the cold. 'Most I could ever manage was to skim the stone once or twice.'

'Want me to show you?' asked Peter.

Kenny laughed and another small healing took place between them.

'Met anyone else yet?' Peter asked.

Kenny shivered, his teeth knocking together in the cold. He smiled at his father.

'C'mon inside, Pete.' He put a hand on his father's shoulder. 'It's freezing.'

Acknowledgements

I'd like to thank my first readers on this project, Bill Kirton and Sara Bain. Thanks guys, you kept me on the straight and narrow and called me out when it was required.

Big thanks also to the gang at Saraband.

Bob McDevitt

Michael J Malone is the author of two previous crime novels featuring DI Ray McBain – *Blood Tears* and *A Taste for Malice* – as well as *The Guillotine Choice*, a novel based on the incredible true story of an Algerian who survived more than twenty years on the infamous Devil's Island after being wrongly convicted of a murder (co-written with the survivor's son).